Retrogenesis 3: The Legacy

By Robert Swann

www.newgeneration-publishing.com

New Generation **Publishing**

BY THE SAME AUTHOR:
RETROGENESIS 1: The Anomaly

A fantastic new technology is discovered which can be of greater significance to mankind than any previous innovation. The advantages it offers could make the entire world a better place in which to live but there is a dark side to the technology which, in careless hands, could destroy civilisation - completely. The challenge the creators of the technology face is to have it embraced by the rest of the world as a heaven-sent opportunity to help all countries whether rich or poor. Unable to find safe hands to protect against the misuse of the power of its dark side, they have no option but to physically create a new safe haven by utilising the phenomenal power of their technology. This would prevent misuse of the anomaly by greedy super powers having an unsavoury interest in the dark supremacy that this powerful tool also possesses. This is an epic battle between grasping, power-hungry governments and the will of the few who care deeply for humanity and will sacrifice everything, except their integrity, to safeguard the future of their discovery.

Julia Ann Chapentier of ForeWord Reviews:
With this the author has a gem in the making.
Formidable and strange.
A mesmerising concept.

MJ Grogan, screenwriter:
Compelling characters with an intriguing plot.
An imaginative thriller with a difference.

RETROGENESIS 2: The Journey

This the second part of the Retrogenesis Trilogy traces the fortunes of the new society which is self-sufficient and continues with their vow to share the benefits of its incredible technology with the rest of the world. Superpowers continue unwaveringly in their quest to wrest control of the technology from the new society by any means, in order to acquire the greater supremacy and unbeatable global control that ownership would bring. That the superpowers have no conscience is clearly demonstrated and it is clear they will stop at nothing, despite past failures, to continue to strive to gain control of this potentially dark gift in their quest for absolute domination. Can this small embryonic nation continue to resist the relentless probing of World Super Powers? Who will succeed in the epic struggle will it be the legendary David or will it be the mythical Goliath? Will the traditional outcome of this epic legend prevail or will the myth be rewritten?

ABOUT THE AUTHOR

Born and educated in London, he started working life as a student civil engineer in the Atomic Power Division of a major British Engineering Company. He progressed his career options and ventured into the field of logistics management and into logistics consultancy, firstly with a British company and then as Vice President of an American consulting group in their London office.

Ultimately he bought out the London practice and formed a close friendship and a joint working agreement with an American business entrepreneur; they continue to work collectively and individually and have worked in around forty different countries.

He feels eternal gratitude for the opportunities that he has been fortunate enough to enjoy through his extensive world travels. This literary work is heavily influenced by an amalgam of many of the fascinating people he has had the privilege of meeting, both socially and professionally, and the truly wonderful and sometimes extremely challenging countries it has been his great fortune to visit.

ACKNOWLEDGEMENTS

Concluding this trilogy has been a labour of love with all the highs and challenges of such an intense undertaking. It could not have been achieved without the support of so many people; family and friends old and new and of course those readers who have enjoyed the fruits of my labours thus far have been generous in their encouragement. My eternal gratitude goes to my wife Jenefer without whose support and phenomenal attention to detail, none of this would have been achieved.

Guidance in the portrayal of a situation borne of pure imagination is by its very nature difficult to find and it is with this in mind that my thanks go to those offered their invaluable advice on matters of style, perception and substance. Support was gratefully received again from Terry Thurston and Tony Bungey who gave their valuable time and the benefit of their considerable experience. My continuing thanks go to Elizabeth Capper and Andy Davis, their intuitive insights added greatly to the whole of this work and to the NGP team. Last but not least my thanks to Charlotte Bowes for her sterling work as publicist, reader and supporter.

I am also grateful to many airlines in many different countries whose broadcast message to frustrated travellers waiting in departure lounges began... 'we regret to announce'... The inevitable delays and cancellations that this phrase heralded led to me and my trusty lap top producing the foundations for the trilogy which this work now completes

For Ella, Josef and Charlotte

One

The man on the control tower roof was virtually invisible; he wore dark, patterned off-Island clothes which blended in with the dappled shade of the overhang of the roof. Sixty feet below him and five hundred feet distant, four figures descended from an executive jet with its distinctive tail decoration showing the curiously regular silhouette of the Island superimposed on a blood-red setting sun.

From his elevated, prone position he pushed the long muzzle of his rifle through the safety railing and switched on the infrared range finder. Through the scope he could see the three men and a dark haired young woman quite clearly and could also see the red dot of the range finder in the centre of the chest of his target. There was a robotic buzz as the scope adjusted to raise the barrel giving the correct trajectory for the distance calculated by the laser range finder. The light breeze which eddied around the convoluted shapes of the towers superstructure ruffled the sleeves of his bomber jacket and his short hair but did not detract from his concentration to keep the red dot steady in the centre of the target's chest

The rifle, which had been manufactured in Nuovostan, was a suppressed sub-sonic sniper's special or 5S as it was known to its few specialist users and was almost silent when fired; the specially modified projectile it fired travelled at less than the speed of sound and did not produce the customary sonic boom. The sniper rechecked his aim so that the dot positioned exactly in the centre of the target's chest. Before squeezing the trigger he switched on the vision and sound recording device which had been added to the rifle at the insistence of the sniper's paymaster.

Escaping gas hissed angrily through the barrel tip vents; a bullet leaving the muzzle and travelling at around seven hundred miles per hour would take less than a second to travel the distance from muzzle to target.

"Bang," the sniper whispered softly, fractionally before he made the shot.

Through the scope he saw blood blossom crimson on the chest of the target as he staggered backwards and fell. His three companions, after a shock induced momentary pause, dragged the supine figure under the fuselage of the jet and out of further harm's way. Pressing the rewind button in the stock of the 5S he looked at the full colour high definition record of the assassination. Satisfied that the images and sound were clear and definitive he began the task of dismantling the rifle.

With measured haste he packed the rifle back into its snag proof bag and descended the tower through the internal stairway down to ground level where he paused before carefully opening the personnel door which gave access to the smooth seamless surface of the apron. Within moments he was inside warehouse 26C which was situated on the western perimeter of the apron; he felt his way in the darkness of the closed up building and located his means of escape.

Even had the light been good he would not have been able to see the outline of the door crafted into the side of the crate. He located the door by finding by touch a knothole in the centre of the top loop of the R in FREIGHT made discernible with the aid of a weak LED key-fob light. Once inside he deposited the rifle in a lock box which snapped shut and locked automatically, the next segment of his task would be boring in the extreme. He strapped himself into an airline style seat which had been fitted with a vacuum chamber to take care of comfort breaks during the long flight ahead. All he had to do now was to wait until morning when the crate would be loaded into the hold of the cargo plane which would take him to Madrid. He fell almost immediately into a deep sleep, demonstrating that he was totally untroubled by the assassination he had just carried out.

He was awoken refreshed the next morning when the crate was lifted by fork lift and trundled across the apron and into the cavernous interior of a cargo plane. His task was complete and had been carried out nervelessly and with military precision. The period of boredom he had anticipated had been mitigated by his deep untroubled sleep and he was now one million US dollars richer and had the satisfaction of having achieved exactly what had been expected of him: to help rid the world of somebody whom he had been told was a despotic dictator. He did not see how life could get better than this.

The unlikely beginning of the events which had culminated in a plan for assassination started during post-graduate research work for the British MoD, many years earlier, carried out by Chester Gilliland and Bruce Crook, two talented young scientists who had discovered an amazing scientific anomaly which could do so many things to help to mankind. Conversely it also had the capacity to destroy every last vestige of the human race or any point between the two extremes. In essence they had devised a radar projector which fired waves of energy directed by computer-controlled nanobots. The nanobots were programmed to transmit energy waves from a table top projector to a pre-determined distance before returning back to the projector, rather than travelling in a straight line into

8

infinity if it failed to detect an object in its path. Their original experiment failed to accomplish its intended purpose but it did lead to the discovery of the powerful anomaly which, when its unbelievably powerful capabilities became known, attracted the interest of unsavoury characters and governments.

They had at first been able to keep their eerily frightening discovery a secret from their unprincipled employer, Colin Wilson the then UK/DDP (Director of Defence Projects) who was a civilian adviser to the MoD, knowing that, because of his demonstrated lack of integrity as a civilian political advisor, they were unable trust him with the potentially destructive power of their revolutionary technology.

Despite wracking their collective brains they were unable to identify an alternative government or country which could be trusted with the destructive power of their discovery. Further problems came to light when the characteristically self-serving actions of the DDP forced the abandonment of their research project just as it was about to reach a conclusion. Clearly his intention was to sequester the original technology for his own advantage, probably by selling its benefits to the highest bidder. They were thankful that he was, in the beginning at least, unaware of the existence of the unexpected additional power of the anomaly. They remonstrated with him about the wisdom of the untimely cancellation of the project, code-named Broken Arrow and in response he terminated their contracts and threatened to ruin their professional standing leaving him to continue developing the originally intended advanced radar capability for his own aggrandisement.

Being a vindictive man and wanting to further his lofty ambitions, he endeavoured to have the two scientists branded as traitors and actually had them

9

imprisoned with the intent of spiriting them away and eliminating them away from prying eyes. After a nerve-wracking escape, aided by Silas Pettit, a soldier of fortune, who had originally been charged, by Wilson, with capturing them, they eventually reached a bolt hole on the Azores island of Flores. From this location the three men, joined by Penny Caine, childhood friend and now partner of Gilliland, in a relationship which flourished and bloomed during their university years together where they developed what had been until then an embryonic plan for constructing an island and forming an alternative society. Using the anomaly's extraordinary power they found it necessary, in order to protect their powerful discovery from misuse, to create a new land mass in the middle of the Atlantic. This step in the development of their new society was furthered by populating the new island with carefully chosen, like minded, engineers, scientists and specialists who were selected from the best available free spirits in the world.

For those selected a totally new way of life was offered, allowing them the freedom to develop their specialities unhindered by interference or monetary constraints. Creating the breathing space that they required to develop their plans unhampered by those forces wishing to possess the new technology, the four feigned their collective demise and leaked the misinformation to their sworn enemy Wilson and in doing so succeeded in diverting his spoiling tactics based on his hatred of them.

The new technology giving them this incredible ability was 'BAM2', an acronym for Broken Arrow Mark 2, the unexpected outcome of a radar research project which they carried out for the MoD and which proved to be a truly revolutionary ground breaking discovery. Its anomalous nature enabled them among many other things to create controlled magma eruptions enabling them to form their island home. Their new home came to be known as Recovery Island because it was recovered from the seabed at a location shown on Moses Pitt's world map of 1681 and that of the renowned map maker Gerardus Mercator as Las Maidas. The island disappeared beneath the waves at some unknown time during what must have been a cataclysmic geological upheaval.

This course of events formed the foundations for a society which could, if given the freedom to flourish, produce a world-changing society for the benefit of the whole of mankind. However, there are those who have a different agenda and who could and if given the opportunity would introduce opposition, pain and anguish at every opportunity.

Two

The surgeon in creased and overly tight green hospital scrubs peered over the top of his binocular spectacles at the face of the woman who lay sedated on the operating table. He was the only person in the operating theatre with her. This was not the standard procedure laid down by the Island's Surgeon Director, Professor Doctor Carlina Tanterelli: there would under normal circumstances be an anaesthetist and attendant medical nurses, but these were not normal circumstances, the surgeon's unofficial benefactor insisted that there should be no witnesses to the minor procedure he was about to undertake. What Dr Tanterelli didn't know about was of no matter to him; his only concern was for the rewards he would receive.

He had no qualms about going against Dr Tanterelli's procedures but he had no intention of doing the same with the diktats of his benefactor, not just because of the vastly inflated fee he would receive directly into his illicit off-shore bank account but also and equally strongly because he was scared stiff of the repercussions which were implied in the meticulous instructions he had been given. This was a new experience for the surgeon; it was the first time he had been able to see the face of a 'special' patient sent by the benefactor. Normally his task was, bafflingly, to apply discreet tattooed symbols on the patients whose faces and bodies were covered when he entered the operating theatre so that he could not identify them. The generous payments he received more than compensated him for the unethical work he carried out.

The face of this patient was required to be uncovered simply because the procedures were to be carried out, unusually, on that part of her anatomy and in any case he had consulted with her prior to the operation to determine the one-off procedure required. Now, as she lay on the operating table she had not been fully anaesthetised, simply rendered comatose; she still needed local anaesthetic to dull the pain which might easily have woken her from her light medication which gave him anonymity.

The more delicate of the two procedures was undertaken first, it involved the insertion of a sophisticated disc camera lens into her right eye. The lens which was the same size and colour as her eye pupil was surrounded by a fine thread of gold; he had been instructed to implant it with great care so as not to disrupt the circuit it formed. This was the longer of the two procedures which was made more difficult because he had to stop frequently to bathe the eye with a saline solution, this would normally have been carried out by a nurse, but there was no nurse, as the benefactor had insisted. The second and final minor procedure was quick and simple; it involved the insertion of a tiny receiver/transmitter in her ear lobe; this would receive images and then transmit them onward; to where he did not know or care.

He completed the procedures and checked to make sure that the eye and earlobe were clear of seepage and appeared clean and healthy. Satisfied with the results of his labours he pulled down the sheet covering her. She wore a surgical robe which opened at the back and had been tied by a pair of tapes at the top. He lifted the hem of the robe to reveal her nakedness and his breath caught at the perfection of her young body, the kind he yearned for but which was unattainable to a man of his unfortunate body shape and his rampant halitosis. He dared not do anything other than look; it was just possible that his benefactor was watching remotely; he was after all, the surgeon knew, an electronics genius. Just in case he was being watched he picked up a stethoscope and placed it between her breasts while pretending to listen to her heartbeat. Never had he taken so long to listen to so healthy a heart. To make absolutely and unnecessarily sure that she was in no danger he took her pulse and finger tapped her chest conscientiously to make sure that her lungs were clear. Reluctantly, not able to find any other reasons not to do so, he finished and covered her up.

His final act was to secure his surgical instruments and switch off the lights before leaving the theatre. Somebody else would collect her and make sure that she recovered from the anaesthetic; they would then pass her along to a third person who would make sure she was returned to her apartment and put to bed to recover. There was always someone else but he never knew who and it was of no consequence to him.

Daniel Pierson sat in the eastern promenade of the Island in the dappled shade of a young date palm. He was sipping iced tea. He was very easy to ignore; everything about him was understated. From his indefinite hair colour, quantity and texture to his bland physiognomy, his whole being was anonymous. Exercise was not one of his strengths but despite that, his build bordered on the cadaverous, but even this obvious fault did not make him noticeable. Had anybody been looking at him, they might have been puzzled by the strange emotions flitting across his otherwise immobile face but nobody was looking at him. Nobody ever did.

Despite his total lack of presence he was a man of great talent and was an internationally acknowledged successful scientific engineer. Some two years previously he had been invited to the Island by the Ruling Council through his demonstrable skills in the field of communications which had fired the imagination of the world's press. His cellular personal communication system had been developed for a major communications corporation in the United States and had broken new ground that rendered obsolete the old fashioned and cumbersome cell phone concept. The communication units were powered not by battery but by the body heat of the user and the two major components of the equipment, the audio receiver and transmitter, were invisibly body mounted. Incoming communications could be heard through a receiver implanted in the ear lobe and a miniaturised transmitter which was imbedded inside the mouth under the flesh of the cheek enabled voice transmission. The new system was activated by the utterance of a personal password which was filtered through a voice recognition application to prevent accidental activation.

Development of this innovation had given him the opportunity to join the Island community, by invitation, as an honorary citizen and also gave him access to the unlimited development funds which was a consequence of their technology fuelled economy; a freedom which was the envy of any innovator anywhere in the world. He was in the end stages of developing 'Spy-Eye,' an exciting new adjunct in which implanted retinal cameras projected holographic images which were only visible to those users implanted with matching Spy-Eye reading capabilities. At the moment this embryonic capability was limited to himself and a single 'guinea pig' that was unaware of her own involvement in the experiment. Visual images received by her were transmitted to him and he could tap into these at will by voice command from his embedded Spy-Eye master controller. He was able to view the holographic images, which were invisible to everybody else, and could still function visually by altering eye focus by look through the images and ignoring them when more demanding issues so dictated. This technology he had unashamedly based on the selective use of old 'heads up' screen displays used by air force fighter planes subsequent to World War 2 – but without the necessity of a screen for the projected image. The heads up technology had been abandoned by the time of the Great Global War, which had led to the world-wide financial collapse, when aircraft were no longer manned but had once more come into its own to serve his latest invention. *What goes around comes around.*

Strange emotions flickering across his face, which nobody had noticed, were caused by the projected holographic images before him. The images he could see were being transmitted from the retinal camera implanted in the eye of one Colleen Brogan, the unwitting guinea pig. Being androgynous the nearest he had ever got to being emotional was when, moments earlier, he had given the vocal command to activate her camera for the very first time. Sharp and clearly in focus images of what she was seeing spread out before him in glorious perfectly defined colour but the images had a flat aspect to them as if the layers of image were made up of 2D moving photographs presented in a 3D format. What made the amazing sight more special was that Brogan had no idea that he had hacked into her visual life in real time and could see what she could see. Being androgynous, his interest was not voyeuristic; he was only interested in the quality of the transmissions. That she was a woman was a matter of chance and of no importance to him. He made a mental note to consider how the projected images could be enhanced to show realistic 3D representations. On the whole he was satisfied with the success of the first trial run of Spy-Eye and with characteristic decisiveness decided to improve the image quality by having a companion camera implanted into Brogan's other eye to give the image the illusion of depth.

Her unwitting foray into Pierson's experimental world was the result of covert work by her consultant surgeon Mr Preece Cole who claimed, truthfully, that he had detected vision impairments in her eyes and persuaded her, at Pierson's instigation, to have corrective surgery. While she was under sedation she had a retinal camera implanted in her dominant eye and at the same time a transmitter was inserted into her inner cheek above the tooth line. She did not have a receiver fitted and was unaware that her vision could be accessed remotely or that her conversations could be overheard.

The procedures were minor and she suffered only mild discomfort but was puzzled by her mouth and ear being sore when it was her eye which was operated on, but she did not feel enough discomfort to raise the issue with the surgeon. The slight discomfort was entirely overridden by her being able to see clearly, through one eye at least, for the first time after many years of gradual, almost unnoticed focal degradation.

Pierson watched the world through her eyes; she was lunching with a man friend with whom she obviously wished to be more than just a friend. She had animated discussions with her companion on a whole range of subjects while skirting around the central issue of developing their relationship on a physical, touchy feely, plane. Pierson, in his androgyny, could not understand why people who were attracted to each other found it so difficult to make their feelings known. He felt attraction to no person but if he had he was sure that he would pursue the interest without the inhibitions that both Brogan and her partner showed; such reticence was beyond his focussed understanding.

Brogan and her partner finished lunch and went their separate ways with demonstrable joint regret, which he recognised by the way her eyes followed him as they parted company and the way he looked back at her, that their attraction was mutual. He was vaguely puzzled that a person so focussed and dedicated in other ways should be so juvenile about her feelings but it was not something he dwelt upon.

He walked with her, figuratively speaking, down the wide Boulevard exchanging nods and, to him, muffled greetings. The replies she received were difficult to hear and he made a note to adjust the receiver sound levels to enhance all-round quality, this he thought would be achieved when her second eye was treated. He switched off the images by voice command, not because he had seen enough but because he was beginning to suffer motion sickness. She was walking and he was sitting still and his inner ear was having difficulty in coming to terms with the conflicting signals; he was also not accustomed to being under the controlling influence of others.

The value of his published communications work had been recognised by the Island's Ruling Council as being pivotal to the development of their emerging society which was why they had invited him onto the Ruling Council. He accepted the position but showed no gratitude or interest in corporate matters as he focussed entirely on his speciality of advanced communications. His being obviously unmoved by the coveted honour being bestowed on him by such rapid elevation to the status of the council member caused some hilarity in the ranks of his fellow council members. Unaware or more accurately unconcerned that he was the butt of their amusement, he continued on his morose way undaunted and unaffected.

Finishing his iced tea, he walked at a leisurely pace to his laboratory in which technicians were in the process of further miniaturising and improving the components he had designed. Each component stood alone and the technicians working under his direction had no knowledge of the part that the component played in the make-up of the finished system, as far as they were concerned they were refining the mobile cellular telephone system. Their disinterest was one of the reasons he had selected the workforce which meant, because of their psychological make-up, that they had no wish to know of the use to which micro cameras and transmitters and receivers were being put. With the potential for more sinister application, neither did the Ruling Council.

Back in the privacy of his office he fantasised, as much as his emotionless persona would permit, about the advanced inside knowledge to which he would have access and which he could use to his advantage. He was so innocuous that even those employed in his laboratories looked straight through him; this was another situation which suited him ideally; his aims were clearly focussed and entirely self-centred.

***

To Pierson's satisfaction the Spy-Eye technology was developed at a fast pace and soon reached the stage where it could under normal circumstances be released for general use, had he wished to; but he did not. His previous life in the USA had taught him that the early disclosure of new and radical technology did not necessarily serve his personal interests. What had started out as a universally beneficial experiment had

19

turned into something which could be used to benefit him alone.

Two more guinea pigs were quickly selected and operated on. They had been fitted with retinal cameras in both eyes, an improvement which corrected the flattened 2D effect of fitting only one eye with the camera. This enhancement also reduced significantly the nausea experienced while watching the remote motion through somebody else's eyes. The applications for this innovation were sometimes obvious and sometimes subtle. Obvious applications were, as simple examples, the ability of parents to monitor the activities of their children and the ability of the security services to monitor the activities of those who had committed offences and who required to be under surveillance while on probation or under house arrest. The same technology could be used educationally by, for example, sending a human camera to remote locations to enable others to experience travel without leaving their home.

The positive uses of this technology, of which he realised there were many, could in future be used in ways which would be contrary to his interests; Pierson's reasons for keeping the innovative technology under wraps was simply that what he wanted it to do could, if revealed, prevent him from achieving his personal aims.

Three

Carlina Tanterelli disturbed him, not because of her undoubted exotic beauty but because she seemed to be able to read his mind with startling clarity and his less than platonic thoughts about her were not something he felt comfortable sharing. Carlina was not his idea of a Medical Director either in looks or by the way she dressed; her one piece, unique to the Island, Reco-fashion body garment was matt black and figure hugging and the top did little to camouflage her figure; it was carmine red matching her lipstick and was startling when contrasted against her alabaster skin which had been purposely denied exposure to the strong mid Atlantic sun.

"I'd love to continue this subject, Mark," she interrupted his private thoughts, "but you should give some more thought to this opportunity. I can assure you that you, in common with almost all people, are using, at best, one tenth of your brain's capabilities. The other ninety per cent is lying dormant and will continue to do so for the rest of your life, unless of course you choose to do something about it." She paused and regarded him through inquisitive eyes, "I recognise in you the ability, perhaps the same as mine, to access your untapped potential."

"I don't understand why you've selected me for this." Mark Lawson composed his demeanour so that she would not see that he was mightily flattered by being compared favourably with somebody who was as obviously capable as she.

"You were recommended to me by one of my fellow Ruling Council members and she thought - probably rightly - that you would be a prime subject for development. There is an adage that I use which characterises this: there are three kinds of people in this life, those who can, those who won't, and those who can't. For those who can, be thankful. For those who won't - educate them until they can. Those who can't should be encouraged to find another, more appropriate, path to follow. Without question, concerning the full use of your brain power, you fit into the second category".

"I'm not sure that I like the idea of being categorised as a prime subject and I can't imagine why you or whoever else it was that recommended me would think that I am anything other than an ordinary bloke." More than anything he was uncomfortable at being the focus of any discussion by those who ran the Island.

"It would be pointless to force you into anything that you don't feel comfortable with, but you would have nothing to lose by joining me in my little experiment to see if we can unleash some of your hidden talent; it could be fun for both of us." She looked at him enquiringly with one eyebrow raised.

"Tell me again what it is you want to try and get me to do, I couldn't take it all in first time round." They had been in conversation for more than an hour and his flagging concentration was being further diluted by her increasingly disturbing presence and the intensity of her gaze.

"We were given brains with a capacity which vastly exceeds that which we naturally use," she summarised. "We have at our disposal this enormous untapped power, for reasons which I don't yet understand but it is safe to assume that it is possible, under certain extreme circumstances, to tap into it, even if only temporarily. We can work *with* your considerable strengths and *on* your incidental weaknesses."

"What circumstances might they be?" He was not convinced by the logic of her assumptions.

"Examples?" She narrowed her eyes in concentration as she searched her mind. "A man has been known to lift a ton of automobile to free his trapped child. Another has halted the progress of a terminal illness to attend his only daughter's wedding and after achieving that seemingly impossible task - which flies in the face of conventional medicine - relinquishes the power of the cure and simply dies. These are rare and extreme cases but they do happen. There are so many things which are not so dramatic." She searched her mind again. "We all have a similar brain capacity so why should it be that one person can play the violin with ease when others can't? What is the trigger that enables a person to play something as involved and complicated as the violin but not to untangle the solution to a complex mathematical problem? Einstein was a genius as was Steven Hawking and at a guess I would say that they only used eleven per cent of their brain instead of the ten that most others use. That's a guess by the way." She laughed and lightened the mood which had become very intense.

"Are you saying that you think I could be an Einstein?" he chided her mischievously.

"In the fullness of time possibly yes, but I think that's a long way down the line," she matched his mischievousness. "The aptitude you have shown in some of the tasks you have carried out, I'm thinking of the choices you made during the drilling expedition to China and the debacle with Wilson in the control room during his failed attempt to take over the Island. You demonstrated a rare ability to tap into extra reserves and think on your feet when the demand is important enough. Tell me," she changed tack seamlessly, "can you solve a Rubik's Cube?"

"Can I what?" He was startled by the unexpected change of subject.

"Can you solve the puzzle of Rubik's Cube?" She picked up a cube from her desk top and threw it to him. "I use that when I need to focus my mind." She held out her hand and he threw it back.

"I tried one a few times but it's beyond me my brain doesn't work that way."

She took the cube and inspected each of the six colour scrambled faces. Looking at her watch she noted the time and began solving the Cube with incredible speed. She paused after fifteen seconds and once more inspected the six faces. The puzzle was solved inside twenty seconds.

"Fantastic," he said when she had finished and he saw that each face comprised a single colour.

"Now how about this!" She manipulated the cube with amazing speed and threw it to him.

He caught it and saw that five of the faces were symmetrical the outside borders were of uniform colour which was different from the centre square; the sixth face was all one colour. "Impressive," he admitted, "but what have you just proved?"

"Like you I was unable to do that when I first tried. I watched an expert do what I've just done and asked myself the question why, then, couldn't I also do it. I reached the conclusion that I couldn't do it because I wasn't allowing myself the freedom to do so. Then I freed my mind of its inhibitions and looked at it logically and used imagination and spatial awareness. Hey presto, by convincing myself that it was possible, I did it." She smiled at his obvious scepticism. "Would you like to be able to do it?"

"I would, but I just don't have that ability."

"No, that is self-evident, you don't yet have that ability but what would you say to my teaching you to teach yourself to do it within one week, two at the outside?"

"I don't think it's possible."

"Are you willing to give it a try?"

"I'll try anything once."

"That's good." She smiled gently. "Who knows where it might lead?"

***

Lawson's next task, after his slightly disturbing session with Tanterelli, was to talk with Silas Pettit, founder, Security Director and influential senior member of the Ruling Council. Lawson was flattered, not for the first time, to be in the presence of such an iconic man but at the same time was still slightly intimidated by him and by their chosen venue. He sat in the lounge of The Atlantean, Recovery Island's only Country Club situated on the Southern slopes of Central Mountain. The panoramic windows looked west to the open Atlantic across the lower slopes of the mountain which were covered in a profusion of sub-tropical vegetation and over the western dwelling area and the gardens of remembrance and out to the silver spangled dark blue sea beyond.

Although the Atlantean was open to all residents of the Island it was, by mutual voluntary acceptance, used only by those who enjoyed the soubriquet of 'elite' in the hierarchy or perceived social standing of the Islanders, even though the Island's population was intended to be classless, established perceptions are hard to counter. There was no rule governing this throw back; it was simply woven into the evolving culture of the citizens and their new nation.

25

A little ahead of the time that they had agreed to meet, Pettit walked into the great room and made directly for the table at which Lawson sat. As he walked across the room he was greeted by several people, some with easy familiarity but mostly with deference.

"Mark." Pettit smiled and extended his hand. "Good of you to come, I hope I haven't kept you waiting?"

"No sir, I arrived a little early." He was both flattered and at the same time a little in awe of the presence of one of the now legendary founders, which was fuelled by this being his first ever visit to the Atlantean Club.

"Mark," he chided gently, "after what you and we went through during the Chinese oil drilling debacle, which I still remember so well, you should drop the formality—it's Silas." He left the sentence hanging in the air. Looking around at the occupants of the adjacent tables, he said softly, "I think it would be wise for us to go to somewhere more private and comfortable to have our conversation."

"If you say so…Silas." He was uncomfortable with the familiarity as he followed Pettit through a nondescript looking unmarked door and mentally castigated himself for his mawkish behaviour.

"Take a seat and please relax, I don't bite." Pettit indicated one of the two soft leather seats at an informal low table in one corner of what looked to Lawson and was, unofficially, a private and very exclusive lounge. "There's a task that I would like you to consider and it could be of vital importance to our Island; let me give you a little background to the reason for our getting together." As was typical of him he launched into the subject matter without the hindrance of further pause. "It is a fact and you are probably aware, that the pressure for us to share BAM2

26

technology with outside influences is being increased but no formal approach has recently been made to us directly or indirectly. In other words they, probably the Federation and maybe others, are still up to their old tricks; they know we won't share so they are exploring other means to acquire it. It does not bode well for us, that they're not being open about their aspirations and probably means that whatever it is they intend to do will not be welcomed by us."

"I understand what you are saying but I don't understand where I come into this?" Lawson was puzzled.

"All in good time," Pettit smiled bleakly. "You spent some time with Carlina Tanterelli this morning talking about development of natural ability." It was a statement rather than a question. He raised his eyebrows and looked questioningly at Lawson, tilting his head to one side waiting for a response.

"Yes, I did," Lawson said hesitantly, wondering what would come next.

"Don't look so concerned," Pettit said mildly, to put Lawson at his ease, "I discussed your meeting with her shortly after it was over but not in detail. Your consultation with her is ethically protected and she would not reveal details of your conversations without first getting your consent and I would not ask her to do so. She merely indicated to me that she felt that you were a prime candidate for some very interesting developments which we have in mind."

"She said the same to me, more or less, and as I recall I said to her that I didn't necessarily relish the idea of being thought of as anybody's prime candidate for anything," Lawson's brow was creased with a concern, "and I still don't understand what it is you want me to do?"

"Carlina is advancing her research into the enhancement of mental acuity and I - no we - would like you to consider working with her to improve and hone the untapped natural abilities that she assesses you undoubtedly and obviously unconsciously, possess."

"I still don't see what the threat to our security and my abilities, tapped or untapped, have to do with each other."

"We need to combat the threat that we believe to be out there and from whatever source it comes. You have already demonstrated your ability to handle difficult situations pragmatically and decisively as they develop." He paused and looked intently at Lawson. "My question to you, before I explain the connection between the two, is - will you be willing to help us to deal with the possible threat and come to our assistance as you so ably did with the Chinese expedition and Wilson's takeover bid?"

Without pause Lawson's autonomic response was "yes."

"That's good," Pettit said softly, "who knows where it might lead?"

Pettit had expressed the same 'who knows where it might lead' sentiment as Tanterelli and Lawson began to wonder where it might lead and was nervous about the possible destination but at the same time felt a piquant frisson of excitement. His autonomic *yes* response had committed him to tacit acceptance of the task without knowing the details of what it would be.

What seemed to him like an interesting and diverting proposition would turn out to be, for him and the rest of the Island population, a life changing moment.

Four

Much to Lawson's astonishment and delight, a week after the meeting with Tanterelli he was an aficionado of the Rubik's cube. Tanterelli expressed no surprise at his momentous achievement; her feelings on the matter were secretly celebrated by a fleeting, Mona Lisa-like smile. She was inwardly amused by his puckish look of pride when he returned to her, completed, the jumbled cube she had thrown to him just thirty seconds before. "Wow." She gave him a look of admiration. "You are even more adept than I thought, just one week and you're a world class cube master."

He laughed to cover his embarrassment at her praise and tried to look nonchalant. "Must be because I have a good teacher," he mumbled in his embarrassment, wondering with immediate alarm whether he was being too flirtatious.

"A teacher is only as good as the talent of her pupil," she matched his self-deprecation, "but let us not dwell on that. Silas tells me that he spoke to you about the help we think you could give us in the intelligence field. Have you reached any conclusions about the offer?"

"It wasn't really an offer it was more of a philosophical discussion." He was being unnecessarily defensive for reasons he didn't understand.

"Silas doesn't do philosophical discussions; he's a straight up military man. In his own way he was offering you the chance of becoming somebody of importance on the Island and that is a rare opportunity."

She poured two cups of delicate white tea from a traditional Chinese willow pattern, tea pot which sat in a soft woven vine nest on her desk and pushed one of the cups in its nest towards him. "Let me make a suggestion to you." She nodded towards his cup of tea and took a delicate sip of her own. "I believe that you can do the job that he was talking about, we are looking for somebody who can use their intellect to find out who, if anybody, on the Island is leaking information to outside sources. Something is going on, we don't know what but obviously it doesn't bode well."

"Being able to master Rubik's cube qualifies me for such a task how?" He peered at her over the rim of his teacup as he gave an experimental sip. "Um," he said. "I don't drink unsweetened tea without milk usually but this is good."

"Glad you like it, this is really the only way to enjoy the subtlety of the flavour." She returned him abruptly to the point of her discussion. "You have the capability to do this job and please believe me when I tell you that. I've sifted through scores of potential candidates for this task and you're the only one who has the specific mind-set to do it, you were a long way ahead of the best of the others."

"I'm flattered of course that you should think so but what is it about my possible abilities that you think qualifies me for this job?"

"I believe that you have the ability to get into somebody else's mind and think like them. You showed that with the cube, you were able to get into my mind and think like me and solve the riddle of the cube by osmosis. You can do this but you must want to; do you want to?"

"If I have the ability that you assume the answer is yes but I still don't really understand how it qualifies me for a job in intelligence?"

"Now we're getting somewhere." She showed obvious signs of relief as though he had made a fundamental decision. "You will need to get inside the

30

mind of the person or persons who wish us harm to gain something by gathering information from them without their knowledge. If you can do this we will be well on the way to identifying and dealing with situations of potential danger."

"Just supposing that what you say is true, I sense a dichotomy. I need to know the identity of the person so that I can get into his mind in order to find out who he is?"

"Very logical." Her sudden tinkling laughter distracted him. "You have actually taken the first step in the deductive identification process."

"But it doesn't get me anywhere. He furrowed his brow in perplexed concentration. "I started out not knowing who he is or they are and I've ended up not knowing who he is or they are and in the meantime I didn't pick up any clues on how to find him, or them."

"You are actually further forward than you think. You have accepted that whoever he, she or they are, they do exist – even if it is just in your mind."

"I'm completely lost; this is all too tenuous for me. I prefer clarity."

"Then make it clear to yourself."

"How do I do that?"

"Apply your intelligence, think outside the box."

"That's all very well but I still don't know where to start."

"Let me give you a hint to get you started. How do you think you can find them when you don't know who they are?"

"I don't know." He was becoming exasperated and his voice sharpened.

"Think outside the box. If you can't find him what is the opposite tactic that you must employ?"

He frowned and looked uncomfortable and then his look changed and realisation dawned. "I must get them to find me." His eyes widened at the thought that had just released itself from his unconsciousness.

"Eureka." She sat back in her chair and gave him a warm smile.

His look of satisfaction blossomed and then evaporated. "How do I do that though?

"You've jumped the first hurdle and now you must consider your next moves. The answers don't come without a lot of thought. Go away and think about your next steps, only you can decide what they are, I cannot do that for you. One further thing which I have already mentioned, you need to get into the head of somebody like this and think the way they think. To do that you have to subvert your own rationale and adapt to the persona of a renegade citizen of this Island who has the aim of destabilising our society."

It occurred to him as he left her consulting rooms that in accepting the challenge he had tacitly confirmed his acceptance of the job in Island intelligence.

Tanterelli's words echoed through his mind '*think like the enemy – get into his head.*' If he was in the position of somebody who wanted to disrupt the workings of the Island community how would he proceed? Was this just one person or was it a group and if a group, how would they be recruited to the cause? How could he find this out and how could he lure this person or group out into his purview?

His first shallow thought was that he had to find out if the foe was an individual or a group; there was no obvious way of identifying the enemy. Thinking more fundamentally he realised that whether he was dealing with a group or a single infiltrator did not actually matter, one would lead to the other, if the situation existed. '*Think like the enemy,*' Tanterelli had said, so he dismissed his own slant on things and engaged the persona of an enemy who needed to remain

32

undiscovered and who needed to be able to infiltrate the inner structure of the Island's administration. In that position and with those aims, what would he do?

It was some hours after he had ended up thinking in circles that the method he would employ if he were the enemy unexpectedly burst into his consciousness. It was suddenly blindingly obvious and a hasty telephone conference with Silas Pettit and Carlina Tanterelli confirmed that his proposed methodology was, they both thought, intuitively brilliant.

Five

This particular series of court proceedings against Paul Zen had caused anger among the activists of the Island's society; they recognised that a hitherto unknown miscreant was being given some unreasonably harsh treatment, in fact he was being pilloried by the official judicial apparatus and there were growing accusations of a witch hunt or a personal vendetta; neither of which were customary in their utopian society. The person on the docket, it emerged by rumour during the proceedings, was a past associate of the infamous and reviled Jacques Pantin, the traitorous Recovery Island National who had worked with Colin Wilson, the conscienceless rogue politician who, after a failed coup to take over the Island, had used his evil powers to subjugate the citizens of the newly emerging nation of Nuovostan, formerly part of Eastern Russia, and take over as their president. Pantin had fled the Island under Wilson's protection when the attempted coup failed catastrophically at the very last hurdle.

Recovery Island activists were unhappy that the exaggerated case against Zen was based solely on his previous association with Pantin and not on the seriousness of the misdemeanours for which he was being accused. That Silas Pettit, Director of Security, was personally chairing the proceedings attested to the seriousness with which the Island's Ruling Council viewed the case. Zen was accused of breaches of protocol in which he had used his Reco-card, the Island's substitute for currency, to aid those who had had their access to certain classes of what were considered to be frivolous products, such as alcohol and tobacco, rescinded because they had in some way transgressed the laws of the Island. This misdemeanour was quite common among some sections of Island society where there was considered to be an '*honour among compatriots*' code of practice. The apparent over-reaction of the administration in Zen's case caused a stir and an atavistic interest which filled the small hearing room to way beyond its usually permitted capacity.

One of the spectators sat unnoticed at the back of the court. He watched and listened to the proceedings intently but calmly, without the show of emotion which obviously infused the majority of the others present. The hearing lasted two days, an unprecedented time for such a low profile misdemeanour. On both days the anonymous watcher sat in the same seat and observed the proceedings as they unfolded.

Common practice in the Island's hearings procedure was observed; the accused was permitted to represent his own interests and the supposedly unbiased adjudicator was, as in this case, the chairman of the hearing, Silas Pettit, the Island's Director of Security. It was clear to those watching the proceedings that Silas Pettit, who was normally a person of strict neutrality, had an axe to grind, probably, it was thought, because of his pathological hatred of Pantin as a cohort of the reviled Colin Wilson. Customarily there was no jury required for misdemeanours and guilt or otherwise, and punishment if appropriate, was determined by the Chairman. The verdict, as was also their custom, was reached by him in private and was given to the accused in person also in private. The punishment meted out, if required by a guilty verdict was a matter between the Chairman and the accused and would not, as this was classed as a simple misdemeanour, be shared with the rest of the community. Island law observed that if punishment of any kind was required, it was applied and after its completion the wrongdoer was fully exonerated. Neither the verdicts nor punishments were published and were matters which would not be divulged by the administration although the wrongdoer could do so if wished. Some elements of the society were violently opposed to what they viewed as feudal injustice, but there was no effective means of countering it under Island law save for deciding to leave the Island to pursue the matter from another land. None of the activists had so far decided on this radical course of action.

At the end of the hearing there was unrest among those who had witnessed the trial, the majority of whom thought that Zen had been treated unfairly, particularly after Pettit's scathing and, to the more militant observers of the process, obviously biased summing up. It was generally agreed that for such a minor offence there was a high degree of over-reaction; the hearing was adjourned for the verdict to be considered in private and disquiet among the activists' grew exponentially.

The verdict and punishment were dealt with very quickly and within a short time Zen was, in an initially limited way as was customary, back on the street while unresolved matters were considered by Pettit. The Island did not possess a jail; the only form of detention was for the guilty party to be banished to a day holding-room within the precincts of the court, for a judicially determined period of time. This form of punishment required the guilty party to be in the day room by 7.00 am and to stay there until 7.00 pm for the duration of the period determined.

A vociferous minority waited outside the building for Zen's reappearance. When he emerged looking ashen faced, they descended on him like a pack of ravenous hyenas baying for information to fuel their passions. Questions were hurled at him. Most of them were provocative and designed to inflame the situation and the baying grew louder. Zen protested noisily at the way he had been treated and he angrily accused the Chairman of the hearing to be biased. He vowed revenge for the harsh and unjust treatment he was about to receive.

The protesting and potentially dangerous crowd was dispersed by uniformed security forces which relied initially on their ability to withdraw Recocard privileges from the protesters should they fail to obey the dictates of the security forces, rather than rely on the application of physical force. The crowd was sullen as it dispersed muttering that the security forces were part of Pettit's domain and therefore prejudiced against them and the unjustly accused Zen. Zen for his part continued vociferously to contest the treatment meted out to him and lamented his unfair treatment.

Pettit stood at a second floor window and watched the dispersing crowd, some of whom showed signs of being prepared to incur the wrath of the Ruling Council by civil disobedience. The feeling did not ultimately take root and the last few dissidents retreated with surly glances over their shoulders at the stoic security forces.

"What do you think?" Pettit asked Lawson who stood looking out of the window out of view of the dispersing antagonists outside the court.

"Only time will tell, but I would say that these protesters are feeling angry and I can't help thinking that they have been pushed too far for them to retreat now. I think they will probably grow in number unless we do something about it." Lawson looked pensive and chewed his bottom lip.

"And if we don't do anything about it?"

"We'll just have to wait." Lawson muttered darkly and then brightened as he realised that Tanterelli had really made a difference to his way of thinking. Before her guidance he would have said of a failure, which might be the fate of this current thinking, that there was no other avenue but to accept defeat, now he was prepared to meet the possibility of defeat with the consideration of an alternative plan. Now he was much more optimistic but at the same time he recognised that if his plan didn't actually work he had no currently plausible idea about what he could do to achieve his objectives.

Six

Zen had plenty of time to consider the situation in which he found himself. The day holding- room in which he had been incarcerated as an initial punishment while consideration was given, unusually, to further punishments had little by way of distraction. There was a disturbing rumour of the possibility of Zen being deported, a first for any Islander, which was fuelled by his newly acquired supporters approaching the point of insurrection. They could not understand why Zen was being dealt with so harshly; clearly Pettit had a hidden agenda of hate against him which fanned the flames of their discontent and led to dark mutterings among the practicing activists.

One of the features of the room in which Zen was being held was that one wall, which faced onto the little used Piazza adjacent to the court buildings, was almost entirely of reinforced translucent one-way multi-carbonate sheeting from floor to ceiling. He could see anybody passing by though they could not see him. The reason for the wall was to remind the offender that life outside continued but that the one being incarcerated could see but not participate in or communicate with life outside; it was a strong psychological reminder of the folly of breaking Island law. Zen felt a powerful, although unreasonable resentment at the unjust treatment he was receiving and was given great satisfaction at the support he was receiving from this group of people whom he did not know.

On the second boring day of his incarceration a small group of demonstrators gathered in the Piazza outside the glass wall and began a shuffling vigil carrying poorly constructed placards which complained about the justice of the way he was being held. They could not ascertain if their protest was being seen by him and he could not hear what they were shouting but by their expression their comments were not pro-Pettit. At the end of the second day he was told by his wardens that to avoid any further trouble with the demonstrators he was being released on trust, by direct instructions from a Ruling Council official, into the confines of his own accommodation in the Island's eastern domestic dwelling area. He was to be under house arrest.

Two days in confinement, with only educational matter to distract him, had been enough to make him realise the value of the relative freedom he had been unexpectedly granted by being relocated under house arrest. Even so, house arrest for 24 hours each day was irksome and boring. While this situation lasted he had no access to his information portal, the IP, which were his eyes on what was happening on the Island and although his current situation was a vast improvement over the former, his gratitude was grudging – he didn't do boredom with any grace at all. His resentment continued to build.

As he was settling back into the familiarity of his home, much to his surprise, he found a mobile radio communication handset which had been secreted in a delivery of his permitted basic groceries. The typed note in which it was wrapped, read 'Press #'. He did so and after six long rings the call was answered, it was immediately obvious that the voice of the person answering had been electronically disguised, it was hollow and had radio frequency overtones. "Zen?" The electronically distorted voice enquired.

"This is Zen, who are you?"

"We should talk." Zen's question was ignored.

"Maybe, but who are you?"

"I'm the one who arranged for you to be freed from the detention day holding-room."

"I'm grateful but what do you want and why have I got this radio device? You and I know it's against agreed protocol, if it's discovered I could end up being tried as a felon. I really don't want to be the first citizen to be deported, so as I said; who are you?"

"Don't worry about regulations; we can have those taken care of. You've had a raw deal and you will continue to get a raw deal from the Ruling Council simply because you're not considered to be a desirable citizen," he added as an afterthought, "it's rumoured that they are considering deportation anyway." His distorted words were clipped and bad tempered.

"That's between me and them, how do you know about these things? My dealings with them are supposed to be a secret."

"You're wasting time with all these questions you can make a choice, it's either risk deportation or talk to us."

"Who is 'us'? And what's in it for you if you help me?"

"Enough time wasting, you're either with us or I can make sure that you will rot in any God forsaken backwater of the world that will have you. It's up to you." The voice paused and there was a hollow shrilling noise sound that lingered longer than Zen found comfortable.

The unknown voice continued after the controlling pause. "I'll give you a last chance. Think about what I've said and phone me back in one hour. It will be your last chance." The transmission ended abruptly.

Zen sat as still as a statue, trance like, as he considered the implications of the cryptic conversation. The illegal communication was radio based which

41

meant it was not going through the Island's fibre optic communications filter and would be untraceable; that, at least, was an interesting adjunct. The voice had been disguised which of itself was a good indication that not only was the Island surveillance system not aware of the communication taking place but that the person to whom he was talking was untraceable by voice recognition. He was obviously dealing with ultra-cautious people.

He smiled to himself with a feeling of satisfaction, these were obviously the kind of people he wanted to get together with and who would help him in the quest for revenge which they obviously recognised. They appeared to have a sufficiently high level of influence to get him out of the day hold room and had done so impressively quickly. Also he was back in his own home, they were using illegal methods of communication and what was telling and important was that they could influence the outcome of any possible deportation hearing should it take place. He decided that they were his kind of people and to call them back. To establish his credentials and play it cool he called them back half an hour beyond their pointedly stated deadline. He wanted to make sure that he was in control of the situation and that whoever they were they could not lead him around by the nose just because they had given him an escape route. They would have to learn and understand that he was his own man and he had his own standards.

The resultant telephone call was made and a long discussion took place in which he was apprised of the nature of the group who were attending, for the moment, to his wellbeing. They were, he learned, small in number and very focussed in a way which would be explained to him if he managed to meet the stringent demands of full membership of their private association. Until he had proven himself he would not even be told of the name of the organisation. He was told in no uncertain terms that after the completion of this introductory discussion his radio would be remotely disabled and he would be given directions for its disposal.

On the very next day he was told by a senior Security Guard that his case had been reviewed by the Ruling Council and that no further action would be taken providing he refrained from breaking, or even remotely bending the laws of the Island. He was also told by the same guard that his release had been opposed by the Director of Security Silas Pettit who had been responsible for his trial and sentencing but he had been overruled by a Council Welfare Committee. The guard raised his eyebrows as he imparted this information and indicated clearly that it would be in Zen's interest not to stray from the straight and narrow because Pettit was a vengeful man and as hard as nails and he had the memory of an elephant. Clearly, Zen reaffirmed his original thoughts; his interests were being taken care of by a very influential and as yet unknown guardian.

Despite successfully recruiting Zen there was, frustratingly, still a shortage of human resources required to meet the private group's objectives. There were a growing number of followers but on the whole their use was limited. Generally they were unprincipled enough to carry out the tasks set for them but they all had their own specific agendas which were not necessarily driven by the aspirations of the group. What the group needed was somebody who would follow orders but who would be capable of independent action should the need arise and who would not be diverted by personal issues. Trawling through the available information on file for every citizen on the Island yielded nothing. His efforts were frustratingly unrewarded and he gave more lateral thought to a way of achieving his aim.

It had been fortuitous that the group leader was in a court when the last of Zen's many transgressions was being heard. It had taken him a while to discover suitable hunting grounds for potential members but once he had selected the courts hearing rooms for this purpose it was simply a matter of being patient and although patience was not one of his many strengths, he metaphorically bit his lip. With great care and after listening to many cases he selected Zen as being the most likely first candidate. He was Island-born, which meant that his dissidence was natural and not inherited; in his late twenties he suddenly commenced a life and record of petty crime and antisocial behaviour.

Contacting him after the completion of his hearings had been simple and he was receptive to the intriguing overtures made to him which would appeal to a career petty criminal. The sentencing process had culminated in his being denied a whole range of Recocard transactions a situation which would do nothing to encourage him to be supportive of the Island's regime. In common with the rest of the Islanders the Recocard was the only means available to him of making acquisitions of any kind; luxury items were now excluded and only minimum basic purchases were possible. His only access to anything other than basics could only be achieved by persuading somebody else to acquire them on their own Recocards and pass them on to him. But this was the very crime that had landed him in his present mess and because of the publicity his case had received he could not imagine anybody else risking the recently heightened wrath of the courts by duplicating his misdemeanours.

Zen was harvested with no difficulty apart from his one puny attempt by responding to the recruiting conversation half an hour late which was immediately recognised for what it was by his interviewer: an attempt to give himself the appearance of being a hard man to control by making inappropriate demands of the organisation, which were immediately slapped down. He was recruited swiftly and allocated a code number of 66 by the disembodied voice over a secured telephone which identified him as a member of one of the cells with the position of 6th member of Cell 6. As he only ever received telephone calls in which the voice patterns were distorted, he had no means of identifying or contacting any other members of his or any other cell. Communications were instigated by 61, his group leader, always by means of secured radio telephone conferencing. All discussions took place through the chairmanship of 61 and only code numbers were ever used as a means of identification.

Initially he was given a number of low-grade tasks which he performed more than adequately by using initiative when the intended plans, which were disappointingly very light in strategy, began to unravel. Thinking further about the inept instructions he received which were at odds with the quality of the subterfuge employed by the group, he deduced that he was being watched closely to see how he would apply himself to completing the allotted task by using his own initiative to overcome the tardiness of the task planning.

Intuitively he overcame the shortcomings in the methods given him by applying his natural cunning and completed the tasks set efficiently. His guesswork proved to be accurate when out of the blue he was contacted by number 11. He assumed correctly that 11 indicated that his contact was number 1 in cell 1,

45

clearly the head man, what 11 had to say gave him a buzz of anticipation, he was to be given a task of supreme importance and he was ready for it.

Number 11 had thought of including 66 into Cell 1, in view of his impressive lawless track record, but decided that six in a cell was the optimum number compatible with security and clarity of communications and had placed him temporarily into cell 6 as the sixth member. 66 was, when research by accessing what were supposed to be strictly secured files told them, an overtly unsavoury character who was obviously unstable in a way which would be highly suitable for RIR, Recovery Island Rebels, the name of the private group and he was attributed with being out to avenge the exile of his hero Jacques Pantin, now considered to be the mythical forefather of the revolution. His involvement in what was almost the capture of the Island by Wilson was now written in Island underground folk law. The hero worship did not dwell on Pantin's lack of basic intelligence and morals.

Much to Eleven's delight, 66 turned out to have close contacts with some unsavoury elements from the outside world, no doubt from his association with Jacques Pantin who had, after fleeing the Island to exile in London, changed his name to Jack Pain. Zen was put to the test by being tasked to source a top class contract killer. Clearly Zen was a dark horse, despite his undoubtedly being watched by security elements of the ruling council he had still somehow managed to maintain off Island contacts. Zen seized the opportunity with minimum delay and used the contacts carefully nurtured and researched by him to strengthen his lawless aims and he was able to introduce to the RIR a thoroughly unprincipled professional killer. 'A' was the anonymous code name used by the assassin, who naturally guarded his identity to the point of paranoia, was approached by Zen and agreed to undertake the tasks set for him. Zen's immediate success impressed Eleven, the speed with which he moved when he identified and was able to contact an off Island professional assassin by means he did not care to share. Zen's decisive actions heralded a previously unheard of fast track into RIR active ranks. He would undoubtedly be a useful asset to the organisation.

Eleven had made contact with Wilson ostensibly to help the Nuovostani President to exact his revenge on the founders but, in reality, it was to serve his own purposes. Additionally he wanted to distance himself from the plan to assassinate one of the founders and allow Wilson to carry the can should the plot be uncovered. 66 contacted Eleven and identified the assassin to him by his epithet of 'A'. Eleven contacted Wilson to advise him of the availability of 'A' and Wilson would pay 'A' for tasks carried out. Eleven was happy that the trail had been adequately obfuscated and he was satisfied that his long term plan to gain control of the Island had taken one further giant step in the direction of his devious goal. All of this had been achieved without their physically meeting thereby preserving the anonymity of both Eleven and 'A', a situation which pleased him mightily.

Seven

Pantin's first departure from the Island was intended by him to be permanent but had ultimately turned into a brief visit to the UK. He had been the sole Islander who volunteered to leave during the Federation's first full siege of the island in an attempt to force capitulation. He had been thoroughly disillusioned by what he judged to be the disrespectful treatment he received once he reached the UK compared with the level of nurture he had been led to expect; that la dolce vita awaited him.

He was devastated by the offhand treatment he had actually received. The promises made to him by Wilson and more especially Julia Hammond, which had prompted him to depart the Island and become an informant for Wilson, had not come to pass. He was not shown even a hint of the high life he had been promised and which he expected as a reward for helping them. The promise of a passionate relationship with Julia Hammond, the tabloid journalist who was in cahoots with Wilson and was instrumental in his departure from the Island, was a further casualty of their agreement.

On departing the Island at the start of the first Federation siege he had been flown to a military airfield in the middle of what he perceived to be nowhere and had been dumped in a military hostel in a god forsaken cold and windswept corner of Scotland where he was interrogated by a bunch of stiff necked soldier clones who had spent much of the time grilling him about what went on the Island. They tried every interrogation technique in the book to get him to tell them Island secrets but acknowledged in the end that he knew nothing of secrets and cared even less. The

48

uniforms they wore were strange looking and the wearers lacked the control that he would expect from professional soldiers; clearly they were a group which was not attached to a recognised national army.

His dream of free movement, after the stifling restrictions of the Island, and a scintillating social life - especially at night - was shattered. Recreational activity made available to him was exclusively on base and involved a lot of drinking strange beer and playing pool or darts in a soulless mess hall. Life soon began to pall, at least on the Island he could please himself where he went and when he slept and ate. Here, life was regimented, meals were at set times and, horror of horrors he was expected to rise at 6.30 am, take a cold shower and eat a healthy breakfast after indulging in calisthenics. He was accustomed to none of these things and soon descended into grudge laden trouble making mode. The trouble making days were terminated by his being thrown into the brig; very soon he realised that he had swapped one form of hell for another worse and more unyielding regimented regime. What, he wondered, had happened to the indulgences that Hammond and Wilson had hinted and on which he had become so reliant.

It had come as a great relief to him when he had been contacted by Julia Hammond, and told that he was required to return to the Island and that he had an important task to perform after which he would be free to travel extensively and freely throughout the free world – no more military camps. He had jumped at the opportunity all the more readily because Hammond said that after the completion of his task he and she would get together for some serious social interaction. He was spurred on by this offer but at the same time was vaguely uneasy about the likelihood of the implied promises actually being fulfilled.

With the original coup attempt, success had been within sight after he played his part in smoothing the way for Wilson to take over the Island. It had all gone horribly wrong when the Islanders had scuppered Wilson's plans at the last moment. The attempt ended ignominiously and culminated in Wilson fleeing the Island in total disarray aboard the hijacked Island plane and in the process taking him along for part of the way of Wilson's escape to Nuovostan. He was abandoned in North Africa and told to make his way, under his own steam with cash which had been supplied to him by Wilson, to the UK and, he hoped, the waiting arms of Hammond. No mean feat for an Island boy who had left the Island briefly and only once before to go to Scotland where he had not been required to fend for himself.

After Pantin had fled the Island for the second and final time from which there was no possibility of his ever returning when Wilson's attempt at a personal takeover failed. Wilson, taking a confused Pantin along for part of his journey of escape had made a headlong flight to the safety of exile in Nuovostan abandoning Pantin along the way in North Africa with enough money to get himself to the UK. Pantin was stunned by the culture shock of this alien land, the clothes and the people had been a shock; the women were covered from head to toe in shapeless black tents. The men were different, some wore clothes that he recognised from the American movies he had watched on the Island as being Western in style and some, more traditional men, wore paler and briefer versions of the women's garb with the addition of baggy trousers and those who did wore full and unkempt beards. It was all so unlike the clothing worn on the Island— at least there one could tell the sex of a body by its shape.

His first task after arrival was to abandon his Island clothes in favour of the more westernised garb which was locally available. The newly acquired clothes felt loose and coarse after the tailored, softer Island fashions, but at least the local people were no longer staring at him and in some cases spitting contemptuously.

Among the more startling of his first impressions were the noise, the surface traffic and the unsavoury smelling crowds. He had no understanding of Arabic and few of the local inhabitants he encountered spoke English. Most of them spoke French and when they discovered his name, much to his distaste, would speak to him in that language; he ignored their overtures. The French part of his heritage had been buried in the past.

His natural cunning came to his aid once he had settled temporarily into his new surroundings. Having no passport was a definite problem and he decided, before his money ran too low, to acquire one. He had a contact telephone number for Julia Hammond, the journalist of questionable integrity who was responsible for his former liaison with Colin Wilson; through her contacts he was put in touch with the local underworld. He was, by extortionately expensive bribery, able to get a virtually undetectable forgery of a British passport in his chosen name of Jack Pain. Having no concept of the value of money he paid very dearly for the illicit purchases he made but was unaware of it much to the delight of the document purveyors.

Using his new passport in his new name, Jack Pain, he flew from Algeria directly to London arriving at Heathrow in the middle of a cold wet afternoon. His first impressions of London were not good. The coach journey into the capital was punctuated by the steady slip-slap of the windscreen wipers which shuttled mesmerizingly, remaining vertical, from side to side across the vast curved windscreen. At first it was a novelty for him to be able to watch the buildings and open land flash by the windows of the coach. On the Island all travel was by subterranean Transfer Car, TC, which had no external view and of course gave no impression of speed. The exhilaration soon palled and he slumped down in his seat despondently. His journey was slow at the London end as they inched their way along the M4 over the crumbling Chiswick flyover to descend into the dark forbidding streets of outer West London. Buildings, as in heavy traffic they slowly crawled past, were distorted by the streaming raindrops on the windows and they looked shabby and down at heel.

Victoria coach station was, to him, a mess of people, noise and traffic. Most of the traffic was stationary and most of the people were scurrying aimlessly in a zombie like trance, neither communicating with nor acknowledging their fellow human beings. He did as he had been instructed and took a taxi to the unremarkable hotel in an uninspiring back street on the south side of Vauxhall Bridge. It was the same hotel in which he now sat ruminating on his present day fortunes and misfortunes.

Now at last after all the trials and tribulations, with a new name and passport, he was finally in England the country of his choice. His introduction to his chosen place did not, on reflection, fill him with joy as he looked morosely out of the rain bejewelled window of his downmarket London Hotel which had been allocated to him through Hammond by Wilson, and cursed his luck.

There were highs and lows; mostly, he thought, lows. He had found it difficult to handle the concept of money having lived his life using the Recocard for all his needs. The concept of receiving change when he made purchases made his brain ache; mathematics was not his strongest suit by any stretch of the imagination. At first he marvelled at the differences between Recovery Island and the wilds of Scotland and now this new alien land, ultimately it was all so alien ...... and to his surprise and disappointment − so infinitely boring!

When he had first arrived at the hotel he excitedly waited for Julia Hammond to visit him in his room. It was not the setting he had imagined for their meeting and at which he hoped to have her fulfil the promise of 'personal service' made by her when he had been of so much assistance during the, unfortunately failed, coup by Wilson in his attempt to take over the Island. As it turned out the setting did not matter.

She walked into his room like a breath of beautiful fresh air and flung her business suit jacket onto the bed. He lunged forward intending to kiss her; she stepped back and held up a discouraging hand.

"Hold back," she said arching one eyebrow. "I'm on my way to a function and my makeup must remain un-mussed."

"What about your promise?" He was deflated by her response.

"There's time for that later. First I need you to talk to me about some Island stuff, well not to me but to one of my people. After that maybe we can get up-close and personal."

"I've been waiting a long time for you," he said darkly. "I don't feel like talking until my itch is scratched." His look and inflection was unambiguous.

"Tell you what." She smiled at him disarmingly. "I'll get one of my assistants to see you; she could scratch your itch and ask you questions at the same time. I told her about you and she was very keen to meet and she thinks you're sexy," her words hung in the air as he considered their meaning.

"Is that a guarantee?" he said, licking his lips.

"Nothing is guaranteed," she said softly, "but I can tell you which of her buttons to push so that she will do what you want."

"Deal," he said moving forward to seal it with a kiss.

"Deal," she replied stepping back from his intended embrace. "Make-up is still a muss problem."

His disappointment flared and just as quickly subsided. "When do I get to meet her?"

"I'll talk to her now." She used her mobile phone by touching a speed dial button. "Diana, it's Julia," she didn't wait for a reply. "Jacques, you know the hunk I told you about…"

"My name is Jack Pain now; not what you just said." He intruded into her conversation angrily.

"Anyway," she said unfazed by his reaction, "Jack would like to meet you to exchange ideas and have you get to know each other more intimately." She listened to the response and turned to 'Jack'. "How about tonight at her place, ten o'clock, it's just a short taxi ride from here?"

"Done," he said hastily.

"Done," she repeated into her phone.

In his new persona as Jack Pain he stood outside the door to her apartment, the piece of paper with the name Diana and the address at which he now stood clutched in a hand that was wet with anticipation. Never before had he been so high up in a building. His first trip in a lift was something of a let-down; it was dirty and smelled of urine and other things he didn't care to identify. Stepping out of the lift he looked dizzily over the chipped metal handrail which was all there was between him and a ninety feet sheer drop to oblivion.

"'Ello," a bright cockney voice greeted him through the door which was secured by a short security chain.

"Hi, I'm Jack." he said, wondering what the initials L and O had to do with their meeting, it was just another of the phrases with which he was not familiar and which he found baffling.

The door closed momentarily and reopened once the security chain had been disengaged, he found the concept of the chain yet another puzzling facet of life in this outside world about which he realised he knew less and less, rather than more. Diana stood in a dimly lit vestibule holding the door open for him to enter. He looked at her in the low light and was surprised by what he saw. She appeared to be in her early teens and was dressed with far less than the minimum required for decency especially in the country he had just vacated. She went ahead of him and opened the door into the apartment switching the vestibule lights off as she did so. The inner light was on and as she walked ahead of him he could see the shape of her body through the minimal gossamer clothing she wore, there was no indication of under garments.

"Wow," he said softly to himself as she half turned giving him a revealing side view of her slim body through the back lit filmy material.

She fascinated him; it was almost as if she spoke a different language. He had always been told by his Island teachers that he spoke lazily by shortening words and slurring them together. She was something else, she seemed incapable of starting a word with the aitch sound and she missed out the 'g' any words ending 'ing'. She liked drinking illicitly brewed Alco-pops, with which he was not familiar, and did so in large quantities, he stuck to local bitter beer which, he soon found, was obviously an acquired taste.

Over a long period of time he enjoyed many meetings with her and although he never stayed the night he did, for a few hours at a time enjoy her to the full. Their meetings, always at her place, assumed a familiarity which he relished and with which he felt comfortable. Without fail they started off with a few drinks in what she called her lounge, which was always dimly lit. The room was always in deep shadow which gave her an air of mystery. She would then ask him a series of questions about the Island customs, controls and defence systems – among other topics, in much the same way as his interrogators in Scotland had, but he felt more inclined to respond to her. They would then adjourn to her bedroom where, completely uninhibited, she would remove the few clothes she wore and then would remove his for him. One of the buttons, to be pressed, that Julia Hammond had told him of, was Diana's fetish about undressing her partner after she had blindfolded him and thereafter doing everything by touch slowly which was more for her benefit that that of her partner, although as a partner he relished the rush it gave him.

The meetings and the questions continued twice a week for almost four months. During the productive part of their meetings she asked questions from a prepared list but did not make notes about his answers. There were times when the questions were, according to his memory, repeated. When his answers became staccato and disinterested she would call a halt to the questions and begin her physical interactions – which, when she was in control, she seemed to enjoy at least as much as he did.

After their thirty fifth or sixth meeting, when the questions and the interactions of that moment stopped, she became suddenly impersonal and business like. He was uncomfortable at the sudden change and waited with anticipation for her to resume her usual intimate persona. When it was clear that she had suddenly changed he wondered what it was that he had done to incur her displeasure. Meticulously he recounted all the tips that Julia Hammond had given him; the undressing fetish, the giving of sensuous massages, the gentle stroking of the hair, wild words of endearment at the moment of crisis and numerous others. In fact he had been given a new tip for each of his visits; tonight's had seemed strange to him. He was told to suggest that they go away for a two week holiday – he had also been told that it would be paid for by Julia Hammond. He had not liked the idea himself. He was quite happy to get together with her for short evening sessions in the gloom of her apartment but the thought of two continuous weeks was not appealing, although the idea of a change of scenery did pique his interest.

His reluctance at spending two continuous weeks with her, day and night, was based on his once having secretly visited the apartment block during daylight. He was surprised to find that she had many visitors, all men, who stayed for up to an hour but mostly for half an hour. When they left they were mostly furtive and scurried to the lift with their hands in their pockets and their heads down. As he was about to leave her door opened and she emerged into the daylight; he pressed himself into a recessed doorway from where he observed her getting into the lift. He was shocked by her appearance, in unforgiving daylight her youthful face and girlish figure suddenly changed into a face riddled by, what he later learned was drugs, and a body which bordered on the fragile border of anorexia. He no longer wondered why she insisted on a blindfold whenever they were physically close and why during the light summer nights she kept the curtains closed and the soft subtly coloured lighting on.

Much to his relief she declined his invitation to join him on holiday pleading previous unchangeable commitments. When she bade him farewell they did not make a further appointment which had been their habit until now. He slipped his coat on and left her much earlier than was customary, realising that their liaisons were at an end and also realising that he didn't really mind.

When he had left and she had the apartment to herself she retrieved one of the two tapes of their conversation from the lounge where they started their evenings and did the same with the tapes in the bedroom. The two tapes were placed in an envelope addressed to Julia Hammond; the two duplicates were placed in a lock box which was bolted to the concrete floor under a shoe rack in her rickety slightly off vertical wardrobe.

She smiled to herself humourlessly. It had been fun while it lasted but the twice weekly visits severely cramped her style and interfered with her freedom to offer appointments to her regular customers. Still, she mused to herself, the financial rewards more than trebled her income over that period. She had almost been sorry when he had invited her for the holiday it was the signal from Julia, who had insisted that they should have no verbal or physical contact during the period of the transactions that her intelligence gathering was at an end. Her copy of the tapes was a form of insurance which could, if the opportunity arose, be useful as a money earner.

Eight

Zen stood outside the London hotel which was occupied by, among others, Jack Pain, barely two hours after leaving the modified freight box in the cargo hold of the contract aircraft which had transported him from Recovery Island to a private airfield, clearly Eleven's influence did not stop at Recovery Island's borders. The neon hotel sign was unlit and had obviously been that way for some time; this was evidenced by the shroud of spider webs which somehow perversely softened its abandonment. The courtyard leading to an unimposing entrance which comprised of a pair of grimy Georgian wired glass doors which, like the neon sign, was covered in arachnid filaments He entered the sloppily painted entrance porch which led on to a poorly lit reception area. He wrinkled his nose in disgust at the unsavoury odours assaulting him. Like Jack Pain he was not used to the sounds and smells of this foreign land.

Squaring his shoulders he prepared himself mentally for his encounter with Pain. He was fully aware that he was treading a fine line with this encounter, the failure of which could be terminally bad news for him and his objectives. Eleven was under the impression that Jack Pain alias Jacques Pantin was a personal friend and this had been a vital part of Zen gaining an entrée into the ranks of RIR. The fine line which Zen trod with Eleven was that his friendship with Pain was a fiction which had been invented by Pettit to strengthen the court case against Zen. It was a myth which it suited Zen to nurture as long as it supported his credibility with Eleven whose influence was vital to him and his aspirations.

Eleven, who had personally identified him as a recruit, knew his name was Zen while other members of RIR only knew him as number 66. Shortly he would be meeting Pain face to face, he thought it prudent to preserve his identity but could hardly call himself 66, while trying to worm his way into Pain's confidence to get the information that Eleven wanted about Wilson and his intentions, so he abandoned the name Zen and adopted the alias of Anton Wright. If his attempts at infiltration went wrong he could kill off the imaginary Anton Wright and perhaps protect himself from exposure by so doing.

The reception desk of Pain's hotel was unattended and a handwritten notice on it invited visitors to dial zero for assistance. He declined to do so and instead elected to ascend the dark stairway to the fifth floor where, out of breath, he knocked sharply on the door of 'suite' 511 which Eleven had informed him was Pain's suite number, the word suite being inappropriate he was to discover. Receiving no immediate reply he rapped sharply on the door once more. After a further delay there was the sound of movement inside and the security eyepiece in the door lightened and then darkened again as the occupant peered out through it. It darkened again and a muffled voice from within asked with rancour. "What do you want?"

"Julia Hammond suggested that I should contact you." Yet another lie which he would have to cover quickly; he had never met Hammond but obviously needed an entre of some kind and Pantin's crush on her was common knowledge according to Eleven. He felt uneasy and exposed by the weakness of his position.

"About what?" The answering voice was surly.

"I've got some problems with people from the Island and she thought you might be able to help me." Zen's response was light and friendly.

"Why would I want to do that?"

"Maybe because I can help you get your own back on the Islanders for what they did to you and I can do the same - for what they're doing to me."

"OK, so why would *you* want to do that and why would *I* want to help you?" Pain's reply was dogged.

"Can we do this inside?" Zen allowed a measure of exasperation to creep into his voice. "It's hard work having a conversation through a closed door and some of the things I want to say are confidential and anyway what have you got to lose?"

There was silence and a long pause before the door to the suite opened a fraction and Pain looked out with one suspicious eye which looked him up and down slowly. "OK, c'min." He was already unconsciously assimilating the London vernacular. He opened the door just enough to admit the visitor and closed it swiftly after he had entered.

"I'm Anton Wright and I'm working closely with Eleven of the RIR, he told me that you could be trusted." He didn't offer to shake hands; it did not seem to be an appropriate gesture with somebody like Pain. He noted with satisfaction that Pain recognised the term Eleven as a name and he seemed relaxed enough not to be bothered by the mention of it.

"She's a great girl, is Eleven." Pain adopted a cunning look and peered at Zen through narrowed eyes.

"Obviously I know her better that you do – she's a man."

"OK, OK just testing. You can't be too careful." Pain picked up an almost empty bottle of beer and drank it down in one overflowing gulp; he took a deep breath and belched noisily wiping his hand across his beer wet lips and chin. "What do you want, I'm busy tonight and I don't have much time to spare. I'm going to meet a honey and she and me are raring to go." He

61

took a jacket from the back of a battered wooden chair and shrugged it on. "It's good to hear that Eleven thinks I can be trusted but what is it you want me to be trusting about?"

"Eleven is doing some business with the President of Nuovostan and you know both men well enough to understand that when they do business with somebody they don't know they do research into their background to make sure that they're kosher."

"Don't know much about Eleven so can't help you there but I'm pretty close with Wilson, him and me are like this." He held up his hand and showed his index and second fingers crossed.

"I work for Eleven so I don't need to know anything about him but I would like to learn about Wilson."

"You and a lot of others." His face took on a look of cunning, "you're barking up the wrong tree, I don't give up confidential information about friends, especially ones as dangerous as Wilson. He's a friend but he's also very dangerous when he's crossed."

"Now you see you've just told me the sort of thing I need to know."

"What do you mean?" He peered suspiciously at Wright.

"You've told me he's dangerous."

"Huh, everybody knows that."

"I didn't know, so why not tell me the things you think everybody knows. That would be a good start."

"What's in it for me?"

Wright's face remained impassive but inside he was jubilant he had already completed the first phase of his planned task, he had got Pain talking. "The gratitude of Eleven for a start." He suggested as an inducement.

"Oh great," Pain grimaced. "I'm going to spill the beans for the gratitude of a dude whose real name I don't even know. Get real."

"I hear tell you've got the hots for Julia Hammond."

"So?" His voice turned even more surly, "what has that got to do with anything?"

"How about if I help you along that avenue and get you the chance to sample her charms?"

"I don't need no help," Pain said sullenly, "I'm doing OK as I am."

"I'm sure you can do better with her and I'm sure you can do better than this." Zen looked disparagingly around the shabby room. "A man of your calibre deserves better. You should be in a nice riverside apartment living the high life after the way you helped Wilson."

"I'm doing OK, I've got this place free and I've got access to as many honeys as I need. What more could I want?"

"Well, for a start if you lived in a more upmarket place you could attract honeys of your choice rather that those who would not be put off by where you live. They could be younger or older, fatter or thinner, nymphomaniacs or first timers or whatever you desire. You name it."

"You could do that?" His interest was sluggishly awakened. "And with Julia?"

"I could and I will if you'll work with me; you help me and I help you maybe we could get Julia to let you into her inner sanctum."

Pain didn't fully understand the subtleties but he got enough of the gist to renew his interest. "So what do you want me to do?"

Wright breathed a sigh of relief; the second stage of his approach had been accomplished with equally little effort as the first, much less so than had been predicted in the briefing before he secretly departed the Island. Pain could obviously be manipulated to perform any thoughtless task providing that the carrot of inducement was juicy enough. Wright would pass on during his telephone reports to the Island later that evening that he had established contact with Pain, through whom he would make contact with Hammond, and that the agreed plans would be progressed on schedule with the most beneficial effects.

***

Diana held the digital recordings of Jack Pain's indiscretions in a hand that was made unsteady by the rapidly diminishing calming effect of crack cocaine in her blood stream. She had listened to a selection of the information that Pain imparted under her seductive influence and found it all incredibly boring. Her fractured thinking was unable to come up with a way of cashing in on the information for which Julia Hammond had paid her so much.

Her one o'clock was due and as usual was late. She was feeling itchy all over and to perform well she really needed a quick rock of bliss but until he came she did not have the money to purchase one. It was catch-22 really, she needed the rock of bliss to be able to perform and she needed to perform to earn the money to buy the rock. She had tried offering her services to her supplier in lieu of payment but he had seen her in the cold light of day while she was low on drugs and he was not tempted to take her up on her offer. He was a strictly COD man.

After performing her duties quite badly with the one o'clock John she went straight to her supplier and within minutes was floating on the euphoric cloud that the rock induced. That the effect of the highs was becoming shorter and shorter in duration was obvious to her and was beginning to cause moments of panic. Her best thinking was done as the all-enveloping influence of the drug began to wear off and she began descending back to the plains of normalcy. At the height of her mental acuity as the rocks affect began to diminish but before depression set in, she decided to camp on Jack Pain's doorstep to see who it was that visited him and maybe could lead her to a visitor whom she could tap to make money from the recordings. Even in her most lucid moments of drug induced awareness she realised that the likelihood of success was at best remote but it was the only plan she had and she stuck to it with the tenacity of one staring into the chasm of despair.

On the third day of her patchy surveillance of Pain's hotel she recognised a hunky-looking visitor whom she had seen once before. Whether he was a friend or an enemy or just a visiting salesman she did not know but she decided to follow him to see where it might lead her. Fortunately the visitor was a walker so she was able to pursue him with comparative ease. She deduced that he was unlikely to be a friend of Pain; he was far too well dressed and had the air of a man of substance.

He walked across Vauxhall Bridge to the north side of the River Thames into an area which was both alien and familiar to her. Alien because it was stratospherically far above her social standing and familiar because she had been there before—it was where Julia Hammond lived. Her interest waned in the value of continuing with this surveillance, if he was a friend of Hammond his value to her was likely to be zero.

She was about to abandon the observation when, instead of visiting Julia's house, as she had expected, he stared at it for a long moment before crossing the road and settling himself at a small table outside a café from where he stared fixedly at the house until interrupted by a waitress to take his order. He opened

65

up a newspaper which had been left on the table, courtesy the café owner, and appeared to any casual observer to be reading it. Diana knew better, he was actually observing Hammonds home. It looked to her as though he was prepared for a long wait.

His actions gave her hope. He obviously knew Pain and equally obviously he knew that Pain was connected with Hammond, but he didn't appear to know Hammond, otherwise he would have visited her rather than keep her under surveillance. Finding out the scale of their relationships was her next task and she realised that she couldn't stand on the pavement observing, she would stick out like a sore thumb, looking and dressing as she did.

As she crossed the road to sit at the only other table outside the tiny café she made an unlikely and desperate-looking figure; her drawn skeletal features made her look like an impoverished street urchin. From a distance she looked like a school girl, but in nearness she aged considerably and she looked like what she was— a drug-fuelled woman desperately in need of a proper meal to keep her alive; she sat at the second table so that he was between her and Hammond's house and watched him avidly.

The waitress came out and looked at her with disapproval; apart from the distasteful physical ravages she was dressed like one of the 'come-on-in' girls outside the strip clubs of Soho. "Can I help you?" Her demeanour was matched by her clipped voice.

"Tea," Diana said, irritated by the waitress's attitude.

"What kind of tea? Lap san…" What was to have been a litany of exotic choices was cut short by Diana's strident cockney voice.

"Tea, I said tea, darlin'." She snapped, because she was entirely out of her element, more forcibly than was necessary or warranted. "Not anything special, just tea, strong, three sugars, in a big cup, no saucer needed."

The waitress walked haughtily back into the café without a backward glance.

The man Diana had been following turned to look at Diana and said with a smile. "Did she upset you or did you upset her or did you upset each other?"

Completely taken aback at being addressed by him she struggled to respond. By the time she did she had modified her response by editing out the expletives thereby reducing it by eighty percent. "Stuck up cow." She mumbled. "She's nothing special, only a waitress in a greasy spoon. I'm a paying customer, I am."

Zen was shocked by how rattled this girl of indeterminate age was, but he did not show it. Having somebody else with him made the watching vigil less obvious and would also help to pass some time by alleviating the boredom. He had no idea whether Hammond was at home and likewise no idea how long he should or could stay at this convenient vantage point without arousing ire and suspicion. He had been shown a photograph of her from some years before, taken when she visited the Island, so he was pretty sure that he would recognise her if she put in an appearance, she was a strikingly attractive woman.

Diana for her part thanked the gods of good fortune for smiling on her. Getting to talk to this man was achieved at a stroke and had not taken the protracted time she had anticipated. Clearly he was not a man she could attract in the way she normally attracted men; she realised shrewdly that he was obviously too discerning to be tempted by her usual brassy approach.

She was rapidly exercising her mind, which was becoming less sharp as the drugs in her system began to drop below the tolerated level, to devise a way of opening up conversation with him which would be to her advantage. To her surprise he began to open up a conversation with her; he was playing right into her hands. She was painfully aware that he would not be swayed by her offering her services to him; quite the reverse but he had taken the initiative.

"Can I interest you in another cup of tea and," he looked pointedly at his watch, "as it's nearly lunchtime, perhaps a snack of some kind?"

"Dunno," She looked at him suspiciously, she was not used to being offered anything like this unless the asker wanted something unusual or painful. "Wocher got in mind?"

"A sandwich or a light snack maybe in exchange for you telling me a little about London, I'm not from around here and I know very little of the life of Londoners."

She acquiesced and chose a light snack from the limited menu which she hoped would help her navigate to the next drug fix. Large meals were a thing of the past for her, the ravages of her lifestyle had taken their toll. While they waited for the food to arrive, the door to Hammond's residence opened and she stepped out into the street looking right and left. She hailed a passing taxi cab which already had a fare and watched in frustration as it sailed past ignoring her request and she started walking south towards the bridge, glancing over her shoulder in search of transport. Dianna watched with interest as Zen took a photograph in profile of Hammond, using his digital phone, as she marched resolutely along the road.

"Junoerr?" Dianna mangled the language in such a way that Zen had to concentrate and translate the meaning of the single word by splitting it into four words.

"Do I know who?" He said after untangling the mangled sounds.

"The tart you just took a picherov." She continued mangling.

"The photo I just took was of a black cab, we don't have taxis like that where I come from."

"Wherezat?"

"Oh you won't have heard of it, very few people have."

"Iynower." She spoke quickly and quietly.

"You know who?" He enquired mildly after once more translating her inarticulate pronunciation.

"The tart you jus' took a picherov."

"Do you now." His voice took on the hint of a menacing edge. "How come you think I don't know her and how do I know that you do?"

"Kostcher." She said cryptically, unmoved by his threatening tone. She had been threatened by professionals and this one was certainly no professional.

He looked at her fiercely but soon realised from her pugnacious look that she was used to being intimidated and had no fear of the implied threat while they were in a public place. He finally deciphered what it was she had said. "Why would I want to buy anything from you?" He realised as he said it that he was adopting the same tactics as Pain by answering a question with an inane question to which a reply was without value.

Throwing caution to the wind she looked at him through narrowed eyes. "Dunno oo you are but I seen yer comin' outer Jacks 'otel morun once. I know Jack an' I know Miss 'ammond but I dunno you 'cept I realise you know 'er but not good, but you would like to."

"I don't know who Jack is and I don't know who Miss A Mond is, just like I don't know who you are."

"Very funny but I'm not laffin it's Miss 'ammond wiv a aitch and Jack is Jack Pain and I are 'is main 'unney.

Zen found it interesting that she should declare herself to be his honey because it was the same phrase 'honey' as Pain used to describe his conquests. She obviously knew both Pain and Hammond but he could not imagine how she would know that he was interested in them.

"Cat gocher tongue." She broke his thought filled silence.

"What makes you think I know this man Jack or that I would want to?"

"Seezy, I was watchin' Jack's drum when I see you go in an' out, like I said an' I see you come an' go a couple er times."

"I was in the Hotel but it's nothing to do with this Jack character, I was visiting somebody else."

"Toff like you wouldn' visit a fly blown 'otel like that. Anyway I see inter Jack's room fru th' winder an' I see 'im talkin' to yer like you was bosom mates."

"Okay, so I know Jack." He admitted, it seemed useless to do otherwise and I also know Julia Hammond. Why would that be of interest to you?"

"I don't give a toss about if you do or don't know them but I got somethin' you might be in'erested in."

"And what might that be?" His interest was piqued by this encounter but the episode was disturbing in that a complete stranger, who was not exactly Mensa material, had figured out very accurately something about which he was very curious. He also wanted to find out if this was just a random happenstance or whether his cover was blown.

"You a private dick or a copper?"

"No I'm just somebody on holiday."

"OK I arst yer the question and you said you aint no copper so if you are anyfin I say to yer will be inadmissible in court."

"Inadmissible, now there's a long word for such a little lady." He laughed to relieve the tension that he was feeling. "I am definitely not a copper, I'm not even a British national."

"I'm not daft." She scrutinised him closely as she said this and was alarmed by the speed at which the drugs were losing their potency and that she would need a top up very soon. "You're playin' hide and seek with yourself so she don't see yer lookin at 'er so I'm guessin' that you're tryin' to get summit from 'er for Jack oo mus' be your frien' an' I fink I know what it is." She gave him a cunning smile and sat back to measure his response.

"Then you know more than I do." He was mystified by what she said.

"Gottem right 'ere," she said as she rummaged around in her tattered handbag which had been defeated by time long ago. She withdrew her hand from the bag's interior and showed him three double digital recorded discs with a snort of triumph.

"And what might that be?" He was truly puzzled by what she was offering.

"You know somethin' you're really 'ard work. 'Eres me tryin' ter do yer a favour an' 'ere's you doin' yer bes' ter roon it." She took on the look of a teenager frustrated at the lack of comprehension by an adult. "These discs is what I recorded of the sessions 'im an'me 'ad at mine when 'e spilled all 'is countries secrets. You can 'ave 'em fer a fee, a big fat fee." She folded her arms across her chest which had once been ample but was now a drug wasted asset. "This could be yer way inter meetin' Julia 'ammond," she added provocatively.

"I'm not really interested." He stood after tidying the used crockery on the small table and folded the newspaper neatly before placing it on the table. "But it's been nice talking to you. I hope you enjoy the rest of your day." He turned to leave.

"This is all yours for a fousand smackers," she shouted after him. "An' if you buy 'em I'll make sure Julia never gets to hear about your interest in 'er, or that you bin seein' Jack."

He turned round alarmed at the intuitive potency of the threat mainly. As a RIN he was not welcome anywhere outside the Island and he was travelling on false papers which, if discovered, would lead to a great deal of trouble and at best deportation and Hammond was an investigative reporter whom he did not wish to be investigated by.

He took his wallet from his pocket and counted out a number of notes. "Tell you what I'll do." He waved the notes before her. "I'll give you this hundred....smackers," he used her slang awkwardly, "if you give me one of the packs to listen to, to see if what they say is of any interest to me."

"No chance!" She snorted derisorily. "Lemme tell yer wot I'll do, I'll lend yer one o th' discs fer two 'undred smackers an' if they're good you can 'ave the rest fer fifteen 'undred. Woja say ter tha," The more confidence she gained the more grasping she became.

"OK I'll give it a try and I'll telephone you after I've heard the information."

"OK," she took a telephone box card out of her handbag and handed it to him. It carried an impossibly lurid naked photograph of somebody looking nothing like her which bore the legend *'Diana's discrete and relaxing service 24 / 7'* her telephone number was in blue script at the bottom of the card. *'Call any time, if*

I'm engaged you can leave a message and I'll get back to you. Don't hold back and I won't.'

He took the card and one of the discs and parted with two hundred pounds. Diana departed a happy woman; she had expected to be beaten down considerably from the thousand she had demanded but had ended up with a potential of seventeen hundred. Zen was happy, not because of the recordings but because he now had a source of information motivated entirely by cash who knew Hammond. Potentially he could save a valuable amount of time.

Nine

The assassination of Chester Gilliland had been organised with clinical precision and was clearly the work of a thoroughly professional organisation. It was the considered opinion of the small inner circle of the Ruling Council, to which news of the assassination was limited to prevent wholesale panic, that at least one organiser of the deed was a resident of the Island working with an organisation from the outside world who had somehow managed to smuggle a fire arm onto the Island and recruit a professional, probably off Island, to carry out the assassination; the inner circle made it a priority to identify both at all costs. Considering the off Island element, there was no doubt in anybody's mind that they would probably not need to look further than their old enemy Colin Wilson. The on-Island contact was a different consideration; the inner circle had no idea where to start looking.

That an assassin had been able to import both his or herself and a weapon of death with apparent ease was a savage blow to their confidence in matters of security and as the one responsible for Island security, Silas Pettit criticised himself openly. He had come over the years, he confessed, to rely on the good advice of Chester Gilliland as a loyal friend far more than he would have been possible in his former, singularly isolated, military life. Some of the decisions he was now making, he also confessed, would have benefited greatly from Chester's solid analytical wisdom. But now he was no longer there to be consulted. One of the most difficult things he had to do was to lie to the good people of Recovery Island by telling them that Chester had gone away on holiday. The lie was not sustainable and to his discomfort, would not stand the scrutiny to which it could possibly be subjected. Hiding the assassination from the Islanders was intended to protect them from the despondency they would feel and to prevent giving their enemies hope of success in their endeavours.

Getting used to his not being there was uncomfortable and the lie was contrary to his newly adopted lifestyle as an open and honest practitioner, a philosophy he had adopted since becoming one of the group of four and for the first time in his life having close friends on whom he could rely without question. It was obvious to him that for Caine it was even more difficult; Chester had been her companion since their childhood in Denver and her constant companion during and since their university days when they had become intimate partners. She still looked dazed a week after that terrible day at the airport and she was sorely missing his presence. The vision of his being dragged under the fuselage of the aircraft and the smear of blood that tracked across the apron were branded in her thoughts for ever and when she thought of it, which she did unconsciously often, a cold numbness enveloped her soul.

It was important that the Island should continue to function efficiently without him and that the Islanders should not, at this time, be traumatised by being told about the airport incident. That the problem had a root somewhere within the Island was without question; somebody within their borders was trying to sabotage their way of life and it was for them to discover who the perpetrators were and to stop them before they could do any more damage. Worse as the perpetrators of the deed had found a way to bypass what they had thought to be impenetrable security their presumed invulnerability was shown to be smoke and mirrors.

Clearly Wilson was the likely antagonist in this further invasion of their lives but he could not have achieved this without significant help from insiders; isolated as Wilson was in his Nuovostani eyrie. The assassin, if he had been a non-resident, had been able to get onto the Island and be supplied with a deadly snipers weapon and given the place and an opportunity and time to carry out the evil deed; even worse, he had been able to escape undetected, either back into Island society or back off Island.

Who could have known that the founders would be at the airport on that day at that time? How could they have known that the airport would, at the time of their arrival, be deserted so that there were no witnesses to the act? There was no doubt they were harbouring vipers within their bosom who were threatening the very existence of the Island society by supplying the weapon and arranging for the assassin to gain access to the control tower and maybe to depart from the Island undetected. It was a time of worrying uncertainty.

Mark Lawson had been given the task of tracking down the suspected dissident group which had found a way of hacking into the Islands restricted information system. The crash course with Carlina Tanterelli had prepared him, in part, for the mission. She had enabled him, with her prodigious mind-influencing techniques, to access parts of his inherent capabilities hitherto untapped and to use his newfound skills to think like the assassin and the assassin's motivators, significantly more than he would formerly have been able to do.

The intention was to focus on all Islanders old and new to find out who might be involved with the dissidents and in what way. With the addition of four more outlying Islands; Leisure Island, Farm Island,

Factory Island, the plans of which had been released to the Islanders and the fourth secretly called Hold Island, the use of which was not being heralded but which would soon become an important part of their society, there had been a significant influx of qualified newcomers and their families for the building and operating of the new facilities required by their ever growing population. The newcomers were a potential source of unrest and the task of weeding out potential trouble makers was daunting as it was baffling but nevertheless he pursued it doggedly. Tanterelli had taught him that patience and focus would succeed where haste and shallow thinking would fail. In his new position as head of Internal Security he would need to be calm, to neutralise his natural integrity, and *think like a rebel.*

Ten

In the President's palace in Nuovostan City, Wilson paced the floor of his tastelessly ornate suite, on his face there was a fierce look of tortured concentration. His hold over all aspects of Nuovostani life was now complete and with former factory Manager and now State Minister, Yuri Kurakin, who was incontrovertibly corrupt and whom he had totally under his dominant thumb, he ruled the country with a rod of unyielding iron.

He was now free to pursue the aim of territorial expansion from his newly 'acquired' country which had emerged bloody and even more corrupt from the collapse of world finances, splitting away from Russia's wild eastern expanses - without resistance. His acquisition had been bloody and had cost him a significant sum of money and a promise to Kurakin that he would hold a position of power in the new Nuovostan.

The area now occupied by Nuovostan was isolated in the far eastern side of one of the most barren parts of old Russia. It had no natural resources and was low in agricultural capacity and was therefore not sought after by anybody else. Wilson's take-over of the territory that had formerly been Russian was not perceived as a threat, rather as the removal of a territory which would have been a drain on the currently limited Russian financial resources. What they had failed to take account of was that what was now Nuovostan had been a dumping ground for unwanted and unsafe nuclear devices which were of great value to Wilson's plans of territorial expansion.

Wilson was wily enough not to want to antagonise the countries surrounding his fiefdom; they were in a position to overpower him at will with their superior might were they not otherwise engaged. His sights were set not only on Recovery Island but also on continental and peripheral Europe which was still endeavouring to come to terms with the collapse of their economies and struggling with the destructive and demanding Chinese demands which made them weak, distracted and vulnerable.

"My dear," he turned to Irena Pelochev his 'Personal Assistant', "have you been able to speak with the contract man yet?"

"Nyet." She emphasised the word in a harsh way which belied her sultry feminine looks. "Man is hard to finding but am look every which-way." Her 'Rushlish', as the President liked to refer to her highly personalised mixture of Russian patois and Americanised English, was liberally peppered with phrases picked up from the Hollywood films which she watched voraciously.

"That's not a bad thing I suppose," Wilson said, aggrieved. "If a contract killer was easy to find he would be behind bars or executed. Keep looking my dear, use as much of your charms and my money as required, but find him quickly. I am becoming impatient." He could not understand her response as she muttered it darkly in Russian, which he did not speak. "Don't forget that the official language of Nuovostan is now English so, less of your home spun gibberish, but for my protection you would be jailed for not speaking English."

"Cullin," she fluttered her eyelashes at him, "is hard for me to say all time English, particular when we are make out." She concluded with a coquettish wiggle of her hips.

"You have my dispensation at such times." He said dismissively.

She could not understand the individual words he had used but she could recognise the intent.

Pelochev just stopped herself in time; she had been about to start gnawing on her thumb cuticle, a sure visible sign that she was frustrated. Her frustration was that she was finding it impossible to make direct contact with the assassin and she really needed to get an update on his progress. The President was fuming at the lack of information coming from the Island about the assassination and was making her life uncomfortable because of it. Her only means of contacting the assassin was via the head of the Recovery Island's rebels who, for reasons of his own safety, controlled their discussions on his terms rather than hers. She felt a swelling of pride in her breast as she recalled the seminal moment when she had revealed the presence of rebels on the Island to Wilson. He had rewarded her most generously – a rare moment that she had savoured with relish.

The Recovery Island rebels, the RIR as they called themselves, were growing in numbers but the growth of the movement was slow because of the need for absolute secrecy in what was to her a ridiculously open society. Although the Island's laws did not permit capital punishment the RIR had no wish to be banned from the Island and banished to a life in exile, which would certainly happen if they were discovered.

Pelochev tried the number one more time and was about to give up when the connection was made. "Here is Pelochev," she breathed huskily into the mouthpiece.

"You are becoming a nuisance." The answering voice was both mean and testy. "What do you want now?"

"Wanting update," she snapped at him not being accustomed, now that she was a person of significant influence in her world, to being treated so tardily. She was after all the President's consort with secret but never-the-less active aspirations of replacing the President when the time was right. The Islander to whom she spoke was what she thought of, in Rushlish, as a '*sneak in the glass.*'

"I'll tell you once more, and this will be the last time, that when there is progress to report we'll let you know. Until then you will just have to wait." He unceremoniously disconnected the call and she listened, with unsuppressed anger, to the static hissing through the earpiece.

"There is not yet some news of the killing, why is it so?" she gabbled in her frustration.

The head of RIR threw the secured telephone onto the table without answering her question, and cursed. Pelochev was becoming a damned nuisance, no doubt because she was being pressured by the megalomaniac Wilson. For once he felt some distant sympathy for Wilson who had to put up with the irritating woman. He too was aggravated by the lack of communication from 'A', he would talk to Zen during their next telephone conversation and make sure that 'A' realised who was paying for his services and who was calling the tune.

There were many things to consider. The assassination planned by him, despite what Wilson might think, and carried out by 'A' had been hushed up which was not, at all, the intention of the exercise. He had hoped to spread panic throughout the Island by the assassination but the news blackout put paid to that. Enquiries through the Island's IPs, the Information Portals, had simply said that the founder was taking a well-deserved holiday and that the other three founders were looking after the interests of the nation in his absence. He repeated the enquiries for a week with the same evasive results. He had misgivings about using 'A' because he didn't know his true identity and he had no individual means of initiating contact except via Zen. Not being in control of the situation was a position he did not relish and would not tolerate for much longer. A further frustration was that he could not instigate an Island wide leak of the assassination without significantly compromising his own anonymity.

The RIR had been thirty five in number and were split into five cells of six and one of five, but now, with the addition of Zen, was at full cell strength. Each cell knew that there were other cells but had no knowledge of how many there were or of names or code numbers of members outside their own immediate group. Eleven, the founding head of RIR had personal control C1 the first and controlling cell. The five other members of cell 1; Pietor Kwietakovsky, Jon Webber, Colleen Brogan, Spencer Ngomo and Arlene Dickinson only knew him as Eleven and were not aware of each other's identity. As founder of the RIR he had chosen his team carefully to ensure that they were all genuine rebels and that they were all fundamentally radical. They were all - including him, although he did not recognise it in himself – 'dangerous psychotics'.

Their constitution was simple; they vowed to replace, by whatever means necessary, the original founders and the Ruling Council in favour of a more radical committee which could realise the potential of BAM2. Use of the technology in a more commercial way would give the Island the clout that Eleven thought he and it deserved, under his leadership naturally. As far as the other cells were concerned, their aim was to take their proper place in the world as a viable nation and the unfettered freedom of movement that could be encouraged by sharing the technology with carefully selected and equally focussed allies. These unreal aspirations were far from the true motivations harboured by Eleven. Having recruited Zen he was tempted to incorporate him into Cell 1 because Zen, with the right incentives, had the makings of a good number two; he had shown himself to be resourceful and self-motivated. Ultimately he decided against doing so believing that his membership of one of the more lowly cells could be used to give Eleven more insight into the real aspirations of the peripheral members.

Reality was entirely different; Eleven intended to do what Wilson had tried, so far unsuccessfully to do, to gain control of BAM2 and to use it to further the aims of RIR, or more specifically himself, to become an organisation of international significance and influence. His cell was peopled by those who considered themselves to be the victims not particularly of Recovery Island but of the world at large. Naked ambition was Eleven's sole and driving reason for being a rebel; he owed allegiance to no man.

Piotre Kwietakovski, one of the earliest members of Cell 1, was radicalised by the chequered history of his family's country, Poland, which long ago had been sucked into the old European Union and divested of its history and culture. His dream was to restore his homeland to its former identity by pulling out of the corrupt and increasingly more decadent European Union and to become once again a proud and independent nation.

Another member of the cell, Angus Webber, a tough and soulless Scot, was radical for the sake of being radical, driven by a pathological suspicious hatred of all nations which were not Scottish he used his radicalisation to justify the streak of cruelty that ran through him. His aim was to have the freedom to pursue his unsavoury predilections and depravities in whatever way he wished and the RIR, when they were successful, would give him the opportunity, he assumed, to do so.

The fourth member, Coleen Brogan, an Irish Bostonian, was lost in the previous century when the hated English and the glorious Irish were at war and her grandfather had worked tirelessly to raise funds for the soldiers of freedom. He had moved in shady circles in the raising of funds and had his life cut short by a bullet to the back of the head, execution style. The family did not know who the assassin was but the thought that it was not the English in some way or other was not considered a possibility. Her aim was to have the freedom to trace the killers of her grandfather and dispense summary justice on their surviving families. No need for courts. She did not care about the Island or the aims of RIR her sole interest was revenge – whatever the vehicle being made available through her membership of RIR.

Kwami Ngomo's reason for being RIR was simple. Brought up in the slums of Lagos he had a tough early life, in his younger days, life was not considered to be a sacrosanct commodity. It was something to be preserved, in his case, and in others made use of and discarded when it ceased to be of value to him. Membership would ultimately give him the money and power to live his dream of excess in every facet of life.

Jolene Dickinson was a much more complex person. Her antecedents were of somewhat vague background. Her father believed himself to be of Dutch Canadian stock, although as he was brought up in a foster home he could not be exactly sure. Her mother was Filipino with probably some American blood from a grandfather she had never met and who had apparently disowned them. Her aim in life was to be able to afford to research her background and to bring to task all of those people and families who had abandoned her to a desperate life in the slums of Saigon.

The dissidents in Cell 1 were representative of the members of the other cells but were at the more extreme end of the spectrum of unrest. Hand selected specialists who had been recruited in the first place to carry out the foundation tasks required to establish Island life and who chose to stay on when their tasks were completed were permitted to invite dependent relatives to join them and to establish an inclusive family unit on the island. Some of the add-on members of family units were a mixed bag. Like any mixed bag there were less desirable elements and it was some of these who chose to join the ranks of underground dissidents. Additionally some of the specialists selected were chosen more for their immediate capabilities in their particular disciplines sometimes at the expense of fitting in to the developing society. This rag bag of citizens was growing in number and in some areas of life actually outnumbered the more settled citizens. This was the hotbed from which additional threats to the Island's continuing peace would eventually be launched.

Eleven

Three weeks after the assassin had completed his mission on Recovery Island, 'A' was in Nuovostan in the private suite of the President at his palace in the country's capital city. He was showing the moving images he had captured of the assassination of the target. The President looked dispassionately at the record and watched it several times before he commented on it.

"This is all lies." Wilson threw the accusation at 'A'. "According to news coming out of the Island Gilliland is away on holiday, not assassinated."

"You can see the evidence for yourself; do you want to see it again?" 'A' showed no signs of unease as he thrust the hand held digital re-player towards Wilson.

"So you think the camera never lies?"

"No, cameras can be manipulated far more easily than people − but in this case the camera image is exactly what it looks like. Look again, see for yourself, hear the gun shot see the target hit, look at him fall, look at the reactions of his colleagues, see the shock on their faces. It's all real, I was there, I did it and I recorded it." 'A' was clearly exasperated and his patience was being sorely tested. "Anyway," he continued with his tirade, "how could I possibly have the ability to persuade the four very influential people involved to act out this scene?" His look at Wilson was hard and unyielding. "I'm a professional assassin, not a magician."

"Man is speak trueness Cullin." Pelochev tried to relieve the tension that had pervaded their huddle.

"You should have prolonged his death." Wilson made yet another of his startling changes of tack which

'A' found it difficult to process. "Maybe a shot to the neck or better still the stomach would have been more satisfactory. A lingering death is what he deserved after what he did to me." Wilson settled himself comfortably in the overstuffed leather chair. "What do you think, my dear?" He turned to Pelochev, his eyebrows raised in enquiry, his wild eyed look for the moment subdued

"I am think you enjoy anyway." She looked dispassionately at a further rerun of the death images and heard again the softly whispered 'bang' and the vicious hissing sound of escaping propellant gasses from the 4S rifle on the sound track and then turned with a more appreciative look at the assassin. "Why you did not make more pain?" She looked at him with her head tilted to one side.

"Nobody asked, I was just told to kill him specifically and leave the others alone," he replied in a flat voice, "and if you wanted that you should have asked, but if you had it would have cost you more." He found the turn of the conversation bizarre. "I still don't understand why you wanted just one killed. Sounds crazy to me."

"Not to using words like crazy, makes Cullin angry." She hissed at him with her head turned away from Wilson so that he could neither hear her nor read her lips.

"Leave the strategy to me." Wilson' voice was petulant. "I want to pick them off one by one for reasons of attrition which will allow me to interrogate however many remain after the attrition succeeds to give me chapter and verse on how BAM2 works. If one man is left standing it will be Crook, he is the main instigator of the technology. After I get the information he will be of no further use"

87

"Cost is not of problem." Pelochev steered the conversation back to its original course. She said this while waving a well-manicured hand dismissively.

"Don't be so free with my money." The President turned to her with a sickly and insincere smile. "You can pay for the extras for the next one."

She was aware that this directly contradicted his earlier conversation giving her financial carte blanche but made no comment about the ambiguity.

"You are not give me money for this," she said petulantly. "You not give enough to buying dresses even." She indicated with an elegant wave of her hands the monstrously expensive haute couture she was wearing. "What you are think?" She asked the assassin.

"I'm not paid to think about fashion. All I know about clothes is camouflage and fatigues," he responded in his customary flat voice, his unfathomable accent was, or had been at some time in the past, American. She found his unemotional treatment of the moment both chilling and exciting.

"Enough of this!" The President expostulated having been out of the conversation for what he considered to be an unacceptable length of time. "How did you manage to get onto the Island with a gun and how did you manage to get out again after the assassination?"

"That would be a trade secret." The assassin looked directly at the President with cold eyes. "Trade secrets are what you hire me to employ. The less you know the better it is for you and for me it is a prerequisite."

"What's the problem, don't you trust me?" The President narrowed his eyes.

"No, I don't trust you," 'A' replied without rancour, "you have my loyalty as long as you pay for it and I'll have your patronage as long as you need me. Trust doesn't come in to it, we are not friends, we have a contractual understanding and as long as it suits both of us we will continue to work together, once the mutuality goes we will never meet again."

"Is good business to do this way Cullin." As usual she mispronounced the President's given name while looking at the assassin with other than platonic interest.

"Irena," the President said with distaste, "drag your thoughts up above navel level and be objective. You should know that I demand loyalty from my employees."

"That's OK then." 'A' ogled Pelochev while addressing the President. "You can have loyalty from your employees but that's a condition that would not apply to a freelance specialist like me, I am nobody's employee, I'm a specialist for short term hire."

"I decide whether you are an employee or not," the President said imperiously.

"On that point we obviously differ." 'A' shrugged dismissively. "Just make sure that you transfer the second half of the fee to my private account and we can part and need never see each other again. As far as I am concerned we have never met and I have never been to Nuovostan."

"Not finishing yet." Pelochev smiled at the assassin lasciviously, "more killings to be doing."

"Leave this to me Irena," the President said testily. "I'll decide if I want to employ him for other work we can't be sure that he has completed the first task yet." He waved his hands vaguely as if to waft her away. "Meanwhile go and get us some Vodka and then leave us to the men's talk."

She flounced off muttering darkly in a patois, which neither man understood, returning almost immediately with two bottles of Vodka and four shot glasses. Handing a filled glass to each of the men, she poured two more glasses - one from each of the two bottles –

and drank each one down in one go muttering each time, "bottoms out." She misquoted and spun on her heel leaving the office in one fluid movement with a revealing swirl of her expensive dress.

"Down to business," the President poured himself another drink. "How do you feel about four more jobs? And if the answer's yes, I expect a quantity discount." He smiled unattractively at what for him passed as a humorous comment.

"One at a time and fifty per cent up front as before; who are they?"

"They're all heads of state and they will be easier to get at than the one you just did." The President paused and looked thoughtful. "I had a hell of a job getting onto the Island on my first visit and just as difficult a job getting off but you seemed to do it with ease. What's the secret?"

"Like I said; tricks of the trade and it's not what you know but who you know that makes many things possible. There's no need for you to know so let's not go there." He settled back and savoured a second shot of Vodka, safe in the knowledge that Irena Pelochev had been used as a taster to make sure that the bottles had not been adulterated "A head of state is a head of state no matter how easy or difficult they might be to get at. The price is the same, no discounts offered."

He left the President's office some two hours later with his next job lined up. Irena Pelochev was sitting in the anti-office outside the President's suite and she looked up expectantly.

"Meeting are finishing?" She asked.

"Yes meeting are finishing," he mimicked her. "The President is having a little sleep, maybe it's better to let him get over the meeting slowly."

"Too many of wodka." She shook her head. "Cullin no good at drink the wodka. He getting fall over very quick." She brightened up and smiled at him. "You go you Hotel?"

He nodded in agreement.

"I get 'leemo' to take us we can speak and getting to know on way to hotel in comfort." She licked her lips. "You have deal with Cullin." It was a statement rather than a question. "How many jobs he give you?"

"I told him 'one at a time'."

"We go you room in Hotel and have room services and romantic dinner. Yes?"

"Sounds good to me." He could think of worse ways of spending an evening in this boring and inhospitable country, she was after all extremely desirable in the most unsubtle of ways.

"What is job you are getting for doing?" She enquired with a coquettish smile.

"The British Prime Minister," he said with a shrug.

She showed no great surprise at his staccato statement, she was contented by finding out who was next on the list which seemed to her to be getting longer as time went by.

They had dinner in his room but afterwards she didn't, as she said she would, stay for the evening - she stayed for the night.

Twelve

Caine looked pensive as she waited for Creswell to pick up his private and personal scrambler-phone. She had a favour to ask of the UK Prime Minister which would strain their friendship up to and maybe even past its credible limit - but still she had to make the call, so much depended on it. After what seemed to be an interminable time, because of her heightened sense of trepidation at what she was about to ask, his cultured voice came through loud and clear.

"Hello my dear, so nice to hear from you." He recognised from the encrypted caller ID who was calling him.

They exchanged greetings, a convention which was usually accomplished easily but on this occasion was tinged with certain unease. Following the greeting there was a pause fractionally longer that was usual and which alerted Creswell to the unaccustomed discomfort which Caine was feeling.

"James…." She hesitated.

"Come, my dear, nothing you can ask of me will be too much, you must know of the gratitude that I feel to you and the others for saving my bacon when I could have been taken down by Wilson. Just take a deep breath and ask."

The incident he referred to took place in the early days of the formation of Recovery Island when Wilson had created a matrix of lies and innuendo about Creswell in an attempt to overthrow him as Prime Minister of Great Britain. It was only with the help of the Islanders that Creswell had escaped from Wilson's clutches unscathed and led to Wilsons flight to Nuovostan.

Caine smiled wryly to herself fleetingly thinking that she had taught Creswell the art of understanding the meanings behind speech nuances. "Very well James, I do, as you have so rightly surmised, have a favour to ask of you that I cannot fully explain and it is an unquestionably outrageous request. You are of course free to make your own choice but I hope that you will ignore what logic tells you and believe that I would not ask this unless it was vitally important."

The rest of her conversation was, considering its content, relatively brief. At its conclusion she let out a long sigh and was conscious of Creswell doing the same.

"I'll be damned," he exclaimed, "I've never heard anything like it in my life, most extraordinary."

She could, even at this great distance, imagine his look of amazement at her request just as she could imagine him shaking his mane of wavy, well coiffured, silver hair and raising his expressive eyebrows.

"I'll be damned," he repeated. "Most extraordinary thing I ever heard – and I've heard some extraordinary things in my life, as you know only too well."

There was another pause and Caine waited with bated breath for his answer which she thought at best would be that he would think about it.

"I may live to regret this my dear but whatever I can do to help I will do." He laughed when he heard the explosion of released breath from Caine. "I'm sure that you appreciate that doing this has enormous international implications. The planning will have to be meticulous and if it fails it will without doubt end my career, political or any other calling."

"James, you're a darling." Her eyes blurred with tears as she fully realised the depth of gratitude that this man, this gentle man, felt for what they had done for him in his most dire time of need.

Creswell sighed as he placed his telephone back into its belt holster. He was flattered to be asked to assist Caine and the Islanders who had been so helpful to him but her request, which she was unwilling to enlarge upon, was bizarre in the extreme. Absolute secrecy had been insisted upon and he was forbidden to mention their arrangements to anybody – even the most trusted of his family, friends and colleagues. He had been deeply moved by the tension in her voice and the spilling of tears he could sense in her words.

There were a number of things he had to accomplish without alerting anybody to the nature of his task. He alone could identify and make the arrangements required and they had to be completed within just a few weeks. Implementing his plan of action without delay he cancelled all forthcoming appointments by unloading a raft of Prime Ministerial tasks onto his deputy and his secretary, without explaining why. There was one task that he could not avoid; it was official launching of the British designed and built Federation submarine the *Neptunium* on the River Clyde. It had been in his diary for some time and it was well known in reporting circles. To cancel such a well-known event would have caused rumblings which would have been a significant embarrassment to him and it was essential for him to keep a low profile before launching himself into this bizarre operation.

Of necessity others were involved in these complex arrangements but they were to be kept to a minimum and kept in the dark and they had to be relied upon to carry out his orders without questioning or revealing any part of what they were doing, to others. He considered using Lord Roland Clearman, the Lord Chancellor who had been so supportive in the past, but decided against doing so because Clearman's character was such that the unusual nature of the tasks ahead would have been more than his delicate, nervous system could take.

A light of discovery came on in his mind when one name came to him. The person concerned owed him a debt of gratitude for having helped him to extricate himself from the deadly clutches of Colin Wilson the ex DDP who had now imposed himself on the hapless citizens of Nuovostan a fate which nobody deserved. When approached, the one he had chosen to assist him expressed astonishment at what he was asked to do but, rather like Creswell had with Caine, he felt honour-bound to come to Creswell's aid. He in turn had some arrangements to observe the same requirement for secrecy as Creswell. Very quickly the die was cast and the arrangements were put in place and the plan to come to the aid of the Islanders was developed in total secrecy.

Cradock, who like a pop star was known only by the single name and who had defected from Wilson's private army and security force after assisting the Islanders and playing a major part in thwarting Wilson's plans, was grateful for Creswell's past intervention with MI5 and MI6 in absolving him of any blame during the failed invasion of the Island. It could have been sticky for him if the government had pursued his felonious actions even though he was only following orders. When, out of the blue, Creswell asked him for help with the delicate matters which he could not trust to his own staff he was flattered.

Since the failed invasion he had settled on the Island and worked with Mark Lawson on the Islands defence control system and he had resigned from the British army to devote his full time to life on the Island. His immediate family had joined him and had not looked back on their decision. Cradock was disappointed when he learned that his task in helping Creswell would mean his having to leave the Island and return to the UK but comforted himself that his time away from the island would only be a matter of weeks and that the hated Wilson was no longer a factor, his being exiled in Nuovostan.

He carried out the allotted tasks with dedication although he understood very little about what he was doing or why. With his accreditation as the Prime Ministers special advisor he found that doors normally closed to him were suddenly opened and his life took on a whole new and powerful meaning.

Thirteen

The river Clyde, Creswell noted as he stepped from the specially adapted ministerial Jaguar under the cover of a large umbrella, was an uninviting grey brown soup, the bouquet of which was not at all appetising. The umbrella was wielded by an equally large but less waterproof naval aide who appeared to think that the wetter he got the more effective he was being. Creswell smiled to himself at the transparent opportunism of his escort.

There was little ceremony to herald his arrival; the press had been given free reign at the dockside and they took full advantage to throw questions, very few of which related to the reason for his visit. He made no attempt to answer the questions merely indicating that the press should accompany him onto the platform which flanked the *Neptunium* and gave access to its functional elevated conning tower.

"Ladies and gentlemen of the press," he addressed them when they were fully assembled in front of him. "It gives me great pleasure to welcome you and to have you join in the ceremony of inauguration of this magnificent vessel HMS *Neptunium,* the latest in the British contribution to the navy of the Federation of Nations joint task force. What you see here is the culmination years of innovative design of which we are justly proud. Not only is this an engineering wonder, it is also testament to the dedicated workers whose unstinting hard work has produced this magnificent feat of technology which will serve to defend us against all enemies. In view of the compact nature of the submarine your number has been strictly limited but you are all free to come aboard with me and view the marvels that *Neptunium* represents. You are free to take any photographs you wish and, within reason be allowed to visit any part of the vessel you wish. I must, however, ask you to submit all copy and photographs for inspection by the naval intelligence service to ensure that we do not give any assistance to those who do not have our best interests at heart." He stepped back from the lectern and by gesture invited the captain to address the journalists.

"Thank you Mr Prime Minister. As captain of *Neptunium* I join the Prime Minister in welcoming you on board." He baulked at what was a total misrepresentation of his actual position, as soon as he had been told that the PM intended letting the press on board he had protested vehemently citing the need for secrecy. His misgivings were aired through the department of the navy who, after a delay, overruled him. It was therefore a bitter pill for him to offer words of welcome to any civilian, let alone the press. "Before we go aboard I request that the Prime Minister be gracious enough to carry out the inauguration ceremony."

In accordance with the newly established protocol of the Federation this was no champagne launching. A ten-man contingent of the crew stood on the elevated deck forward of the conning tower with stubby assault rifles pointing skywards from where they nestled on the shoulders of the submariners. They waited patiently for the signal to commence the ceremony.

"I have the honour," Creswell stepped back to the lectern, "to perform the naming of this magnificent craft of the Federation task force. May she serve and protect our free democracy and may all who sail in her be true to their task of defending the Federation by following the orders which promote Federation interests without question. I name this submarine *Neptunium*, may she rule supreme." He hated the words for their blatant and controlling insincerity but they had become implanted and were accepted protocol. There were three sharp and rapid salvos from the ten men on the deck after which their fire arms were held diagonally across their chests. They stared steadfastly ahead waiting patiently for the order to dismiss. They were dismissed as soon as the last of the visitors had disappeared through the door which led to the interior of the vessel.

Nobody noticed that they were, in the confusion of dismissal, joined by an eleventh man when they broke ranks and followed the visitors through the door to the interior of the vessel. The eleventh man was slightly stooped to disguise his very noticeable height difference. The other ten men were all of different build and colour but were all of about the same height, as dictated by the Federation to prevent the lesser stature of the Chinese contingent from being an embarrassment.

Inside *Neptunium* the sighing of the air purification system was accompanied by the vibrating hum of the fusion beam power plant which propelled the vessel and kept everything functioning, a task it would accomplish for the next ten years without replenishment. Lighting was soft and calming and the red glow of the instrument array was also strangely soothing so that even the journalists were caught up in the atmosphere and chose to talk in hushed tones. Journalists and photographers were paired and accompanied by an officer who would act as guide and answer any acceptable questions that might arise.

James Creswell was shown into a small executive cabin which was intended for the use of visiting dignitaries. He made himself comfortable and sat on a captain's chair which dwarfed the tiny desk on which sat a coffee maker, a selection of cups and an assortment of highly calorific biscuits. He tried the coffee in an unsuccessful attempt to wash away the distaste he felt for the words of inauguration, dictated by the Federation, that he had been required to spout. No mention of King and Country no mention of God blessing those who sail in her, just the lie about democracy and the requirement to follow orders without question.

The eleventh matelot in ceremonial navel uniform was carrying an assault rifle which had been, now that he was separated from the rest of the uniformed naval contingent, fitted with a suppresser, also a camera with lighting; he silently opened the door to Creswell's cabin and slipped inside. Creswell looked up from his desk initially with a look of annoyance which changed rapidly to alarm when he saw the gun wielded by a balaclava masked sailor.

"What…" Creswell said with a look of horror before his voice choked off.

"Bang." Said the gunman, with a devilish grin, just before he squeezed the trigger. Gasses escaping the suppresser hissed angrily and Creswell's dress shirt blossomed crimson as he jerked back in the chair which spun on its axis and deposited him on the desk, face down. The assassin swivelled the gun mounted camera around the small cabin before returning to the supine figure of Creswell and switching it off.

He switched the camera to playback and watched the screen to admire his handiwork. Satisfied with the results he removed the camera from the gun barrel and the suppresser and placed them in his pocket. He dismantled the gun and placed all the parts into a drawstring sack which he swung nonchalantly over his shoulder before opening the cabin door a crack to make sure that the coast was clear before he melted away into the environs of Clyde Side where his Chinese naval uniform was a common sight and his unusual height was less obvious because he kept away from other people and things which could be used as a comparison.

On the very next day there was a hastily prepared announcement in the press that the Prime Minister had contracted a viral illness which was very contagious and would be out of circulation for at least ten days and that his appointments would be kept by the Deputy PM as indeed they had been in the period immediately preceding the sudden viral attack.

Fourteen

Eleven's plan was simple, as all good plans should be. He had studied the failure of Wilson's 'bull in a china shop' approach to get control of BAM technology as a consequence of Wilson's scientists not being unsuccessful in carrying out duplicate experiments to recreate the anomaly. This he had gleaned from discussions with Pelochev whom he found alarmingly indiscrete by the revelation of the ignominious failure of the first attempt for which Wilson alone, despite his protestations to the contrary, was entirely responsible. His second attempt to unearth the secrets using Nuovostani scientists had led to the annihilation of the team together with the laboratory and the precious experiment notes. This was not a course of action that Eleven would choose to follow; it had already proved to be costly in time and personnel and the fact that Wilson was considering a third attempt underlined his 'bull in a china shop' approach to what had become his blind and illogical obsession.

Indulging in experimentation with all the tribulations was something that he could not understand and did not care to think about— it was unstructured and was just not Eleven's way of doing things. His intention, rather than recreating the original experiments with all its obvious faults, was to use the carefully chosen members of the RIR cells to gain access to one of the back-up dormant BAM2 units stored below ground which would not be missed immediately. Being an Islander he could take this option which Wilson could not from the remoteness of his eyrie in Nuovostan.

Cell 1, comprising the radical dissidents who had personal axes to grind with the world in general was very useful for carrying out the less ethical of tasks without any reservation. He recognised that they were not satisfactorily useful when any form of imagination or subtlety were required but under his direction their prejudices could be put to good use. In his cell there was a member of Pettit's security staff, not a senior member but one who would nevertheless be useful in circumnavigating at least some of the heavy security which protected the hallowed BAM2 units. The cell also included a middle ranking member of the physics research team who would be invaluable in helping him achieve his aims. Eleven had selected them purposefully and carefully to be in his cell.

The outline of his tactic was clear to him but in the interests of total security he shared it with nobody else. Cell contributors to his plan of action would carry out their part in complete isolation and would have no knowledge of the actual strategy he intended to employ. He alone would be in command.

There were three basic phases to his plan: To short circuit the security and acquire a BAM2 unit; to disable the unit to prevent it from the self-destruction for which it was programmed and finally; to dismantle and extract the secrets while it was still disabled. This simple expedient would give him the leverage that was necessary for him to blackmail all-comers into total acceptance of him as undisputed leader in the revolution against the Island. There were many it would give him great pleasure to dominate but none more so than that bumbling arrogant fool President Wilson of Nuovostan who had wasted so many good chances of success and made it so much more difficult for Eleven to achieve his goals.

Contacting, separately, the two cell members he had selected to help him achieve his initial goals, he set them to work researching the details of their allotted tasks. Eleven had devised a way to acquire and disable the unit but he wanted his chosen helpers to try and come up with a better alternative than the ones he devised, he resisted mentioning to them that he had devised a system which he thought was brilliant in its simplicity.

He was satisfied when they failed to come up with an acceptable alternative means of meeting the objectives. After all, if they in their relatively lowly positions had been able to access protection protocols and manage the acquisition of BAM2 in the same way that he proposed, the systems would surely have been in place to prevent it. Without delay he set his proposals in motion, with each of his chosen helpers being given only part of his overall plan. He urged them to make all haste with a promise of great rewards in the outside world. Mentally he carved another notch on his hypothetical weapon of conquest which moved him one step closer to fulfilling his ambitions.

Fifteen

The barman, who was perched on a stool behind the bleached yellow wood counter of the Beach Bar Resort on Coral Island in the heart of the Caribbean, flicked lazily at flies which used the bar counter as a landing strip. Being off-season, the barman was also standing in as the manager, the receptionist, the cleaner and the cook. His lifelong familiarity with Coral Island had robbed the location of the charm which was so much appreciated by the procession of rich and foolishly extravagant holiday makers during the season. The unexpected arrival of his only two guests, when the season was officially finished, was a bonus which provided him with a trouble free way of earning a few more dollars. This was a bonus which the owners and financers of the bar, who spent the off season away from the island, did not need to know about.

Coral Island is remote and idyllic. Green palm thatch on the bamboo roof framework shaded the veranda from the sapping heat of the Caribbean sun which continued to be strong, even off season. The resort's only two guests sat in the shade sipping ice cold cocktails of random ingredients of uncertain origin. The younger man, in his thirties or forties, was dark haired and weather tanned; his older companion probably in his late sixties had a shock of grey hair which was unkempt as it was constantly being teased by the salt laden onshore breeze. They were, the barman thought originally, probably drug gangsters hiding away from the police.

They were comfortable with their own company and their discussion was easy but furtive, they stopped speaking whenever he was near but failed to realise that the strange acoustics of the bar enabled him to pick up stressed words from their whispered conversations. It was obvious to him after listening to their hushed tones that the two were probably not drug runners but more likely film producers who were discussing a plot dealing with evil doings and deception on a massive scale and that their nervousness was occasioned by their wish for secrecy as they discussed their proposed movie, rather than the fear of the police..

The barman continued half listening to their conversation and decided that one of the men was English and the other American— recognising accents was a skill he had picked up when trying to determine which of the guests would get special treatment because they were likely to offer the better gratuities. The bits of the plot they were discussing which he could hear was a no-go as far as he was concerned; the American film-makers who frequented Coral Island in season would never have entertained the idea of such a weak plot. This was probably, he presumed from within the meanderings of his fantasy world, why Hollywood was bigger and more influential than any of the other film centres in other countries. The snatches of conversation he picked up seemed to be weak and lacked the necessary hint of conviction required by a blockbuster. He watched them with growing disinterest as they picked up their drinks and moved further away from the bar.

"I think we'd better move away from the bar," the younger man whispered to his companion. "I think he might be eavesdropping." He inclined his head towards the barman on his perch.

"Looks to me like he's asleep," the older of the two men looked briefly at the relaxed barman. "But let's not tempt fate."

They hand signalled the barman, who snapped by autonomic response out of his reverie, to refresh their drinks. Once replenished they moved away from the bar to a table closer to the hot white sand of the beach and where their conversation would be covered by the rhythmic whispering of the waves as they lapped softly onto the beach and the sucking sound as the water retreated over the white sand and tumbling seashells. Their conversation of the plot continued in privacy but they seemed to get stuck in giving it a satisfactory ending. Like the barman they gave up in the end and succumbed to not having anything of great importance to do or say but they gave off an air of tension which was beyond the comprehension of the Coral Islander. Rich people of European descent were a mystery to him, especially those who made movies.

Sixteen

Zen in his guise as Wright continued to develop the interaction with Jack Pain; it was an excruciating process because of Pain's basic lack of intelligence. The third stage of his plan was to plant information into Pain's befuddled mind with a view to extracting from him inside information about Wilson as well as finding a way to get to know Julia Hammond, the tabloid journalist whose part in the machinations was hinted at but was not clear. It was hard to understand what was in this for her; she was a successful journalist with a well-known if somewhat tarnished tabloid newspaper and her connections to Pain and Wilson were beyond Zen's understanding. This understanding was what he was required by Eleven to determine. His quest was to gather as much useful information about the knowledge of the workings of the Island as understood by Wilson and Hammond and was the reason he had been smuggled off the Island. Eleven believed in comprehending the strengths and weaknesses of his apparent friends as well as his enemies. Zen also had another agenda of which Eleven knew nothing.

Zen's illegal absence from Recovery Island was obfuscated to a satisfactory extent by his Recocard being used by one of Eleven's men to make random and appropriate purchases which would mask his absence from the Island. If this deception were to be discovered it would make his position very precarious. Eleven had thoughts of elevating Zen to a senior position in RIR and had used his considerable influence to cover Zen's tracks for his own reasons.

The frustratingly slow progress with Pain gave Wright time to look at London as a tourist. Unlike Pain he saw through the grime-laden buildings, which flanked the major routes through the city, to the history beneath the coating of time. Mostly he did this on foot and instead of limiting himself to observations from street level— he lifted his head to see the time worn, somewhat neglected, grace of the upper stone facades. Like Pain he found the noise and bustle of surface transport distracting as well as dangerous and malodourous. Similarly he found the use of money extremely inconvenient and soon after arriving requested, during one of his updating calls to number 11, that credit cards be made available to him. Eleven was as good as his word and with amazing speed was able to fulfil the request. There was a marked improvement in his financial transactions because of its similarity to using a Recocard. Even so it was not possible to use a credit card for all transactions such as buying a newspaper or something from a street vendor or paying some taxi drivers so it was still necessary for him to use the unfamiliar cash.

He had, despite the misconception that he was Island-born, spent the first ten years of his life living in London with his family before they were invited en-masse to migrate to the Island when the Islands administration had been looking for computer specialists; his father was a recognised and very able advanced practitioner. His memories of London were those of a ten year old; now some fifteen years later he had recollections of the buildings which now seemed so much smaller and less threatening than he recalled from his childhood. The noise of the traffic was greater than he remembered and the pollution was horrendous after the cleanliness and relative quiet of the traffic-free Island of Recovery.

The biggest change, to his earlier recollection, was in the people; they did not look happy and they appeared to be in a hurry to be somewhere else – there was, it seemed, no time to admire the time worn beauty of the architecture, the plethora of national costumes, the cluttered gaiety of the myriad, almost anarchically dissimilar, shop windows. For all their unhappy appearance they were actually cheerful and engaged with relish - given the opportunity. Despite what he had heard to the contrary people on the street would exchange greetings when prompted and would help if asked. Visitors would be left to their own devices unless they sought assistance and it was given freely.

Living in London was so different to life on the Island where every day things were not conducted at such a frenetic pace. On the Island coffee was often consumed cold – simply because it was enjoyed over a long relaxing time. In London's coffee houses the rush to be elsewhere meant that very often a half cup of coffee, still steaming, would be abandoned on the table because of the baffling time constraints which were levied. Here too patrons left their used dishes and utensils for others to clear away and they were actually washed to be reused, a practice he found particularly distasteful; on the Island the used items were cleared by the users to renewing stations where crockery was separated from cutlery and put into an appropriate disposal chute where it would be sanitised by super steam treatment and then ground down, super heat-treated again and reformed into new items which were produced as required rather than being stored in less than sanitary conditions.

***

110

Julia Hammond was a completely different proposition when compared with Jack Pain. She certainly was not, like Pain, unintelligent. She had the reputation of possessing a cunning which she used to great effect. Wright had to tread carefully with her, unlike Pain whom he could manipulate with relative ease. Being an off-Islander, intelligence about her was less prolific than that for Jack Pain. Zen's instructions had been plain: *"Get to know her any way you can, find out as much as you can from her about what Wilson is doing and about this assistant of his – we need to be one step ahead of them at all times."*

His instructions were that he had to make haste to infiltrate the world of Jack Pain and Julia Hammond because there was intelligence that told of Wilson being up to no good and Pain and Hammond could be a useful conduit to him. Because of Hammond's absence from the country on a task for the PPA, the Popular Press Association, he had to deal with Pain and Hammond in reverse order to that which he would have preferred. It was not ideal and Wright had to take care not to expose to Pain that he did not yet know Hammond. If he were to learn of that fact Wright's plans would collapse without hope of recovery. The Machiavellian twists and turns of events left Wright feeling uncomfortable and uncertain.

He had listened to the recording sold to him by Diana in which Pain gave away the limited and often inaccurate or invented secrets about life on the Island. The knowledge Pain had given away could potentially be of marginal interest to off-Islanders but to those on the Island it was of no value and was therefore of no value to Zen and subsequently Eleven. He did not break his contact with Diana but he did string out the purchase of the other discs by offering to buy them one at a time to 'check out their value'. In his conversations with Diana he slowly extracted information about Hammond's likes and dislikes. She liked money, the pampered life and notoriety but did not take to sharing any journalistic advantages she might gain by whatever means at her disposal. Hammond pursued her objectives coldly and calculatedly and was not known to take prisoners.

With some surprise Wright had to admit that the cover that had been put in place for him was a stroke of genius the background established him as an influential under-cover investigative reporter who undertook freelance projects for the New York Times. In this guise he contacted Julia Hammond when she returned from her overseas tour. Initially she brushed off his overtures to meet him as a fellow journalist. In her opinion any other journalist who wanted to meet her was after something she had and which they wanted. She was no philanthropist and what is more she had just returned from a long and tiring trip and had promised herself a few days of self-indulgent bed rest.

Learning this, Wright made her an offer she could not refuse, using information about her character gleaned from Diana and RIR files. He tempted her with a free long weekend in 'The Place'; the most expensive health spa in the country which was located in the heart of London's Mayfair. Her reluctance wavered when he mentioned that he was with the New York Times and evaporated completely when he offered her a long weekend at 'The Place'. The die was cast and, suitably attired in formal evening wear they met in a bar in the Park Lane Hotel and consumed a few relaxing cocktails before taking a cab for a brief ride to 'The Place'.

The exterior of the august Place establishment was disappointingly unimpressive; it was six ugly storeys high, but interior was another world, marble floors and columns were polished and precisely matched, being the finest that Italy had to offer. Ceilings were high and ornate with fine well forged renaissance paintings bordered by dark wood frames. Doors were huge and of hand carved oak, lovingly polished – their heaviness was not a problem, each door was attended and opened, as required, by a liveried attendant, who impressed the over indulgent and over rich patrons.

They were both overawed by the spa, which for him was grander than anything on the Island, and Hammond's sparkling eyes showed that she too was impressed by the overt if somewhat gauche grandeur. She was even more impressed when he checked in by simply saying that their suite had been reserved for Anton Wright by the New York Times which would be taking care of all expenses incurred.

The checking in process was personalised. They were taken to a small sumptuous reception room where an attractive senior stewardess sat them down in comfortable winged leather chairs and placed two flutes of champagne on a silver tray before them. The fine crystal flutes were lightly misted but not running with condensation as they would have been had the champage been at too low a temperature.

Also placed before them were two red hand tooled leather folders embossed in gold leaf with the legend 'Monarch's Suite' which the stewardess opened with some reverence. Each of the folders contained a gold digital key secured to a white gold necklace. There was also a selection of velum sheets with information about the services available in the establishment and a slim gold Wi-Fi telephone for use in the event that they should require anything from the establishment, anything at all, at any time.

They and their luggage were taken up to the Monarch Suite by two scantily uniformed attendants. Male for her and female for him, both attendants were obviously chosen for their looks as well as their ability to converse politely and easily with their overly pampered clients. Their luggage was placed on an ornate gold and red porter's trolley which was pushed by a traditionally attired bell boy. Once inside the suite they were shown two interconnecting bedrooms with sumptuous en suite bathrooms, a dining room with a business centre alcove, a mini gym, a drawing room and a small fully equipped kitchen complete with wine racks and a fully stocked cocktail cabinet. The compact but fully equipped kitchen, they were assured, would be operated by an attendant in the event that they wished to use the room service facilities rather than one of the formal dining rooms.

"I think I'm in heaven," Hammond said dreamily when the attendants had left after unpacking their luggage. "Have you ever seen anything like this before?" She twirled around in the middle of the drawing room under a crystal chandelier. Despite her assumed air of sophistication she was mesmerised by the grandeur.

Wright smiled to himself at her childlike glee; she was not at all as he had expected. He decided that he would enjoy her company a whole lot more than that of Pain. 'In fact it would be,' he thought quizzically, 'No *pain* at all.'

They dined simply in their suite on tender steamed salmon fillets accompanied by lightly sautéed sliced new potatoes and buttered asparagus spears, followed by syllabub all of which was accompanied by an award winning fragrant light English sparkling wine which put even the finest champage to task. They were both tired; she from her travels and he from his demanding meetings with Jack Pain and they both agreed that they would retire early and enjoy the facilities all the more after a good night's sleep.

114

Much to her surprise he made no overtures to join her in her bedroom. She caught their reflection in a full length seductively flattering mirror; they made an imposing pair dressed in their finery. He in black tie and dinner jacket, she resplendant in an off-one-shoulder, full length, deep red evening gown. They both looked around the same age, although she was ten years his senior. They were both tanned from their various travels and she looked at their reflection and saw how beautifully matched they were together and turned to him with a frown. "You didn't suggest joining me in the bedroom, are you...I mean ...do you? " Her voice tailed off as she left her thoughts incomplete

"Nothing like that. Would it bother you if I did whatever it is you think?" He arched an eyebrow quizzically.

"No." She arched an eyebrow in return, "but I think it would be a terrible shame if you did....whatever it is I was thinking."

"Tonight we sleep separately," he gave her a satanic smile. "Tomorrow, who knows?"

"Maybe you won't get a chance tomorrow." She said as a throw away comment as she turned to leave him.

"And maybe I will." He smiled wolfishly at her and turned towards his bedroom.

She entered her room and switched on the low side lights. Reaching behind she dragged down the zip and let the soft material of her dress pool on the floor around her feet. Under the dress she was completely naked; she admired her tan in the mirror which showed no pale parts of the body where the sun had not reached. "Just look at what you're missing, Anton Wright." She whispered to the mirror, turning away with surprised embarrassment when she saw the reflection of disappointment on her own face.

115

Seventeen

Feeling that he had trodden softly as long as was necessary to establish his basic contact, Anton Wright decided to step up his assault on both Pain and Hammond. To get to Pain he decided to use the influence of Hammond whom Pain coveted in the most obvious and unsophisticated way which had laid him open to manipulation. To get to Hammond he arranged to lunch with her at a fancy restaurant which she had mentioned to him in glowing terms during their weekend of luxury. This was their first meeting since spending the long weekend together at 'The Place'. Their intimacy had developed no further than overt and obvious flirting during their weekend together, although he was sure that had he pressed the matter it would have been possible for him to have got to know her in the physical sense so desperately sought by Pain. His decision not to do so was based not on a lack of desire on his part but on the feeling that had he taken advantage of the opportunity she would, later, have backed off and that did not suit his purposes at all, better to keep her on tenterhooks, a thought which made him feel arrogant but which he had been tutored to ignore.

Lunch was lengthy and suggestive. She was clearly used to dining lavishly and what he had intended as a light repast allowing wide ranging discussion turned into an alcohol fuelled contest to see who could stand the pace longest. She was clearly more used to this sort of occasion than he and it became clear that she would win the competition unless he mounted a defence against the alcoholic assault.

This objective was achieved with comparative ease by his excusing himself from the table on the pretext of a comfort break. Once out of sight he collared their wine waiter and with persuasion, and the judicious offer of a large denomination bank note, persuaded him to serve ginger ale when he ordered whiskey but to continue serving his companion with whatever she ordered, in double measures. The waiter gave him a knowing smile and tapped the side of his nose to portray understanding. He resisted the temptation to tell this customer that he did not need to get her drunk to take advantage of her, it was well known to the staff of the restaurant that when she liked somebody she was very free with her favours – and it was clear from the way she looked at him that she liked him, very much.

At the end of the meal she was slurring her speech and slightly unsteady on her feet. Zen emulated her but was comparatively sober. He steered her towards a secluded table on the terrace overlooking one of the many coils of the River Thames and ordered coffee for them both. His conversation started off generally by discussing nothing of any noticeable importance; slowly he introduced the subject which was the whole object of their lunch date.

"I'm going to be writing an exposé on Recovery Island and you are one of the few who have been there. How about giving the lowdown on the bits you didn't put in your article?"

"I don't do sharing information," she was immediately sobered and suspicious.

"We could share a by-line in the New York Times that would do your career no harm at all." He admired that even when she was drunk she kept tight rein on the control of her journalistic interests.

"Tabloids are more my forte." But she said in such a way that he could read into her words that the thought

117

of moving up market was appealing to her and would enhance her journalistic standing.

"Don't sell yourself short," he admonished her gently. "You have so much more talent than a tabloid hack requires to function and having an explosive front page article in the NYT will move you up several notches." He watched the myriad emotions flit across her face as she wrestled with the concept. That he would actually be unable to deliver the promise was not a matter of regret to him.

Her eyes, which had been clouded and slightly vacant cleared and became focussed. "I looked you up on the net but I didn't see any reference to articles written by you for the NYT, as you call it, so what's that all about?" She blurted this information out in an attempted diversion to give herself more time to develop a plausible response without actually committing herself.

Momentarily he was panicked; this deception had been arranged so hastily that Eleven's techs had failed to take care of this vital aspect of his cover. Cold shivers ran up and down his spine, he had been caught out in an exposed position which she had, despite being impaired by alcohol, revealed. The whole deception began to unravel and failure at this point would close the doors to the information he so badly needed. He felt the cold hand of failure descend on him. All, he thought with absolute despair, was lost because of a simple oversight.

The panic he felt when Hammond so casually exposed the flaws in his cover story prompted a sudden rush of adrenalin which caused everything to unfold in slow motion except for his thoughts which accelerated to many times its normal speed. There was no doubt that her thought processes were impaired by the alcohol she had consumed and he looked closely at her to judge the intensity of her concern. Her eyes were glazed and unfocussed; she shook her head as though trying to recapture a thought that had slipped out of her grasp and he was relieved to see that whatever the thought was it continued to escape and was lost without trace.

"Time for us to go," he stood up and walked around the table to take her elbow.

"Are we done?" She looked confused.

"Yes, we're done especially when you can't even work out the simplest of reasons for being unable to understand why my name doesn't appear on the NYT website. I need anonymity to carry out my job as an investigative reporter, if I advertise my trade and become famous, how can I investigate undercover?" Had she been entirely sober she would have questioned the flaws in his argument and he would have been hard pressed to counter them, but she wasn't. "Time to go home," he coaxed her out of her chair.

As they left the restaurant the wine waiter opened the door, observing that Zen's hands were full of Hammond who could hardly stand. As they finally left the waiter said under his breath so that only Zen would hear. "I think you over did the happy juice, she can't walk, she can hardly talk and she is certainly not in any state to make out. Tough luck!"

Eighteen

Eleven was taciturn when he took a telephone call from Irena Pelochev; he had repeatedly asked her not to make contact with him, a requirement which she completely ignored. His telephone was security protected but he was reluctant to use it with any regularity, especially to talk to somebody as devious as Wilson's PA whom he knew would throw him to the wolves without hesitation should it suite her purposes or those of her mentor Wilson.

"Have special ask for you," she mangled the incomplete sentence in a way he was learning to decipher.

"What is it you want of me, you know I do not like you to call me."

"Am knowing this, just so. Mr President is wish to have talking with you on things most grave, but not on telephone you must coming with Nuovostan for talking."

"No chance." He said abruptly. "Leaving the Island is not an option."

"Mr President is thinking you will say this and he say that you cannot do the things you want to do without other help. We can give other help and you can make lot of influences."

Eleven was silent while he considered the implications of what she had said in her unique way. So far the RIR attempt to acquire the technology was going well; Kwietakovski had exchanged a working BAM2 unit for a dummy. His final act in the process was to remove it from the confines of the silo and to a place where another cell member could retrieve it when shifts worked in their favour.

If Eleven were to fail in his attempt to get the BAM2 unit opened up without it self-destructing he would need a plan B. "OK," he acquiesced after a long pause in the telephone conversation with Pelochev, "I'll make travel arrangements and let you know." Wilson had, for the moment at least, become Eleven's plan B and he was only too aware that if it ever became necessary to employ plan B he would be on very shaky ground but, he thought, *needs must when the devil drives.*

"Is good," she acknowledged his unexpected capitulation with a high degree of suspicion; it had all been too easy. In her mind she was formulating a plan in which she would tell Wilson that she had had to be very persuasive and had offered to pay for his travel to Nuovostan and his accommodations. Mollified by her plan, she reported to Wilson and laboured the point of how difficult it had been to get his agreement to come but that in the end she had been successfully persuasive. Wilson was indifferent to her attempt to impress him and dismissed her with an imperious wave of his hand.

By meeting in Nuovostan, the plans of both Wilson and Eleven were, unwittingly to each other, fast tracked in one fell swoop. It also gave Pelochev pause for thought; she could see a future for herself without the encumbrance of Wilson or any other man of dubious competitive ambition. She thought that an ideal partner for her would be 'A', whoever he might actually be; he would protect and nurture her because like all the professional murderers of her acquaintance, and she knew a few, she perceived him to be of limited intellect and imagination and she would bestow upon him delights which she doubted he could get elsewhere. Her understanding of the psychology of people was of the

121

same quality as her lamentable understanding of philanthropy.

The meeting between Wilson, Pelochev and Eleven was disjointed and peppered with bad tempered spats. Their tripartite agendas were in dire but unspoken conflict— Wilson wanted the total destruction of the Island after he had made BAM2 his own, Eleven wanted BAM2 and its Island base and Pelochev had aspirations to sell on the technology to the highest bidder and live a life of luxury, with her partner of choice – 'A' or maybe even somebody else, on the proceeds. They were all conscious that they had divergent agendas without knowing what their rival's schemes actually were.

Although the outcome of their discussions were inconclusive each of the three felt that they had moved some way towards realising their aims. The one area in which there was general acceptance if not total agreement was that the Island's Ruling Council should be disabled and that the best way of achieving this was to bring about the removal of the remaining three founders after which the rudderless Council would be easily neutralised.

Their discussions about achieving this goal were a bizarre mishmash of hare-brained ideas from the two men without rationale or any kind of finesse, varying from blowing up the Island's administration building while the Ruling Council were in session to lacing the food at one of the official dinners with deadly poison.

Pelochev was not in agreement with what she thought was their scattered approach. "Shootings are the answer." Pelochev grew tired of the irrational ranting of the two men. She laughed inwardly at the look on their faces that she a mere chattel should have any input into their deliberations.

"Shut up Irena," Wilson said with ill controlled fury. "You're not part of this conversation."

In her newfound boldness brought about by her resolution to be the victor in this battle of wills she looked haughtily at Wilson with all the pride of her Siberian antecedents and did something she had never dared before, she stared him down. "I shut up when you are speak sense. Now you are not to speak sense so I must for you."

Wilson broke eye contact and half rose from his chair, lunging towards her. Eleven interceded and stood between them physically separating them. "Take your hands off me you commoner," he spat at Eleven. "You are here at my whim and you are a long way from home and you are in no position to take the risk of incurring the wrath of the President of Nuovostan." His psychosis had advanced to the stage of his speaking of himself in the third person.

Undaunted by the overt threats, Eleven pushed Wilson back down into his chair and indicated by the inclination of his head that Pelochev should resume her seat. She did so slowly and insolently, her cheeks were flushed and her eyes were sparkling, not with tears but with the excitement of this challenging moment which gave her a shortness of breath and a feeling akin to the approach of ecstasy. She had at last got away with standing up to Wilson without being harmed.

"President Wilson." Eleven's carefully modulated soft voice defused the situation in an instant. "Please accept my apologies for becoming physical. We are all excited by the opportunities that we have and a little calm will help us reach the conclusions we seek." He indicated by the direction of his gaze that the decisions would be made by the two men. "Let us listen to what Miss Pelochev has to say before dismissing her ideas

123

out of hand." He turned to Pelochev and indicated that she should speak.

"We have kill two people by shootings." She was slow to speak as she translated into Rushlish from her native language. "This we know from kill videos we have. We tell 'A' to kill other three on Island and others can kill later."

"We've already tried that with the two we had assassinated and it didn't work." Wilson dismissed her ideas before they were formulated.

Pelochev looked at Eleven as if asking for permission to continue. When he nodded to her she did so. "We kill people we want to and video as it happen then we show videos on Island information systems which are possible because Eleven has way break into the televisions and, how you say it, insert pirates?"

Eleven watched various emotions cross Wilsons face. He realised quite clearly that his thoughts about Wilson before they had actually met were correct; he was a fully-fledged and unstable psychotic in the advanced stages of delusion. This supposition was confirmed when Wilsons face broke into the semblance of a grin and he looked with some fondness at Pelochev. "There," he said as though speaking to a child. "I knew that if I trained you well enough you would eventually come up with a good idea. I have done well." He turned to Eleven as though the incident of anger had never occurred. "What do you think of my protégé, isn't she wonderful?"

Eleven thought it best to agree with him in the interest of harmony. Pelochev had assumed a look of burgeoning fear, in all the time she had been with Wilson he had never before threatened her with physical violence and more frightening he had never praised her for anything she had done but the fear turned to triumph when the threat diminished. She

124

realised in that instant that he had finally snapped and was clinically certifiable. She realised that he was still an unstable threat to anybody who crossed him but now she had the measure of him she could use damage limitation.

He had finally lost all vestiges of humanity and had crossed the line into the tangle of the twilight zone.

Nineteen

What was very clear to 'A' was that arranging a meeting with Wilson in Nuovostan, ostensibly to be briefed on the next assassination, would further his cause. The real task was for him to find out more about who was actually behind suppressing the two assassinations and why. Eleven could not understand why anybody except Wilson would choose to hide the facts of the assassinations and had tasked 'A' to elicit the reasons by any means necessary. Eleven had dismissed Pelochev's suggestion about releasing the information about the assassinations over the Island's IP's because any input to the system was by the nature of its security systems, traceable and in any case would be filtered out.

At Eleven's instigation 'A' made a telephone call to Irena Pelochev which was very well received, largely because he had made contact without being asked to do so which caused her to think that he was contacting her in the hope of further personal favours from her, she was after all very good at it was she not?

Pelochev's representations to Wilson were not fully reflective of the facts. She told him, in much the same way as she claimed credit for persuading Eleven to visit Nuovostan, that with great personal effort she had tracked down 'A' and demanded that he should come to Nuovostan, at his own expense, to report on his failure to produce the evidence they required to verify that he had actually carried out his allotted tasks.

Wilson was delighted that she had achieved this coup but as usual was not willing to give her any credit for it and instead of praise he castigated her for taking

126

so long to carry out this simple task which he could have carried out in a fraction of the time, he had reverted to type. He openly revelled in the look of disappointment on her face as she listened to his dismissal of her assumed efforts. Belittling her was one of the highlights of his existence and helped to alleviate the boredom caused by his being a virtual prisoner in his own castle. Travel to or through other countries was not easy for him, he had so many sworn enemies and there were so many international warrants being out for his immediate detention. Even travelling in his own new country was fraught with danger posed by the majority of citizens who hated what he had done to their country, language and culture; such as it had been.

When 'A' finally arrived at the President's palace he was greeted with undisguised pleasure by Pelochev and apparent indifference by Wilson. He was shown to his accommodation where he showered and changed from his travelling clothes into very expensive casual clothes which befitted a man who was so successful in his chosen profession and was intended to impress his clients. He joined his two hosts in the ridiculously opulent dining hall which, he estimated, could hold between two and three hundred people.

There was an uneasy silence between his two hosts who were clearly not enjoying each other's company, a situation which was becoming more frequent as time passed. They spoke to him separately addressing only him, not each other and they seemed to be following different agendas.

"Their assassinations have still not been announced," Wilson said angrily. "Why is that? Are you sure that you have actually done this work?" He threw his linen napkin down on top of his untouched repast. "You'll get no more work from me until the announcement of their deaths is made." He hit the table hard with the side of his clenched fist causing crockery and cutlery to rattle.

"That's your choice President Wilson," 'A' said with what Wilson considered to be unacceptable calm.

"My choice, my choice," he repeated through clenched teeth. "You have been paid a King's ransom to carry out two simple tasks and you've failed. I'll have you flung in jail, tried for treason and shot as a traitor. You're in my country now and my word is sacrosanct."

"Really?" 'A' raised one eyebrow quizzically and smiled a cold and controlled smile. He had been briefed on Wilson's idiosyncrasies and how his maniacal outbursts should be handled. "I should advise you that if I fail to return to my home in the next few days documentary evidence, including videos, of the assassinations and the part played by you will be sent by my legal representatives to all major governments and news outlets across the world. If I do return there will, of course, be no repercussions." He sipped his glass of deep red wine and held the glass up to the light. "Congratulations this is excellent claret – one of the best I have tasted for a long time." He smiled disarmingly at Wilson.

Wilson's demeanour and attitude changed completely and he smiled, although the smile did not reach into his being. "I have specialists who scour the world for the best of everything. This claret is produced in a small private family vineyard in the southern cape of South Africa. First I bought the whole of the vintage and it is so good I bought the vineyard. The owners didn't want to sell but a series of unfortunate accidents befell them and they were forced to relinquish ownership." His confession of wrongdoing was not made with any regret for his actions.

'A' was stunned by the sudden change in Wilson and was hard pressed to hide his astonishment even though he had been warned that Wilson was precariously balanced on the edge of reason. He became aware that Pelochev was studying his face intently and that an evil smile played about her sensuous lips as she saw his fleeting reaction to Wilson's words.

Later that evening when Wilson had retired and 'A' and Pelochev were enjoying a cocktail in the privacy of her apartment she placed a hand on 'As' shoulder and whispered conspiratorially. "Have never seen any person deal with Cullin like you, he is pussy cat in your hand. He is going from jailing you and killing to tell you about things he does not tell even to me in bedroom. I can see will have to watching you from getting things about me," she simpered and shuddered as she tussled with a private internal turmoil.

"What is there to know about you, what secrets do you have?" He smiled flirtatiously and placed his hand over hers. "Are you going to tell me something that will mean that I can own you as my slave?"

She shuddered once more at his words. "Not being a slave to any man," she insisted but her words and eyes did not match. His inferred meaning had set her imagination on fire.

He marvelled at how easy it had been to manipulate Wilson and now her; the reasons were very different, Wilson was easy because he was a maniac but Pelochev was far more complex. He had implied domination of her without physical or mental harm; she needed to be dominated in a way which did not belittle her and which she romanticised as being true affection. His task now was to manipulate her into giving him the information he had been charged with gleaning and he began the task with a relish that was tempered by an uneasy feeling that this manipulation was unfeeling and divisive. He comforted himself by thinking '*such is the lot of a paid assassin*'.

Twenty

The plans for the acquisition of a BAM2 unit were developing to Eleven's satisfaction. His clear instructions were being followed by the two chosen Island infiltrators he had planted and were coalescing as he had expected. The sequestered member of Pettit's security forces was primed to disable the principal security protection of one of the standby BAM2 projectors and via a member of the maintenance staff, pass the unit to the third RIR member who was part of the main physics research team. This would give them the opportunity of accessing the unit in its security box by disabling the booby trap that was its secondary means of protection.

The scene was set; it only remained for the renegade security guard to be assigned to guard duty of the targeted BAM2 unit. No attempt was made to hurry up his posting as guard, a duty which was prescribed on a random basis and without warning, in order to avoid suspicion and possible discovery. Likewise the physicist could only have unsupervised access to the laboratories necessary to disable the booby trap within the box when he was assigned to the graveyard shift. The maintenance duties with which he would be charged would give him the opportunity to use the specialised equipment without which disabling the booby trap was not possible.

Peotre Kwietakovski accepted the coded passkey from the second shift security guard and began his stint in the graveyard shift. Normally this was a quiet, largely unnecessary, shift spanning from midnight to 8 am. Time had little meaning in this secure silo which had no external windows and was deep underground. This, as far as Kwietakovski was concerned, would be a shift with a difference. Number 11 had given a simple but vital task, to remove one of the backup BAM2 units and replace it with a dummy that would stand the brief scrutiny it normally received during security rounds. He had smuggled into the silo the components which would be assembled into the dummy over a period of five days and had stored them in disparate locations but in plain sight in such a way that if they were found they would arouse curiosity but not suspicion.

Removing the last piece of the assembly from the haversack which contained his mid shift meal when he was sure he was alone, he began the task of retrieving the components from their holding places. He had to exercise caution because, in line with security policy, there were two guards in the facility at all times which made the task of assembling the unit more challenging.

Choosing the right night to undertake the task was considered carefully and this particular shift had been chosen because his fellow guard was a rookie who was known to be a slacker who could easily be diverted from his task. He sent the rookie off to do a check of the whole of the silo. This was strictly against the rules which stated clearly that the guards must always work in pairs to ensure that neither of them could steal or damage any of the BAM2 units or other valuable pieces of specialised machinery stored there. The rookie was heaven sent as far as Kwietakovski was concerned, with him out of the way his task was so much more simple.

He set about the task of assembly as soon as the rookie left their guard post office. The BAM2 units were contained in custom-made insert wooden boxes some nine inches cubed. The cube itself was genuine and it had been acquired, by another anonymous cell member, from the physics laboratory where the BAM2 units were assembled under close scrutiny. The units were scrutinised and checked carefully but the wooden cube components were not considered to be a security risk.

He grinned wolfishly to himself and luxuriated in the inefficiency of the cretins who ran the Island. Had this installation been in his homeland of Poland such slackness would not have occurred. Assembly of the cube was simple and took no great skill and it allowed him to dream about what he would do for his old country when number 11 achieved his goals and gave him the promised finances and influence which would allow him to make a difference. Once that had been accomplished it would be simple for him to acquire his own BAM2 unit and the controlling computer for the greater good of his first love - the PFM, Polish Freedom Movement. Poland would then be able to break free of the European yolk and would assume the independence which had been lost after the death of their great compatriot Jan III Sobieski, the King of Poland in1696. The Island and the RIR were of no consequence to him; his homeland and its heritage were everything. His present activities were simply a means to an end.

Completing the assembly of the dummy cube he carried it to the backup BAM2 storage unit which bore the same recognition number as was stencilled on the dummy. Using his security access card he unlocked the door to its small holding pen. He held his breath involuntarily as he opened the door; had the security alarm not been deactivated he would be discovered and there would be no escape from the consequences of discovery by the authorities but more so from the RIR who would be merciless. The door swung open silently and he let go of his breath in relief at his silent success.

The next phase was to smuggle the unit out of the silo. It could not be dismantled by him, that task could only be carried out by qualified physicists in their dedicated laboratory. The method devised by number 11 was simple, effective and to implement it he hid himself behind a storage shelf stack which was just inside the entrance to their security lodge and waited, a balk of timber in his hand – and waited.

Footsteps echoed along the corridor leading from the storage area to the security lodge heralding the return of the rookie guard. As he entered the lodge Kwietakovski stepped out behind him as he passed and struck him a fierce blow on the back of the head. The rookie fell to the floor, unconscious before he landed on the hard stone surface. A quick check of the pulse showed that he was still alive; had he not been it would have been of no consequence to Kwietakovski who continued with the pre-determined plan

To cover up the attack he arranged the supine guard as though he had been struck by the storage unit which he unscrewed from the wall and allowed to fall on the inert figure. The contents of the shelving were spread out over the floor and allowed to form a natural pattern, A small adjustment to the position of the felled guard made the scene more convincing. The final two stages of the plan were then put into being. Taking the stolen BAM2 unit from the office he opened up the security door which led into the silo from the entrance chamber and slotted it into an empty CPU processor casing on one of the storage units similar to the one he had just collapsed. It looked just like the other ten or so units contained by the shelving. The final part of his task was to contact security central and tell them of the terrible accident which had rendered his companion guard insensible.

At the end of the graveyard shift when the injured guard and the debris of the accident had been cleared away, a second standby guard had been appointed and in accordance with security protocols a full inventory count was carried out on the equipment stored. The substituted dummy BAM2 unit passed muster.

Kwietakovski whistled tunelessly to himself as he left the silo to report his success to number 11. One more, he thought, to Poland and another blow to the despicable enemy among which he included number 11.

Twenty-one

Mark Lawson was deep in meditation; he used the mind focussing technique taught to him by Carla Tanterelli which he had modified to suit his own strengths and understanding. Each bout of meditation lasted for a mere 5 minutes of deep concentration in which he normally indulged twice each day and sometimes more frequently when the need arose. Having completed the meditation he spent a further few minutes relaxing and bringing his consciousness back into the physical world.

He reviewed his knowledge of his adversaries which had grown to the point where he knew for a certainty, because of the intelligence he had received from one of his primary under-cover security agents, that they existed and he knew that they went by the name of the Recovery Island Rebels, RIR, and that they comprised an unexpectedly large number of members. He now knew that the leader was referred to as number 11 but he did not know the identity of the person the sobriquet obscured. Knowing that they existed was a start but they had to penetrate the organisation in depth in order to combat it.

Using Carlina Tanterelli's teachings he put himself into what he thought would be the mindset of number 11. Clearly he and his henchmen wanted either to overrun the Island or steal BAM2 technology or, more likely, both. They were clearly responsible for what had happened to Chester Gilliland but why they should also subject James Creswell, the British Prime Minister, to the same fate was a puzzle.

Keeping quiet the news of the assassinations could only last so long— the cover used for both men was very thin and would not stand up to scrutiny. It was puzzling that those who had ordered the shootings had not leaked the information of Creswell's fate to the UK media. Not releasing the news of Gilliland was a little more understandable, any news release on the Island was traceable and whoever number 11 was must have been aware of this.

So the task remained for him to put himself into the mind-set of the RIR, specifically that of number 11. Physically taking over the Island would require a military force that RIR did not appear to have at least within the shores of the Island. This left only one avenue open for them to achieve their aims; they would have to gain control of BAM2 and its operation. But how could they do that with the fool-proof security measures which were in place?

He cleansed his mind of its 'fair play' inhibitions and tried to think as a lone rebel would think. His understanding of this technique of the imagination was still in its infancy and he struggled with the concept of not having to consider normal social parameters in identifying a means of achieving the desired aims. He failed to connect with this mythical creature which probably had no conscience and no morals and was centred on reaching his, or her, objectives without deviation. Wrestling with the problem got him nowhere and Tanterelli's words of advice came back to him *'When you start thinking in circles and you come back to the beginning of the process for the third time, you should consider a new beginning.'* He contacted Tanterelli and arranged another session with her.

Tanterelli regarded Lawton with an open gaze which encouraged rather than admonished him for his failure to apply fully the techniques she had taught him.

137

"Please do not punish yourself for not being able to achieve your aims so early in the learning process. This ability will develop over time to the point where you will be able to teach me your slant on the technique," she smiled gently and continued. "It is extremely difficult to think so basically out of character, but remember you have already done this successfully in planting agents into the fringes of our enemy. Remember how you achieved this and how you succeeded in out thinking you adversary."

"Maybe that was a lucky guess," Lawson said in a rare moment of dejection.

"As has been said so often '*the more I practice the luckier I get*'. Don't think in circles, think in a straight line and you will reach your objective. It never fails if you allow it to work."

"What you're saying is don't panic, relax and all will be revealed."

"Do you believe that to be the case?"

"I suppose I do." He looked a little less uneasy.

"Then you have reached the next stage; so go out and practice your beliefs take the path down which they lead you, follow them through to their conclusion." She looked at the expression on his face, "you have just answered your own question, trust in your ability. It is there, all you have to do is allow it to prevail."

After he had left she stared at the door as it closed behind him. For all her apparently unflappable confidence she was acutely aware that she was straying into the unknown with Mark Lawson. In telling him how to approach his problems she was painfully aware that she could not actually achieve what he was, she felt sure, going to achieve. The testosterone levels required to solve these problems were insufficient in her but, fortunately, abundant in him. But only time would tell.

Once more, back in his own domain, Lawson cleansed his mind once more of its 'fair play' inhibitions and this time actually thought, in his trance-like state, as a lone rebel would think. Everything hinged around the acquisition of BAM2. It was not possible to get a BAM2 unit which was actually in use in the defence and running of the Island so the alternative, he dreamed of in his 'think like the enemy' state, would be to get one that was either only used infrequently or was in back up storage.

The light suddenly dawned; all unused and stored units should be gathered together in one secured location and protected by a BAM2 dome which could only be operated by the four founders in unison. His thoughts were uncannily accurate but what he did not and could not know was that the BAM2 unit had already been stolen and that good as the proposed security was—it was too late, the barn door had already been breached.

Twenty-two

Wilson's psychotic episode had at first bothered Eleven, but on reflection he realised that he could use it to his own advantage, a process he began to develop on his long and boring journey back to the Island. He would get number 66, Zen, to go to Nuovostan and by fuelling Wilson's paranoia, persuade him to accelerate the assassination of other world dignitaries to deflect Wilson's attention away from the Island and enable RIR to pursue their aims unhindered. To do that it would be necessary to enlist the aid of 'A', and 'A' could only be contacted through Wilson or Pelochev. Making contact was the task he gave number 66, it would be simple for 66, his being the sponsor of 'A'.

Zen was not happy about the interference with the tight schedule of requirements which he was personally pursuing in addition to his role for Eleven and it certainly did not include flying half way across the world to a god forsaken place run by a maniac. He was not ready to interact with Wilson before completing the interrogation of Pain and Hammond which he believed would give him valuable background for the more effective interrogation of Wilson. To refuse to go to Nuovostan at Eleven's direction would compromise his ability to learn more about the identity of the RIR leader which was one of the many challenges he had set himself, such knowledge would be invaluable to him. He had to see where this new course of action would lead him and he hoped shortcutting and going straight to the horse's mouth, the horse being Wilson, would in some way hurry up the process and at the same time would fit in with Eleven's plans.

His introduction to Nuovostan was a meeting with Pelochev who immediately dismissed him out of hand; she assessed that number 66 was subservient to the man she knew as number 11. She took it upon herself to interrogate him about the purpose of his visit and in a distracted way was very thorough about the process. Her quaint handling of the English language amused him but it was the only thing about her that did; he deduced that she was, under the primitive beauty of her exterior, a callous and unyielding woman. Surviving the initial cursory interrogation, he breathed a sigh of relief but inwardly cursed Eleven for putting him in this invidious position before he was ready for the task ahead.

The Wilson he saw as President was almost unrecognisable from the one he had seen just briefly a few short years before. He was considerably heavier and the sparse combed over hair that stuck unhealthily to his bald pate was liberally peppered with iron grey. Although Zen had played no part in Wilson's failed coup he was relieved that Wilson showed no signs of recognising him, had he done so it would be difficult if Wilson learned that Pain knew him as Anton Wright. In fact Wilson showed very little sign of recognising anybody at this moment in time, his look was vacant and he seemed to be having difficulty in focussing on anything tangible. He doubted that he would be able to do what Eleven had demanded of him, to divert Wilson's efforts away from the Island and concentrate on the other assassinations, but he had to try, failure was not an option Eleven would tolerate.

Ignoring the difficulty in having a rational conversation with Wilson he launched his offensive by feeding Wilson's megalomaniac aims which still bizarrely included aspirations of world domination, it seemed to Zen that the only productive route for him to pursue. He did so suggesting that for Wilson to achieve his aims he should further destabilise the Islanders by completing his round of assassinations. Softening up the Islanders could best be done by RIR because they were there on the ground and ready for action. At mention of the Island Wilson was stirred from his almost comatose state and his dull eyes began to sharpen.

"His words are good, Cullin." Pelochev had also observed that Wilson was in a more wakeful state. "You can be master of much if we take care of other leaders and let RIR look after Island for us." She spoke persuasively but her real aim was to divert Wilson away from the Island in much the same as number 66 was, her reasoning was uncomplicated and different. It was her intention to get 'A' to assassinate the remaining three of the Island's founders and for her to be smuggled onto the Island with him so that she could get control for herself with 'A' as her generalissimo. She had yet to deal with how control would be achieved but she had no doubt that with the total destabilisation of the Island's Ruling Council and with A's help she would be completely victorious. In her own mind she was a brilliant strategist who could not possibly fail.

Number 66 was thinking furiously, Pelochev was obviously not sure of or at best was unwilling to reveal the identity of Eleven which was one of the tasks that he had in mind. The name Mr Da Neel, whoever he might be, slipped out in conversation but he was reluctant to press her openly on the matter. He was grateful that Pelochev had, unwittingly, helped him in diverting Wilson's attention away from the Island and would delay interrogating her until a more appropriate moment. Whatever her motivation any involvement from her would not bode well for the Island but at least

142

she was rational enough to be second guessed, unlike Wilson who was less predictable than an out of control ballistic missile.

Later that day Zen spoke by protocol-secured digital radio telephone to one of his Island contacts about the inadvertent disclosure of the name Mr Da Neal and set in motion a search for a person of that name. It was suggested to him that he should talk confidentially to Pelochev to see if he could get more information about the name. Saying that getting anything from her would be difficult because he was not high enough up the tree to be a person of interest to her, he was further advised to get her interest by whatever means necessary. It was suggested that he tell her 'in confidence' that he was much more senior in the hierarchy than he was prepared at the moment, to reveal.

Pelochev was so self-centred that it proved to be easy get her to open up. He told her that he was travelling incognito and was really the supreme leader of RIR and as such he hinted openly that he could be of great value to her. As predicted the ruse worked; she immediately became more attentive and warmed towards him to the point of fawning over him.

She began to open up and talk to him more freely but it was necessary for him to direct her thought processes. Treading carefully so as not to cause any suspicion on her part he moved the conversation round to what she knew about RIR, this being the main purpose of his visit. With extreme care he turned the conversation round to a name, which had featured several times in her muddled conversations with him, Mr Da Neal. As she believed him to be the head of RIR he could not simply ask the question 'who is Da Neal?' He had to be more circumspect.

"I would value your opinion of Mr Da Neel." He used his opening gambit with feigned nonchalance as if he was taking her into his confidence.

"Mr Da Neel pretend to be top man of RIR so is liar." Her demeanour showed that she did not appreciate being duped by this imposter. "Would be better to working with you not number second in organisation." She hit down hard with the side of her fist onto the table top.

His mind was working overtime the name Da Neel meant nothing to him but it seemed that he was the actual head of RIR. He would need to use his contacts on Recovery Island to trace this character. He was, in anticipation, considering how he could firstly identify this man and how he could use the knowledge to his advantage. He was reluctant to interrogate Pelochev further because it might lead to her becoming curious at the line of questioning.

He became aware, as he emerged from his reverie that she was staring at him with her head questioningly on one side. "Irena, I think you and I can work very well together." He noted with satisfaction that she was visibly jolted by his use of her given name. "For the moment it is better that you keep negotiating with Mr Da Neel and you must not let him know that you are aware that I am head of RIR, that is a secret between you and me. You are the only person in the world, apart from myself of course, who knows who I am." He watched her carefully realising that she was immensely flattered by this knowledge and that she was already formulating ideas for cashing in on the knowledge. "RIR is a very secret organisation and as its head I must remain incognito."

"Liking you to call me by Irena - is my name - what means incognito?" With rare candour she admitted that she did not understand the word.

"It means you must never reveal who I am to anybody else. If you do you will die," he said this with indirect menace and smiled inwardly as she shuddered in ill-concealed pleasure at the implied brutality of his threat.

Twenty-three

Dessertes Kingdom Valerie, he of three names of undisclosed gender, sat in the comfort of his Kensington apartment admiring a limited view of his part of West London. *'It may be limited'* he thought to himself *'but at least it is mine and belongs to nobody else'*. He was in mellow mood as he savoured a balloon of fine brandy and listened to soothing Liszt on his over indulgently expensive sound centre. The sound centre was not his only indulgence his significant other would be appearing shortly, he looked at his watch – she was, as ever, being fashionably late.

He heard a key in the lock of his apartment door and felt a tremble of pleasure run through his entire being as her sensuous voice called his name softly. He rose from his chair and embraced her as she walked into the room; she returned his embrace and they lingered for a moment savouring the feel, touch and fragrances they shared.

"I've missed you," he breathed into her hair.

"And I you," she kissed his ear.

They were neither in the first flush of youth. Caroline Pelham possessed in maturity an extreme sensuousness which captivated red blooded men of all ages, from those in their twenties who fawned over her ethereal beauty to geriatrics who adored her – mostly from afar. DK, as he preferred to be known, was older than she by a handful of years but did not, he thought, possess the handsomeness that her beauty deserved, nor had the years been as kind to him as they had to her.

She was slender and aristocratic; her proudly held head was crowned with blond hair in which the many

146

threads of silver only served to make her more alluring. Her willowy almost fragile body was attired in a long evening dress which had its origins in the early part of the last century. It clung provocatively and with promise and hints of hidden delights to her slender frame. On anybody else it would have looked old fashioned perhaps even drab, on her it took on a whole new opulence. He, on the other hand, was losing his hair and what little he had was a mixture of black and iron grey rather than distinguished silver. Where his waist had once been was now a thickness which joined his hips and the rest of his body without a discernible change of contour.

She was dressed formally, not because they were going to the opera, she had already been there with her husband, a Cabinet Minister who had found it necessary to return to the House of Commons for an all-night sitting. DK and Caroline had been lovers for many years despite their incompatible appearance but it was not their intention to destroy her marriage in order to be together. DK's marriage had failed long before he met Caroline and the parting had not been amicable. For a number of years he descended into alcoholism as a defence against the pain of the rejection he felt after the departure of his former wife. He had no wish to visit that problem on any other person especially not Caroline's husband, whom he actually admired, hence the clandestine and opportunistic nature of their liaisons. They had both tacitly agreed, when their attraction became obvious to them both, that they would not destroy her marriage but would meet, with measured discretion, whenever and wherever the opportunity presented itself. This night was one such case; her husband being called to the house was perfect for them. She had told him as he departed that rather than make the journey alone back to their home in

Berkshire at this late hour she would stay in London and do a little shopping and would see him later on the next day.

Both savoured these moments because they had deep feelings for each other and because the fact that they could seldom anticipate their stolen moments together made them more immediate and passionate. Part of the game when they were together unexpectedly was to build up to a climax of feelings slowly and sensuously. They would drink a little but not so much that their senses would be dulled. They would talk a little, sometimes seriously but mostly their conversation was light and frivolous.

Frivolity was not a natural part of DK's life as a broadsheet journalist specialising in the sciences. There was little to laugh about in serious science and humour was not a natural ingredient of the academic world he inhabited. His time together with Caroline was like a welcome breath of fragrant fresh air and he was able to give free reign to the fanciful thoughts which were stifled in his working life.

Their discussion on this unexpected evening together strayed into territory which they seldom inhabited. Some years before, in the heat of early passion, they had been indiscrete. They had, in their euphoria, exchanged letters which were totally compromising. These letters, by calculatedly devious means, had fallen into the unprincipled hands of Colin Wilson who had used them to extract privileged information from DK. It had given Wilson, a means of using DK's serious journalistic contacts and outlets for biased viewpoints which he wished to give a national airing.

Both DK and Caroline, at that time, were desperate to keep their relationship out of the press so DK had gone along with the blackmailer whose demands became ever more unreasonable. Ultimately their blackmailer, who was now amazingly the President of Nuovostan, and who had been blackmailing others for many different reasons, came unstuck when he went an extortion too far. Thanks to James Creswell, the British PM and Chester Gilliland the head of Recovery Island, DK and Caroline had been freed from the bondage of the insidious blackmail that had been slowly but inexorably destroying them.

They touched on the subject of Creswell because of the news item that said Creswell was very ill and was receiving treatment for a serious problem which meant his isolation for a long course of treatment. Since receiving help from Creswell, DK had kept a watching brief on him by dint of his press contacts; Caroline did the same but through her husband, his being a Cabinet Minister. As far as she could tell her husband was not aware of her association with DK and he certainly did not give any indication that he was.

They were enjoying a close moment when the telephone rang. He was tempted to ignore it but succumbed to the curiosity which his love of journalism engendered.

"DK," he said in a neutral voice. Listening for a moment his brow creased and he looked momentarily indecisive. "OK, but it'll have to wait until tomorrow. Book the flights; I'll pick up the tickets from Heathrow in the morning."

"Something serious?" she enquired as he put the telephone down.

"Could be," he said distractedly.

"Do you want me to go?" she looked genuinely concerned at his demeanour.

"Yes." He said and he laughed at her look of disappointment before changing his stern demeanour.

"I do want you to go......I want you to go straight into the bedroom, I've got to leave at crack of dawn tomorrow and I don't have time to be subtle."

She laughed as she half ran to the bedroom tugging down the zip at the back of her dress as she disappeared through the door. He joined her and there was a shriek of girlish laughter which was cut short before it reached its crescendo.

She didn't ask him where he would be going tomorrow or for how long. She was the wife of a politician and she was accustomed to being told what was going on only when she needed to know.

**

The gaudy red and white Catalina PBY-5A, one of the few remaining but beautifully maintained sea plane relics from the middle part of the last century, approached Coral Island from the west. This late in the day, it was silhouetted against the diffused orange glow of the setting sun and appeared to hover, like a sea bird with its legs extended ready for a water landing, as it approached the beach heading directly for the Coral Beach Bar Resort.

Two men who were the only guests at the resort watched in fascination as the strangely ugly but graceful bug eyed aircraft drifted down to sea level in the placid shelter of the bay where it kissed the calm surface twice before settling down into the deep blue water; the wake was spangled with phosphorous as the craft powered slowly and noisily towards the beach.

A six-seat rigid inflatable boat, a RIB, with a powerful outboard motor appeared from the resort's ramshackle boat house and made its way to the aircraft which had come to a standstill and was nodding gently in the light breeze. The boat's pilot was the resorts off

150

season factotum who was fulfilling one of his many seemingly endless duties.

The two men who were sitting under the cover of the palm thatched veranda which stretched down to the white sands of the beach, watched with some trepidation as the lone passenger and his single piece of luggage were transferred unsteadily from the Catalina to the RIB. The newcomer was clearly visible to the two men on the veranda but at that distance and with the shade of the brim of his panama hat obscuring his features he was not recognisable. He was, they could see, not dressed for this remote tropical location; he wore a travel crumpled city suit. They exchanged uneasy glances; this location had been chosen because it was off-season and the two men had expected to be the only occupants. With some unease they watched the newcomer as he alighted the RIB and followed the factotum up the beach to the palm shack which was used as a reception area; the door was a locally woven blanket fixed to the lintel and the unglazed windows were topped up with rolled up rattan blinds which, judging by the delicate flowers which grew from between its strands was seldom used.

Some minutes later the newcomer, carrying his single piece of luggage walked from the reception to one of the close by Rondavels into which he disappeared. The Rondavel, similar to those occupied by the other two guests would, presumably, be as much a surprise to him as it had been to them. The thatch clad wooden frame was clearly sourced locally and would have been unbearably hot if it were not for the air conditioning which hummed gently in the background and was set by thermostat to twenty Celsius. Warm by the standards of the country he had just left it was slightly chilling to him, after the heat he had experienced on arrival. He looked around his accommodation with some surprise, the inside and outside belonged to different cultures and centuries. The furnishings were simple and elegant with the copious use of hand crafted wood and animal hide. Cushions and floor rugs were of the same local style as the curtain which had covered the door opening into the reception area; its influence was adapted African.

Once unpacked, showered and changed he left the Rondavel and ventured out into the descending gloom of approaching evening. The air was heavy with the blossoming scent of night flowers which breathed out their enticing perfumes to attract the night flying insects which either helped with the pollination of benign plants or provided a delicate meal for those of a more carnivorous nature.

Lights around the canopy of the small bar attracted more flying insects most of which were hypnotically attracted to the blue lights of the insect zappers which flashed and crackled with each kill. The barman smiled in welcome and deferentially slid off his stool to lean on the bar and welcome the new guest who looked as though his drinking habits would include imbibing some of the more exotic offerings of the islands.

"What's local, unusual and strong?" he asked.

"Well sir." A wide and welcoming white toothed smile split his face. "I can recommend the Coral Island Slammer made from things you aint probably never heard of." His wide smile turned into a full bellied laugh. "But I must tell you that the limit set by the management is three slammers, but most give up, or fall over, after two." He always found it best to exaggerate the potency of the drink as a challenge to ensure the sale of the third, extortionately expensive, drink was taken before the reality of the price persuaded them otherwise.

Still wearing large sunglasses and a panama hat the newcomer took his drink over to a table near to, but apart from, where the other two guests were sitting. They looked at him uneasily and talked to each other in soft tones. He studied them casually through the foliage of his Coral Island Slammer. Satisfied that he had been given accurate information by his informant, he watched them for a while. They made a great show of not taking any notice of him and continued with their soft conversation glancing with studied indifference in his direction.

The factotum sat behind the bar lazily polishing glasses and observing the three guests. There was something strange about the first two guests who had arrived within a week of each other; they were unlike the usual people who came to the island to drink, eat and usually to cavort with the girls from the main island. They had obviously known each other before arriving but had been reserved with each other as though they shared a situation with which they were uneasy. Now he looked at the third man; in age he was between the first two and like them he had a natural affluence not necessarily borne of wealth but simply by what the British used to call class.

Smiling to himself he finished polishing the glasses and poured himself a generous measure of white rum to which he added a splash of pomegranate juice. He watched as the newcomer picked up his drink and walked steadily and with focus to the table at which the other two sat. Pausing before them he exchanged what appeared to be pleasantries, removing his hat and glasses, a move which provoked a marked reaction from the two seated men who half rose. Flapping his down turned palms he placated them and they slumped back down into their chairs.

153

Observing their deep and concentrated conversation the barman lost interest and, leaving the bar, returned to the reception area where he slid open the drawer which held three passports, one American and two British. The older British man and the younger American were Mr B Boss and Mr R King. The latest British man was a Mr D.K. Valerie, a journalist, probably, the factotum mused, a film critic who had surprised the two film makers who clearly did not expect visitors in this remote backwater. The factotum hoped that he would dissuade the two film men not to make a film with such a weak plot.

Twenty four

At Lawson's suggestion both Crook and Pettit began to develop a more secure way of safeguarding the BAM2 units against theft. They had thought that the existing methods were secure enough but Lawson with his heightened awareness of probable dissident activity was agitated by the thought that whoever was trying to steal one or more units would be able to penetrate the existing precautions. They had after all been able to manage the fate of Chester Gilliland with seeming ease by making light of the established security protocols so it was quite feasible that they could do the same with BAM2.

Pettit took care of identifying the new protocols and Crook took care of the technology to satisfy them. It soon became clear that the potential weakness of the current system was that it contained an unreliable element – the human being. Eliminating this element using BAM2 technology was as simple as it was effective.

They would keep the backup and infrequently used units in a simple building that was not overly secure but was waterproof and would provide the right environment. Security would be provided within the building by covering the contents with a BAM2 security hemisphere which would take care of access to the secrets should anybody gain access to the storage building. Any attempt to breach the hemispherical shield would result in the instant deconstruction of whomever or whatever tried to pass through the shield, the result was unequivocal and irreversible.

Breaching from below by excavation was a different matter. To simply complete the protection by transforming the hemisphere into a sphere would have a very unfortunate side effect; the shield would break all matter down to its atomic level, the complete sphere when activated would, under the force of gravity, simply eat its way through whatever was underneath it. With its self-contained power unit it would simply disappear through the earth's surface and continue to descend for as long as its power source was able to withstand the searing heat produced by magma.

To overcome this catastrophic disadvantage they projected the lower half of the sphere as an open grid, the apertures of which were smaller than a BAM2 unit. This allowed the protection required from underneath while still allowing the substructure to support the weight of the contents of the protection system. Whenever Crook worked on this type of BAM2 problem he recalled vividly how he and Chester Gilliland had so nearly vaporised themselves during the initial experiments when they had been so close to reducing the projected hemisphere down to zero with themselves inside it. They would have been converted into a small heap of disparate atoms and their disappearance would have been more inexplicable than that of the crew of the *Marie Celeste*.

Once they had started to consider greater uses of BAM2 they continued to investigate other areas of development. Carla Tanterelli had relentlessly pursued its use in the field of medicine, Ed Pickering was their manufacturing guru and he began using it to drill, rout and shape. Moulds were made which allowed the finings which were the by-product of sculpting volcanic rock, to be cast into building blocks and paving.

Their development work was not limited to the practical only. Some of the younger members of the

156

Main Island community decided that the facilities on Leisure Island were all well and good but they were not so easy to get to quickly at the end of a day's work. They approached the Ruling Council with a proposal to create a waterfall with lakes connected by a river system, on the south side of central mountain which would give them the opportunity to indulge in various water sports; they had in mind swimming but they also thought that white water rafting would be a very therapeutic pastime.

In the interest of keeping the thoughts of the youth of the Island diverted away from the tribulations of world politics the Council gave permission with all haste. Using BAM2 technology and a team of willing volunteers they cut a spillway into the south face of Central Mountain. After carving out collecting pools for the series of waterfalls they constructed a zigzag river course to mitigate the steep gradient of the descent of the mountain side, they formed interconnecting flowing streams and rapids some of which flowed more gently to a meander which took the course of the river to the west through the garden of remembrance via a tranquil pool to a final waterfall which spilled out into the sea some thirty feet below.

The flow of the water could be regulated using the valves to control the influx of water from the natural water reservoir which emanated from below the mountain. The water flowing into the reservoir and spilling over into the newly constructed waterway was warm and although it cooled somewhat by the time it reached the sea it was still as warm as any tropical sea. Fast-flowing white water rapids were interspersed between wider stretches of quiet water which were in turn interspersed between tranquil pools. All of this was accomplished in the mile and a half between the summit of Central Mountain and the sea defence wall.

It was a tremendous success and using BAM2 took only a few days. Perhaps the most difficult part of the exercise was creating and manoeuvring the boulders which created the white waters. Within days there were plans to build cafes and restaurants along the banks of the new river which its builders had named Westfall River.

The influence of the tropically warm water stretched for a mile or so across the shallows of the Island's margins and out to sea and would in time form a small and unique tropical enclave. Within a very short space of time marine biologists detected many unusual species of sea life which took possession of the micro-environment and made it their own, much as the Islanders had done by constructing their Island home.

Twenty-five

Pelochev's meeting with Mr Pain and Mr Da Neel, as she referred to them in a hybrid mixture of Anglo Russian vocal protocol, was progressing to her satisfaction. Believing that Mr Da Neal was not the head of RIR gave her greater courage in her negotiations with him more forcefully. For his part Mr Da Neal was taken aback by her sudden lack of subservience. Their deliberations were rudely interrupted by the door to their room being flung open to crash against the wall.

"What's going on?" Wilson was wild eyed as he looked suspiciously at Pelochev and her two guests. "Why am I the last to know what's going on. Who are these people?"

"Cullin," Pelochev placed a hand on Wilson's shoulder, "please being to sit down and having calmness. Have asking Mr Da Neel and Mr Pain coming here to meeting with Mr A so we can get plans up and on."

"I don't know these people, except maybe you." He pointed a quivering finger towards Mr Da Neel." Then turning to Pelochev and looking confused asked, "who is Mr A?"

"Mr Da Neel was here a few days ago to talk making movies to show on Island. You agree OK, remember? Mr A is still here for talkings about other killing wants."

"Killings and movies of killings. Yes," he straightened his shoulders. "Of course I remember."

"This are Jack Pain, you are know him by first name of Jacques Pantin, you escape recovery Island with him. They are here to talk Chicken."

"Talk turkey, turkey—not chicken." Some of Wilson's old rage propelled character was beginning to emerge. "When will you learn to speak English properly?"

'A' was not happy that he had been instructed to come to Nuovostan and help Wilson to develop his plans. He found the strain of the assassinations impinging more and more on the rest of his life, it was no longer his own but there was little he could do about it. To get to Nuovostan he had to fly from Denver to Moscow via London and pick up an internal flight to Barnaul in Siberia from whence he was shuttled to Nuovostan by President Wilson's private jet. Having a stopover in Moscow meant that the journey took him three long and tiring days. He arrived in a foul mood, in the half wakeful state during his long journey, in his mind he kept replaying the assassinations and the stark blood stains on his victims, they had made for fitful and unsatisfying sleep.

Pelochev was clearly pleased to see 'A', she even gave him a hug; her actions were out of character and he wondered what, apart from the blindingly obvious, it was she wanted from him. Wilson looked terrible and was distracted enough to need to be reminded who 'A' was.

"The President doesn't know who I am which doesn't surprise me considering the state he is in but what bothers me is that I don't recognise the people who are in the room with you and Wilson. I saw them as you opened the door; I've told you that I don't want to meet any other people, the fewer who know who I am the better."

"You are not knowing who they are?" Pelochev was clearly puzzled.

'A' looked blankly at her.

"Knowing them, is a must." Pelochev was mystified

"Never clapped eyes on them before." 'A' said testily. "Your security is slack. My identity is supposed to be protected."

"If you are not knowing them, who you are then?"

"You know who I am and what I do."

"Yes; you say you are Mr 'A' and maybe this is not so. We contact you through Mr Da Neel and Mr Pain. If you are not knowing him I am again ask who you are?

"Oh I see." There was a look of relief on his face as the light suddenly dawned on him. "I know him only as contacts, in our business it is best that we don't meet. I always deal with intermediaries he is just a voice on the telephone."

"You are not meeting before?"

"No, I am not meeting before and I don't want to meet them now. My discussions are with you and President Wilson and nobody else."

"Is OK for me." She looked relieved at his explanation. "But Cullin is sick and maybe has crazy ideas which not to work. You and me will speak in loneliness and not with Cullin and the other two. I have idea that is good for us." She winked conspiratorially.

"You want to make other plans?"

"Yes, just on our own by ourselves. Not having with the others."

'A's' allotted task had been to help Wilson with his plans and divert him away from the Island but it seemed that Wilson was slipping away from reality and that Pelochev had her own agenda. It would do no harm to listen, he supposed.

Not only had he now seen one, possibly two members of RIR but he had in the few brief moments

161

that they had been together managed to take photographs on his watch-cam. Later he would access a computer and file the images in a secure cyber-vault for future reference He smiled grimly at the paradoxes of life he was working potentially with three groups whose ambition was to be sole owners of BAM2 technology.

Twenty-six

Life in the tropical paradise of Coral Island had lost its glitter. Endless days of sunshine and unbearable heat, eating strange foods and drinking strange drinks and also having no structured work to do was beginning to take its toll on the two men whose previously normal everyday life had been full of challenge and decision making.

In the short time they had been on Coral Island they had acquired healthy looking tans and both enjoyed the muscle toning early morning and late evening swimming in the warm Caribbean waters. Apart from their normal working environment the thing they missed most was news of the outside world. They had no idea about what was going on in the worlds of politics and finance; they even missed the continuous droning of repetitive news telling the same stories every fifteen minutes sometimes unchanging for days on end.

On this particular evening they watched as the tiny spec on the horizon of the dimming evening sky began to grow and take shape. The Catalina PBY-5A once more skimmed gracefully over the calm waters of Coral Bay, skipped several times leaving a foaming broken line on the smooth surface and settled down to cruise towards the shore. The engine note increased to a scream as the pilot slowed the craft and came to a stand-still in the shallows.

The six seat RIB nosed its way towards the open door of the sea plane and as the Catalina had done executed a dead stop with the screaming of the engine under reverse. Both pilots acknowledged each other in flamboyant Caribbean style as DK Valerie scrambled gracelessly from plane to RIB. With a wave of the arms the boat and plane separated, one heading towards shore the other heading out into the bay to turn into the wind for take-off.

The Catalina wallowed as it turned across the tide and after a pause settled down into the water as the engine was accelerated and suddenly lurched forward as the thrust of the prop caused the surrender of the inertia of the beautifully ugly bug eyed craft. Gathering speed it lifted gracefully into the air; banked left and flew low over the beach residence wagging its wings as it departed back the way it had come. They watched the spec get smaller and smaller until is disappeared into the descending gloom of the evening horizon.

Dessertes Kingdom Valerie, DK, alighted from the RIB demonstrating the ability that this second attempt gave him, without getting his feet wet. Leaving his suitcase in the tender care of the Barman he trudged up the beach to the table under the palm thatch which was occupied by the island's only other guests. They exchanged greetings and were presented with three exotic drinks in full regalia by the Barman who had left DK's suitcase leaning up against the bar.

"To what do we owe the pleasure of your company?" the older of the two men enquired. "Nothing wrong I hope?"

"You may have to re-emerge. Things are happening which you both need to defuse. Your cover could be blown at any time and it is better that you take control rather than having discovery thrust upon you with all the repercussions that would bring."

"How may our cover be blown?" the younger of the two asked with one quizzical eyebrow raised. "Unless of course it is blown by you?"

"Not by me," he looked offended. "Somebody is about to release these digi-videos on national television and, well, I leave you to draw your own conclusions. He removed a generation 10 digital viewer from his breast pocket and switched on the digital-video app. The backlit screen sprang into immediate life and showed five figures leaving an aircraft. A scarcely audible voice said 'bang' the screen jumped and one of the figures fell as the picture zoomed in to show the blood speckled shirt front and the inert form of Chester Gilliland supine at the bottom of the wheeled steps. There was confusion and panic as the three other, joined by a forth woman milled around the fallen figure.

The screen went blank momentarily and then jumped back into life. This time it showed James Creswell sitting at a desk in a cramped room. He had a look of great surprise on his face and his eyes widened in horror as he realised that he was face to face with an assassin. Again a scarcely audible voice said 'bang' and the screen jumped and instantly Creswell's white shirt front was suffused with crimson blood. He was slammed back into his seat and recoiled forward to end up face down on the table.

From behind his bar the stand in keeper of the resort watched the three men as they looked intently at the device being held by DK. They were shocked at what they were watching and even from that distance he would have sworn that under their tans their faces were grey. He didn't care as long as they stayed, even one more day would help his finances but he had a feeling that he would soon be calling Coral Airways to get the Catalina to the island to take them away.

The three guests walked past the bar, ignoring its occupant. They were deep in conversation and really didn't notice him. He heard the one called Valery, *strange name for a man* he thought, as he went past; saying to them "Unless you do something to defuse this all hell will be let loose and you will both be in big trouble." Mr Boss and Mr King agreed with him but were not happy about it. He revised his opinion about them being film producers, they were most probably, he thought, gangsters.

Twenty-seven

As predicted by the Coral Island barman, all three of his late season visitors took the Catalina to the main Coral Island having first given him a generous tip with instructions to forget they had ever been there which changed his mind about their being movie makers back to their being gangsters. From Coral Island they boarded a flight to Miami and from there to Paris where they split up. DK and Creswell were going to London and Gilliland to Lisbon. In their guises as Boss and King they wore floppy hats and sunglasses so that they wouldn't be easily recognised and hurried telephone calls were made to their destinations to arrange for discrete transport to collect them. To their relief they avoided recognition in the melee of Miami Airport and Creswell because of his diplomatic connections with the US administration had enabled them to board their flights incognito and without going through the normal checks and channels.

On the following day there were choreographed news reports from London and Recovery Island to say that their leaders were back in harness having either convalesced more rapidly than expected or returned from holiday earlier than expected. Gilliland and Creswell, looking tanned and well, appeared separately on screen saying that they were well and rested and were looking forward to being back in harness. Creswell's news conference was carried by international media sources; Gilliland's return was less fully covered.

Eleven was incandescent, which was not a condition to which he normally subscribed, when the shock of the

167

news of their resurfacing reached him in Nuovostan. He ranted at Wilson and Pelochev in a way that reminded Pelochev of Wilson in full fury before he had gone off the rails. His plans were seriously out of sync. He still had a BAM2 unit but Gilliland's survival was a deathly blow to his plans for destabilisation. Worse, he no longer knew how secure RIR was thanks to the traitorous behaviour of the Nuovostani's against whom he intended to exact revenge for their obvious leakage of information which had unveiled the assassination attempts and caused them to fail – probably by the use of body armour.

Gilliland returned to normalcy as though nothing had happened. As far as the Islanders were concerned he had simply had a holiday off Island and had returned looking rested and healthily tanned. The same misconception was true for the bulk of the Ruling Council which welcomed him back and congratulated him on his fitness. The three other founders together with Mark Lawson and Carlina Tanterelli and a small management committee were the only ones who knew the truth of what had really happened; the as yet unidentified leader of RIR had not been one of those in the know. Panic had been averted but a by-product of the revelation was that the RIR and whoever else was involved in the assassination plots were warned, their existence and activities had been rumbled. It would now make uncovering them even more difficult.

***

The eight hundred series Boeing Cargo plane appeared, for a moment, to stall in the air as it slowed and descended towards Recovery Island Airport. The sole passenger among the webbing which restrained the items on cargo pallets glanced eagerly out of the window as she settled precariously into a single person string sling which was attached by lanyards to the side of the fuselage and the overhead hitching rail.

Slack in the lanyards was alternately taken up with a snap and then released as the aircraft banked to line up with one of the two recently extended runways. She was oblivious of the uncomfortable jagged swirling motion of the aircraft as it banked more sharply and then levelled out into the descent path. The landing was smooth and oddly ponderous as the huge aircraft settled onto the runway which, being free from expansion joints, added to the gentle unreal silence of the landing which was punctuated at the end by the banshee roar of the reverse thrusters' which wound slowly down to a halt before being silenced.

Disembarking down the wheeled steps, which had been pushed into position by a ground crew, she waved at the assembled crew who recognised her instantly; she was extremely easy to identify even without the dark long haired wig that she wore on dressy occasions. Her tightly curled black hair was like a skull cap it was so precisely cut, her skin glowed golden brown from the Thai part parentage and her eyes, apart from being a startling blue from an unknown part of her family tree, were slightly almond shaped from her Chinese ancestors.

An electric luggage cart was used to ferry her to the TC, Transfer Car, station which she entered and then with a key pad programmed to take her to the administration building. With almost indecent haste she skipped out of the TC station and ran across the polished floor of the atrium into the first of the unoccupied lifts. Her eyes were sparkling mischievously as she left the lift and hurried along an internal corridor; she burst through the door into

Crook's office. "I'm here at last," she squealed in a high girlish voice.

"Yah!" Crook uttered the pet name he used for her in amazement. "You're a sight for sore eyes, what happened I didn't expect you for another two days?"

"I talked to Adie about getting transport and he told me there was a transporter leaving from Nematasulu today and he managed to get them to give me a lift and promised not to let on to you." She flung her arms around his neck and kissed him, noticing as she did so that there was another person in the room. "Oh, I'm sorry it was rude of me to rush in without knocking, but I'm so excited to be here." She looked chastened.

"No need to apologise." Juilietta Gray extended her hand.

"You must be Juilietta Gray," she said breathlessly, "I've heard so much about you; it is a great pleasure to meet you this day." Katya, in her haste and excitement stumbled over her English which she had not used much during her time in Borneo. "You must call me Yah." She looked at Gray with a smile that lit up her face. "All my friends do and I know that you are a good friend to Bruce which means that we should be good friends also."

"I'm sure you have a lot to talk about." Gray gathered up her papers and headed for the door. "How long will you be here for, maybe we could spend some time together; get to know each other?"

"Love to and the good news is I'm here for good, my project in Borneo finished early and I'm a free woman."

"Not for long." Crook gave her a great bear hug. "I'm going to be using up all your time; there won't be a moment to spare."

"Catch you both later," Gray said as she left the room; she smiled gently to herself, she had never seen

Bruce look so contented and happy in all the time she had known him. Turning as she closed the door she saw that they were joined as one and oblivious to their surroundings.

Katya did not get the opportunity to settle in gradually. After a single day of grace she was given some important tasks. Nematasulu had become an important part of the development of the Island system of administration without being run in the same way as Recovery Island. The use of the equivalent of a Recocard was not a practical proposition because of the nature of the country and its level of technology. Bartering was equally not a practical proposition because so many of the population did not actually produce anything they could barter so it was necessary to introduce a financial structure based on value. Being paid a wage for the people of Nematasulu was not customary; theirs had been an agrarian society but was rapidly becoming more technological. One of the first tasks given to Katya was to introduce a welfare state which meant a taxation system had to be put in place.

Applying her speciality as an anthropologist she had many lengthy long-distance discussions with Tembo Mbunani, Nematasulu's Homeland Minister and long-time friend of Chester Gilliland to establish the parameters of the taxation system which she intended to make simple. The complicated thinking which she applied to produce a simple system of taxation was not cluttered by political or any other leanings or biases and enabled her to pander to the societal aspirations of the people of Nematasulu.

Taking the projected national income of Nematasulu she broke the earnings down into how much would be earned by which group. The upper echelon of the country which comprised half a percent of the population would earn seventy per-cent of the available

171

income. This was not a statistic she supported but realised that to get the support of the Nematasulanders she would need to observe the unequal division of wealth which was an accepted part of their culture. The next third would earn twenty per-cent of the available income and the remaining sixty or so per-cent would share the balance of around ten per-cent. The simple result of the complex calculations, which partly mitigated the inequality of reward, was that anybody earning up to the national average wage would pay no income tax at all; the tax burden would fall on the five to six per-cent of the population earning over the average. The earning disparity was that the highest paid earned one thousand times more than the lowest paid and had deducted from their earnings, at source, a fixed percentage taxation of earnings above the average. This was used to support the whole of the country in terms of the welfare state and all other national expenditure including health care. No taxation applied would be allowed to take earnings to below the national average.

When this was presented to the population those who were among the lower paid were delighted to get a wage of any substance which had never happened before. Those who were well-off were prepared to pay tax because it showed that they were recognised as being successful, taxation became a badge of office – the greater the tax the more the attached kudos. All of this was possible for the government of Nematasulu because of the income from diamonds and general trading for and with Recovery Island who had opened up the wealth of the mines by the use of BAM technology.

To celebrate Katya's return to the Island the four founders, accompanied by Juilietta Gray arranged a dinner party in one of the more intimate dining rooms attached to the council chambers. The conversation ranged over a wide spectrum which of course included some of the adventures that Katya had in Borneo. She also learned more the more developments which had taken place on the Island.

She was particularly interested, being an anthropologist, in the way the Island's society had begun a process of natural polarisation. RIN's, without any prompting from the Ruling Council, had separated into two basic camps. The more sophisticated citizens gravitated to the western side of the Island while the remainder, in general favoured the east. All RIN's had the right to choose the district in which they were to live. Housing was of the same standard in either area, there were no living costs as all items of subsistence were free of any cost to the citizens and there was no distinction between the facilities provided for those providing the most menial of services by way of voluntary occupation compared to those performing more skilful tasks.

By this process selective polarisation occurred naturally and was the cause of some concern for the founders. The outward appearance of the polarisation was in some cases obvious and in others more obscure. In the east a greater percentage of citizens chose not to undertake work of any kind. This included not taking care of the cleaning of the squares and streets, a task which was undertaken by volunteers from the west side of the Island. There was a higher preponderance of excessive alcohol abuse and the violence which went with living in the eastern side. The gulf between the two sides of the Island was being widened by the emergence of an Island patois which was a form of back-slang used by many of those from the east and seldom if ever by the westerners. Some second generation citizens actually chose the patois as their

173

first choice language, with English coming a poor and strangely accented second.

These anthropological developments were of great interest to Katya and became the main topic of conversation as they remained at the dining table long after the meal had been consumed, which everybody but Gilliland joined in. Gilliland's reluctance to join in was occasioned by his inability to come to terms with what was happening to the Island's society. It had been his dream that a truly egalitarian society would develop if political uncertainty and money pressures were eliminated; that his hopes in this direction had been dashed was, in view of the present conversation, self-evident.

He was disturbed by these thoughts and his first instinct was to stop the entrenchment of polarisation by decreeing that all areas of the Island should be populated by a balanced mixture of citizens to prevent the formation of ghetto areas. This thought disturbed him even more. If he were to intervene in what was happening he would be guilty of social engineering a thought which was abhorrent to him because it was one of the main planks of the societies which he was fighting so hard to resist. To change human nature was God-like and he was not and would never be a God like entity. His deep gloom was interrupted by Katya.

"Chester, you are not being good company tonight what ails you?"

"Nothing that you can do anything about," his voice was flat, emotionless.

"Chez, that's not very nice. Katya is concerned for your welfare," Caine scolded him.

"Sorry Yah, I didn't mean to be rude but there are some things that I need to sort out for myself. No offence meant," Gilliland's voice was still emotionless.

174

"Offence not being taken," she said in the light Oriental sing song voice she used when trying to inject humour or calm into a situation. "But I think I know what it is that has caused your melancholy. We were talking about the Island having two classes and that is against your wishes," she observed astutely.

"Maybe."

"Absolutely and you don't know how to counteract this in a way which is acceptable within your philosophy and conscience?"

"Maybe."

"Absolutely, again, don't even try to meet this head on, the more you try to control it the more resistance you will meet from both sides of the divide. Society all over the world adopts a two or three tier system which comprises the haves and the have-nots and sometimes the underclass. The haves become leaders and are influential and the have-nots become the drones and worker bees; fortunately we don't appear to have an underclass. You cannot change that, nobody in the world has ever been able to change it. It is the human condition. Take it away and you will have a society in a leaky vacuum."

"So you're saying we should live with a flawed system of social inequality."

"No such thing." She frowned and shook her head. "Without something to aspire to the drones and worker bees will become trouble makers, the underclass if you like. They can aspire to become one of the people of influence and this for some is a goal which leads to progression. Those who choose not to move up into the ranks of the influential look to those of their kind who do and realise that they too could achieve this elevation if they so chose. They can see that it is possible for themselves to succeed if they really wanted to, but maybe they think it could be achieved some time later,

175

they would have seen by example that this was possible."

"It's all out of control, it's a kind of social fibrillation, everything fires off at random. Not a satisfactory way to run a nation."

"Wrong again Chester, there is something you can do about it. Using your analogy of fibrillation you could, just as with the heart, apply medicine which doesn't necessarily cure the ailment but does alleviate the symptoms."

"Give them a pill?" His voice took on a lighter tone and he gave a wan smile.

"In a manner of speaking," she joined him in the smile. "What you do is give the easterners some pride in their emerging culture. Structure the language they are developing, embrace the emergence of an accent in the way they speak English, it's all part of their Island identity. Give them pride in what they do and you might find that some of those of the west culture might choose to join those in the east and those who remain in the east do so by choice."

"Fascinating," Gilliland's former gloom lifted a little more. "And how do we do that?"

"Give me free reign and I'll do it, it's my speciality."

"Feel free."

Katya (she did have a family name but nobody could begin to master its pronunciation) was a breath of fresh air to the ever more inventive and active female population of the Island. She joined them in reshaping Recovery Island and three of the other four outlying Islands. They were told that Hold Island was not a candidate for change and that they should concentrate on the other three; Leisure Island, Farm Island and Factory Island. her work in Borneo over the previous four years was anthropological in essence but had

176

actually translated into the restructuring of Borneo's society and infrastructure which had been less influenced than most countries by the global financial collapse.

She and her group of island re-shapers embarked on an orgy of gentle geologic manipulation. The manipulation of the shape of the Islands was made possible by the use of their amazingly versatile technology and the extensions to the island land masses was made by tapping and harvesting raw magma which was made habitable by the use of unique capillary cooling.

Recovery Island itself was by far the biggest challenge and was left 'til last and they concentrated on the other three. Agriculture Island was the largest of the three and was rectangular in shape, measuring some four miles by one, with a huge dock to the South which was used for loading and unloading ocean going vessels. The other two Islands located to the east and west of Agriculture Island, Leisure and Factory Islands, were equal in size and about one mile square. A fourth island, Hold Island was something of a mystery and was excluded from the geological work.

They set about changing the shape of the three Islands within their remit by making their outlines irregular and adding coastal and hinterland contours to them so that they were no longer uninteresting flat lines on the ocean; the coast lines were given coves and bays. They added long shallow beaches in some places and cliffs in others, there were rivers flowing down to the sea from newly created hot freshwater springs from deep within the bowels of the earth. The two flanking Islands were changed in shape from squares to more aesthetically pleasing irregular lozenge like shapes that were extended north, south, east and west and the three islands which were originally separated were joined by

177

causeways of banked tidal sand spits. The long beaches were planted with palms which would flourish in this climate which was more northern that they would normally tolerate but would do so because of the subterranean warm springs which fed the rivers and therefore the coast lines. Each of the islands including Hold Island had a centre of learning designed to provide secondary and tertiary education suited to the specialities of each island.

A further feminine influence was to change the names of the Islands from the utilitarian ones chosen by the original engineers and scientists who had engineered the initial designs. Recovery Island maintained its name but two of the other three in their remit were renames as; The Isle of Plenty, the Isle of Creation. Leisure Island retained its working name if not its working shape. Another step had been taken in the move towards a truly independent nation.

Twenty-eight

Zen's report to Eleven on his task of gathering information from Hammond and Pain had proved to be a frustrating dead end. After the expenditure of a lot of time and money it turned out that neither of them, despite the current rumours, had any influence over Wilson and they were merely pawns in Wilson's game of domination. He philosophised that they had at least been eliminated as a source of either information or danger to RIR. It also meant that Wilson had no spies either on or off the Island which could be a source of danger. He reasoned the failure of the mission to be, after all, a success.

Eleven felt the need to progress not only the planned access to his BAM2 unit but to begin to test the mood of the more disaffected members of the population, without implicating or in any way identifying himself. The solution came to him in a flash of inspiration. Paul Zen about whom he had been ruminating could be the catalyst to promote RIR's aspirations and the way to do it was so simple. Zen would be promoted to cell 1 so that Eleven could communicate more freely with him and they could in the fullness of time form an association which would promote the involvement of ordinary Islanders.

For Eleven it was a short step from starting a benign association that he admitted to into a fully-fledged militant trades union. They could pick a name that was innocuous and would not arouse the suspicions of the Ruling Council who were for ever carping on about trade groups being formed to give collective strength to empowered working groups. Zen might arouse some reservations within the Council, but if a cap was kept on his more radical activities he would be given some latitude because he was ostensibly supporting the diktats of the Council, especially if he was promoted as a reformed bad boy. While satisfying the broad outline of the Council's wishes he would also be able to attract some of the more militant Islanders and they could go off piste and follow a different agenda. This agenda represented Eleven's real interests, providing it remained under his firm control.

The first move was to bring him into Cell1.The cell already had a full complement of six so Eleven created a secret seventh position the existence of which he would keep under wraps until such time as he chose to reveal his master stroke. Zen would become member code 17 and would be answerable only to Eleven. There was another reason that Eleven wanted to pursue this course of action; since he had brought Zen on board he had been impressed by the independence he had shown and at the same time bothered by that same independence. Keeping him under close supervision he would be able to ensure that his own position would not be jeopardised and that Zen's contacts, especially with 'A' would be at RIRs disposal, it still rankled with Eleven that his attempts at direct contact with 'A' had been rejected. There was also the matter of the failure of 'A's' assassinations which could not with any accuracy be laid at the door of 'A' he was after all just a tool in Eleven's arsenal, this would be something else for Zen to unravel.

Within a short space of time the association which they named innocuously, PRICE, the Progressive Recovery Island Change & Evolution movement, became active and attracted a surprisingly large number of members. By surreptitious means and careful interrogation Zen was able to separate the radical from the passive members; the passives were elected onto the management committee and set about doing good things for the population in general. Radicals were collected together and met separately and in secret and were encouraged to strive for more individual freedom than they were currently afforded by the Ruling Council and to discuss how they could wrest some of the power away from their oppressors.

Both Zen and Eleven were surprised by the number of radicals that were unearthed. One in five of the Islanders joining them were radical to some degree and a third of them were bordering on being anarchists. Most of the anarchists were incomers, that is they were not Island borne but were brought in by the specialist member of their family who had been recruited because of their specialist skills These were people who had lived in the outside world and felt claustrophobic in the cloistered existence of their newly adopted society had no wish to give up the many and considerable advantages that the Island offered but wanted what they considered to be the freedom of the outside world.

***

The surgeon was dressed from head to toe in a pale yellow one piece surgical suit of the kind that was worn when the operation did not include the incidence of blood. A hood covered his head and the small circular opening which enabled him to see was obscured behind a tinted visor of polarised polycarbonate.

His patient was supine on his back beneath a surgical sheet which covered all of his face and his body with the exception of his left foot which stuck out incongruously beyond one folded back corner of the sheet. His breathing was regular and untroubled and the instrumentation showed that his blood pressure and heart rhythm were normal for one at rest.

Commencing the procedure the surgeon picked up what looked like a dentist's drill with a shaped bottle of parchment coloured liquid attached which formed the handle. An air-line ran from the instrument to a small compressor which hummed steadily. Using a surgical clamp stand the surgeon separated the great and second toes so that the inside of the great toe was exposed. In the concentrated light the number 66 showed up clearly.

Depressing the trigger on the instrument caused the compressor to change to a more laboured tone as the air drove a vibrating needle at the business end of the instrument. The needle traced over the number 66 and the parchment coloured liquid was injected into the epidermis. After fifteen minutes or so the number 66 had disappeared and that anything had been there was only discernible by the slight discolouration where the number had been.

It was thanks to his boss, Dr Carlina Tarrentini, that this procedure was possible. She had developed this means of obscuring tattoos after she had succumbed to a dare after an excessive graduating party on the campus of her university in Australia. She had lived to regret what she had done and had spared no effort in devising a procedure to eradicate the indelicate tattoo in its indelicate place. Removal of a tattoo at that time was difficult, painful and expensive – none of which options she cared for. Typical of her nature she applied herself to the problem and devised a technique which was as pain and risk free as the original tattoo had been. Her technique was being applied by the surgeon to his supine patient with the application of an anaesthetic which was necessary only to protect the identity of the surgeon.

The solution was logical and, for her, easy. She developed a synthetic polymer skin in liquid form and added enzymes that enabled the synthetic implant to mimic the colour of the skin into which it was infused. By doing this the covering would be all but invisible and it would change if the body became tanned either naturally or unnaturally.

Leaving the operating theatre after the completion of the first stage of the operation the surgeon found a quiet place to enjoy an illicit cigarette to calm the tension he always felt after completing an unauthorised procedure. As he pushed up his polarised visor and lit the cigarette he felt uneasy, he knew only too well the damage that smoking could do and had seen the resulting, potentially fatal, damage that was caused to otherwise healthy tissue by the habit. Pulling back the sleeve of his surgical suit he noted that ten minutes had elapsed and returned to the operating theatre. Washing his hands fastidiously he dried them using an air dryer in which the hot air was infused with an antiseptic moisturiser which enabled him to pull on his surgical gloves with minimal resistance.

Removing the bottle of parchment coloured liquid from the instrument he replaced it with one containing dense black liquid. The compressor changed to its laboured note once more as he began the final task of replacing the number, which he had just obscured, with a new one, seventeen. He applied the ink, wiped away the resultant moisture and applied more ink. After a short time he gave the site of the tattoo a final wipe and inspected his handiwork with a small magnifying glass. Satisfied with the result he dismantled the instrument he had used, including the bottles of liquid, and placed them in a small zipped bag which he locked. Taking a last look at the instrumentation which monitored his patient's condition he picked up the bag and left the theatre allowing the double doors to sigh closed behind him.

He had no idea why he had changed the identity of his patient and cared even less. His final task was to deposit the locked bag of operating paraphernalia into a hopper marked hazardous surgical waste and left the theatre complex. In all the procedure had taken a little over half an hour and in that time he had met and talked to nobody. He had no idea why he had done what he had done and to whom but was happy that, apart from the person who had instructed him in what to do nobody else knew that he had done - whatever it was.

The net result of his labours was a generous deposit into his French bank account which would enable him to indulge in the excesses of his wildest dreams during his next holiday in France – without having to explain to the Island Finance Committee why he required so much currency for a simple holiday.

Twenty-nine

Katya was truly fascinated by the way in which the Island had developed. Some of the developments she recognised as being a natural consequence of the need to sustain themselves in times of deprivation and some which were unique and perhaps frivolous. She went on an early shopping expedition which was the alternative to ordering through the Information Portal, feeling the need to see and feel the goods she required.

The IP had changed significantly since her last visit; it was no longer the large, cumbersome screen on the wall operated by a physical remote control. She activated the new portal by pressing the international 'on' symbol on what appeared to be a ceramic desk top which immediately became an image generated key and symbol board, softly lit. The view screen was an image projected onto the blank wall in front of the desk. The symbols on the desk top were the same as the original hand remote of the old portal but in addition there was an alpha numeric keyboard which enabled more subtle interrogation of the system a feature which had not been available during her last visit some two years earlier. She adjusted the size of the keyboard to suit her hand span and vision capabilities.

Having looked up what was available and where it could be located, she selected the appropriate dispensing market and made her way there by TC. She found the market disappointingly clinical; it comprised banks of dispensing windows for smaller items and dispensing bays for the larger items. She collected a shopping cart for those items she wished to take home with her; the rest would be delivered by TC to her home.

The shopping cart was fitted with a receiver into which she slotted her Recocard and which enabled the goods in the market to be assessed and attributed. The system used 'safeTscan' which had recently been installed and tested by its inventor, the Island's communications director. To acquire the selected item she simply had to press the purchase and quantity buttons for the items to be dispensed directly into the safeTscan cart the front panel of which was lowered by the dispensing mechanism so that the selected item did not fall into the cart and be liable to damage. When the safeTscan cart was full, whether by volume or weight, the Recocard was ejected and another cart could be selected so that the process could be repeated. Larger items available through the dispensing bays offered the shopper the opportunity to have the item dispensed or automatically delivered to the purchasers address.

Having completed the initial foray into the world of Reco-shopping she decided to make her way to a coffee shop in the west of the Island and sent the items that she had purchased to her apartment via an automatic Transfer Car. The shopping would be waiting for her on her return home. The storage of the purchased items awaiting her return did not need to be secure; there was little likelihood of it being pilfered from within the confines of her apartment block. It exercised her professional mind that the lack of the need for money made bank robbing impossible and meant that all things were freely available for all people, stealing served no purpose. The reverse side of this coin was that mans need to strive for improvement was subverted and she wondered what form the relief from this condition would take.

Yah decided not to accept the invitation to join the ranks of the Ruling Council feeling that it would inhibit her ability to research the Islands anthropological development in respect not only of the language but all other aspects of her speciality. To pursue her objectives she needed to merge into the background, a task made difficult by her exotic appearance which was only partially diminished by the disguise she adopted. She dressed in the dark blue of an artisan and wore a medium length wig to hide her striking skull cap hairstyle.

She sat outside a café in the outer margins of the Eastern domestic area which was populated by the section of Island society which led a life less embroiled in matters of the Island and its welfare. This was the active heart of the area in which the Island's new language was emerging. Although she understood the mechanics of the new language she found it difficult to decipher audibly. The young people sitting at the tables around her were talking animatedly at a speed which made translation into any of the four languages she spoke fluently, an impossible task. When addressing older members of the community the youngsters spoke English with a noticeably staccato cadence, showing that English was to them a second language choice. For Yah the difficulty with the language was that she had to translate English into Gne-shil by mind mechanics, which was a slow process. Those islanders who spoke both languages treated them as that; two languages – meaning that they did not have to perform a clumsy translation as she did.

"Foc-ee, on klim." She said asking for *'coffee no milk'* with some hesitation when the table attendant raised an surprised eyebrow.

"Muk-gni pu" She responded by saying *'coming up'* with a bright smile. "Ton nem-ee dlo-see kaeps Yi-dnal tap-raw." Yah watched the girl walk away and congratulated herself at the visible success of her first use of *Gne-shil*. She had rehearsed the words she spoke until she could order '*coffee no milk*' by reversing each of the syllables so that the order became 'foc-ee on klim.' Recalling phonetically the girl's responses she finally deciphered that she had said. '*Coming up*' and '*not many oldies speak Island dialect*'. She laughed out loud at being referred to as an 'oldie' when she was only ten or so years older than the attendant.

Her peel of laughter obviously annoyed the man sitting two tables away in the shade of a date palm; he tutted and showed a great deal of annoyance at her disruptive burst of sound. She toyed with the idea of apologising to him for the intrusion into his contemplations but decided against it as being just a further intrusion. She studied the man covertly as the coffee she had ordered arrived.

"Rooy Foc-ee," the attendant said, '*Your coffee*' as she placed it on the table.

"Knath-ooy," Katya responded politely, '*Thank you*'.

"Ruy lew-moc.," '*you're welcome,*' the attendant responded as she walked away.

The tutting man was of professional interest to her as an anthropologist. He was in a public place where noise was inevitable but he obviously thought of himself as being above the others around him. He was a strange almost invisible man who appeared to be responding to a stimulus that she could not see, his eyes were unfocussed but his facial expressions were reacting to the stimulus which she couldn't see. He was something of an enigma— he wanted privacy in a public place, a place which was in the heart of the artisan section but he was not dressed as one. Covered by the pretence of making a telephone call, she took his photograph.

The object of her interest stood up, brushed crumbs from his lap and walked with the unsteady gait of an inebriate through the maze of tables. He was not concentrating on where he was going and seemed almost to be navigating on a different plain.

"The man who was sitting there?" she asked the passing waitress. "Do you know who he is?" she asked in plain English.

"No." The waitress looked at the table and then the disappearing man and frowned. "He comes here on most days but doesn't interact with any other regulars. He's a bit creepy though he watches people and listens to what they are saying but never talks to them. What's even creepier is that he seems to go into trances where he's not with us but in some other place. He's not the usual customer we get here but then, neither are you; you're dressed like a labourer but you've got the hands of a beautician. You speak Gni-shil even if it is with a funny accent and you're a lot older than the usual Gni-shil speaker. We get all sorts here but I can't help you with the odd man except that he comes here two or three times a week and he is definitely a Western Islander."

Katya looked long and hard at the photograph she had taken of the tutting man. He was so insignificant that it looked, curiously, as if he were out of focus on the photo-screen, there were no distinguishing features; his large peaked cap threw his face into shadow. She would have been hard pressed to describe him to anybody else. Had she realised the importance of the photograph she would have been able to prevent a lot of heartache but she did not and a golden opportunity was lost.

Thirty

Finding the source of the RIR problem and doing something about it exercised the minds of the founders. They chose not to share their thoughts with the Ruling Council partly because they did not wish to open up the options for a solution to an endless inconclusive debate but mainly because, through vigilant intelligence they had learned that number 11 was an influential Islander and could possibly be part of, or bring influence to bear on, the Ruling Council. They also did not wish to decrease their options for a permanent solution by pursuing him, if they were able to find him, as a single element of the illicit organisation. As it is with a worm cutting off the head could cause the body to grow another one and little or nothing would have been achieved. Reeling in number 11 would also drive RIR further underground, thereby increasing its potential danger.

Those in the know about the situation were the four founders, Mark Lawson, the head of External Security, selected members of his staff and Carla Tanterelli. It was their intention to neutralise the RIR activities without general Council involvement. This gave the founders a feeling of profound unease. They were being secretive by keeping the Ruling Council in the dark and their actions were in direct contravention of their stated rules of open and honest governance.

Silas Pettit insisted that they should be prepared to develop an alternative plan in the event of their failing to recognize the full implication of the intentions of RIR and Nuovostan in a way which assured them of a successful defence. But no alternative plan was readily obvious; the threat was from two fronts – one from

Island sources and at least one from a foreign territory or territories. They had to assume that the Federation of Nations had not given up their aspirations to gain control of BAM2 and there was, of course, the ever present threat from New Russia.

Gilliland, rested after his enforced holiday in the Caribbean, thought laterally. He suggested, much to their collective surprise, that they adopt the maxim 'if you can't beat them, appear to join them,' by which he meant that they should form a possible co-operative relationship with an adversary. Pettit saw the potential immediately.

"Let's give this idea some thought." Caine extended her hands palms down in a flapping motion to calm the others who were showing signs of dissent.

Pettit suddenly came to life. "If I read what Chester is saying correctly, we could approach Russia or the Federation about a joint defence capability - I exclude Nuovostan from this for obvious reasons. Such an approach would afford us protection without increasing our isolation and would offer our chosen partner the comfort of knowing that they were safe from their adversaries gaining ascendancy by acquiring BAM2."

"Silas you've done it again," Caine laughed delightedly, "you've developed Chester's concept before anybody else has." She turned to the others, "what do the rest of you think?"

"I'll go along with it until it falls over and if it does I'll try to come up with a revised alternative plan," Crook said this with a beaming smile.

"Who's going to choose the partner to come in with us, our choices are limited to the awful and the disastrous?" Gilliland shook his head slowly.

"I'd go for awful over disastrous any day," Pettit responded.

"That means that we throw our hand in with the Federation," Caine emulated Gilliland and shook her head slowly. "I can't believe I'm saying this. What happened to us wanting to go it alone and to hell with the rest of the world?"

"That policy has not been noticeably successful so far but I don't see that we have a choice," Gilliland said with a reluctant shake of his head.

"Let's start the process as soon as we're through with this discussion." Caine looked at them all expectantly. "My guess is that our meeting is over right now."

She was right.

On his return from Nuovostan, Eleven was nervous and his adrenalin level prepared him for fight or flight. It soon became obvious to him that his intentions remained secret when nobody showed any suspicion about his motives when he returned to the Island. In fact when he saw Gilliland at the next Council meeting he was asked if he had enjoyed his brief holiday away from the Island.

His next and immediate task was to complete the next stage of his acquisition of the BAM2 unit which still resided in a dummy CPU mini tower in the store room outside the BAM2 storage facility. Another of the cell members was part of a cleaning crew which did not have access to the storage facility but who did clean the external store room. Security in this area was not tight— old and disused CPUs and ancillary equipment were not considered to need any special attention.

The CPU purloined and exchanged by Kwietakovski, was retrieved from its plain sight hiding place by Webber, the soulless Scot who was part of RIR Cell 1, and transferred by him to a similar storage facility, the cleaning of which was part of his duty, outside of the physics laboratory. A third member of the team, Colleen Brogan, was part of the physics lab team because she was a computer geek of unsurpassed excellence. She collected the dummy CPU from the storage room and walked into the lab unchecked, there was no ingoing security and in her case very little by way of egress checks.

At her work station she was able to open up the CPU casing and check that the boxed BAM2 unit was inside, a CPU case on her desk would not arouse any suspicion but a BAM2 box would. She would have to work on it during the grave yard shift and even then she would have to exercise extreme caution.

Her opportunity came during her very next shift; the only other person on this graveyard shift was heavily involved with maintenance work and to all intents and purposes was not a problem. Having freedom, Brogan removed the BAM2 unit from its hiding place and plugged her computer into the box port using a URL. The enabling programme told her that the unit was inactive and that all defence protocols were in place.

Peering at the data screen she looked carefully at the options offered. She had never tried to wake up a BAM2 unit and she had not seen the enabling programme before, it had been acquired through number 11 and passed to her only the day before. The first option she chose was 'Disable security protocols', the screen went blank and immediately refreshed with the instruction 'Enter disabling code'. She had been told that there were only two opportunities to enter the code correctly and despite her normally cold and inhuman persona, she felt her palms moistening; if she got this wrong an Island-wide alert klaxon would sound. She entered the number she had been given and flicked the return key. The screen went blank and then returned with a message in red, 'Incorrect entry – try again. If another incorrect entry is made a general alert will activate a lock down procedure.'

She wiped her sweating palms on her overall and dabbed her brow with a paper tissue. They had said that this was the correct code, maybe she had entered it incorrectly, she counted the asterisks on the code screen there were the same number of asterisks as there were numbers in the disabling code. Maybe she had entered the code incorrectly; she hit the try again option and waited for the flashing cursor. When the cursor activated she entered the ten digit code with extreme care. Hesitating before pressing return she counted the digits and the asterisks, they matched. With her eyes closed she pressed return and waited, eyes closed and nerves tingling for the alert to sound.

Thirty-one

Moments of lucidity for Wilson were interspersed with ever lengthening psychotic episodes. The occurrences were strange and frightening for him; it was as if he was watching himself from a distance and could see his disassociation from the decisiveness that had until so recently been his driving force. His real self shouted to the other self to get out of the way and let him get on with his plans. But the other self was not always listening.

When lucidity returned momentarily, he recapped his situation. As he did so his anger began to mount to a crescendo which he now knew would lead to another bout of wild disassociation. Breathing deeply he calmed himself and tried to think more rationally. The plans he had so carefully nurtured to bring about the assassinations of his adversaries had failed miserably.

He blamed the failure on 'A', whoever he was, and Eleven and Pain whom he had unwisely trusted to fulfil their part of the bargain in exchange for a great deal of money. Curiously it was not the loss of money that bothered him, he had more of it than he knew what to do with; his loss was the failure to acquire more power. He calmed himself once more when he felt his paranoia rising to engulf him.

Pelochev watched him with some alarm. He was clearly struggling with his inner demons and in her view he was losing the battle, slowly but surely. Seeing that he was at least partially in control she decided that now would be a good time to lay the foundations for her own future security.

"Am thinking, Cullin, that we are not needing these people who letted us down. We are not needing them but do requiring partners we can control and who are free to move over world in freeness."

"What are you talking about?" He peered at her as though looking through a thick fog.

"Must go to neighbours next door into Russia and work with."

"Work with the Russians to do what?"

"Making up BAM2 units, is obvious. They have top good scientists who can working better than the ones who let you down and disappeared." She referred to the Nuovostani scientists who had correctly interpreted the notes made by Gilliland and Crook but had failed to realise that there was a deadly outcome when they got the final stages wrong. "You still are having copy of notes from original experiments, yes?"

"Of course I have," he said testily. "What makes you think the Russians would be any better than the scientists I chose?"

"Not better but they keep going until finding out what goes wrong in end. Russia has many scientists; too many maybe. To lose a few in experimenting is not a problem. They go on until they get right." She smiled in triumph at the undoubted wisdom of her words.

"That would give the Russians the technology but how does that help me?"

"Easy to tell," she giggled coquettishly. "We have all scientist notes before experiments made, so will know how success is reach. Means we have secret and if Russian Presidium decide to go alone we can sell to others the methods. We can also to make us safe from outside by use technology to give defence to Nuovostan."

Wilson's frazzled mind was able to assimilate the meaning of her plan and he began to adopt it as his own, guided by the clamour of voices in his head. With this plan to occupy him he began to return to the old vitriolic Wilson which was not good news to any other person, including Pelochev. Seeing his immediate return to his twisted world she smiled secretly to herself and visualised the document that she had prepared some time ago, before her own plans had begun to form properly. The document was in a safe in her apartments which nobody but the specialist who had forged them knew about; she had imported him from the Ukraine paid him well and sent him back into obscurity.

Simple but effective, the document in the safe recorded the marriage of Irena Pelochev to Colin Wilson, President of Nuovostan. She did not care that Wilson knew nothing about it; the signed and witnessed document would not be revealed until after the death of the President. The will which he had not actually made would entrust to her and her family in perpetuity the hereditary Presidency of Nuovostan. She had learned about forged documents and signatures from Wilson in his former dealings with Creswell. She had turned the tables on him and used his wiles to her advantage; she was satisfied with what she had done.

Thirty-two

The Russian President, Boris Lebedev, was not at all interested in meeting with Wilson. He told his equerry that it would not be possible for at least three months and probably not even then. The equerry spoke into the telephone and then listened intently. His brow creased and his eyebrows came together as he listened to the response to his dismissal of the meeting. Placing his hand over the mouthpiece of the old fashioned telephone he turned to address Lebedev who was annoyed at yet another interruption.

"Sir, I think you should hear this," he addressed the President in a quivering voice.

"What is it?" he said tersely

"The Pelochev woman says that the President of Nuovostan has access to the secrets of BAM2 and is willing to share them if the right deal can be struck." He raised his eyebrows at the expectation of a sign of interest.

Lebedev took the phone from him and used his disinterested voice to carry on with the conversation. "What is this nonsense Pelochev, why are you bothering me with these fairy tales?" Although his disinterested voice was feigned, his face was actually alive with interest. He listened for a moment and with the same voice tone said casually: "It so happens that I have had a cancellation in my diary for tomorrow. I don't think I have any interest in what you have to offer but you can come and talk to me if you wish but it will probably be a waste of your time." He put the telephone down and turned in agitation to his equerry. "Cancel all my meetings tomorrow, it doesn't matter who they are with, I need to have my diary cleared completely. Oh and get the guests suite ready for our visitors…and arrange for a formal dinner to extend a welcome to our Nuovostani allies."

"But sir, the President of Nuovostan is not a friend of Russia, he is on our most wanted list."

"Then have him removed from the list and arrange for a welcoming party, he will arrive tomorrow in his private Presidential jet. Make sure all necessary clearances are made for his arrival and for his transport from the airport to the Kremlin." He looked at the open mouthed equerry. "Now comrade, what are you waiting for?"

The equerry scuttled off to make the necessary arrangements, he shook his head as he left; he would never understand politicians, they could and did reverse critical decisions with a speed that left him breathless.

Pelochev fussed around Wilson as they took the eight hour flight from his private air strip on the outskirts of Nuovostan City to Moscow. She was concentrating hard on making sure that Wilson was kept calm so that he would remain lucid. Before leaving she had contacted 'A' using the number that he had, much to her excitement given her, shortly before his return to the USA. She was preparing him for the task she had lined up for him after the conference with the Russians which she alluded to but of which she gave no detail. One of her aspirations remained to have him for herself; he would be an invaluable ally.

The obvious questions she asked herself, and then by telephone call she asked 'A', was about his motives and why he had agreed to rig the assassinations. He had said that he knew nothing of the deception; he had been provided with weapons and the time and place and that he had done what was asked of him. He had no knowledge of the who and the how of the fake

199

assassinations. He pulled the trigger and took the video. The fixing must have been either from the Nuovostanis or RIR. She had passed this information on to Wilson who immediately assumed that this betrayal was the work of RIR. It did not occur to him that RIR had nothing to gain by such actions. Pelochev knew that they, the Nuovostanis were not involved in the deception and determined that she must find out who was behind it.

On their arrival in Moscow they were met by troops in full regalia forming lines on either side of the Presidential jet's covered stairway. As Wilson left the aircraft a military band struck up a raucous, slightly discordant, march and the guard of honour presented arms. President Lebedev himself greeted Wilson effusively and, to Wilson's disgust, kissed him on the lips. Pelochev received a cold and formal handshake and was thereafter dismissed by Lebedev.

The effusiveness of the reception continued when they reached the Kremlin. There was a further guard of honour which Wilson was invited to inspect. Such a reception, much to Pelochev's delight, put Wilson in a good mood and boded well for the forthcoming discussions. Wilson revelled in the importance which his visit engendered and became almost statesman like in his approach to his duties. Since assuming the Presidency he had been a prisoner in his own country and had become, despite his wealth, very isolated.

"I told you my dear," he muttered to Pelochev out of the corner of his mouth, "that my idea of befriending the President of Russia would be worthwhile. You should listen more carefully to my ideas, you could learn much."

Pelochev made no comment about the total inaccuracy of his words— she was satisfied that when he adopted an idea as his own, he would follow it through.

Thirty-three

Explorative approaches to the Federation by the Islanders promoted an explosive reaction. With an uncharacteristic turn of speed the President of the Federation of Nations, Jan van der Linde, let it be known that he would agree to a meeting at any time in any place. It was agreed that investigative discussions would take place in a neutral location; the location which was mutually acceptable was the Azores, paradoxically the scene of the first encounter between the two factions at the beginning of the Island's history.

The founders were amused, but not entirely surprised, by the alacrity with which their offer was taken up. Recovery Island was still blacklisted by the Federation territories but it was clear that the Federation would not be averse to a meeting on Recovery Island; it was the Islanders who were averse to their proposed venue, on the grounds of security. There was no quibbling concerning the agreed location of the meeting; the lack of success from their first meeting on the Azores seemed not to bother the Federation at all.

Within two days the time and exact location of the meeting was agreed and no restriction was placed on the number or disciplines of people attending from either side. The immediate agreement to meet meant that the Federation were unable to assemble a military force in the vicinity of the Azores as they had done at the time of the first meeting. Gilliland and Caine flew to the Azores in the Apache Chieftain and Crook and Pettit took their newly acquired smaller and faster Apache Warrior.

The Warrior was a smaller version of the Chieftain and was equipped with long range tanks giving it a flight distance of four thousand miles with a cruising speed of eighteen hundred miles an hour. The two flights ensured that the founders could fly separately in the interests of security. Acquisition of the Canadian built Warrior, a fighter bomber modified to carry eight passengers, had not been easy because of the ban on the sale of strategic aircraft to the Islanders; they had used Nematasulu their West African affiliate country, to make the purchase on their behalf.

The initial suspicion of the Federation was overcome within minutes of the talks opening. The Founders had decided that it would be better if Caine took the lead in representing the Islands interest. It was perceived by the Federation that she was less threatening and certainly less belligerent than any of the men who completed the Island's representative negotiators.

Van der Linde was tripping over his words in his haste to secure the right to use BAM2. He caveated his approach saying that he presumed that this meeting was not merely cosmetic as former meetings had been when they had agreed to meet with the Federation on the understanding that nothing would be resolved. He received assurances from Caine that it was the Islanders hope that they would reach agreement on the use of the technology to safeguard the Island and the Federation territories against incursion.

Caine opened up by laying the Island's cards on the table. "I should explain to you why we have chosen to approach you about a pact of co-operation. You will know that it has been our aim for some time to be able to interact with the rest of the world without let or hindrance. This has never been possible since the formation of the island and we feel that it will be better for our development as a nation and for the good of our allies in the rest of the world that we enjoy collective security and the freedoms that will bring for you and for us. We are accustomed to being safe from external aggression but lack the freedom of movement we desire. You, on the other hand have the freedoms offered by your society but are not so secure from external aggression. Therefore it is in our joint interest to co-operate; we will get the relative freedom of international travel through that part of the world, over which you have influence and you will get absolute geographic safety in all of your territories. There is another reason for us wishing to take this course of action. We believe that The President of Nuovostan is about to join forces with another country or alliance to somehow acquire the technology. We have presumed it is not the Federation in view of the bad blood that there is between the Federation and President Wilson. If we can agree on that then we have the makings of a deal."

Still falling over his words in his haste to achieve what had so far eluded them, Van der Linde broke in almost before she had finished her introduction. "I can assure you, Madam that we are at one with you in this matter. We will have no truck with Nuovostan or its President who are enemies of the Federation. Rest assured that we of the Federation will work closely with you to ensure the safe use of this fantastic technology for entirely peaceful means."

"Good," she said brightly. "We will draw up an agreement to formalise our partnership in the use of BAM2 technology that is our legal people will, together with yours, agree.

Van der Linde was beside himself with glee. He had exceeded even his wildest dreams and had pulled off a coup that would assure his ascendant position in the annals of Federation history, as the man who had given the Federation the tools to achieve absolute global dominance. He hoped that nobody had seen that his fingers were crossed under the table when he promised the peaceful use of BAM2. That of course would never happen. They, he thought, were so other-worldly, so naïve, so stupid.

***

Shortcomings in the security system highlighted an ironic inconsistency in the application of BAM2. It could do impossibly complex things but it was not the be all and end all. It could vaporise mountains, dig tunnels, protect the planet against asteroid collisions and create and control volcanic eruptions but it could not prevent itself from being terminally destructive. It could not detect the intentions of the user and therefore prevent itself from being used for the wrong reasons.

What should have been a great boon to mankind could in many ways be a disastrous millstone around the neck of its inventors, the custodians of the key to its capabilities. For every advantage it presented there were many accompanying problems the most fundamental of all the problems was that, no matter how hard they might try to control it, it remained a machine capable of death and total destruction.

Thirty-four

Colleen Brogan opened her eyes slowly, the alarm that she had dreaded activating when she attempted to open up the BAM2 system had not sounded, not that she would have heard it had it been activated – she would have been immediately annihilated - the cursor on the reactivation screen winked provocatively at her. So far, so good she was into the programme but now she was on unfamiliar ground— she had to fly the rest of the way on a wing and a prayer. She scrutinised the menu which filled the screen:

Type of activation   *

Security Code
                                                                        *
Engineering
                                                                        *
Remote
                                                                        *
Manual
                                                                        *
User type
                                                                        *
Range
                                                                        *
Delay Parameters
                                                                        *
Failsafe Parameters
                                                                        *
Auto destruct
                                                                        *
Armageddon

Her palms were sweating again; she had no idea what the menu meant and no idea about how many attempts she would have to get into the system before it would freeze or set off the alarm which would lead to her being revealed as a traitor to the Island. It would have to be trial and error. She selected each one of the types of activation and studied the sub menus which were offered. Unless she had help, she realised very quickly, she might destroy the chances they had to control a unit and that would scupper her real agenda of earning the freedom and the money to find out about the people who betrayed her grandfather and punish them with the same fate, only more slowly and painfully.

Eleven was disappointed by the telephone call he instigated with Brogan. She had told him that the menus were difficult to grasp and she was reluctant to delve further without more information because of the likelihood of freezing the system with little hope of recovery. It was all moving too slowly for him now. He realised with frustration that the Spy-Eye with which she was fitted did not allow him to see her expression and judge the integrity of her words. He could only see what she could see and as she had no idea that she was fitted with spy-eye he could only see what she chose to look at. A mirror would have sufficed but he had no way of getting her to comply.

***

Eleven's last visit to Nuovostan had caused him great anguish, he wasn't sure if his cover had been compromised by the hastily ill thought out visit. He wasn't so much worried about Wilson and Pelochev knowing who he was, they had no axe to grind and no international presence. He was mildly concerned that

Pain who could now recognise him but at least he was in exile in London and did not pose an immediate threat. He was concerned with the assassin 'A' because he didn't know who 'A' was and didn't know which country he came from, there was a hint of an American accent when he heard him whispering to Pelochev in the next room but that was no help, he also didn't know where 'As' loyalties lay. The fake deaths of the two who were supposed to be assassinated had, it seemed likely, required 'As' collusion but if it did why he had done what he had, was a mystery?

Putting aside his reservations about 'A' for a moment he considered his options: The activation of the BAM2 unit was slower than he had hoped, maybe Brogan was being over cautions but on the other hand rushing it could prove disastrous. Unbeknown to her he had been watching her progress through Spy-Eye and had seen enough to be aware of her lack of courage. One option was to get the deactivated BAM2 away from the Island which he could do and use external specialists to decode the situation. The question he asked himself was; who could he get to do the decoding without them wanting to wrest control away from the RIR. He answered his own question; *nobody*.

Only one course of action was open to him, as far as he could see. He would have to throw his lot in with Wilson; the man was completely mad, which was both a bad and good thing; bad because he was unstable but good because he no longer had the intelligence to defend himself against an organisation as committed as RIR. At the back of his mind was a niggling concern about Pelochev but that was a bridge he would have to cross if and when he came to it.

In parallel to his interaction with Wilson and Pelochev he was progressing the development of PRICE, the Progressive Recovery Island Change &

Evolution union. This was something he could do more openly than was the case with RIR in which secrecy was everything. His intention was to promote a movement for change and as part of the recruitment process, identify those members who were more radical and of that group, those who were candidates for aggressive change and potentially membership of one of the RIR cells. Pierson could not, as a Ruling Council member, front the organisation and he had no intention of exposing Zen as a founding member because of his court record.

He chose Jon Webber, the disaffected Scot to be the nominal head of PRICE. Webber, a member of Cell 1, was a cold and remote individual whose hatred of the way Scotland had been destroyed and bankrupted by ineffective government, was only slightly greater than his hatred for the way the Island was being run by, in his words, a mish-mash of unelected upper middle class losers.

Zen had identified, for him, a number of the Island's citizens who were critical of the way the Island was being run and these names were passed on to Webber. Approaching each of the 26 names that Zen had identified, Webber was blunt in his initial discussions making no bones about his intention to get a better deal for the citizens of the Island by any means necessary. Of the 26 he found 4 who were ripe for subversive activity. The other 22 he approached, under Eleven's direction, with a sanitised version of the true intentions of PRICE; the sanitised version lived up to the acronym which had been selected, concentrating on the Progressive and Evolution components.

PRICE was developed with two distinct components; one was for the benign and idealistic more open approach, the other was for the fanatics with a closed approach. These would be the public and secretive faces of the movement. Of the two the fanatical element was developed fast track while the benign element was allowed to bumble along in its idealistic way. The aim was to get enough support for them to have a voice for change and evolution and Eleven could, safely, champion the cause by promoting the benign openly while secretly nurturing the real core of the movement.

Thirty-five

Running in parallel with the meeting between the Islanders and the Federation in the Azores, was a similar meeting in Moscow between Wilson and Lebedev. Their meeting, like that in the Azores appeared on the surface to be calm and cordial, but beneath the calm duplicity seethed on both sides of the discussion.

Lebedev, knowing Wilson's weaknesses, suggested that they observe Russian protocol of imbibing good Russian Vodka at the start of, and throughout the duration of, their discussions. He was amused when Pelochev took the first glass of Vodka from the bottle before Wilson and drank it down; she waited a minute or so before nodding her head at Wilson and muttering "Da," from behind almost closed lips.

"I suggest," Lebedev spoke in very good slightly American accented English, "that we have a constructive meeting in which we deal with the general points and leave the details to others after we have agreement." He regarded them both over the rim of his shot glass as he sipped the potent liquid. His glass was less full than that of Wilson and the Vodka in his bottle was diluted by a third with distilled water.

To Lebedev's surprise the presentation was made to him by Pelochev in Russian because, she said, they wanted to be absolutely clear about the proposal and did not wish language to be a problem in respect of clear understanding of their Russian host.

"*Comrade President,*" she began formally in cultured Russian. "*It is our wish to come to an agreement with you about access to BAM2 technology, with which I am sure you are familiar. You will also be familiar with the fact that President Wilson,"* she looked at him as the mention of his name penetrated his Vodka-impaired brain, *"has twice attempted to emulate the experiments of Gilliland and Crook which produced such valuable results. What you don't know is that the first experiments failed because the scientists were working with incomplete data and the second failed because it succeeded."* She paused to let her provocative words take effect.

"Failed because it succeeded?" Lebedev looked puzzled. *"Perhaps it would be better if you explained that in English,"* he said with a smile, "it makes no sense in Russian."

"I think not," she continued in Russian. *"The scientists succeeded in emulating the results of Gilliland and Crook but somehow managed to destroy themselves, with the technology they evoked, in the end process."* She conveniently avoided telling Lebedev that the damage caused to the infrastructure in Eastern Russia and the disintegration of two Russian air force jets was down to the experiments carried out by Wilson's scientists from the lake laboratory in Nuovostan. *"The notes they used can be made available to you if we can reach an agreement. President Wilson has made an understanding with some freedom fighters on the Island and they can be our eyes and ears on the ground there. The advantage is that we can keep a watch on what the Islanders are doing while we complete the BAM2 experiments. The freedom fighters have captured a sleeping BAM2 unit and are working on re-activating it."*

"So you have a plan of action which seems to be sound, so," he paused reflectively, *"why do you need us?"*

"So simple," she reverted to English, at which Wilson stirred from his reverie, "we needing are better science and better of military capable of being world power. We are not trust the Federation they are snack in glass."

"Snake, I keep telling you, it is snake in the grass, snake in the grass, not glass," Wilson mumbled in his half waking state.

"Is what I am said," she shot a withering look at him as he absorbed more Vodka.

"Can we trust these freedom fighters and, more importantly, do we really need them?" Lebedev asked casually, he reverted to Russian.

"Are needing them because is no good if we have BAM2 and they too. BAM2 only good if had by one people otherwise it is same as old nuclear deterring. Both sides have, no side can use. Stool mate is no good." Seeing his puzzled look she repeated her response in Russian.

Wilson mumbled "Stale mate, that's what you mean, stale mate."

"If the freedom fighters already have a BAM2 unit why do they need us, they could go it alone."

"Their organisation is too small and there is no guarantee that they can make the BAM2 work"

"Do they need to be represented at our meeting?"

"Not necessary," she punctuated her words with a knowing wink, *"they are only useful if we do not succeed with our experiments. Once we have the BAM2 their use is very limited, if you get my meaning."*

Lebedev smiled his avuncular smile and nodded in agreement with her unstated sentiments. Behind his friendly exterior he recognised that this woman would have to be watched. He recognised her as a 'snack in the glass' par excellence.

Thirty-six

The euphoria expressed by van der Linde at the culmination of the meeting with the Islanders evaporated when he received the draft of an agreement from them. It did what the Islanders had said to him in their preliminary discussions but there was a caveat that he had not considered; it said in unambiguous terms that BAM2 would be made available for use in Federation territories but that its operation would be carried out only by Recovery Island personnel and that the units would be fitted with a remote self-protecting mechanism of the kind that had been used during the China drilling incident should it fall into the hands of other than an Islander.

Van der Linde was fuming at what he saw as the lack of trust being shown by the Islanders, especially at this early stage of the negotiations President Chung of the Chinese People's Republic was also not amused by the caveat that the technology would be shared in the same way with the Russians to ensure even handedness. The unspoken facts were that although the negotiations were being carried out under the auspices of the Federation it was actually the totalitarian Chinese administration, as the biggest economy in the Federation, who were calling the shots and they had no intention of sharing anything with the Russians.

Negative responses from van der Linde's legal department, at the insistence of President Chen, were sent to the Island's administration. The Founders response was straightforward; they insisted on keeping control of the BAM2 operation to ensure that it would only be used for the purposes of defence. The response from the Federation said that if they were to join together to police the rest of the world there would have to be trust between the two factions.

The response from the Federation underlined how far apart they were from the Islanders. They had missed the point of the discussions entirely; it was not the intention of Recovery Island to police the world; that was solely a Federation aspiration. The Islanders intention was to offer the safety for the Federation and Russian territories in exchange for free movement of the Recovery Island citizens within their relevant territories.

Looking very uncomfortable, the four founders analysed the situation. The Federation had not changed its stance and they had to confess that they, on behalf of the Islanders, had not substantially changed theirs. True they had offered the protection of BAM2 to the Federation and would do the same for Russia but the caveat of the control staying entirely with the Islanders was obviously a condition too far for China.

Worse news came during the course of these deliberations in the form of an explosive intelligence report that RIR has somehow managed to steal a disabled BAM2 unit and smuggle it out of safe custody but at the present time were unable to access the unit; their capacity to activate it was just out of reach, for the moment.

Pettit was more relaxed than the other three about the missing unit. "The unit is switched off." He looked at them from under raised eyebrows. "It means that they can't operate it because they lack the expertise. We can track its whereabouts using the GPS feature, if that's what you want to do, and/or we can activate the self-destruct and *voila*, the problem is gone. Why are you all looking so glum?"

"If only it were so simple," Crook said wistfully, "problem is that the unit is switched off, not just asleep." He turned to Pettit. "What that means Silas is that we can't track it and we can't initiate self-destruct – to do that it needs to be asleep, not switched off. Essentially if they can crack the access code they will have access to the technology. That's bad enough but what is worse is that if they activate a BAM dome anywhere near us and expand it, it will pass through our domes and annihilate us. There is no protection against it. That is its strength and its weakness"

Pettit looked pale. "Did you ever consider telling me, the one responsible for the security of BAM, that this was a potential weak point? Had I known I could have done something about it but I'm not clairvoyant; what possessed you to keep it a secret?" His words were cold and unyielding.

"Calm down Silas," Crook was placatory

"Calm down? Calm down? What kind of advice is that? Potentially the most dangerous weapon ever devised by man is in the hands of maniacs." His voice and face were full of impotent anger.

"Silas," Caine interrupted the moment. "Don't take it out on Bruce; this is not his fault any more than it being your fault that it was possible to remove the unit from the secure storage area in the first place. The reason you were not told about this problem with the design was that the fewer people who know about it the better."

"You mean you didn't trust me with the information?" He glared at her.

"That's enough Silas," Gilliland burst into the conversation. "Nobody's blaming you for the gap in security and it is unfair for you to blame anybody else for what's happened. The fact is it's happened and we have to limit the damage that it can do. Although we don't know where it is at the moment we have every reason to believe that it has not yet left the Island and as long as it's here we are relatively safe. Its use within the Island could eliminate everything including those who have stolen it and they must know that so they are unlikely to experiment."

"My apologies," Pettit looked embarrassed. "It was unreasonable of me to criticise anybody else to cover up a lapse in the security I designed and it was down to me to hunt out the possible weaknesses. But we do have to address this situation without delay. I'll seal the port and airport so that nothing unwanted gets in or out."

Prevention of a breach of the BAM2 safety protocol was now on a knife edge. It might take time, but with a working unit on the loose which was soon to be or perhaps already was in the hands of the computer techs of a foreign power, a breach could result. It was their worst nightmare. Because the unit was switched off and not in sleep mode they could neither track it nor could they switch it on remotely to enable them to destroy it as they had with the units that the Chinese had sequestered in the early days of its development. Crook and two other high end computer gurus were concentrating on finding a way to detect the remote activation of the unit and countermand the instructions it had been given.

Although under extreme pressure to succeed, their endeavours were not rewarded with success.

Thirty-seven

Acting on curious information received from Lawson's Intelligence Department as part of the on-going security initiative, Tanterelli instigated a medical alert which was issued to all Islanders between the ages of eighteen and sixty. Attendance was, without exception, obligatory and a potential health hazard was cited as the reason for the diktat. Despite the ensuing grumblings the selected citizens were pursued relentlessly, without regard for the seniority which would normally excuse them from participation to ensure full participation. The inspections, which took place under the watchful eye of Carlina Tanterelli, were brief and to the point requiring the inspection of the body's extremities. The outcome of the investigations was a great surprise to Tanterelli and the founders and gave rise to acute concern over the welfare of the Islanders in general. Their discomfiture at the outcome was not voiced in public but had a drastic influence on the course of intelligence gathering.

The unexpected findings of the medical alert caused a radical rethink of the course of actions being considered to allow a certain amount of integration between the Islanders and outsiders. What was revealed by the tests was disquieting and led to the inevitable conclusion that the threat they had begun to uncover was made by incomers who were generally but not exclusively from the add-on families of the specialists invited to join the Island as a valuable asset.

***

The Islanders' overtures for sharing and cooperation were still being looked upon by the Federation as a sign of weakness rather than the olive branch which was intended. There was no sign of movement in the ultimate acquisitive intentions of the Federation even though they had been offered use, if not control, of BAM technology which would assure them of protection against Russian territorial aspirations and vice versa. Tanterelli's conclusion from the tests carried out on the Islanders was that any intermingling of Islanders and non-Islanders could increase the threat to security uncovered by the tests.

To reduce the threat and as a consequence of the intransigence of the Federation, negotiations for the sharing of the technology outside the Island were curtailed, it was decided to call a halt to the negotiations. Responses from the Federation when the breakdown of negotiations was announced became obvious. The Federation naturally assumed that it was the intention of the Islanders to continue talks with the New Russians and reach with them an exclusive agreement with regard to facilitating BAM2. Denials by the Islanders fell on deaf ears and the Federation recommenced their former threatening behaviour both to Recovery Island and to New Russia. There was, however, no inclination to offer any kind of deal to the Russians because they felt an even greater suspicion of Russian motives than they felt for the Federation and the Ruling Council had no intention of reaching agreement with one of the super powers without the other

Both the Federation and Russia made further threats of dire retribution over the stance taken by the Islanders. The Federation threatened reprisals for the Islanders and to those countries which supported the Island by trade exchanges. They cited Nematasulu and the countries around it which gave succour to the Islanders as being hostile and therefore being legitimate targets for harsh consequences, with immediate effect and without warning. In a strange way the banning of both powers from BAM access brought them closer together than they had ever been before but not so much that they became firm friends.

The war of wills moved into new territory; the threat to those countries friendly to the Island caused a drastic rethink among the majority of Ruling Council members. Peaceful resistance was being reassessed; the use of BAM2 as more than just a means of defence was discussed openly among the Council members. With the exception of Pettit, the founders looked upon this change in stance with alarm. Pettit was on the side of those who supported the use of the technology as a lethal deterrent to the threats of their enemies, although he did not voice his support openly.

The founders, without the inclusion of the Ruling Council, considered their options in a private session outside the normal protocol of having formal discussions of any kind recorded. It was decided to enlist the aid of a communications professional to counter the wild accusations being made by the Federation in particular, which continued to feed misinformation to the citizens of their various countries and nurture the fear and paranoia which they would use to inflict military action on Nematasulu and other nations friendly to the Island.

There was an obvious candidate for this task, one who was friendly to the Island and who had the means of accessing the organs of public information; Dessertes Kingdom Valerie, DK. He was contacted by secure telephone and arrangements were made for him to meet with Mark Lawson in London. The meeting was convened before the Federation could tighten up

220

their travel net which would make open travelling more difficult.

DK not only supported the altruistic motives of the Islanders but he felt he owed them a debt of gratitude for having liberated him from Wilson's clutches. He listened intently to what Lawson had to say and undertook to give the tasks one hundred percent of his time to the pursuit of the objectives he was set. If he was unable to help them stem the tide of vitriol from their enemies they would let it be known that, as a last resort they would destroy BAM technology and deny the world the salvation it represented.

Time was of the essence and DK was contacted and rushed to the Island for serious talks on recovering the situation which the Islanders had handled so badly. Their attempts to promote harmony and safety had backfired to such an extent that relations between the three interested parties had deteriorated as far as it was possible to go without invoking an open declaration of a three sided war.

The proposal that DK should take up residence on the Island, for the duration of his PR exercise, was immediately vetoed by him. Such an action would separate him from Caroline, the love of his life, and he reasoned would brand him as an Islander with no hope of his being seen as even handed or of his even being listened to. It was agreed that he would continue to be based at his London flat and would work from there as a neutral investigative journalist.

It was suggested to him that he should call on the assistance of James Creswell to give DK a more trouble-free segue into the world he would need to inhabit to assist the Islanders in their cause. Once more he rejected their proposal and explained that any assistance from the PM would taint his impartiality in the eyes of all the other participants. He undertook to help them only if they gave him free reign as far as methods were concerned. With some reluctance the founders agreed to give him carte blanche providing he were kept informed of the strategy and process that DK intended to pursue.

After they had reached agreement with DK the founders sat in joint silence, each having their own thoughts on the step they had just agreed. They had put the immediate future of the Islands international relations into the hands of one off-Islander.

DK took his task seriously not only because he was a journalist on a mission but also because he truly believed that the Recovery Island society deserved an opportunity to state their case once again to a world being misled by political opportunists. He could do that via his articles in the broadsheets but as a scientific correspondent he was straying beyond the bounds of his remit and would need to harness the support of somebody of political influence.

On returning to London from the Island he contacted Caroline Pelham to arrange a meeting with her as soon as she was free to do so. It was during the course of an all-night sitting in the House of Commons, requiring her husband's presence, a week or so later that the opportunity to meet presented itself. They met once again at DK's Kensington flat and as soon as she arrived she sensed that the meeting was not entirely about the usual reason for their get-togethers.

They kissed and embraced on meeting but the encounter was without the usual urgency, DK was being unusually reserved and looked uncomfortable.

"What is it darling?" She enquired as she separated from him and settled onto the generous sofa they usually occupied together. "You are not your normal sparkling self," she observed.

"I have something of a problem and I don't really know how to deal with it because it involves you in a capacity which we have tacitly agreed, without actually saying it." He passed his hand wearily over his face and then shook his head with a grimace.

"Are you going to share this with me or are you going to keep me guessing?" She took the sting out of her observation by softening her voice and smiling. "I had hoped that we were past this point in our relationship." She became more business-like and added, "as long as you are not going to ask me to desert my husband and move in with you, which I have made clear I will not do, there are no tacit agreements we have made which are likely to cause problems between us."

"This may not be an implicit agreement but it is implied." He took a deep breath and launched his proposition to her. "I want you to use your influence on your husband to get government support for my friends on Recovery Island. I had promised myself that I would never use you to get to your husband but these people need my help to put right the unreasonable misinformation which is being spread about the intentions of the Islanders which is denying the poor nations of the world the help they so desperately need."

"I'm not sure that Rupert is the right man to give support to what he considers to be a rogue nation hell bent on using their technology to get their own way." She arched an eyebrow and looked at him with some surprise. "I'm surprised that you have decided to support a regime which is undemocratic and totalitarian."

"We've never talked about my time on the Island during the visit by the world press, I suppose," he chuckled lasciviously, "because we have other things in mind when we get together.

223

She joined in his laughter. "True, we are usually preoccupied with more physical than political pursuits. But maybe the time has come to broaden our horizons."

"Heaven forbid," he shook his head in disbelief at the altered course of their conversation. "I don't want our relationship to change and I wouldn't normally ask this of you but I have promised to help my friends and this is one course of action that I feel I must pursue."

"Do you think it's reasonable to ask me to help you with something when I don't share your beliefs about, what appears to me to be, this unstable nation?"

"Of course you're right," he looked defeated. "I'm asking you to take my side in a situation with which you are uncomfortable; it is entirely unreasonable of me to expect you to go along with it. Don't worry about it I just have to find another champion for my cause." He said this to stop any further erosion of their relationship but at the same time was at a loss to find another sponsor.

Thirty-eight

Eleven, after his return to the Island, made a secure conference call with number 66 when it became obvious that Brogan had lost her nerve and was unable to unlock the acquired BAM2 unit - not because she did not possess the ability to find her way through the control protocols of the unit - but because she was petrified that a wrong move would bring about her immediate demise. This was a thought she shared with nobody but Eleven was astute enough to know when she had lost her nerve; he had the added advantage of being able to access her attempts through the Spy-Eye of which she was unaware.

Zen was distracted by the discomfort he felt that was caused by the work he had had done on his toe during the second bizarre tattooing ritual, which was insisted upon by Eleven whom he now knew to be Mr Da Neel but despite his efforts Mr Da Neel remained a mystery. Something had gone wrong with the tattooing process and inflammation had set in, when he looked at it before treatment began he was unable to distinguish what change had been made to the recognition symbol which he had been given as soon as he had been recruited.

Their discussions on the next step to be taken in re-activating the unit were inconclusive. Zen would, of course, do what he could to facilitate the process but he did not possess the skill necessary to undertake the task himself, to help he suggested that another source of expertise should be sought. Eleven was eager to shortcut the process in any way possible, especially as he had already told Wilson that he had a BAM2 unit and Wilson had become very excited by the prospect of achieving his number one dream. He was less impressed when he learned that they were unable to access it and feared that it might disintegrate if they failed to countermand the self-destruct mechanism.

Zen contacted Pelochev and gave her the opportunity of finding a team of scientists capable of opening this modern Pandora's Box thereby allowing her to lay claim to a share in the resulting financial rewards. The suggestion fell on fertile ground and with anticipated speed she came up with a solution which Zen thought he could sell to Eleven. In reality the work of finding a competent team had already been accomplished. The expedient was the unexpectedly rapid progress that had been made during the meeting in Russia with Lebedev. The Russians had agreed to supply Wilson with any technical support that was required to carry out another series of experiments to discover the secrets of BAM2. A laboratory had been made available on the same day as the agreement had been reached and Wilson handed over a copy of the notes made by Gilliland and Crook during their experiments on the Isles of Scilly and at the stone cottage on the Moors.

Eleven reluctantly accepted that there were two things that RIR could not do: They could not raise enough numbers to take over the Island without assistance and secondly they could not, without outside assistance, unravel the activation of the BAM2 in their possession. Thinking it through and with some covert hints from Zen he concluded that he would have to join forces with somebody who could offer a solution to both problems in one fell swoop.

Choice of partner was limited to Russia or the Federation or even the emerging Arab nations which, for the first time in their history, had decided to band together to pool the wealth of their oil reserves and to

226

protect the Arab world against the aggression of the Federation or Russia. As ever there were two factions: The enlightened Muslims and the Muslim fundamentalists. The two factions could find no common ground and had aligned themselves with the two main powerhouses of the Federation and Russia. He discounted Nuovostan because it had no credible military presence outside Nuovostan and very limited credibility within it.

He eliminated throwing his lot and his BAM2 unit in with either of the Muslim groups. History showed that they were unstable and likely to go off at a tangent and either became rabid enough to join forces with the Taliban or laid back enough to join in with the capitalist West where they were at a loss because of the basic cultural differences. The remaining two choices were not much, if any, better. The Federation was brutal and Russia was, as ever, totalitarian. On balance he decided that Russia would serve his purposes better; the Federation was cunning and Russia was dogmatically rigid – which gave him the benefit of being able to think faster than them.

A telephone call on the next day to Pelochev amused him. It had been his intention to inform her that he had decided for tactical reasons to join forces with the Russians and to work on the BAM2 unit with them. Before he could unfold his story to her she told him in detail of the meeting with President Lebedev and how they had reached agreement on experimentation and power sharing. Eleven told her that it was only possible for the RIR to work on the unit when the Island laboratories were on graveyard shift and that even then they had to be careful not to be seen doing so.

He proposed to her that the BAM2 unit should be sent to Nuovostan to be opened up by expert computer engineers who could work without looking over their shoulders. She thought quickly and said that instead she would arrange for it to be sent to Russia where expertise could be employed and, if need be, replaced. His agreement brought a smile to her face. She had a great opportunity to claim that she had persuaded Eleven to relinquish control to her and that she had decided to give Russia the opportunity to work on an actual unit as well as conducting their own separate experiments. They would have two bites of the cherry.

Thirty-nine

Tasked with uncovering all the other members of RIR under Eleven's leadership, Lawson set about using all means at his disposal to identify them. His aim was to move against them only when he had identified enough of them to render the organisation ineffective which meant identifying the leader who remained a mystery. Even with the help of his undercover agents the task was daunting; they had no means of measuring the numbers involved and for the moment there was no obvious way of getting the information.

The irrefutable information they had at their disposal was that Zen had been recruited by the RIR after his high profile court case. From the same undercover source they knew that he had been given the number 66 which, it was correctly assumed, indicated that he was the 6th member of group number 6. If they assumed that there were ten members per group and that he had been one of the last to be recruited, assuming that his group was the last group formed, it would indicate that there were 60 or so signed up members of RIR. Lawson was painfully aware that his reasoning was insubstantial and subjective; it could, of course, be that Zen had been fitted in to an unexpected vacancy in a mid-range group in which case there could be twice as many groups or that each group comprised 20 members which would double their original estimate. His random thoughts got him nowhere.

Carla Tanterelli was called in to the discussions to bring her psychological expertise to bear on the problem and to report on the findings of the medical alert which she had instigated to uncover the potential size of the membership of RIR. She could only report limited intelligence gathering from the medical alert inspections because the methods she was forced to employ was shared with the minimum of practitioners commensurate with security requirements. The number of people being dealt with in this way was significant and the limited resources she could employ were unable to meet a compressed time frame.

As a result she too had difficulty in establishing from the facts at their disposal how many RIR members there might be and suggested a review of the whole of the information that had been collected from all sources, some of which were of questionable provenance. After several hours of lateral thinking they were no nearer to finding a solution and they still didn't know whether they were dealing with a platoon or a regiment.

Eleven was looking out of his office window south across the docks where he could see Wave Walker the yacht on which Gilliland, Crook, Caine and Pettit had planned and implemented the building of the Island. The vessel was now a museum and the history of the Island was taught to young eager school children and older students by extoling the virtues of the founders' philanthropic aims. The words accompanying the tours promoted the good intentions of the Island and how it was hoped that at some stage in the future the benefits of BAM2 to the Islanders would, one day, be shared with the rest of the world.

Eleven shook his head as he considered the weak other-worldliness of the founders who had failed miserably to develop the influence of the technology for the benefit of all Islanders. They had stared opportunity in the face and ignored it. He would, once he had harnessed the technology, use it to better the lot of himself and his faithful followers - to an extent yet to be decided by him. From that position once he had assumed control of this small but immensely powerful empire, any benefit to the people of the Island would be coincidental to the power that he would wield throughout the world. He realised he was emulating what Wilson had tried and failed to achieve but comforted himself with the thought that he, unlike Wilson, was not a fool. The difference between himself and Wilson, he mused, was that whereas Wilson was weak and unfocussed, he was exactly the opposite which meant that he was bound to succeed where Wilson was bound to fail.

Eleven was joined in his office by Preece Cole, the RIR surgeon who was the only other person on the Island who knew the true identity of the head of RIR. His knowledge was based on the fact that he was the surgeon who had worked closely with Eleven in the early days before the formation of RIR on the corneal implant research techniques required by the Spy-Eye technology which had since been implemented. Cole had been astute enough to realise that this work was being carried out without the knowledge of the Ruling Council of which Eleven was a member. The relationship which blossomed from their interdependence meant that Eleven was beholden to Cole because he knew about Spy-Eye and Cole was beholden to Eleven because of Eleven's knowledge of Cole's illicit offshore bank accounts and his illegal activities in Paris. Offshore accounts for Islanders were strictly forbidden because the account could only be fed from the proceeds of the Island, which was money-free and therefore involved fraudulent misappropriation. Eleven's funding of this was a result of the income he still received from patents and royalties received in the USA which had been in place prior to settling on the Island and still continued to yield significant sums.

"You look as though you are planning something momentous," Cole broke into Eleven's reverie.

"Preece," Eleven looked indolently at the newcomer, "I'm just jumping ahead, in my thoughts, to our bright future. Have you given any more thought to how we can unlock the unit?" This was a matter they had discussed during their last exchange.

"I've tried," he lied, "but I have no contacts in that respect. If you want somebody immobilised or you want some restricted drugs I'm your man – but computers?" He shrugged and sighed.

"I thought you might say that so I'm also thinking about the next steps to progress." Eleven was hesitant; he was not comfortable talking about such important matters, even with a confidante like Cole because of his paranoia about being discovered. Cole may not know much about computer technology but he could be relied upon to be thoroughly unprincipled; just Eleven's kind of man.

"What steps might they be?" Cole said casually as he stood with his back to Eleven, staring out of the opposite window down into the well of the atrium. Before Eleven could answer Cole stiffened, he prided himself with an eidetic memory when it came to faces and was alarmed when he saw a total stranger striding from the Transfer Car station to the lifts. "Who is that?" He pointed a finger at the tall figure as he entered the lift.

Eleven turned and had a fleeting glance of the figure before the lift doors closed, he watched the figure ascend to the fourth floor where the lift stopped and the single occupant alighted and disappeared into the interior. He closed his eyes and concentrated. He opened his eyes and looked jubilant. "That, my friend," his eyes narrowed as he continued to search his mind, "is the same mystery visitor I saw briefly in Nuovostan during my meeting with Pelochev. He wasn't exactly introduced and I only saw him from the back when Pelochev left the room to talk to him, but I got the strong impression that it was our mystery friend 'A', the assassin. What could he possibly be doing here? I need to find out."

"Not yet." Cole restrained Eleven by placing a restraining hand on his shoulder. "He might recognise you from Nuovostan, in the same way that you recognise him, and that would not be good for you, or," he added quietly, "me. Let me see what I can do."

It was Eleven's turn to reciprocate. "The same might apply to you; I'll get somebody else to do some ferreting for us. If this man is 'A' he's an assassin. What could he be doing here; maybe he's here to finish off the job he started so unsuccessfully?" He picked up the telephone and keyed in a number from memory. "Number 61," he didn't bother to identify himself, "there's a visitor on his way to the fourth floor in Admin. I would like you to find out who he is and who he's seeing and what he's doing here and I mean right now. No excuses just do it and let me know." His instruction was clear and cold.

"Can we trust whoever that is you were speaking to?" Cole looked uncomfortable.

"Number 61 is a cell leader and completely reliable. He doesn't have a lot of intelligence but he has cunning and is loyal for as long as it suits him. I make sure that it suits him in all kinds of ways, I can see that his weaknesses are pandered to."

Number 61 reported back very quickly after visiting the suite where the unexpected visitor was closeted in with the founders. He had been unable to ascertain the name of the visitor but had been able to elicit that he was visiting from the American government with which the founders were in negotiations about secretive trade deals.

Eleven instructed Cole to intercept the visitor with a view to finding out as much as he could about who he was and what he was doing. On reflection Eleven's view that Cole could compromise their anonymity was swept aside as being unlikely because it was as dangerous for the assassin to be exposed as it was for RIR and that they should make use of the stalemate to gather what information they could.

Positioning himself outside the administration area Cole waited patiently for the mysterious visitor to reappear. After an hour, the statutory time limit for meetings on the Island, the visitor appeared and headed towards where Cole was standing, on his way to the TC station. 'A' looked suddenly uneasy when he realised that somebody was waiting for him. He froze and looked at Cole with trepidation.

"It's OK, I mean you no harm but we should talk. I think you should meet one of my colleagues. He has some questions for you." Cole looked around furtively to make sure they were not being observed. "So, who are you?" Cole said when they were in a secure location out of the way of prying eyes.

"You know damned well who I am." 'A' hissed through clenched teeth. "And I know who you are; you are part of the RIR and Wilson just like I am but for different reasons." It was a shot in the dark which was rewarded by the reaction of the man to whom he was speaking.

"One important question for you; why did you stage the assassinations that way, what was the point?" Cole guessed correctly that 'A', and he was now sure that's who he was, thought that Cole was Eleven.

"I didn't stage the assassinations any way at all. As far as I was concerned I did what I was paid to do, I set up the victims using RIR for Gilliland and another organisation for Creswell. I agreed the set ups with both organisations and used the guns provided by Wilson. I did my bit. Why it happened the way it did is of no importance for me, I did it, got paid and that is that."

"Aren't you at least curious about what happened, I mean like – how did someone get Gilliland and Creswell to co-operate in the scam? They must have been in on it."

"Don't know, don't care, I'm done with that."

"So what are you doing here on the Island?"

"That's need to know and you don't need to know. I'm on a new job."

"Doesn't anybody here know about you, apart from me and my boss?"

"Your boss?" He looked puzzled. "You mean you're not Eleven?"

"Correct, I'm not Eleven, but I know a man who is." Cole smiled at his own quip.

"In answer to your question; no nobody here knows about me and if you have any fancy ideas about the situation I suggest you forget them. In my profession I can't afford to leave any live loose ends? If you get my drift?"

"I get your drift, OK, and your secrets are safe with me – we would be wise to keep each-others interests at heart. Do you get my drift?" He countered grimly.

"Best if we part then and never speak again. That will be the safest way."

"Not quite," Cole gave him a penetrating look, "there is one thing that you could do which will help us both."

"Really, and what might that be?" He looked sceptical.

"It's something which is very simple and it will earn you a lot of money, with little or no effort. You seem to be able to come and go to the Island at will with or without RIR assistance, is that so?"

"I have my ways but you should know about that; your boss has arranged for me to get in and out. My current sponsor is part of the government of the good old US of A so I guess you could say that I have alternatives that give me the option of coming and going just about at will."

"How come an assassin has the ear of the USA administration?"

"I am a facilitator for corporations and governments. My input is usually commercial but sometimes I have to enforce the will of my clients by resorting to more physical tactics. Resorting to the physical forms only a small part of my professional life and what you have seen on video are two remote examples of this."

"As I said I have a simple but very rewarding task for you which will not require the more extreme of your talents. Are you interested?"

"Probably not but go ahead if you must."

"I have something that needs to be removed from the Island without anybody knowing about it. It's small and weighs just a few Kilograms and it needs to be spirited away to a part of the world where you have done business before and it will be cash on delivery."

"On whose behalf is the delivery being made?"

"That's not important to you for the moment but if you do this your secret will remain safe with us."

After a few moments of thought 'A' sighed heavily. "OK on the understanding that after this we have nothing to do with each other ever again, I'll do it."

"Consider the deal to be sealed."

Cole made his way back to Eleven at breakneck speed the news he had to impart, he knew, would meet with grateful approval. "Great news," he said as he burst into the office, "I've got a way of getting the BAM2 unit off the Island without any problems."

"How so," Eleven looked intrigued, "there is a big security lockdown, the Ruling Council don't know yet but I believe that somebody has discovered that a unit is missing and they're stopping everything going in and out of the Island."

"Could be but I've had a word with 'A', it was him we saw going into the Council chambers. He's here as a representative of an American government agency and he has free passage on and off the Island. I told him that we would protect his identity if he takes the unit off the Island and delivers it COD."

"Can we trust him?"

"He's a hired mercenary and he was tempted by big money which would only be paid when we receive confirmation that the unit has reached its destination, he has to trust us because we know who he is and what he's done."

"Don't forget he reneged on two assassinations."

"No, he explained that to me he did his job; the treachery lies somewhere else in the chain of events."

"What are you suggesting he does?"

"I suggest we seal up the unit and get him to put it in his diplomatic luggage. He can take it to Wilson or whoever else you please and they can keep it safe for us. It's disabled so nobody can get at it without the control software which only we will have. Once we get the BAM and its software together with top experts we can crack the codes at leisure."

""Great idea," Eleven's eyes gleamed, "when's he leaving the Island?"

"I don't know exactly but there are no aircraft due in here until tomorrow so he can't leave until then at the earliest."

"I'll get Brogan to take it from the lab and we'll deliver it to 'A' before he leaves. I'll make the necessary arrangements," Eleven gloated. Once more it was all falling into place; with the unit off the Island and the control software in his possession in a compressed memory drive he could develop his objectives at leisure. His desire for the ultimate acquisition of power had taken another huge leap forward.

Forty

Beverley Olsen sat demurely across the desk from Jon Webber; her dislike of the man was instant. He had no regard for personal hygiene and no dress sense and in the confines of his small office the lack of hygiene grossly offended her olfactory senses. Under normal circumstances she would have made her excuses and declined to take the job; but these were not normal circumstances.

Jon Webber ran his fore finger and thumb across the bristles of his chin stubble; they could both hear the audible rasp. He looked at the young woman under lowered eyelids and took in and enjoyed the contours she showed in her one piece Reco-fashion body garment. His thoughts were less on the job she was there to be interviewed for and more on the development of a personal relationship. Initially he had resisted employing her because she had been recommended, rather than being chosen by him but his mind was changed as soon as he saw her.

"Do you have a boyfriend?" He asked bluntly.

Her response to the unexpected question flustered her. She quickly composed herself. "Not anybody special, but why do you ask?"

"I ask you this because of the job," he lied blatantly. "It will be very demanding and can lead to long hours of work at odd times." He once more observed her from lowered eyelids. Despite her Scandinavian name she was obviously English born and bred; with rapidity he temporarily suspended his pathological hatred of the English and all they stood for. With a Scandinavian name she was clearly new to Englishness, he rationalised, and he would not hold it against her. "I

239

think you'll do this job very well. You can start immediately." He stood up and terminated the meeting without giving her a chance to respond. "Your office is through there until I can get a better unit where we can share the same office."

Unabashed by the dismissive arrogance he showed, she headed towards the door he indicated and said over her shoulder, "I've got friends in administration who can probably find us better accommodation; do you want me to contact them?"

His response was an immediate, "yes," and in his imagination he was already forming a relationship with her which could not in any way be construed as professional.

Her contacts came through with a suitable office space which was part of the administration block. Webber was delighted and surprised at the speed with which she had achieved the first of what he hoped would be many objectives. There was little to move from their old location; PRICE, the Progressive Recovery Island Change & Evolution union, was still only formed in Eleven's mind. Such rapid progress had not been expected but was very welcome. He advised Eleven of the progress which had been made and Eleven congratulated himself on identifying the right person to fulfil the post of Secretary to the union as the acceptable face of an unacceptable philosophy.

Olsen set about acquiring furniture and office equipment which was moved in immediately and within one day they had opened up the PRICE office and equipped it. Webber sat in his new office behind a large desk which fed his self-aggrandisement and looked with anticipation at Olsen who shared his office and was directly in his view from where he sat. Over her shoulder was a view to the south where he could see the Wave Walker museum and beyond it the sparkling silver and blue green of the Atlantic Ocean.

Without delay Webber set up files and information systems for two disparate groups of members that the Union would sponsor. One group he called the 'citizens action group', the other he called the 'citizens activist group'. Unlike trade unions all over the rest of the world there would be no subscriptions and the union would have no assets; one of the features of a cashless society. The only investment that members would have to make would be a donation of time to carry out union policies.

Olsen was given the task of arranging the 'citizen's action group'. The sister group was to be administered solely by Webber and the records for this group would be held separately and securely by Webber. Olsen set about contacting those who were recommended as prime members of the action group. Interest from this group was immediate and a core of members were called to an inaugural meeting at which it was intended to set up the aims and agenda of the organisation. A nucleus of members soon formed and the constitution was outlined for discussion.

The members determined that the aims of the union should be stated in the simplest of terms and made available to all RIRs, Recovery Island Residents over the age of eighteen – which Webber thought to be a clever twist because it also stood for Recovery Island Rebels. Agreement was reached concerning their statement of intent: *PRICE is a collection of citizens who will give voice to ensure the momentum of the Island's development is not inhibited by unnecessary restrictions which impede progress. PRICE will work together with the Ruling Council to ensure that the interests of the Island's population as a whole are served faithfully and effectively for the good of all.*

Webber read the statement, which had been given to him by Olsen, and smiled to himself. His separate group was the antithesis of hers; its sole purpose was to destabilise the Island's population and make preparation for the RI Rebel takeover. Unlike her he did not rush into setting up his group; he would allow the benign setting up of the public face of PRICE while he worked at leisure, with his different radical agenda. The activist group would not have a written avowal, it would be too restrictive; what Eleven wanted was a dedicated group of dissidents who would change what needed to be changed whenever it needed to be changed. From the security perspective it would be better for them to resist putting anything in writing.

PRICE's statement of intent was sent to all citizens of the Island, including the Ruling council members as well as the Founders. The responses were in excess of their wildest hopes; hundreds of citizens expressed an interest in the sentiments that the document outlined but felt that it did not go far enough. There were of course dissenting voices who suggested that the aims of the union were counter to the interests of the Island as a whole and that moves should be made to nip the union in the bud before it could do irreparable harm to their society. Such is the way of the world: Inexorably to every action there is an equal and opposite reaction.

Eleven observed the action and reaction with satisfaction. He had never even considered for a moment that there would be any objection to the formation of the union; not only did he now have a core of people spreading dissent at every opportunity but his enemies, those who would never support his ideas of trades unionism, were also spreading discontent by making his moderate supporters stand up and be counted. Everything was continuing to fall into place;

his aims were ever closer to fruition and he was leading a charmed existence.

* * *

At the same time as Eleven was plotting to undermine the fabric of Island society DK Valerie was moving a step closer to healing the rift with the outside world. Rupert Pelham was on another foreign trade mission, this time to Australia and would be out of the country for a week as part of the PM's team. DK had persuaded Caroline Pelham to accompany him on a covert trip to the Island. His hope was that when she saw how the Islanders conducted themselves she would be more amenable to his cause.

Caroline Pelham was impressed by the courtesy she was shown during the flight to the Island and by the easy going manner of the air crew. She was even more impressed when they arrived by the efficiency with which they were shepherded through customs and immigration departments and by how they were transported to the administration block by Transfer Car. Being a woman of high fashion she was somewhat taken aback by the Island's fashion statement; although she had a figure that would be complemented by the clinging one piece garments favoured by all the islanders she was not convinced that DK would cut other than a figure of ridicule if he were to adopt the fashion.

She was introduced to the founders whom she noticed were on close terms with DK. Having met them it was suggested to her that while the meeting with DK was in progress she might like to have a tour of the Island in the company of Juilietta Gray. Caroline shook hands with the strikingly attractive Gray who was as tall as she and shared in her aristocratic bearing.

"I'm in your hands Miss Gray." She inclined her head towards her tour guide.

"Miss Gray? How quaint," she gave a tinkling laugh. "I haven't been called that for longer than I care to think. I'm Juilietta, but please don't shorten it."

"And I'm Caroline and likewise, please don't shorten it."

They both laughed, promoting an instant bonding.

Two days later Caroline and DK took the return flight from the Island on board the Apache Chieftain, once more enjoying the comfort and luxury of the flight and the close attention they received.

"I must confess that I am totally converted to your way of thinking by this visit," Caroline said after they had settled down into the routine of the flight. "I found them all to be completely open and charming and despite my original expectation of being shown around only those places that they wanted me to see, I was given absolutely free reign to visit whatever and wherever I wanted. Juilietta and her partner Silas were model hosts to me when I was alone with them and to you and I when we were together. I saw how the people live and I was left alone to talk to them without inhibition. Without exception I was shown courtesy and understanding when I displayed quite clearly that I did not understand how their society works. They were hungry to know how the rest of the world works and I did my best to enlighten them. Their responses to my words were polite but I could see that the younger members of the society who were Island-born found my answers beyond understanding; they could not grasp the thought of working for money rather than out of civic responsibility. They could not understand the negative friction of having a transient government which was permanently at odds with the opposition when it was the government that the people had elected and not the opposition. Taxation for efforts made were also beyond their understanding. I tried to explain to them the concept of free enterprise; they looked at me as if I were mentally defective. They could not grasp the logic of the profit motive; all of those I talked to could not understand how everybody could make a profit – for somebody to make a profit somebody else has to make a loss, in their minds there is no equanimity in this. Likewise they could not comprehend the reasoning behind democracy in which the few could outvote the many" She looked at DK with the dawning of concern. "I didn't know how to respond to their not understanding our way of thinking."

"Depends on who you think is right, us with our decaying democracy which is heading for anarchy where the few do rule the many, or with them and their society which relies on the commitment of the individual to the common good. Are they being ingenuous or are we are being cynical? My heart and my head are in conflict over this but one thing is obvious – they have no doubts about which way is right and that is exactly why I want to let the world know about their aspirations and the reasons why their wishes are being resisted."

***

The citizen's activist group - CAG, in secret session, expressed views diametrically opposed to the impressions that Caroline Pelham had formed and discussed with DK during her brief Island visit. The meeting was chaired by Jon Webber and the hard core of twelve carefully selected members did not expect him to pull any punches and he met entirely with their expectations. It was Webber's intention to set precedents at this first meeting which he did with a mixture of blasphemy beer and sandwiches, by the time he opened the meeting the assembled chosen ones had filled the room with pungent cigarette smoke. They occupied four tables to which they had been guided on arrival and they occupied three of the four chairs provided.

"Okay brothers," Webber paused and squinted at his audience, "and sisters," he added as a staged afterthought. "We all know why we're here so let's get right down to it. We all agree that the toffs are running the Island for their own benefit and are they're of touch with reality; it's up to us to do something about it and get some kudos from the technology that they are keeping to themselves. If you don't think so then now is the time to leave before we get down to any details."

Webber looked around the room with a scowl on his face and paused to hear any response. There was no response, as he had expected – his audience had been very carefully selected for their freely admitted extreme views. "This is the only time I expect to hear silence from you, from now on in you make a contribution to our plans. Now that you're in with us there's no getting out, you're with us for life and I'm sure you don't need me to say what will happen to anybody who doesn't toe the line." He stared at the assembled dissidents who returned his stare in silence. He snorted loudly and cupped his ear towards the audience willing them to respond. The more quick witted among them cottoned on to his earlier mention of not being silent and responded to him with, 'I'm in and me too." The slower among them took longer but as realisation dawned they joined in in the chorus of support.

"We've got a big job to do but we have to be careful; to make this technology work for us we have to shake them out of their stupidity and get them to see the

246

sense of using the power of the technology for the good of our citizens. I've broken you into four groups of three. The first group will deal with transport, the second with the supply chain, the third with communications and the last with civil disorder.

He visited each table in turn and outlined the tasks that they were expected to undertake. He stressed that the groups were to decide on their own hierarchy and that once they had done this they were required to work seamlessly together to achieve their objectives.

Forty-one

Dreams of unbridled success washed over Eleven as he reviewed the remarkable progress that had been made in just a matter of days. His dreams of success were no longer on a distant horizon they were here and now and he could almost taste the spoils of victory. Not only was he able to enjoy his brilliantly engineered success, he now had a companion whom he could trust and with whom he could share the fruits of his labour. Until now Preece Cole had been a companion of sorts but his position had been usurped by Zen who was much more of a kindred spirit. The feeling of liberation his newfound protégé gave him was tangible. Their relationship would of course be on his terms; he still intended to retain his anonymity by ensuring their discussions were via telephone rather than face to face but an exchange of secured telephone conversations would enable him to use Zen as a sounding board for some of his more fringe ideas.

The unknowing, simple elegance of the solution offered by Cole for getting the BAM2 unit off the Island was immediately adopted by Eleven as his own and it solved the dilemma of handing over the unit to an unknown courier. The idea was that releasing the BAM2 unit into the care 'A' was not as dangerous an option as it first appeared, they would retain absolute ownership of the control systems by withholding an essential control component without which the unit could not be operated. Without the component the unit was just a collection of worthless junk.

They agreed on a course of action which allowed them to smuggle the unit off the Island with 'A' who had what was the equivalent of diplomatic immunity. He would take it to Wilson who was a guest of the Russian President. This very act would ensure the cooperation of both the Russians and the Nuovostanis as long as they were told that the control system was in the hands of RIR and would be released when a formal understanding had been agreed.

With stunning rapidity the arrangements were made. The unit was retrieved from the physics lab and passed to 'A'. He wrapped it in gift paper and added a happy birthday label and secured it in his hand luggage. There was a moment of uncomfortable hesitation when after a quick visual inspection, his hand luggage was put through an x-ray scanner but any chance of discovery was eliminated by the use of a diversionary tactic. As the first piece of luggage passed through the scanner 'A' nudged a second piece so that it fell off the conveyor onto the floor with a loud crash of broken glass. The scanner operator jumped off his stool in an attempt to avoid being splashed by the alcoholic beverages which seeped across the floor. An innocent looking cleaner emptying waste bins in the departure area observed the ruse that 'A' had used to distract the luggage checker and spoke briefly using his telephone, Eleven received the report with great satisfaction. The tide of good fortune was still running strongly with him.

The trip taken by 'A' was uneventful and boring but he didn't know much about it as he slept all the way from Recovery to Paris in the comfort of the Apache Chieftain and for most of the flight to Colorado via Chicago. It was important that if he was being observed by any of the many groups who were interested in him that they should observe that he returned to the USA.

Once there he collected his beloved Jeep Cherokee from its long term parking and took the Interstate from

Denver Airport to his home in Silverton, Colorado. As he drove along the strip road leading to his property he pressed the remote control and the double garage doors rolled open. The noise alerted Hink, his hound and he bounded out through his special door from the wet room which was his usual home. At a shouted command from 'A', Hink sat down away from the path of the jeep and waited, tail wagging which from his sitting position formed a one winged dust angel, he waited impatiently for his master to free him from the command.

As soon as the car was parked and 'A' left the garage, Hink bounded over to him and after a few ecstatic circuits made to wobble through the motion of his tail he stood up on his hind legs and placed his forepaws on 'A's' shoulders and stared intently into his eyes.

"Down Hink, down boy," 'A' said laughing at the dog's exuberance as he tried to avoid the excited face licks.

Hink reluctantly subsided and once more circled his master making high pitched whimpers of welcome. He rushed back through the dog door and reappeared moments later carrying a rubber bone which he dropped at 'A's' feet and danced back in an invitation to play. 'A' threw the bone and walked back into the garage closing the door behind him. He retrieved his meagre luggage from the Jeep and entered the house through an internal connecting door.

A few hours later a shadowy figure hidden in a stand of fir trees a quarter of a mile from the A frame, watched through binoculars as Hink sat and watched the Jeep drive slowly away down the strip road onto the Highway which led to the Interstate. He threw the binoculars onto the passenger seat of his car and waited for the other car to pass him so that he could identify the driver, before following him on his way to the Interstate. He had failed to notice that Hink had not displayed any distress at the departure of his master, but then the watcher was not a dog owner, so why would he?

***

From the upper storey of the house 'A' watched himself drive away. The apparent 'himself' he had watched leave in his car was actually his identical twin brother with whom he had swapped clothes. These were the precautions of a meticulous man rather than one who was paranoid. If he were being watched he wanted to make sure that the watcher was thrown off the scent. He smiled grimly to himself when he observed that the car being driven by his identical twin brother acquired a tail shortly after he had passed the stand of fir trees that marked the boundary of his property.

He waited for a further thirty minutes continuing to watch the property for other signs of movement, there were none. With a sigh of relief he left the window and descended into the first floor great room in which a log fire in its stone hearth crackled and popped as the wood dried and was consumed by flames. The strain of what he did was beginning to wear him down as the life he was leading was full of tension and danger. He was mixing with powerful and dangerous people whom he realised could carry out the threats they insinuated and they could remain unscathed.

Outside the gloom descended and the temperature began to plummet at a greater speed than the setting sun. The fire, before which he now sat, was soporific and he allowed himself the luxury of gentle descent into slumber as if he were innocent of fault. The dog flap which led into the mud room from the yard creaked as Hink pushed his way through it by butting it with his lowered head. He padded through the mud room and reared up on his hind legs to depress the handle of the door leading from the mud room into the warmth of the kitchen. Passing through the kitchen he moved silently save for the clicking of his claws on the polished hardwood floor and entered the great room where he walked slowly towards his master who was peacefully at rest; with a deep grunt and a noisy yawn he settled himself at his masters feet and joined him in contented sleep. This moment of welcome rest was a prelude to the next round of separation which would leave Hink at home and see his master disappear once more to wherever it was he went.

Forty-two

The newly released Jaguar XX-17C stood gleaming expensively in one of the Island's dockside warehouses. In any location it would have created a stir being as it was one of the most sought after cars in the world. On Recovery Island it was a sensation. Except in the immediate dock area, in which the use of freight transporters were used for unloading goods from incoming vessels or aircraft, no surface vehicles were permitted on the Island so there was a clamour to see a real live road vehicle in the flesh rather than via the information portal. For the adult founding citizens the sight of the vehicle was nostalgic, for those generations born on the Island it was a completely new experience.

Ed Pickering watched the excited hoards parading past the vehicle and touching it with awe and reverence. He joined the group of admirers who were seeing the wonder of this engineering masterpiece for the first time; its sleek lines and solid construction gave this greyhound of a vehicle a special almost mystical presence. He had set up a design office in the warehouse in which the Jaguar was housed and began to outline the tailoring of the vehicle to provide it and its occupants with security when it was used in areas which were potentially hostile to Islanders.

At the prompting of Silas Pettit, the first task of Pickering and his design team was to fit a BAM2 projector in the centre of the vehicle which would cast a shaped protective shield over the car to a point marginally above the road surface on which it would ride. The aim was to give protection while not being peripherally hazardous to the environment in which it was being used. It was considered, for example, that the application of the shield when the car was moving should be selective rather than automatic. In the event of a road accident, which under normal conditions would simply mean that there would be body damage, automatic application of the defence dome would mean that the other vehicle would be turned into the dust of unglued atoms. This and other practical constraints needed careful consideration before the modified vehicle could be unleashed on the roads of the rest of the world. A trickier problem was to ensure the safety of the car's occupants even when the BAM unit was switched off for peripheral safety reasons. This was the requirement which exercised the minds of Pickering and his design team, as usual it was Pickering who came up with a solution outside the box.

There were further requirement if the vehicle was to be used in locations that were hostile to it and its passengers and it related to how they could protect against the privations of running out of fuel while navigating in a hostile environment. Pickering exercised his mind and came up yet again with a typically Pickering solution; clearly using the usual fuel for automobile propulsion be it petroleum, gas or even solar left them open to dangerous exposure. He turned once more to BAM technology and used its unique capabilities to provide endless fuel from the environment. In essence the engine was converted to run on a BAM generated gas mixture. Fresh air would be sucked in through ports in the defensive shield and the air would be processed through a customised min-BAM which would break the air down into its atomic components. The combustible elements of Hydrogen in the main and other volatile components would be assembled into an explosive mixture which would ignite when injected into the engine. The fuel that this would produce would be burned off and the other unused gasses would be expelled through the integrated exhaust system.

A final constraint on the suitability of the modified vehicle was the road testing so that flaws could be identified and adjustments made. Apart from the Island's perimeter road and the airport runways there were no other surfaces suitable for the testing of the vehicle. It was decided that the most convenient place to carry out road testing was on the Azores island of Flores where Gilliland as a legacy from earlier times, owned a beach-side property with a significant parcel of open land and Caine still had the support of the local community. Arrangements were made and permissions granted by the Islands administration for the road trials to be carried out.

Neither of the Islands fleet of two aircraft was suitable to carry the modified Jaguar so it was necessary for them to hire an air freighter for the transfer to Flores. A small sub-committee of the Ruling Council were appointed to arrange and observe. This was done in open committee but was not announced generally to the Islanders.

Eleven was not part of the sub-committee responsible for the implementation of the Jaguar project but he made sure that he was kept informed about the progress and detail of the programme of testing. He saw this as a means of impairing the experiment which would be an additional tool to his aim of the destabilisation of the Ruling Council's ability to administer the welfare of the Island population. When he learned that Ed Pickering was to carry out the testing in the Azores he was at first disappointed; he had been hoping that, if not one of the founders, at least Silas Pettit would be given the task. His interest in who would be accompanying the vehicle to its testing

255

ground was because it was away from the constraints of Island security and would present an opportunity to make up for the failed assassination attempts. Pickering was not a first choice but he was senior enough to create a high degree of despondency if assassinated.

At first Eleven was considering giving the task to 'A' but on reflection he was not entirely convinced that 'A's' excuse for the failure of the two attempted assassinations being somebody else's fault was entirely legitimate. He decided that he would give one of his RIR members an opportunity to make a name for himself. The natural choice would be Zen who had proven himself to be capable but he also wanted to divorce the assassination from any connection with the Island and reduce the possibility of discovery. After consideration he elected to enlist the aid of Jack Pain whose connection with the Island was now completely severed and should he be found out would not be traced back to RIR.

The route used to muddy the trail was instigated by a secured telephone call from Eleven to Pelochev who was bribed to contact Julie Hammond who in turn, for a fee, appointed Jack Pain as the hired gun. The same model 4S, sub sonic snipers special, which had been used in the failed assassination attempts was to be used, but this time with laser guidance inculcated bullets which were checked to ensure that they were the real deal and capable of a kill.

Delivery of the weapon to the Azores was facilitated through an RIR member who was slotted into the test team by Eleven in his capacity of Council member. Dismantled, the rifle components were scattered among the various mechanical parts which accompanied the team of mechanics and engineers. Once delivered the parts of the 4S were retrieved and reassembled by the RIR mechanic and passed on to Pain who had flown to the Azores via Portugal. The same RIR mechanic worked closely with a CAG, civil activist group, member of PRICE, the Progressive Recovery Island Change & Evolution union, he was responsible for the first of the really big disruptive and dramatic actions to be undertaken. This involved smuggling Jack Pain onto the Island and providing him with a newly modified 5S rifle with dot-guided bullets.

Most of the test team were away from the Island for the first time and keeping them focussed was a full time job for Pickering. This distraction made the task of assembling the 5S and delivering it to Pain all the more straight forward and it was accomplished without any hitches. Pain was by no means a marksman but that was not a disadvantage because of the nature of the rifle and the advanced technology of the laser guided bullet. All the rifleman had to do was acquire the target with the powerful electronically magnified scope and ensure that the red cross was projected onto the target and to make sure that after the shot was made the cross was kept on the target for the fraction of time it would take the bullet to reach its intended target. The tiny micro-processor in the tip of the bullet would ensure that the bullet found its mark even if the target was moving erratically.

Testing took place over a two day period and Pain, who was situated a mile from the testing grounds, lay prone patiently waiting for the right moment to make the kill shot. He had been told to acquire the most senior target and to take his time and make sure that the acquired target was not just a mechanic or engineer. He was given photographs of all senior personnel who might be involved and this included the attendance of at least two of the four founders who were expected to visit briefly. He glanced at the photographs and threw them aside; the faces portrayed were all familiar to him.

Patience was not normally a virtue he possessed but he was on a promise from Hammond. If he were to succeed she had made a full and binding promise to him that he would get from her the thing he most desired. It had been a great disappointment to him when she told him after their first meeting on the Island all that time ago that he had possessed her but had been too drunk to remember the event. On that occasion he had been drunk but actually his memory had not been at fault, by adopting devious means she had planted evidence of a night of debauchery which had not actually taken place. The promise gave him the strength to be patient and he luxuriated in the thought as he lay prone in a protective dip in the hillside and felt the warm sun on his back.

He began to feel uncomfortable when on the afternoon of the second and final day of the tests he had not been able to acquire a target of the seniority required by Eleven. The mechanics and engineers were packing their equipment into cases and crates ready for the return journey to Recovery Island. Last minute detailed tests were being carried out on the sleek silver vehicle which glowed with a luminosity that was highlighted in the gloom cast by the lowering sky. The image in his scope became suddenly clear and he saw a woman open up the car door and slide easily into the driver's seat.

He adjusted the magnification and increased it so that he could see details of her head and the fine sheen of her dark hair which was tied back into a pony tail. He switched on the dot light and saw a sharp red cross with a dot in its centre appear in the midpoint of her right temple. Recognition by him of who she was, was immediate. He could see from the number of people in close proximity who were opening and closing the rear doors to adjust the monitoring equipment, that if a

BAM shield was fitted to the vehicle it was currently inactive. He did not touch the trigger until after the faint whine of the servo motors which ensured that the trajectory of the bullet started off straight and true until dot guidance was taken over by the miniscule chip in its nose. In the fraction of a second that the bullet took from muzzle to target he held the red cross steady on her temple, even when she leaned forward to activate the engine ignition. As if in slow motion he saw the passenger side window shatter at almost the same instant her head whipped sideways as the bullet struck her in the centre of the temple.

Mayhem reigned; there were test engineers and onlookers who all converged on the vehicle in a sudden panic. One of the mechanics, the one who had assembled the rifle, looked through the driver's side window and spoke into his telephone. "Pain did it number Eleven, he actually did it, right through the temple – I can see the bullet hole in the passenger side window and I can see the wound where the bullet hit her right in the middle of the temple." He listened intently and then ended the call as he walked rapidly away putting as much distance between him and the murder scene as he could.

Eleven smirked in response to his triumph. He had shown the so called professionals how to do it. He didn't leave things to chance, being the consummate professional he had covered all angles. He had, at last, eliminated one of the founders; his plans were now firmly anchored. Success was within his grasp.

Forty-three

'A' was weary; he was flying again. In the last month he would have earned a lifetime of air miles but for the fact that most of his flights were private using difficult to trace aircraft from little known and virtually unregulated airfields. He had successfully been able to engineer flights for which there were no paper trails but he still maintained a vigilant watch to ensure as best he could that his movements were undetected. His anonymity was paramount. The rewards for his work were huge but with it went the constant strain of covering his tracks and serving more than one master. After his current journey he could foresee two more marathons and then a long period of recuperation which he intended would be as far away from an airport as he could manage.

He arrived at Moscow airport dishevelled and irritable. The surly Russian officials rubbed him up the wrong way and added to his discomfort. They inspected his cabin and hand luggage thoroughly and looked with suspicion at the six inch cube wrapped in gift paper, indicating in grunts that he should open it. He snatched the package from the customs officer who immediately drew his side arm and waved it inexpertly, therefore dangerously, in 'A's' direction.

"Hold on buddy," he shouted at the customs officer while removing a document from his breast pocket. "Take a look at this."

The officer took the document, still waving his gun indiscriminately, and glanced at it suspiciously. When he saw the seal of the President of New Russia he placed his gun on the counter and scrutinised the document more closely. Showing it to his companion he launched into a diatribe in Russian which 'A' could understand clearly without being able to speak a word of the language. Picking up a telephone the second officer spoke rapidly into it and receiving instructions looked at 'A'. "Waiting," he said with a thick accent which changed the word to an almost undecipherable 'Wyatying'.

After a few minutes a third officer appeared on the scene and as evidenced by the embellishments on his uniform was senior to the other two. He took the document which was proffered by his colleague and scrutinised it in absolute detail including, unaccountably, holding it up to the light.

"Passport," he beckoned with all four fingers closed together, his thumb sticking out sideways. He grunted while he looked at the passport which 'A' passed to him. "OK," The fake passport was returned, "all in order Mr Simmonds. You may go." He returned the letter from the President. He was free and clear, the BAM2 unit was in Russia and very soon he would be delivering it to Wilson in the Kremlin and would receive in return a large bundle of US Dollars.

For 'A' there was no military escort to the Kremlin. His mode of transport was more prosaic; the taxi had seen better days and the chain smoking taxi driver did nothing to improve the quality of the ride. He wondered just how he was going to get into the Kremlin to hand the BAM2 unit over and collect his reward.

His anticipation of the difficulties proved to be unfounded when the taxi driver delivered him to an out of the way entrance into the Kremlin the location of which the taxi driver had been pre-advised. They were met at the entrance by Irena Pelochev who summarily dismissed the driver with a hand full of paper money.

"You are having goods?" Was the focus of her greeting to 'A'.

"In here," he held up his small cabin luggage.

"Bringing in," She led him into the interior.

The expectation when he entered the room occupied by the two Presidents was palpable. Wilson looked dreadful, his features were bloated and the florid hue of his face foretold of recent quantities of vodka. President Lebedev was quite the opposite; his lean features were smooth and belied his age. His pale blue eyes glittered brightly but could not fully hide the animal intensity beneath.

"The unit," the President said tersely, holding out his hand.

"My instructions are to deliver the unit personally to President Wilson." He extracted the brightly wrapped parcel and deposited it in front of Wilson.

"President Wilson ails, he is in no condition to receive anything." Lebedev shrugged his shoulders and reached out for the parcel.

"One moment Mr President," 'A' placed his hand on top of the brightly wrapped box and moved it away from Lebedev. "I deliver this in exchange for payment from President Wilson."

Lebedev looked petulant and rattled off a tirade of Russian at Pelochev while gesticulating wildly at 'A'. She listened attentively, responded to the President in Russian and turned her gaze to 'A'

"President is saying you are capitalist hooligan and is considering to have you to be arrest. I say him that you are doing job and must collect reward for the working."

"Just give me the money and I'll be out of here."

"Not to be considered for President Lebedev, we leaving here and I am getting moneys for you." She spoke to the President again and deferentially backed out of the room tugging on 'A's' sleeve in an entreaty for him to comply with her wishes. Even before they left the room Lebedev was stripping the wrapping paper from the cube.

"Should not to challenge President Lebedev; he is most powerful person in Russia and maybe world." She said this knowing it not to be true but aware that walls had ears she felt that it was wise to show obedience. "We have drink for celebrations. This is big day we have BAM unit and soon will be able to work it. Then we can do many things."

"Just give me the cash and I'll be gone."

"Cash yes, gone no. No more flying until unit works. We go and wash and eat and drink and have some fun."

"Whoa," he grabbed her shoulder. "What do you mean no more flying until unit works," he squeezed hard and made her flinch.

"Once unit is work you can go, until that you stay with me." Her smile was truly evil.

"That's not the way it works," he said grimly. "I'm just the courier; it's nothing to do with me I don't even know what it is, let alone how it works and anyway Eleven has the control software and without that you can't make it work."

"Is what Eleven thinks, but Russia has world best computer understanders. With these can fix unit for working."

"Come hell or high water I'm out of here tomorrow – with or without anybody's approval. Come on let's have that drink and some chow and you can tell me how I can get away from here."

'Getting away from here' was not high on her agenda; she wanted to talk to him about the partnership she had dreamt up for them so that she could start again with a new protector. Clearly Wilson was finished. They had a night of Vodka and heavy Russian food and from his perspective not enough sleep. She told him of her dreams and fantasised about the life they could live together when she inherited the Presidency of Nuovostan from her 'husband' and the wealth of the nation became hers – and, she hinted, *theirs*.

On the following day 'A' made contact with Eleven and threatened him with all kinds of retribution if he didn't talk to whoever was necessary to get him out of Russia. The only way to do that was to make the control system available to the Russians and then he would be free to go and Eleven would be free of the likelihood of assassination by Lebedev's minions.

Eleven was not about to relinquish his bargaining chip and made it clear that he would need assurances from the Russians that he would be kept in the loop. In fact what he wanted was to become part of the Russian/Nuovostan alliance so that they could rule in joint harmony. From what 'A' had seen so far there was little if any likelihood of that intention ever reaching fruition.

Pelochev had further discussions with Lebedev and told him of Eleven's conditions. Lebedev just laughed at the request but there was no warmth of humour in his response. There seemed to be impasse, Eleven was adamant, Wilson was incapable and 'A' was stuck in the middle. The only bargaining that 'A' could do was by using the aspirations of Irena Pelochev to persuade her to prevail on Lebedev to let him leave Russia.

Forty-four

There was mayhem around the right side of the Jaguar XX-17C, the driver's window had a star shaped hole which had been punched through the supposedly resistant glass by the depleted uranium bullet. Caine lay on her side with her left shoulder and torso on the front passenger seat; there was an angry red wound where the bullet had struck but there were some things which were not, to Pettit's reckoning, as they should be.

He opened the passenger's side door and felt for a wrist pulse just as the paramedics arrived in their emergency vehicle. Without any delay, at Pettit's instruction, her body was placed on a stretcher and bundled into the emergency vehicle which was closed up and driven away in haste.

Pain observed and recorded the unfolding scene on the digital camera, similar to that which had been used by 'A', fitted to the rifle. He recorded the departure of the ambulance and continued to pan at random around the scene catching the confusion of the onlookers some of whom were talking agitatedly and some who were lost in a motionless world of incomprehension at what they had just witnessed. The last scene he recorded was of Pettit who wandered away from the car in the direction of where Pain was recording the scene. His head drooped dejectedly down, his arms hanging uselessly from his shoulders as he moved at a measured pace forwards. Suddenly he stopped and peered intently at the ground, after a long pause he bent down and picked something up and held it in the open palm of his hand while continuing to stare intently at it. Finally he placed the object in his pocket and taking out his satellite phone he punched in a number and began speaking urgently. After a brief time he straightened his drooping back and squared his shoulders throwing his head back he looked up into the sky as his hand fell down to his side, the phone dangling from its wrist strap.

The last thing Pain recorded was Pettit walking slowly back to the car and poking his finger through the shattered driver's side window. He turned and stared in Pain's direction which caused Pain to shrink away from his penetrating gaze until he remembered that he was observing Pettit through the magnification of the scope of the 5S and from a mile distant it was impossible for Pettit to see him, but he still felt a cold shroud of impending doom. He had a passing fancy to use this amazing gun on Pettit but he had not been given instructions to shoot a second person and his fear of Eleven prevented him from indulging in independent action.

He switched off the digital camera and detaching it from the 4S he slid it into his jacket pocket. He felt good; not only had he eliminated one of the hated founders, he had secured the gratitude of Eleven whom he was sure would become increasingly powerful, even more so than Wilson whom, he had seen and heard was becoming noticeably more unstable. He ran bent over from the hollow in which he had been hiding to where his car was parked. Running in this way was not necessary, at a mile distant from the scene of the assassination; bent over or upright he could not be seen but it seemed to him to be the right thing to do and it gave him a sense of added drama. Within fifteen minutes he was boarding a privately hired speed cruiser which sped him away from Flores long before the authorities could become involved in investigating the incident.

Forty-five

Wilson returned to Nuovostan without Pelochev, who had stayed on in Russia ostensibly to protect their interests but which was, he recognised dimly in the reality which was ever more frequently slipping away from him, probably to further her own agenda. During the six hour flight Wilson brooded about the direction his strategies were taking. After two attempts he had been unable to uncover the BAM2 secrets unaided, so his only course of action was to give the task to a third party which had access to the quality of scientist able to make the discovery without annihilating themselves, or if they did, to be replaced so that they could eventually reveal the secrets. The only practical avenue open to him was the Russians, he did not trust them and knew that they would attempt to wrest the control away from him, but there were no other 'friends' to whom he could turn and his plan was to withhold a vital piece of information which would force them to include him in the conclusions.

In his confused mind he was in command of the situation; he would control the Russians whom he thought were crude and without the sophistication which he possessed. His sophistication would defeat the deviousness of both Pelochev and the Russian President. Wilson would allow them to do the necessary work and step in when they had unlocked the BAM2 unit but were unable to complete the task because he had instructed Pelochev to remove a vital component from the controlling computer, in addition to the information he was withholding, and by activating the one piece of the jigsaw he had held back he would re-assume ownership of the technology. His plan, he thought in his deluded state, was simple and brilliant.

On his return to the President's Palace he dismissed the minions and with the living parts of the Palace to himself he set about searching Pelochev's apartment. He had long suspected that she was double dealing and had decide to leave her in Russia to allow him to search unhindered. It was becoming increasingly clear to him that what had once been fear when she was in his presence had been replaced by an attitude which paid lip service to his authority while at the same time covertly she was endeavouring to usurp him; he vowed to prevent any ambitions she might have by finding something among her possessions which he could use as a lever to promote her destruction. He laughed out loud as he searched through her belongings for incriminating the evidence which he was sure was there and by the application of which he would re-establish his rightful ascendancy.

Several hours of effort yielded very little; there was a significant volume of correspondence but it was in Russian, which he did not understand. His laughter turned to crocodile tears when he finally realised that he was in a hopeless position; being unable to read her documentation without her help was both impossible and destructive to his purpose. With her he could not expand his horizons, without her he could not communicate meaningfully with his staff or his subjects. He abandoned the search, without achieving anything, and resorted to the comfort of Vodka.

There were matters of state, which had built up during his brief visit to Russia, requiring his immediate attention. Without Pelochev to interpret what was required of him he was unable to make any progress. They had developed a system where she explained the questions raised by matters of state and he provided her with an answer. He was vaguely aware that the instructions he gave her were not always adhered to and she made adjustments to them to suit the ever-changing circumstances; in the back of his mind lurked the fear that she was actually taking over his role. He was not too concerned about it but he felt tired and weighed down by the burden of his responsibilities.

He telephoned Pelochev in Russia and ordered her to return to Nuovostan to attend to her duties as Deputy President, a term he had not used before but one which he thought would persuade her to return. Her initial reluctance evaporated when she heard him call her Deputy President, it had a nice ring to it, indicating as it did that she would be taking over the presidency in due course. After the telephone call he felt drained; he celebrated with a further bottle of the finest Russian vodka and his last waking thoughts were that it would be better for him to take stock of his situation at leisure before resuming control of his country. But now was a time for rest, a long and trouble free rest with no interruptions.

Forty-six

President Lebedev was furious at being outmanoeuvred through Wilson's incompetence and by the pitifully insignificant little nation of Recovery Island, an irritation which he felt he should be able to squash with the same ease as he would a slow moving garden pest. The best of his scientists told him that opening the box of tricks without causing massive destruction was beyond their capabilities.

Lebedev had many enemies in the presidium and so far, as President, he had kept them at arm's length by exerting his crushing personality, but the ignominy of his failure to get control of BAM2 had laid bare the vulnerability that his detractors would immediately seized upon when the failure was exposed. Wilson clearly knew that they would fail in their attempts and it was equally clear that he was holding something back, probably as a bargaining chip. It became essential for him to act swiftly to retake the initiative by exacting his revenge on Wilson. He despatched a fully armed and empowered special fast action team to Nuovostan to abduct President Wilson so that he could be dealt with by a high profile show trial after the extraction of information concerning the missing element denying them the success they required. By this means Lebedev would to demonstrate to the people of New Russia that he maintained rigid political and social control over his domain and all those who may have influence over it.

The collapse of Wilson's personality was accelerated by his own irrational actions. He deluded himself into believing that he was omnipotent, as the alternative custodian of BAM2, and had no reason to fear the danger posed by his adversaries. As a consequence he made no attempt to increase his personal security which only served to underline his diminishing mental faculties. He chided Pelochev for her belief that the Russians could come to terms with BAM2 in a more successful way than he could himself. She tried to rationalise his thought processes by patiently explaining that it was not possible for Russia to carry out the experiments successfully unless they had something positive to work with. Wilson dismissed her views out of hand and continued to dream about completing his life mission by his own means without having to share the superiority such an outcome would bring. He decided that the wisdom of the voices in his head should be accepted and acted upon without question.

***

Wilson's capture was swift and clinical in its surgical precision. The twenty man special fast action team lived up to their name by landing in two assault helicopters within the walls of the Presidential palace. Their plan was brutal; they jumped from the helicopters as they were in the process of landing and opened fire without preamble on the surprised and poorly trained presidential guard. Entry into the palace was gung-ho and salvoes of bullets preceded the special forces into the interior of the palace, without regard for who might be killed in the process. Once past the perimeter guards the incursion forces preceded their moves through the rooms of the palace by opening the doors and throwing into each room flash-bang grenades which would disorientate the room's occupants without killing them simply to avoid harming the target of their abduction, they had specific instructions to take President Wilson alive. They moved towards where they knew, from reluctant informants, the presidential quarters to be; disabling possible resistance as they went.

The kidnapping was achieved without resistance; he was in his private quarters when the special troops burst into where he sat, pyjama clad, with Pelochev in attendance having breakfast. He was in one of his less responsive phases and looked at the black suited soldiers more with surprise than fear or anger. A hessian sack was thrown over his head and he was unceremoniously carried out to the helicopter over the shoulder of one of the more powerfully built soldiers.

From the arrival of the helicopters to their departure with a confused President Wilson no more than eight minutes had elapsed. There were no casualties among the fast action team and Wilson was unharmed, just as the Russian President had ordered. The forward side doors of the helicopters were left open and the muzzles of rapid fire canon were thrust out through them to ward off any resistance that might be mounted by the Nuovostani forces. No such resistance was encountered and within minutes the helicopters were over the Nuovostani Russian border and safe from any interference. Lebedev was informed of the success of the incursion and made an immediate proclamation over state television that enemy of mother Russia, President Wilson of Nuovostan, would stand trial as an enemy of the state.

Lebedev smiled mirthlessly to himself when he saw and made a note of the faces of his detractors in the presidium when they heard of the capture and proposed show trial of Wilson. The initiative had been stolen from them, an opportunity to depose Lebedev had been squandered yet again and his detractors knew that their position as members of the presidium would soon be brought to an end. They also realised that the trial would reveal to the Russian people that the attempted sabotage of BAM2 technology was promoted by the unprincipled actions of certain presidium members who would be tried for treason and, as was available under Russian state law, executed military style.

***

The international news agencies picked up and ran with the story leaked by Pelochev, of the Nuovostani President being spirited out of his own country by a special Russian invasion force. Views were naturally polarised. Countries which relied on Russian benevolence to exist came out in favour of the apprehension of the president of another country in pursuit of national security of the Russian motherland. Those speaking out against the warlike actions of the totalitarian Russian state were reliant on the benevolence of the Federation for their continued existence and followed their line that the warlike intervention of the Russian state flew in the face of international law.

Since the total worldwide social collapse, caused by world depression, institutions like the League of Nations and NATO had ceased to exist, leaving a vacuum waiting to be exploited by opportunists. Opportunistically the Federation put itself forward as the champion of the oppressed and castigated New Russia for their inappropriate actions in kidnapping President Wilson. Differences between New Russia and the Federation of Nations, which had been generally dismissive, hardened and heralded the return of the old previous century cold war.

On Recovery Island, for the moment out of the news, the Ruling Council took the opportunity to discuss something other than their own uncomfortable position. It was reasoned that as long as Wilson was the only other holder of information which could possibly lead to the uncovering of the BAM2v secret they were largely safe as long as Wilson was contained. That was the good news, the bad news was that Wilson had been abducted by the Russians and there was no doubt among the Ruling Council members that if the Russians were to gain possession of the information held by Wilson the situation could turn out to be dire.

Pettit came up with a typically Pettit solution: he proposed that a task force of the Island's finest should infiltrate Nuovostan and locate the BAM experimental notes, providing they had not been sequestered by the abductors, which were in Wilson's possession. This posed for them the questions of who the Island's finest were? Citizens of Recovery had been generally selected for their professional, academic or artisan centred skills and they were hardly likely to have the military training necessary to undertake the task of infiltration. A more likely source of candidates was the pool of dependent family members who had accompanied the selected denizens.

Trawling through the population register for likely candidates naturally fell to Pettit and it was a surprise to him that there were a number of potential team members who appeared to have the skills required. He had decided that a small team would be more manageable and he set the number at six. To his surprise the number of obvious candidates was greater than he required and of those there were three who spoke eastern European languages and all were ex-military, although not all were front line troops.

The candidates were contacted and given a psyche evaluation by Tanterelli to verify their suitability. Nine candidates were found and were approached individually by Pettit who told them that there was to be an off Island task which was of extreme importance to the Island. He did not at the initial stage tell them what the task would be.

Induction and training of the task force, because all the selected members were ex-military, was accomplished clinically and swiftly - even then, the candidates were only told that this would be an off Island task and that there would be ever present danger. Those selected and briefly trained were unquestioning about the nature of their involvement which was only revealed when the training was completed - to a man they accepted. The training was carried out on Hold Island, which was the one island in their archipelago to which no function had so far been broadcast.

The islands landscape was still raw and the unfinished buildings were forbidding and sinister and served Pettit's purposes admirably. The selected team were instructed by Pettit to scale perimeter walls and enter buildings contained within the walls through doors and windows where available and to gain entry by more explosive means should no easy access be available. The whole of the team took to the training with enthusiasm and threw themselves into the scenarios set by Pettit.

Pettit, for his part, praised the progress made by the ad-hoc team but was secretly concerned by their lack of front line experience which could only be partly countered by their enthusiasm. He fretted in the days leading up to the selected day of departure about how he could give cover in depth to his team who, without an experienced leader would be ill equipped to complete the task. If he as leader were to be compromised in some way during the course of the incursion the team would fail. The quandary gave him sleepless nights.

The one experienced person he could trust to take his place should it be necessary was Mark Lawson but as head of External security, the Island's equivalent to MI6, he was fully engaged with his important job. It was with a heavy heart that Pettit launched into what he expected to be a battle of wills with the other three founders. As the discussion unfolded he was surprised to find that his colleagues were not averse to his thoughts about the wisdom of a deputy and that Lawson was clearly the obvious choice, but they thought the matter of his inclusion was a matter for Lawson alone. Lawson was also supportive of Pettit's request and agreed without reservation to join the off Island venture. They all realised the seriousness of the operation and were prepared to subvert their misgivings. This operation was vital to the wellbeing of the Island and its citizens.

Forty-seven

President Lebedev was growing impatient and an impatient Lebedev was not good news for anybody. He had ascended to his supreme position as Russian President of this vast country as a result of the global crash, by being very successful in the Russian petrochemical industry which was not known for its gentle business integrity. Blood had been spilt on his way to the top and he was not averse to spilling more to further his grip on his country - and the world.

His scientists were working hard to uncover the secrets of the small, innocuous-looking box which they were treating with the utmost caution. X-rays had been used to better understand the workings of this powerful technology, they knew from Wilson what had happened to the unit sequestered by the Chinese and had no wish to repeat the total destruction that the futile Chinese endeavours had brought about.

Getting into the wooden box housing was a problem because there was a mechanical trigger which when released would cause massive and total destruction of the apparatus and maybe the scientists working on it. There was an external USB port which could be accessed but when activated it displayed a meaningless jumble of code which they were unable to decipher. They studied the information provided by Wilson but as they comprised notes on the original experiment by Gilliland and Crook, they were of limited assistance with the sophisticated unit which had ultimately evolved.

The senior scientist took the view that it would be easier to emulate the original experiments instead of trying to break into the box and set a team to work to follow the same course as Wilson's two previous teams, the first of which Wilson had annihilated and the second of which had annihilated themselves. A fact of some moment which Wilson had neglected to share with them; oblivious of the potential dangers they proceeded to reinvent the wheel.

Pelochev courted the favour of the Russian President by flattering him and offering to help with the unravelling of the secrets they were trying to access. Flattery was not a foible to which he was prone and it had no value to him in their discussions. He was, however, interested in her knowledge of Wilson's attempts to discover the great BAM2 secret, but more so he was interested in finding out why Wilson had been unsuccessful. The lack of success came not from discussions with Wilson but from deducing the oblique meanings behind the way that Pelochev hinted at a mystery, but only when she spoke in Russian.

When pressed by this powerful man she relented and allowed him to extract from her the fate of Nuovostani scientists when they used the information provided by Wilson to carry out the experiments. The President was startled when he learned of the total destruction of the scientists, their laboratory and the whole island under which they had been based. He pressed her for more information and extracted every last fact and supposition surrounding the failure of the endeavour.

It was as if a light was switched on in his mind: he suddenly understood what had happened to the bridge to cause it to collapse and what had caused two of his air force jets to disappear off the face of the earth and all of the other hitherto unexplained phenomena. It was obvious from his epiphany that Wilson's scientists had actually succeeded in accessing the BAM2 secrets and had, presumably unknowingly failed to understand that they had and that lack of understanding had led to their self-destruction. Their tinkering had unfortunately caused the previously unexplained phenomena which had caused the downing of the jet fighters and the collapse of the bridge and the other unexplained things. He shouted his sudden understanding in his native Georgian dialect which Pelochev did not fully understand but she could tell he had made a dramatic deduction. For Pelochev there was a jolt from the past which she could not quite place – and then she remembered it was the same reaction that Wilson had when he had discovered the missing piece of the BAM2 jigsaw. Lebedev had, she realised had an epiphany similar to that of Wilson: he now knew an important part of the secret of the technology.

Pelochev was alarmed by the President's reaction and by the fact that she had not been able to understand what either he or Wilson had suddenly understood. She could not allow him to realise that she did not understand what he had discovered simply because it would weaken her in his eyes.

"Congratulations Mr President, you have joined the very small club of those who understand what this all means. I regret that it was necessary for you to reach this conclusion by your own deduction." She gave him a conspiratorial smile.

"How long have you known this?" The Presidents repost was frosty.

"That is not important. What is important is that you have deduced the answer or at least part of it which means that you are well on the way to success and with my help you will be able to complete the discovery you desire." Her enigmatic words stopped him in his tracks.

He was puzzled; the shoe was now on the other foot; he was now unsure about what she knew and it was necessary for him to tread carefully and to elicit the information she had by whatever means he could employ. He realised that although he recognised her as being Siberio/Georgian lineage that she was of peasant stock and she had great cunning which he would have to watch. He would play her for as long as was necessary and then cast her adrift just as he had, in his own mind, disposed of Wilson. This would leave him as the lone possessor of this so powerful technology which he could use for domination he desired. He was mindful that because of her upbringing which was more Siberian than Georgian and which led to her family fleeing following brutal Georgian persecution; she had an inbuilt steely strength which was underlay by her desirable physical appearance.

The team of scientists and engineers he had assembled to unravel the secrets of BAM2 worked day and night. They had been warned that failure to observe safety protocols in the work they were doing would result in their disappearance and failure to succeed in revealing the secrets of BAM2 would yield similar a result but that oblivion would be slower and infinitely more painful.

By working to the extreme of their ability the scientists slowly teased out the secrets which would lead to the opening of the box. The outer casing was crude as was the self-destruct mechanism; even so, it was difficult to disarm and they would only know if they had been successful if it was not reduced to dust after they had completed their task. There was a great deal of tension in the laboratory when they finally decided to place the unit in a high pressure chamber and use the pressure within to keep the destruction plunger depressed while they removed the carcase. They plucked up the courage to commit to opening the box.

There was a rush of euphoria when the box was opened and neither it nor they were atomised. It was to the head scientist that the task fell of informing the President of the success of their attempts, a task which he undertook with great pleasure. He knew fully that had he and his team failed to open the box the failure of the attempt would not be borne by them and not the President.

When the President had absorbed the news of their glorious success he turned his thoughts to how to exclude Wilson and his irritating deputy from the benefits that he alone would take. He would also see that the RIR would likewise be excluded from the benefits of the captured technology. His considerations were logical but they failed to realise a flaw in his way of thinking - Wilsons scuppering of the Russian plans by tinkering with the BAM2 control system.

Control of BAM2 was greater by far than the 20th century mastery of Atomic power which had led to the ending of World War 2 - but had not prevented World War 3. In Lebedev's hands sole ownership of BAM2 would ensure that New Russia would govern a new world which would be dominated by Russian ideology.

Forty-eight

What really disturbed Eleven, as he listened to the story unfolding in the court room, in addition to finding that RIR was no longer a secret organisation, was that they obviously knew that not only had the BAM2 unit been stolen but also where it had been sent. The alarm bells began clamouring once again. He glanced at Brogan and saw that her eyes were dilated but calmed himself in the knowledge that she was a drug user and that, rather than the fear of revelation perhaps, was the reason for the dilation.

"How we deal with that issue will come later." Gilliland was silent for a moment as though gathering his thoughts. "We do know from the debriefing of one of our agents that there were meetings in Nuovostan which were attended by the head of RIR and one of his Recovery Island National helpers. We also know that an ex-Recovery Islander was involved; his name will be familiar to some of you, he was called Jacques Pantin when he lived on the Island but since being the only citizen to leave the Island by choice, or for any other reason. He now lives in London, following Wilson's failed coup in which he took part and which caused him to flee the Island and he now calls himself Jack Pain and he is persona non grata.

There was a change in the tone of the meeting when Gilliland sat down and Crook took over the narration. "Before Chester loses his voice I think I'd better take over the story and I would like to outline to you the method which we will be adopting for the purposes of this enquiry. We shall be calling on the testimony of some individuals; some who are in this room and some yet to join us. You may recall that we recently had a fungal infection scare and all adults were required to undergo tests in Doctor Tanterelli's clinic. There was actually no infection, general or otherwise present, it was an attempt to help us identify at least some those who were combined against us."

A buzz of excitement ran through the audience, this was better than any Hollywood drama and they were enthralled by the developing solution to the plot. Eleven and the cell leaders were not among those enjoying the unfolding story and the dawning of comprehension could be seen on their faces. They looked around nervously trying to find a means of escape.

Crook continued, "we learned that there is a secret society, as Chester has already mentioned, called the Recovery Island Rebels, but don't be fooled by the comic book lack of sophistication in the name; the members of this organisation have a serious agenda, they intend to destroy the Island society and sell us out either for their own use or to the highest bidder – of which there are many. They were clever enough to outwit our security systems and steal a BAM2 unit and clever enough to export it to an outside interest. But I'm getting ahead of myself; our method of identifying the members of RIR shows that although they are cunning to a very high degree they indulged in an infantile act which will be their undoing. They believed in primitive symbolism and once we ascertained this, identification of the members became relatively simple." He took a sip from a glass of water and surveyed the audience.

Eleven was totally confused. What was this symbolism he was talking about? He was confident that there was nothing in the make-up of RIR which would give them away. "What's he talking about?" he hissed to himself much to the surprise of those within hearing.

Crook continued, "what now needs to be addressed is: How do we intend to identify members of the RIR, what do we do about them once they are identified and what do we do about the missing unit. I'll start with - how do we identify the members. For this I will need a volunteer from the audience." He craned his neck in a mock attempt to survey the audience; his eyes alighted on Coleman the florid surgeon. "You sir, may I ask you to step forward and assist us?" The question was rhetorical.

Coleman stood up unsteadily, wishing that he had abstained from his normal ration of alcoholic beverage at breakfast on that morning, but then he hadn't known that he would be called upon to participate in the proceedings. Taking a deep breath he launched himself towards the main table where the presenting founders sat.

"Thank you for your assistance. Now I would like you to take the witness stand tell us your name and what part you play in the life of the Island." Crook sat down and looked at Coleman expectantly.

"I am Preece Coleman and I am a surgeon on Doctor Tanterelli's senior medical research team." His voice sounded strange to him and he wondered with some dread why he had been selected for whatever it was he would be asked to do. He felt a cold chill at the thought that his illicit offshore bank accounts were full to overflowing. How could they know about them?

"And how long have you been a resident of the Island?" Crook asked from the comfort of his seat.

"I've been here about seven years." His brow was creased in puzzlement.

"And what is it you actually do by way of being a surgeon?"

"I specialise in dermatology but I also handle general surgical procedures, I don't understand why you are asking me these questions."

"Bear with me please Doctor, or perhaps I should say Mr Coleman. Isn't that how consultants are addressed?"

Cole nodded his head and looked miserable. He had no idea where this line of questioning was going or how it had any bearing on his chosen profession. However he frequently broke Island rules, the holding of offshore accounts being the main rule that if discovered could bring about his downfall, probably his deportation and the loss of the easy life to which he had grown so accustomed.

In your capacity as a consultant surgeon do you perform operations only as directed by your superiors and administrators in pursuit of research or cures?"

"Yes, of course – why would I do anything different?"

"Are you saying to me that you do not take on any private work, under any circumstances?"

"Of course not what would be the point, health care is free on the Island, there is no such thing as private work." As alcohol began to fuel his aggression he became belligerent. "I demand to know what it is you are getting at, I have a busy schedule and I need to get back to the hospital to continue with my list."

"Let me explain to you what it is I'm getting at and what it is that you are not keen to divulge." Crook stood up once more. His demeanour had changed to take on the persona of a prosecuting council. "There is evidence that you do carry out medical procedures which are not directed by others in your profession but by people who have no connection whatever with medicine. I am talking about tattoos." He paused to judge the reaction of the surgeon.

There was a murmur from the audience who were intrigued and puzzled by the way events were unfolding. There was, Crook noticed one member of the audience who was visibly shaken by the line of questioning and by the use of the word tattoo.

The light of comprehension dawned on Coleman's face and his mind sharpened at the speed of light. "You must be talking about the repair work that I do in tattoo removal as part of my dermatological tasks." He thought quickly and concocted a cover story in an attempt to mitigate his misdemeanours. "I must confess that I do carry out tattoo removal procedures without going through the normal procedures, I do this to protect the dignity of people who are ashamed of the messages contained in their tattoos – changed partners names and the like but I don't charge the patients for it, I give my time freely as a public service." He began to relax into the half-truth that he presented; payments were received offshore and were not paid by the recipients of the surgery.

"Don't be shy Mr Cole, you do fine work, applying, removing and changing tattoos. The ones I am talking about are those that you undertake by special request from people you could not identify because their faces are hidden from sight. You apply or remove tattooed numbers on the inside of the right great toe where under normal circumstances they cannot be seen. Each number comprises two digits and comprise the identification numbers of the members of the six cells of the RIR movement."

"I did them but I didn't know what they were for. I was asked to do them as a favour." Cole's voice quivered with fear as he fully realised that he had been caught out.

"Thank you, you may return to your seat, but do not attempt to leave this room." He turned to the audience.

"Here we have a man who has been nurtured by the Island and its people and who has undertaken work directed by unqualified people who hide the identity of those who are having procedures performed. We have no doubt that he has received illicit payments for the secretive work he has carried out. We simply followed the trail down which the evidence took us. Knowing that this was the method used to symbolise membership of RIR we instigated an Island wide immunisation programme based on a medical check-up on all adult RINS. This included an inspection for an imaginary foot fungus which enabled our medical crews to identify which Islanders bore the tattoo that branded them RIR. We believe found them all except one and that is number 11, that designation being the first member in the first cell, in other words the boss"

Pandemonium broke out as it dawned on the members of RIR they had been compromised. Eleven heaved a sigh of relief; he had not been discovered.

Forty-nine

As surgeon Preece Cole returned to his seat, his head was cast miserably down. His blood ran cold as he realised that the income supporting his illicit sojourns to Paris to indulge in his peccadillos would almost certainly cease. He was at the same time relieved that although what he had done was not strictly within Island medical code it was hardly a hanging offence and he had gained enough knowledge of Tanterelli's techniques to continue with the good life in the outside world if necessary.

Preece's coming to terms with the situation was not fully echoed by Eleven; his world was tumbling down around his ears and his aspirations of grandeur were evaporating before his eyes. He could see that the game was up but at least he had the satisfaction of knowing that his identity was protected. He had not had the code number tattooed on him because he felt that it was a violation of his body which was, to him, sacrosanct whereas having it done to others merely underlined his superiority. He sat back to watch the destruction of RIR and all of its members in the knowledge that he was safe and would be able to start again. He was after all the possessor of, if not all, at least a lion's share of the ownership of a BAM2 unit – and he had withheld the missing component from the control system that prevented anybody else from enabling it.

His interest in the proceedings now that he was safe from being revealed as the head of RIR took on a new slant. He would find out from this enquiry, the who and the how of the unveiling of RIR and make sure once he had gained control of Recovery Island, the perpetrators of its demise would be brought to account.

Crook continued relentlessly, "those of you who are present in this room and who are members of RIR can make themselves known and may represent their own defence from the witness box. If you make yourself known you will be shown some leniency. Just remember that if you have a tattoo identifying you as a cell member and you have undergone a requested medical examination recently your identity is known to the founders."

A complete silence descended over the watching audience. Most of those present looked intrigued as they glanced around the room at the others present to see who, if any, would admit to membership. For perhaps a minute nobody stirred and then Piotre Kwietakovski stood up looking pale faced and nervous. He had been outed earlier, by clear implication, as being involved in the stealing of the BAM2 unit and there was no escaping his fate. Slowly a second person stood to join Kwietakovski; this time it was Colleen Brogan one of Eleven's own elite cell.

"I will give you a short time to identify yourselves after which time we will identify and detain those who have chosen not to do so. I suggest that those of you who wish to avail themselves of the council's leniency to make your way to the two jury seat areas at the side of the court." He indicated the areas to the right and left of the judgement seats occupied by the founder. Both sets of twelve seats filled up slowly as the RIR members realised that there was no choice but to comply. The last reluctant member to join them was Paul Zen who became the thirty fifth RIR member. As Zen passed by, Eleven whispered softly out of the side of his mouth so that nobody but Zen could hear. "I will look after you and make sure that you are safe from persecution." Already Eleven's fertile mind was formulating a way that, as a senior member of the Ruling Council, he could have Zen freed as an unwitting victim of the despicable organisation. Zen for his part looked startled by the approach from this man.

The two banks of twelve jury seats were full and the well of the court held the other eleven. Eleven breathed a sigh of relief; all of his hard work in keeping his own identity secret was now paying off. He was home and free, he had lost the whole of his carefully nurtured troops but ultimately they were expendable and replaceable, simply cannon fodder. At least he could, from his own senior position on the Ruling Council argue for the freedom of his recently found two IC by offering to sponsor him for rehabilitation as a recent convert, so that they could start over.

"Ladies and gentlemen," Gilliland took up the chairmanship of the enquiry. "There are two other people who have not identified themselves as being members of RIR and after Surgeon Preece Cole has joined the other members who have been wise enough to identify themselves there will be only one, the illusive number 11. He remains unidentified and at large."

"I am not an RIR member," Cole blustered. "I have no tattoo and I do not belong to a cell. You have no right to include me in their number."

"Very well," Gilliland became testy. "You have a choice, join your fellow miscreants and be interrogated or don't join them and be interrogated separately without the offer of leniency which has been offered to them." He looked expectantly at Preece.

After a long moment of inactivity the surgeon stood and walked in slow defeat to the well of the court to join the other thirty five.

Fifty

The modified Apache Chieftain carrying the Island's task force took off pre-dawn and headed south towards the Azores. The unease with which most of the rest of the world still viewed the Islanders made a direct flight to Nuovostan more difficult than they were prepared to countenance. Once on the Azores they transferred to a long range charter aircraft which was piloted by Adie Cox, the Recovery Islands chief pilot, and began a long and tortuous flight which would take them first to Manchuria and then by an overland route to Nuovostan.

Pettit used the boring flight to continue with the briefing of his five man team which with himself and Mark Lawson totalled seven members, five active and two supervisory. They had made use of live digital imaging to study the lie of the land in Nuovostan by hacking into various international visual communications satellites which they were able to watch as they flew, in real time. From the illicit imaging they were able to track vehicle and personnel movements in and around the President's palace. To their relief there was no evidence of military activity of any kind. What little there had been before the President was abducted seemed to have been withdrawn. No President, no guard.

The team travelled across the Manchurian border with Nuovostan in the dead of night. The three Range Rover's which made up their small convoy were GPS guided along tracks which were difficult enough to discern in broad daylight and impossible in the stygian darkness even with full headlights. Their sturdy vehicles made light work of the uneven terrain but the passengers were jarred and thrown around inside the cabs and were forced to slow down to less than walking pace for long stretches of the journey. Shaken and wearied by the constant jolting they at last joined up with tracks which smoothed their journey about twenty miles inside the Nuovostani border.

Wilson's palace came into view as the weak sun struggled above the horizon from behind a bank of solid grey cloud which held the promise of winter rain which, if the temperature dipped any further would turn to snow. The troops were well equipped to deal with the cold weather and part of their equipment was white one-piece coveralls which would be deployed if it did snow. Three miles short of the palace they stopped for a warming breakfast and a final pep talk before breaching the palace walls.

No dwellings or people were visible and the hill on which they had stopped gave them a clear view of their objective; from this distance there was no signs of life within the palace or its compounds, it was as though the whole facility was either still asleep or deserted. Even at this great distance the team felt the need to talk in hushed tones, their breath frosting in the chill mountain air. To an outside observer they looked like a bunch of desperados having lived for the past three days in their black combat uniforms which were creased and dust covered from the un-metalled roads. Four days of beard growth did nothing to make them look more wholesome and the lack of meaningful sleep turned their eyes red and also made them water in the cold breeze.

Before leaving their resting place they scoured the site for any evidence that they had been there and scattered the remains of the cooking fire by throwing the ashes in the air so that they were carried away on the eddying breeze, the scar left by the fire was camouflaged with debris which would protect it from a cursory examination. Boarding the three vehicles they began to make their way to the palace which was located in open woodland a mile outside Nuovostan City on the crest of a hill which gave it 360 degrees of visibility to the city and all the surrounding countryside.

Hiding the vehicles which they had disabled against discovery and theft, they loaded into their back packs and utility belts the weapons and other equipment they would need to gain entry into the palace compound. Pettit was beginning to feel apprehensive, preparation for this exercise had been superficial added to which he had not undertaken an independent military manoeuvre in many years. He looked at Mark Lawson and noticed his pinched expression which gave him concern, and then at his overriding look of absolute determination which gave him great heart. Lawson realised he was being scrutinised and turned to face Pettit, they smiled at each other; Lawson's smile was slightly apprehensive and Pettit's noticeably grim. Their unspoken exchange indicated that they were ready to start their task in earnest.

The seven men loped steadily in single file headed up by Pettit. As they had been taught after twenty paces the man in third place broke ranks and loped towards the back of the file which he re-joined moving in the same direction as his companions. As he joined the back of the queue he saw the next man in the third place that he had vacated earlier break ranks and repeat the run which he had made earlier. This pattern was repeated continuously and provided them with continuous rearward vision for the whole of their yomp without slowing forward progress.

Nine minutes after starting out they reached the perimeter wall of the palace compound. There was no discernible sound or movement from within the walls.

After a pause to make sure that they had not been discovered a telescopic ladder was produced from one of the back packs and extended to a point just short of the top of the wall. Lawson ascended the ladder and cautiously peered over the top of the wall which was crowned with razor wire. He looked towards the palace itself and produced a pair of binoculars from one of the many pockets in his combat suit panning slowly from side to side.

Descending the ladder he huddled with Pettit and spoke in hushed tones. "Can't see any people either military or civilian, the place is a mess, it looks like it's been subjected to an assault using armaments, could be grenades, and certainly small arms. The brick and stonework are badly mashed and a lot of windows have been broken."

The wall scaling exercise was repeated on the other three flanking walls which made up the rectangular compound and each observation yielded the same evidence of damage. Clearly the building had been accessed from all four sides and the main palace doors had been demolished by explosives.

They chose to enter the compound over the wall adjacent to the back of the palace where the grounds were shrouded in trees and they were able to get to the palace walls without being discovered. Treading carefully they traversed to wooded open space making no sudden moves that might attract the attention of any of the inhabitants and moved slowly from tree to tree from the refuge of which they peered towards the palace looking for any signs of movement. No signs were discernable and they bunched together in a small coppice where they were addressed in hushed tones by Pettit. The five man task force looked with overt nervousness to their two leaders for instruction and guidance.

294

"By the looks of it," Pettit addressed them quietly, "they are either still asleep or if not they are waiting for us to make a move before they join in the party, but somehow I doubt they are waiting." He cast a studied look at the facade of the palace which was pock marked by small arms fire and by larger smoke blackened damage of the kind caused by hand grenades. "Looks like we can get in easily enough, most of the windows seem to be broken and the two external doors have been blown in." He turned to Lawson and issued instructions to him. "Mark, you wait here with these two and you three," he indicated three of the team who were huddled together, "come with me. We'll go in through the French windows and if it's okay for you to follow us in I'll let you know. If you don't get to be invited in it means were in trouble and you'll have to use plan B"

"Which is?" Lawson enquired.

"Which is……. you trying to get into the building using a different entry point to see if you can come to our assistance. If that's shaky you get out of here fast, collect the Land Rovers and drive back to Manchuria, then get back to the Island as fast as you can."

The two who were to stay with Lawson looked nervous about the part they were about to play and glanced at each other apprehensively.

"Relax," Lawson said to them in a placatory voice, "our bit is easy. They will do the donkey work, if the lie of the land is clear we can affect a safe entry; if it's not clear we'll know about it and can take the necessary precautions and at worst we can get out fast and report back to the Island."

Using military hand signals Pettit directed his three men. He stationed one man on either side of the shattered French windows and indicated that the third man should accompany him through the doorway and cover to the left whilst he, Pettit, would cover to the right. They both drew cumbersome side arms from side pockets in their combat suits. The side arms were compressed air activated dart guns which fired a syringe containing a powerful anaesthetic which would totally incapacitate an adversary within two seconds of a hit, the magazine of ten darts was held in the butt of the pistol along with the compressed air reservoir. Ed Pickering's gun design was unusual in that it had the ability to harvest spent compressed air and recirculate it back to partially replenish the reservoir. The advantages of using this weapon included that it was almost noiseless, a considerable advantage with an incursion of this type and the fact that the receiver of a dart would be incapacitated but not killed by it.

The room they entered had been badly damaged by grenades, the walls were blackened and what furnishings and furniture had been set up in it was in broken, scattered, disarray. They both checked the room which was not populated; Pettit cautiously opened a door into the next room and peered through into the darkened interior. Seeing no signs of movement he retreated to the French windows and beckoned to Lawson and his men to join them. When they did so Pettit and his men entered the next room and made sure that it was free of danger; the same process was repeated again and again as they progressed through the many rooms they encountered.

Forty five cautious minutes later they were seven rooms into the palace and were beginning to think that it was deserted. Pettit, because of his military upbringing resisted the urge to throw caution to the wind and to breeze through from room to room. His caution was rewarded in part when he prepared to enter what appeared to be the President's apartment, as he eased the door open he could hear raised voices and the distinct rasping sound of a pistol being cocked.

Fifty-one

Pettit slowly withdrew from the door opening and peered through the gap between door and the jamb flanked by the heavy hinges. He could see a man in military uniform standing legs splayed both arms extended as he pointed his side arm at somebody outside of Pettit's field of vision. The shoulder insignias on the gun holder's uniform were in Cyrillic and he was shouting instructions in his strident language, his face in profile was pinched and mean and his vocal tone brooked no argument.

The youngest of the three accompanying Pettit had a fluent knowledge of Russian and he joined Pettit at the doorway in response to Pettit's hand signal.

"What is he saying?" Pettit whispered.

"He seems to be demanding some documents which are the property of President Wilson." The reply was whispered at a barely discernible level.

The voice that responded to the gunman was staccato and cold with fury and was undoubtedly feminine. She rattled off a retort of invectives that Pettit was able to guess at even though he did not speak the language.

At a glance from Pettit the interpreter volunteered an interpretation. "She is saying that she knows nothing about the documents they are looking for and that anyway they are the property not of the President but of the state of Nuovostan. The rest of what she is saying is to do with the lack of formality of the soldier's family structure and makes unpleasant references to his mother's morals."

Pettit grinned momentarily and put his index finger to his lips in the universal symbol indicating the need for silence while they listened to what she was saying. She continued without drawing breath for an astonishingly long time. When she finally stopped to replenish her oxygen to launch into a further tirade the soldier took the opportunity to say his piece. His words were brief and to the point and caused the woman to pause unexpectedly. Pettit turned enquiringly to the interpreter.

"He says that one way or another he will get the documents as directed by Lebedev, the President of New Russia, so either she can volunteer the whereabouts of the documents or he will call in his platoon so that they can all enjoy her feminine charms while he looks for the information he needs."

Pettit frowned: as a military man himself, he did not approve of any tactics which threatened civilians – men, women or children – in the pursuit of any military objective. From what the Russian soldier had said Pettit assumed that his platoon were in another location that was not necessarily close by. To break the deadlock he swiftly and silently opened the door having first levelled his pistol at shoulder height. The door opened silently and revealed the Russian soldier still with his gun levelled at the only other occupant in the room a woman who he recognised instantly as Irena Pelochev, she who had given evidence against Wilson as part of the enquiry on Recovery Island during the tussle between Wilson and James Creswell the British Prime Minister.

She, unlike the Russian, was facing the door and her shocked look as she saw Pettit in the doorway alerted the soldier to another presence. He began to swing the pistol round to where Pettit stood with a coldly calculating look on his face. Pettit squeezed the trigger and there was an almost inaudible but powerful hiss as the gas reservoir was deployed to expel the dart laden with anaesthetic. The delay in activation gave the Russian what seemed to Pettit like an age to aim and fire, especially as he knew that the Russian had already cocked his weapon. Pettit fired and dropped to the floor, reflexively; the bullet from the Russians gun passed where Pettit's head had been a millisecond before and from his prone position he saw the soldier's look of incomprehension as the red feathered dart embedded itself in the side of his neck. Almost immediately his eyes rolled back and he collapsed in an uncontrolled heap on the marble floor.

The noise of the Russian's gun discharge echoed around the marble clad room and left those present with ringing ears and a sensation of disorientation. Pettit's immediate concern was that the noise of the guns discharge would alert the platoon that the soldier had referred to and bring them running. Pettit advanced into the room and turned to face Pelochev who stood momentarily frozen in place at the turn of her fortunes. She had gone from being threatened with multiple rapes to being in the perhaps equal peril from the man she recognised as Silas Pettit, Wilson's sworn enemy.

"Miss Pelochev," Pettit looked at her quizzically.

"Mr Pettit," she replied, recovering from her induced inertia. "What you are doing here in Nuovostan?" She asked the question not because she could not guess the answer but to give herself time to recover from the shock.

"We understand that President Wilson has been taken by the Russians and we know he is in possession of documents which are the property of Recovery Island and we are here to retrieve them."

"So you are want me to giving such documenting to you, I do not have. Is what I am telling this," she pointed to the supine soldier, "that you have killing."

"He's not dead." Pettit looked at her and noticed her calculating look. "He's been shot with a tranquiliser; we're not in the business of murder no matter how much we are provoked."

"But you are soldier," her brow wrinkled in concentration. "How can soldier not be murderer?"

"I was a soldier and now I'm not but I am still a military man and I still believe in military objectives, I just don't believe in killing my fellow human beings."

"Not making sense to be a not killing soldier. How can this be so?"

"No time for all of this. We have a mission which we must carry out at all costs....short of murder," he gave her a cold smile. "We are here for the copy of the BAM experiment notes that Wilson stole."

"Not having these notes as I am telling man on floor, not knowing what you are talk about." Her jaw took on a stubborn and determined set which made it clear that she would not divulge the whereabouts of the notes willingly even if she did know where they were.

"I'm guessing that his team," he indicated the still supine figure by pointing his foot, "are also looking for the documents, maybe we'll just let them find the file and take it from them."

"Is for you to think of. I am not know anything." She smiled knowingly at him; he had made a major mistake to her way of thinking by telling her that they were not prepared to kill their opponents.

"You are an open book and so predictable," he said this gently but with menace and watched her face change from being cunning to being affronted and angry.

301

"What you are mean," she spat angrily. "I am not what you say. I am person who has lost husband to invasion of home and am in sadness for his going." She neglected to say that the marriage certificate in her possession was forged and that no marriage had taken place.

"Your husband?" Pettit was taken aback by her statement. "You mean that you and President Wilson are husband and wife?"

"Why you are not thinking this is possible; I have look after Cullin for many times now and he is needing of me, but the Russians are taking him and leaving these mans to look for documents you also want."

"I just can't imagine anybody wanting to marry Wilson, especially somebody as…er…presentable as you."

She preened herself as she translated his words into her Russian patois and smiled at him coquettishly. She found this man very attractive and wondered if she could use his compliments as a launching platform to help her out of her present difficulties. Although it was not apparent to any observer she had been taken completely by surprise by the abduction of Wilson by the Russians and it left her in a no-man's-land of indecision as to how she could repair the damage caused by his abduction.

The Russians had Wilson but they did not have the vital piece of information which he had withheld. That information, which they now realised they needed to complete the task of redevelopment, was still in Nuovostan but its exact location was known only to Wilson. Even though Wilson's mind was almost completely destroyed, his innate cunning meant that he still held the winning card.

Originally she had been willing to share the spoils from the acquisition of BAM technology with the

302

Russian President but he had grown impatient and Wilson had been abducted without her involvement. This treachery invoked her natural ability to seek revenge and as she looked at Pettit in all his sombre glory she thought that he might be the one to help her in this new quest.

Her sojourn into the realms of fantasy took only seconds and she returned her thoughts to the present situation. "It is a must that I get back my Cullin. We have country to run and much things to doing." She adopted a business-like pose that belied the true reason for wanting to get Wilson back. Without the missing piece of information not only could the Russians not continue with the BAM experiments but neither could she. This thought she kept hidden.

"You have my sympathy but your situation has nothing to do with us we are here for the research notes that Wilson stole from us."

"Is called *President* Wilson, not just Wilson. " She heaved her bosom with a deep intake of breath and looked haughty. "This notes you are talk about is stolen by you, not by President. He was minister who pay for research and it all belonging to him. Not belonging to you." Her nostrils flared and her eyes narrowed.

Realising that this course of action was not going to achieve anything useful Pettit changed tack. "You want to get your husband back and we want the notes back so maybe we can do a trade."

"What you are having to trade?" she asked suspiciously.

"If we get President Wilson out of Russia we will trade him for the notes."

"You getting him out of Russia are not possibility." She snorted contemptuously.

"Is it a deal?" He smiled at her in a gentle friendly way.

"Is a deal that you cannot win – so yes, is a deal"

Pettit noticed a look of absolute horror on the face of Mark Lawson who clearly had no idea of how they could accomplish such a mission. Pettit's only problem was that he didn't know how he could achieve it either.

With Pelochev's collusion Pettit's team were hidden away until the platoon of Russian soldiers gave up trying to locate the research notes for the original BAM2 experiments. When they finally left to return empty handed to Russia, Pettit and his team hunted in vain for the documents which together with the piece of vital information extracted from the documents by Wilson would enable the technology to be rediscovered.

The trial of Colin Wilson, for the want of a more accurate description, was set to precede the New Russia Presidential elections so that the guilt established would support the re-election of a strong President. This gave Pettit some three months to try to do the impossible – to rescue Wilson from the Russian embrace. They searched the President's palace from top to bottom to no avail; the documents were nowhere to be found.

Pettit and his six man team returned to Recovery Island to regroup and plan a way of getting Wilson away from the clutches of Lebedev and the Presidium. Without Penny Caine, the three remaining founders and Mark Lawson and Carlina Tanterelli brain stormed the rescue of Wilson but despite their best efforts the task appeared to be too Herculean. After talking around in circles for several days it was Mark Lawton who came up with further help. He recalled his earlier sessions with Carlina Tanterelli in which she had coaxed out of him the ability to think outside the box and he suggested that Tanterelli be brought into the loop.

She accepted the invitation without hesitation and after being briefed about the situation launched herself straight into solution mode. "What are we actually trying to achieve?" she asked of them all.

"We need to get Wilson and his knowledge of the location of the notes and the vital piece of information he had removed from them." Pettit was the first to respond to her question."

"Must we get both Wilson and the notes?" she enquired of Pettit specifically.

"We must get them both. His copy of the research notes and access to the piece of information he is withholding from the Russians. We must have both," Pettit replied after a moment's thought."

"Where are his notes being held?"

"We don't know; we searched the palace but came up with nothing."

"What did Pelochev have to say about where they are being kept?"

"She knows nothing."

"Do you believe she knows nothing?"

"No."

"Why would she withhold this information from you if she does actually know where it is?"

"She's a devious woman and I have no idea why she would withhold it except, perhaps, it's what she does." Pettit shrugged in resignation.

"Okay, let's get back to that later." Tanterelli opened up the conversation to the rest of the group. "We need to get under our control Wilson, the notes and the missing piece of information he holds." She looked with raised eyebrows at her colleagues who one by one nodded their consent. "Three points and we only know where one of them is, Wilson, and that is an assumption based on Pelochev's information, a woman that we don't trust and information leaking out of New Russia which is hardly the fount of unvarnished truth."

"Are we actually going somewhere with these blindingly obvious statements?" Pettit was becoming testy.

"Silas," Crook admonished him. "We invited Carlina in to help us; at least give her a chance.

Pettit looked rueful and shrugged his shoulders. "Sorry, it's just that I've been thinking round in circles about this for the last few days and what I'm not looking for is an analysis of the situation, I'm looking for a solution."

"Silas," Tanterelli looked at him with gentle fondness and understanding, "I appreciate your frustration but if I am to help I must go over the whole situation even if what I'm doing is in parallel with your own thoughts." She again turned to the rest of the group and addressed them all. "At the risk of incurring further wrath from Silas," she smiled benignly, "it is obvious that the key is to get Wilson out from wherever it is he is being held. The other things, the notes and the missing information are actually secondary. If we acquire Wilson and with him the secrets of his withheld information, the notes the Russians have will be useless. So, getting Wilson away from them before they get the missing information out of him is paramount."

"That simplifies the task," Pettit said with a deep frown, "but it doesn't tell us where Wilson is being held."

"For the moment that is true but what we must ask ourselves is, how do we find out where he is? And having done that we need to formulate a way of extracting him, a task which is not without difficulty and which is, sadly, impossible if he is being held in the Kremlin." She looked at the faces before her and saw a look of impatience from Pettit, of deep thought from

Gilliland and Crook. Her face alone had a look of expectation.

"What are you proposing we do Carlina, to start this ball rolling?" Gilliland relaxed back into his chair and watched the cogs of Tanterelli's brain thinking outside the box.

"Why don't we make a friend of an enemy," she said cryptically. She smiled at the look of puzzlement at the apparent irrelevance of her statement.

"Elucidate," Gilliland prompted.

"One way of finding out where somebody is, is to get inside information and as we don't have any contacts in the Russian hierarchy ourselves we need to nurture somebody who can become one. The obvious person is Pelochev." The room was enveloped in a stunned silence.

"We can't trust her, she's a maverick." Pettit was vehement.

"Absolutely true, Silas, and it's because of that we can trust her. You said in talking about your discussions with her, in Nuovostan, that the Russians had reneged on an agreement with her. Her personality is unable to deal with that sort of treachery – perhaps because it is the kind of thing that she would do without thinking – so she will be open to suggestions which will enable her to get her own back and re-establish her own self esteem."

"Interesting." Pettit prompted her to continue.

"We need to persuade her to approach the Russians with an offer to use her influence with Wilson to find the missing information that Lebedev needed so desperately to get. If they agree to her proposal, and they will, she will need to meet up with Wilson to do his persuading and if he is being held inside the walls of the Kremlin she is duplicitous enough to con them into moving him to a location which is more conducive to getting him to talk."

"I knew she would do it." Lawson leapt from his chair with glee and did a brief Irish jig much to the amusement of his peers.

"So," Gilliland prompted Tanterelli further, "how do you then, after we have taken him out of the Kremlin, get him out of Russia?"

"That," Tanterelli laughed, "is more Silas' domain than mine."

"And I know how we can do it too." Silas looked happy for the first time during their discussion. "I need to get together with Ed Pickering and I need to do it now."

Fifty-two

The last leg of their flight from Harbin in Manchuria to Nuovostan in a chartered ex-military cargo transporter was uncomfortable and it was extremely cold. They had chosen this mode of transport because down at heel and outdated aircraft were the norm in this part of the world. Strapped onto the cargo deck a Land Rover which had been modified by Ed Pickering with his usual flare had also been modified in general appearance. The body-work was battered and dented and the hand rendered paint finish failed to entirely cover the logo on both front doors which with careful scrutiny read, 'state geographical survey' in Cyrillic script. The interior had been tastelessly modified significantly and was liberally scattered with what gave the appearance of, duct tape repairs. One of the changes made was a typical Pickering whim; by throwing a switch on the botched dashboard the engine could be made to sound as though it was about to expire. The original diesel engine had been replaced with a Pickering special liquid sodium powered engine which was extremely powerful and which ran on a hybrid reusable fuel which, when recirculated, enabled them to travel at high speed for up to ten thousand kilometres on a single twenty Kilogram cartridge of enriched compressed fuel.

Nuovostan airport had not received the attention it was due; the runway was too short and the surface had begun to disintegrate in the face of the harsh winters coming to it from Novosibirskiye Ostrova which lies between the Laptev and East Siberian seas. Pettit made a mental note to speak to the pilot, Adie Cox, to make sure that he logged all three of the landings he had struggled to make before coming to a halt at the extreme end of the runway.

The modified Land Rover was driven down the transporter's rear ramp onto the uneven runway where it sat with the engine running. There was no noise coming from the modified engine until the driver threw what they had called the Pickering switch; immediately the engine took on the sound of a diesel engine in terminal distress and there were simulated sounds of intermittent misfiring. The three men forming the vehicles crew laughed at the dreadful sounds but the laughs were tinged with nervousness. Pettit and Lawson were joined by Ernesto Corvelle who was ex-SAS and fluent in Russian and a smattering of an impressive selection of other Eastern European languages.

They were driven under escort to the President's palace where they were greeted by Irena Pelochev. It was clear as they entered the state rooms that Pelochev had assumed the reins of power in the absence of her husband and obviously found the position to her liking. Her staffers were all strikingly handsome males in their mid-thirties who fawned over her as if she were royalty, which she undoubtedly thought she was.

Tanterelli, who had accepted the post of liaison officer had spoken to Pelochev on the telephone and had outlined the plan of attack so that it was not necessary for Pettit to brief her. She shook Pettit by the hand but ignored the other two.

"Am having thoughts about the proposings," she said imperiously. "First part not good. You plan we should drive to Russian border in special car and I go on to Moscow by train. Da?"

"Roughly," Pettit nodded his agreement. "Then when you find out where Wilson is and if it's the

310

Kremlin we will drive to you under cover of night and pick up both you and Wilson and drive back over the border into Nuovostan."

"Not good plan," she said with exasperation. "First border is long way away, will take too much time, not having too much time; second drive from border to Moscow is very long way, will take a week there and a week back. Roads not good, again too much time"

"Time is not the problem. Time we have but we need stealth, we plan to travel at night and hide during the day and stay away from towns and cities." Pettit countered her proposals. "Apart from that there is no alternative means of getting to Moscow or wherever, we can't exactly fly in, can we?"

"Da, can fly in." She gave him an evil smile. "I am personally knowing President Lebedev and can arrange to fly to Moskva in Nuovostan military helicopter, no problems."

"Last time I saw you, you were being interrogated and threatened by the Russian military. Why would they let you fly into the heart of their country in one of your war machines?"

"Simple," she looked at him askance that he did not know how. "I am tell Lebedev that I meet with President Wilson and persuade him to let me have information Lebedev want, but he must let me in to his country."

Pettit smiled to himself and turned away from her so that she could not see the change to his normally implacable look. Carla Tanterelli had been right, had he suggested such a course of action she would have objected but she had come up with a solution herself, which they had subliminally planted in her mind, and would therefore follow it through. Her proposal was by no means as simple as she thought in her shallow way.

311

She knew how to get there but she had no idea how to free Wilson and get him away from the Soviets.

Pettit's plan was simple and fraught with danger but, he thought, better that than complex and fraught with danger. If she could get his team there he was sure, with Pickering's help, he could release Wilson and get him back to the helicopter but he would have to rely on her to get them back to the comparative safety of Nuovostan. One of the more obvious flaws in his plan was that Pelochev could not be trusted; she would change sides at the drop of a hat if it was an advantage to her. He had to find some inducement that she could not resist to make sure she stayed on side.

The Russian made helicopter, with Nuovostani commercial markings, stood on its pad in the grounds of the Presidential palace, its squat body was open at the back end and the loading ramp that doubled as a cargo door was down, its trailing edge on the helipad. Pettit eased the Land Rover up the ramp and onto the cargo deck where it was secured with ratchet retaining straps. A six man team of Nuovostanis hand balled a bottomless, top covered open fronted three sided crate into position over the parked Land Rover. The open front was covered in with a hinged wooden panel which made the whole assembly look convincingly like a freight box; its markings in Cyrillic script indicated that the contents were tractor parts for export.

Pelochev sat in the second pilot's seat while Pettit and his crew squeezed in on either side of the freight box where they sat, uncomfortably, on folding plastic garden chairs. The flight to Moscow was a long one and required two refuelling stops on the way both inside the Russian border. At full speed it took them ten hours to reach their goal. They arrived hungry and thirsty and just before landing Pettit and his team folded the chairs and entered the freight box through the hinged front gate. Folding the chairs they pushed them into the back cabin of the Land Rover and crammed themselves into the front driver and passenger seats. They had closed the front door of the freight box and had to manoeuvre inside the cramped crate space using flash lights.

They listened to the changing note of the rotors and were conscious of the helicopter swaying as it hung in the air preparatory to landing. There was a slight bump as the twin after landing wheels hit the surface and a further gentler bump as the pilot pivoted on the aft wheels and settled the nose wheel. The engine whine slowed down and the separate whump, whump of the rotors could be discerned as they slowed down. After a short while the noise of the rotors stopped and there was an unnatural silence after so many hours of noisy flight.

Within the dark crate Pettit and his two companions waited in silence listening for the next signs of activity. Pelochev could clearly be heard talking in Russian to an official who was charged with meeting her and making sure she was not a threat. Corvelle listened intently to the exchange and translated the conversation in hushed tones for Pettit and Lawson.

"Why are you here?" The Russian asked officiously.

"I came to do my Christmas shopping." She said contemptuously and snorted in derision. "I am her to talk with your President Lebedev as you obviously know, stop wasting my time with your childish mind games"

"Of course I know I am a senior official in the border guard group and I am empowered to ask such questions." His voice was tinged with an insolence that he did not have the courage to express openly.

"I don't mind being asked questions as long as they are intelligent, so far you have failed the test." Her acid tongue cut like a whiplash. "Stop this nonsense; you know who I am and why I am here. Take me to the President without delay."

"What is this?" He kicked the freight box.

Pettit and his two companions flinched in the darkness and held their collective breath. This was the first of what they were sure would be many moments of impending danger.

"As you can see this is a freight box, I had to commandeer this commercial flight to get here and didn't have time to unload it." Again she snorted in derision. "What did you think; that I have hidden away the entire Nuovostani army and all of our tanks and guns to launch an attack on the thousands of armed Russians in Moscow and take over the whole country while nobody was looking, from a box of freight. I at least expected, as deputy president of Nuovostan to be met by a senior person with at least some intelligence. Take me to your superior and be ready to defend yourself against my complaints."

The argument continued as they both left the helicopter to look for the unfortunate senior border guard. The tongue lashing was halted for a brief moment as Pelochev called to the helicopter pilot to join them. They heard a scuffling as the pilot prepared himself and then the opening and closing of the flight deck door as he departed.

They waited a full ten minutes before carefully opening the freight box door and cautiously peering outside. Seeing no immediate danger through one of the side ports of the freight cabin they emerged from the box and squeezed themselves into the limited space between it and the fuselage. The limited view through the side ports showed that they were in a military style airfield and they were surrounded by a plethora of different flying machines, some of which appeared to have been there for a considerable time and were all but leaning against each other for support.

"Now, gentlemen we wait, and I'm sorry to say we're in Pelochev's hands for the moment. So....let us pray." Pettit smiled sardonically; his companions were not amused. "Don't forget, if you can do nothing about it, don't even try, you will probably make things worse.

Fifty-three

Waiting for word from Pelochev was boring in the extreme. The interior of the helicopter cooled rapidly with all systems switched off and within a very short time their breath was frosting in the frigid air. Pettit went over a variety of plans which attempted to cover all possibilities for the extraction and he realised that the task was statistically impossible; nevertheless he pursued it with gusto.

They changed into the cold weather gear which had been stowed in the back of the Land Rover and at Pettit's suggestion they tried to get some sleep in preparation for what might be a prolonged period of nervous inactivity. Lawson took first watch while the others rested; the exercise was futile and although they closed their eyes they were unable to sleep. Their minds raced with infinite possibilities.

Pettit's phone buzzed discretely and the caller ID told him the call was from Pelochev. He grunted in recognition and listened intently to her words, trying hard to unravel her tortured English. After asking a few questions he finished the call and turned to see his two companions watching him intently.

"Game on," he said, his face grim. "Irena has persuaded the President to let her take Wilson to his Dachau which was located 150 Kilometres to the east of Moscow so that she can, in isolation, persuade Wilson to give up his secrets. There is a slight fly in the ointment however the President obviously doesn't altogether trust her. She is to be accompanied by a colonel in the Army Intelligence Corps to make sure that nothing untoward takes place." He observed the

316

looks of concern on the faces of his two man team and smiled sardonically at them. "We are getting to the Dachau in this helicopter or at least within a few kilometres of the Dachau so we're going to have to lock ourselves into the crate again and keep absolutely quiet until after we land and they leave to go to the Dachau."

"And then?" Lawson enquired.

"And then we have to decide how we get to the Dachau from wherever we land, Pelochev doesn't know where that will be. She will let us know by telephone, what the location is and how far away we are and how we can get there. The rest will be up to us." He didn't take the conversation any further because what being up to us meant was still a total unknown. Even Lawson was not in command of the full facts of their capacity to affect a rescue and exit strategy for both Wilson and Pelochev.

Pelochev, Wilson and their single escort boarded the helicopter together with a new pilot. From within the confines of the dark crate they could not see the replacement pilot but they were made aware of the difference by the timbre of his voice and the fact that he showed overt subservience to the Colonel and spoke in clipped military phrases unlike the original pilot, who was more garrulous.

The clattering flight to the Dachau took less than half an hour. After landing there was the noise and chatter of the departing passengers and from within the crate they could feel the movement of the deck as they disembarked and then the slam of the door as it was closed behind them. They waited in silence and in darkness until after the sounds of departure faded away. Pettit moved to the front of the crate and was about to open it when the high pitched whine of the engine driving the rotors began to wind up in preparation for flight. Pettit cursed as the craft rose unsteadily into the air.

As they rose and pivoted the engine noise increased and the steady whump, whump of the rotor blades changed in pitch as they ascended. Pettit cursed and switched on the interior light of the Land Rover which gave enough illumination for him to be able to make out the faces of his two companions.

"This wasn't part of the Pelochev plan." His features were bleak. "She thought that the helicopter would be parked at the Dachau so that we could make a quick in and out but it looks like that part of the plan is a no go. Not a good start," he observed reflectively.

Their flight was of short duration and less than twenty minutes later they landed again and remained hidden away until they were sure the replacement pilot had left the helicopter. When silence settled and remained they cautiously opened the front of the crate and peered through the bulkhead into the cockpit. All that remained behind was the pungent odour of cheap cigars, presumably used by the pilot who obviously did not believe in the in-flight no smoking policy adopted by most of the rest of the world; but then, Pettit mused, they were in Russia where rest of the world rules did not necessarily apply.

Silence was punctuated and underlined by the random ticking of the cooling engine which occasionally erupted into an unexpectedly large ping. Peering out of the side windows revealed an unlit compound which appeared to be part of an abandoned agricultural area surrounded on three sides by ramshackle abandoned barns in varying stages of disintegration; there was no sign of habitation or movement wild, domestic or human. The open side of the compound looked out over an uninhabited plain on the horizon of which was a muted glow, probably Pettit thought the early evening lights of a town.

He took a large scaled regional map of Russia from one of his many uniform pockets and studied it by torch light being careful not to let the weak light be seen by anybody outside. If they had flown north from Moscow the lights he could see would be those of Vologda, south could be Tula or Kursk, east could be Vitebsk or Vilnius and west could be Cheboksary. His calculation assumed average travel speeds and that they had followed a straight trajectory. He gained nothing from the exercise except momentary diversion and sighed deeply, the self-deception had not worked.

Silence within the confines of the fuselage was interrupted by the angry buzzing of the telephone, he snatched it up and prodded the receive button but did not announce himself.

"Is Irena," Pelochev's voice was unnaturally subdued.

"Yes." Pettit's response was non-committal.

"Have not many timing," she hissed, "the machine you giving to me tells location of me."

"What are the co-ordinates?"

"Here are numbers." She read out the co-ordinates from the GPS reader he had given her. "Now you must come here soonly. The President Wilson is not good and the general with me will make him not better with his questionings. I am expecting to ask questions on Cullin but am not given chances. Come to me now and when you arriving send me words not by voice," by which she meant text, "and I will explain how to get us."

"What did she say?" Lawson asked breathlessly.

"That's not an easy question to be definite about but from what I can gather President Lebedev's watcher is preventing Irena from asking the right questions for us and she's worried that this will take Wilson over the top. She wants us to go to her; I gave her my GPS reader and she's given me her position we just have to figure out where we are and we're all set."

"If we don't have a GPS locater how do we do that?" Lawson was not critical of them not also having a GPS reader; they had changed their plans and adopted hers so he was intrigued to learn how they could find their position in a foreign country without alerting the natives.

"We go back a long way in time and techniques," Pettit said cryptically. "We get ourselves out of here and onto a main route of some kind and find signposts which will tell us where we are; then we use the coordinates she has given me to find her."

Lawson looked askance at him. "Are you seriously telling me that is what we are going to do; we're going to look for signposts." He shook his head in wonderment. "I would never have believed it from anybody else."

"If you have a better way of doing it I'm all ears."

Lawson hesitated, thought for a moment and then shook his head. "I'll be damned if I can think of anything better but please don't ever let anybody else know that's what we did – my street cred would drop to below zero." He smiled, suddenly brightening his face. "Did anybody ever tell you you're a genius, because you are."

"Not a genius," Pettit replied evenly. "Just very clever." His laugh was self-deprecating.

Having completed a cautious reconnoitre of the immediate area and found no signs of life or habitation the rear loading ramp of the helicopter was lowered and the packing case opened up to allow the Land Rover to be removed from its confines. Pickering's compressed liquid sodium engine was fired up and Pettit had to look at the instruments to be sure that it was working properly. There was a complete absence of engine noise even when the revolutions were increased, the CLSE was noiseless, the only discernible sound was from the wheels crunching over the debris scattered around the compound as the Land Rover was reversed out.

Dressed in their black combat uniforms the three men were virtually invisible behind the tinted windows which, together with the rest of the bodywork, they had dampened and then smeared with dust. The windscreen wipers were switched on briefly and the dust smears partially cleared to give the appearance of the vehicle having undertaken a long overland journey.

Their first decision when leaving the confines of the horseshoe of buildings was the decision to turn left or right. Pettit opted for the right turn to take them in the direction of what he believed to be the town of Vilnius, the deeply rutted track led to a more substantial road which was wider than the track but not metalled. The Land Rover coped easily with the ruts and undulations and despite the roughness of the terrain they were able to make good progress in the last of the fast fading daylight.

By the time they reached a main rout the darkness was punctuated only by the Land Rover's high energy lights which cut two pencil beams of blue tinged light into the deep gloom. This time they turned left and picked up speed on the more forgiving road surface and within minutes Pettit spotted a roadside marker with worn almost unreadable Cyrillic's. Ernesto Corvelle jumped down from the vehicle and inspected the stone marker. He climbed back into the vehicle and gave a translation of the marker.

"It says that we are 40 kilometres from Velikiye Luki." He looked over Pettit's shoulder at the large scale map of the region. "There's Velikiye Luki," his finger stabbed at the map, "and we're forty kilometres from it."

"Okay," Pettit said with relish, "now let's find another signpost and see if we can tell whether we're north, south, east or west of Velikiye Luki."

They drove to another road junction this time found a signpost which gave them a cross reference to establish their position on the map. The signpost informed them that they were 2053 kilometres from Daugavpils; with this additional information they were able to establish their approximate position on the map. The map grid was marked with a GPS location grid and by comparing where they were with the coordinates that Pelochev had given them they were able to establish a route that they could take and to estimate how long it would take then to make the journey.

Pettit estimated that the journey would take them two or three hours, depending on the state of the roads and whether they might meet obstacles that would cause them to detour. Lawson took the first spell of driving while Pettit assumed the role of navigator. The Range Rover made light work of what would have been for a normal road vehicle hard going. Surface conditions were very variable and the metaled surface frequently gave way to become a rutted rocky track when even the range Rover had to slow down to walking pace.

Forty five minutes into the journey Pettit's telephone vibrated into life. Pelochev sounded nervous and her voice was so low that Pettit had to ask her to repeat herself frequently.

"Am in Dachau," she hissed breathlessly, "President Wilson is sleep for now and Colonel is gone to bathroom, I must be fast before he is coming back. Where you are?"

"We should be with you in less than an hour, I'll call you when we are closer and you can talk us in."

"Not to call me," she hissed urgently, "if Colonel hears phone he is to getting suspecting. I will call you when it safe is and possible. Am not getting anything from Cullin yet, I think he is very sick. Somebody comes...." The call was cut off abruptly.

"What did she say?" Lawson asked nervously. "It didn't seem like a very long call."

"There's a fly in the ointment." Pettit paused in giving his response because he was thinking on the move. "The military escort is proving to be troublesome, it seems like he's interfering with Pelochev's interrogation and is going to be a problem for us. I had hoped we would get a clear run at this but we are going to have to watch out for him and handle the situation as it develops."

They spent the rest of the journey to the Dachau in comparative silence which was punctuated by Pettit giving route instructions to Lawson as they jolted along the unmade surfaces. Their reverie was interrupted by a shout from Ernesto Carville who had spotted activity on the road up ahead which was lit by an emerging half-moon which was fortuitously between clouds when it really counted. Pettit took this to be a good omen, not that the road ahead was active but that the activity had been detected while there was still something they could do about it. Pettit gave orders to his two companions swiftly and succinctly during a brief pause in their journey.

They started moving forward again this time with the engine distress noise turned on and Lawson drove an erratic course weaving about on the road in exaggerated fashion. They navigated a gentle curve in the track and were on top of a small military convoy which was headed in the opposite direction but was currently stationary. This was not what they had anticipated and Pettit hoped that his catch all plan of action would still achieve the desired result.

The Land Rover's powerful headlights had been switched off and the much weaker side lights switched on. Mud smeared on the light lenses dimmed the lights even further and together with the weaving and uneven path they were following and the dreadful noise of an engine in what sounded like a terminal faze they hoped to navigate this potential obstruction by deflection rather than subterfuge. As they approached the military convoy Carville wound down the left rear window and began shouting in loud Russian so that the soldiers could hear him.

"I told you to get the damn car fixed before we left Ostrov, but no you are a lazy son of a cretin," he screamed over the clattering of the engine. "Now here we are in the middle of nowhere with this dying heap of rubbish and we can't even stop to have a pee because we'll never get started again." He gesticulated at the soldiers hanging out of the open windows of their vehicles. "What can you do with a cretin?"

The soldiers were all jeering and laughing at this noisy clown who was at least breaking the interminable boredom of their convoy. An officer had dismounted from a staff car bringing up the rear of the convoy and held an assault rifle across his chest. He stepped out into the road and held his hand up, palm forward to arrest the passage of their vehicle. Pettit and Lawson in the front of the Land Rover had a decision to make, to stop and be discovered or to run the officer down and become instant fugitives. As it transpired the choice was taken out of their hands.

Of his own volition Carville hung out of the window and improvised. He shouted in coarse Russian over the noise of the engine as they slowed down; the induced popping and banging of the exhaust became even more pronounced. "Comrade, we are in real trouble we go to a family wedding but this imbecile didn't fix the car before we left. If we stop we'll never get started again and if we stop I will kill him slowly and get blood all over the place."

The officer grinned and stepped aside waving them through as he did no. Pettit and Lawson let out breaths that they did not realise they had been holding as they passed the tail of the convoy which they watched in the wing mirrors until the curve of the road hid them from view.

"I don't know what it was you said to him," Pettit said with relief and a touch of admiration in his voice, "but whatever it was you are a genius."

Carville told them chapter and verse what he had said and they all joined together in laughter as much in relief as in humour.

Fifty-four

The rest of the journey was uneventful; there was very little traffic on the road and they passed through a number of small communities. Some were so small that they were through them before they had the opportunity to take precautions against unwelcome interest from the natives. When the communities they passed through were made more obvious by roadside signs or by the glow of lit buildings they switched on the engine noise but not so loud as to be obtrusive. Pettit explained to a slightly perplexed looking Lawson that the reason for doing so was that if they were seen passing through a village and their vehicle was making no noise it would arouse suspicion, if they made too much noise it would cause counter-productive anger; getting the noise level just right would prompt irritated acceptance. He likened it to the subtle success of hiding something in plain sight in which the something which was intended to be unseen was overlooked because it was not being hidden from sight in any obvious way.

The Land Rover, now in silent running mode, approached the location of the Dachau along a pitch black narrow ribbon of road. Pulling off the road before reaching their objective Pettit got out of the vehicle and donned night vision glasses; he pulled a black hoodie over his head and pulled the drawstring tight so that his face was entirely covered. To all intents and purposed dressed like this and standing on a black topped road in the dark, he was entirely invisible even to his colleagues who were watching him.

There did not appear to be any external personnel guarding the property, presumably because President Lebedev was not in attendance. No lights were visible in any of the four elevations and the whole building looked to be abandoned; satisfying himself that there was no obvious danger he withdrew his telephone and sent an agreed message to Pelochev. He closed the phone and waited for a response.

The delay in receiving a response was nerve wracking and Pettit continued walking around the perimeter wall of the Dachau as much to fill in time as to facilitate gathering additional intelligence. He was considering sending a back-up message when his telephone began to vibrate.

"You are here now?" Pelochev's soft yet somehow still strident voice came over clearly.

"Yes we are here, what is the situation?"

"President sleeping is, as me was also 'till you woke me."

"You're talking to me so I presume you and the President are alone."

"Is so, I can waking up President and getting him to first floor for escaping."

"First floor?" Pettit queried. Getting from outside to the first floor was fraught with difficulty and something he didn't relish.

"Not first floor English but first floor American, is ground floor English."

Suddenly the perceived obstacle had been removed; they were on the ground floor which made extraction so much easier. "Which elevation are you on?"

"What is meaning elevation I am on?"

"Which side of the building, how can I find you?"

"We are in back, opposite side to main entrance. I will opening drapes so you to see light. But being careful there are soldiers outside my door inside the house, the windows are lock and are having prison bars."

327

"Okay, I'll get back to you as soon as I can get the car to you and I'll call you. When I do you must stand back from the wall and you must make sure the President is dressed and ready to go."

"Da." The line went dead.

He returned to the car and was not seen by his companions until he opened the door and slid into the front passenger seat. "We're good to go." He rotated his index finger which was his instruction to start the engine. The muted dials on the dashboard showed that the engine was fired up and could be seen to be working from the dash board indicators, there was no engine sound. At Pettit's direction they navigated their way to the wall flanking the back of the building and at its centre they stopped with the vehicle pointing towards the stone perimeter wall. He switched on the BAM2 unit.

"All ahead slow." Pettit sounded like a navy, rather than army man.

Lawson headed forward towards the wall and although they knew what was going to happen, the situation still seemed unreal to them. The BAM2 skin shield which clung to the contours of the cars body unglued the structure of the wall and converted its substance into disparate atoms which drifted in a fine almost indiscernible mist on the light breeze and the Land Rover drove through the wall into the modest grounds surrounding the Dachau. As they passed through what had been a solid wall, despite their knowing what was about to happen, there was a collective expulsion of breath

Once through, they stopped and listened to make sure that they had not elicited unwelcome attention. The silence remained unbroken and there was no sign of movement either human or canine. Pettit used his telephone again. "Irena, are you ready?" He listened to the response and indicated to Lawson that he should inch forward. "Stand well away from the outside wall or you will die." His brutal words were delivered without any emotion.

Lawson drove the vehicle through the wall and waited straddling both inside and outside until the dust of atoms settled and the interior became visible. Pelochev and Wilson were as far against the back wall as they could get and were dressed in outdoor clothes and paradoxically with suitcases at their sides. Pettit switched off the BAM2 unit and exited the vehicle after switching the BAM off and reversing the vehicle back from the breach in the wall. He ushered them into the back of the vehicle where they joined Carville and shut the door quietly.

They reversed back out across the narrow compound and back out through the perimeter wall onto the narrow external road. Within minutes of affecting the rescue they were heading back towards where the helicopter was parked. Pettit looked in the rear view mirror and saw that Pelochev was pale faced but agitatedly excited and Wilson appeared to be asleep, his head rolling from side to side with the erratic motion of their ride.

"What's wrong with Wilson?" Pettit enquired of Pelochev while looking at them both through the rear view mirror.

"He is have sleeps pill to make ready for interrogate tomorrow." Her voice was at a higher pitch than was usual and her eyes, he could not help but notice sparkled with intense excitement. "How you are doing this with the motorcar is this the BAM2 I have been hearing of?"

"Yes it is, but more to the point I could see no guards outside the Dachau, how many were there inside?"

"Six maybe seven but three or four will be having sleeps so maybe three to four will be watching at us."

"Any signs of them following us?" He asked Lawson.

"Not as far as I can tell," Lawson responded after checking his rear view and side mirrors.

Is like magic, how you get through walls like that. BAM2 is powerful like they all say." Pelochev leaned forward with her head between the two in the front seats panting excitedly. "Is like magic what you do, yes?"

"Not magic just science which," he paused reflectively and chuckled, "is actually like magic."

She had insufficient knowledge of the English language to understand the subtlety of what he was saying, even had she been concentrating on his words. Having seen a demonstration of the fascinating power of BAM2 at close up first hand, she realised that she wanted to possess this wonder of this science more than ever even more than the Presidency of Nuovostan, which was now within in her grasp. Wilson was slumped next to her, he was out for the count and not only because he had been drugged. His contact with the real world which had been tenuous before his abduction was now on the brink of non-existence. She looked at Pettit's reflection in the wind shield and saw his strong, determined and self-sufficient personality shining through. She thought in her usual way that she could use her wiles to use his strength to her advantage.

Being familiar with the route as they returned to the location of the helicopter they were able to maintain a much higher speed over the rough terrain. The understated sound made by the engine was drowned out by the wind noise and road rumble as they punched their way through the night air and made it feel as though they were travelling much faster that the speedometer showed.

Knowing that they had passed through a number of small villages which had shown no signs of life on the way out they abandoned the furtive driving they had adopted earlier and throwing caution to the wind increased their speed when the road was visible clear to in excess of sixty miles per hour. All was well until they rounded a steady curve at speed on a good road surface and realised too late that they had overtaken the convoy they had passed on the way out. The convoy had been parked on open ground next to the road and all the vehicles were in darkness.

Pettit held his breath and studied the road behind intently, all was quiet and dark and just as he thought they had got away with it he was aware of the staff car at the rear of the convoy had pulled out onto the carriageway and was chasing them.

"We've been spotted," Pettit said through clenched teeth, "and it's coming up fast we need to get away from it, pronto."

Lawson put his foot down and the Land Rover settled down on its rear suspension as acceleration overcame inertia. "I can lose them for the moment but we're only about five minutes from the turn off to where the helicopter is parked."

"Go for it and put as much distance as you can between us and them."

The Land Rover rocketed along the road swaying and bucking as the road surface alternately deteriorated and improved at random. They turned into the track leading to the landing site and executed a four wheel drift which pitched the Land Rover onto two wheels before it rotated back onto four with a loud, bone shaking jolt. The car that pursued them was a standard Mercedes saloon which was less able than them to negotiate the unmade twisting track which led to the buildings behind which the helicopter sat in the darkness before dawn.

Pettit and Carville exited the vehicle before it skidded to a halt and dropped the helicopters rear loading ramp without ceremony. The crate inside the freight cabin was open at the end as they had left it and in moments the Land Rover was back inside the crate and the ramp was closed up, as was the crate door behind it. In the cramped confines the four occupants who were sentient, and Wilson who was not waited, in complete silence. Faint noises from outside heralded the arrival of the staff car and movements felt from within the crate told them that the doors were being tested for access. Quiet descended once more to be punctuated a little later by a voice shouting into a telephone.

Pelochev translated in whispers what she could hear of the one sided conversation. "He is say that helicopter should not be here – what should he do?"

"Who is he talking to?"

"Not knowing," she said testily. She continued to listen intently to the faint voice from outside and she translated in real time. "He asks what should he do. He tells that markings on helicopter are Nuovostani." She paused as the soldier was listening to information he was being given. The voice outside changed from being a telephonic shout to a more conversational level. "He is told that the helicopter is from Nuovostani government is here by agreement of President Lebedev. They are told to leave it and get together with the work of finding the car they are chase because it might be terrorists and this is more important." Doors opened and were slammed and the staff car made a pirouetting exit from the courtyard, its tyres scrabbling for grip on the rubble strewn beaten earth surface.

"Who do you think they were talking to?" Pettit asked Pelochev.

"Not knowing for sure but I guess it was regional army headquarters."

"Is that bad for us?"

"Army is not choose to share thoughts with government or anybody else but themselves. For this moment we are okay but when presidium and army talk together we will be in trouble. We must leave here soon. Dawn is coming, after that danger."

"Where's the pilot?"

"Pilot is back in Dachau under guard so he cannot leave."

"Oh wonderful," Pettit slapped his forehead in frustration. "Where are we going to get another pilot from?"

"Not needing pilots already having one." She smiled evilly to herself at Pettit's confusion. "Coming this way." She beckoned him to follow her into the forward cabin where she hitched up her inappropriately haute couture dress and straddled the pilot's seat from where she started pre-flight checks.

"You can pilot one of these?" Pettit was astonished at the thought.

"Am Siberian woman, can ride horse, drive tractor and fly helicopter, of course." She looked at his expression of surprise and laughed out loud. "Now you go and stop car from rolling around and I will take us away from here." She grasped the control column with her right hand and began activating a series of switches with the left hand. "Now is good time for you to do these things and we go."

Pettit went into the after cabin and began the task of securing the Land Rover in its crate, the floor tilted as he finalised the fixings and the rotors wound up to a vibrating crescendo. As they rose into the air the floor

333

swayed into a level position and then tilted forward and down as the machine accelerated forwards and upwards.

Walking forward quickly down the sloping floor Pettit entered the forward cabin and slipped into the second pilot's seat. Pelochev handled the controls expertly and with consummate confidence. She turned to him and smiled her alluring but evil smile. "Is good yes?" She turned to look at him as she banked the helicopter in a half right turn. "Is good yes? I can teach you to fly we have plenty time to be doing. You would like to fly?"

"You are an amazing woman, you dress like a fashion model and you fly like a cowboy controlling a wild stallion using only one hand. You are sparklingly beautiful and yet you sit there with your knees splayed in a most unladylike way and your mind is in the gutter. I don't know whether to admire you or fear you."

"What you are talking of? My English is good but you are speak very fast. You think I am beautiful and not like lady but like cowboy. You are very strange to me." She stopped talking to him and peered intently at the virtual horizon and the compass balancing the two together to achieve the desired result.

"Where are we going and why?"

"We go to Ural Mountains as far as we can before is getting light. Then we hide during day and carry on at night time to get back to Nuovostan."

"Why the Urals?"

"Plenty of place to hide from Lebedev, trees, mountains and valleys. When guards go in and find us not there they go crazy and Lebedev will go like maniac. He is needing to frame President Wilson in Wallaby court so he can get more years as President of New Russia."

"Wallaby court?" Pettit questioned in a puzzled voice.

"You know it is where decision of guiltiness is made before trial is done."

"Oh, I get it. You mean Kangaroo court." Pettit laughed out loud.

"Wallaby, kangaroo I don't understanding differences." She joined him in laughter and slapped her thigh with her free hand.

Pettit looked at her thoughtfully and wondered how a woman who was so screwed up in her personal and political life could suddenly become fun filled. He realised almost instantly the thought passed through his consciousness that she was entirely alone in this world and was simply not used to conversational interaction in a way which had no acquisitive agenda. The thought filled him momentarily with sadness.

Fifty-five

Just two hours later they descended into the remote wilderness of an isolated Ural Mountain valley. Wilson was still comatose and Pettit thought that it would be better for him to remain that way until they got him back home. Pelochev took a medical bag from her suitcase and gave him a carefully measured injection which she informed Pettit was a morphine derivative needed to keep him under and to control the pain of his ailments.

There was no food and very little drinking water left on board; it had been consumed during the long inward flight from Nuovostan so it was necessary for them to plan a re-provisioning trip. Using the GPS they located their position on the map and looked for the nearest place that they could get food for themselves and Diesel for the helicopter, they were not out of fuel but thought it would be prudent to have a reserve supply. Pettit drove the modified Land Rover and Pelochev was navigator and translator of road signs. They found a road of sorts less than a mile from the helicopter and opted to turn in a direction away from the mountains.

Most of the scattered collections of building which they drove through were too small to have a garage or even a food store and after driving through several without luck they stopped at a road side stall where Pelochev asked the stall holder where they could get provisions and fuel. They were directed by him to a farmers' cooperative general store which supplied the needs of the local agricultural community. On arrival at the store Pelochev was able to negotiate the supply of a small quantity of basic foodstuff, enough for a few days but the fuel was a different matter. Generally the local farmers would drive their tractors to the store and fill them with diesel as required. Landing the helicopter at the store was not an option and the store owner was edgy about these strange people. One of them was, by her accent, Siberian; the other said nothing but the way he was dressed did not scream Russian to him.

The language of business came to their rescue in the form of American Dollars, when the store owner was shown a quantity by the Siberian woman his misgivings were, if not forgotten, at least muted. He agreed to sell them five large drums of diesel that being the maximum that would fit into the back of their Land Rover. The profit he made on the sale was the equivalent to the annual profit on all his other sales; he was a happy man.

As the Land Rover left the store's compound he owner shook his head. The unhealthy noise the vehicle made and the black smoke billowing from the exhaust both looked and sounded terminal, if he had owned the vehicle he would have hesitated to fill the tank fearing the engine would blow up before the fuel was used. His happy feelings about his good fortune did not stop him from feeling nervous about selling fuel to them, they were a strange pair and he wanted to avoid falling foul of the authorities. Shortly after they disappeared from view he picked up his telephone and called the area party representative, outlining the transaction to him.

***

In his Kremlin office Lebedev was fuming. The idiot colonel to whom he had entrusted the custody of Wilson had contacted him to say that both Wilson and Pelochev had been abducted, he was unable to say how this had happened or when. He said that the outer wall and the wall of the Dachau had been breached and the two prisoners taken away by a person or persons unknown. He was ordered back to the Kremlin to personally debrief the head of security and face the wrath of the President.

The military were put on high alert to look out for and apprehend, by any means, the kidnappers and the kidnapped. Lebedev's rancour was heightened by the approaching presidential elections before which he intended to show his control and strength by having a show trial which would clearly show that the shortcomings in the BAM2 programme that he had revealed was due to the duplicity of Wilson not a lack of application on the part of the President. Without Wilson, whose arrest and deportation to New Russia had been widely reported as a coup for the President, Lebedev's position was precarious at a critical time, an event which would count heavily against him.

Military leaders were left in no doubt that their performance was being monitored and that the service which recovered the situation would be rewarded handsomely, the unsuccessful services would be punished by harsh attrition. The leaders of all four services: Army, Navy, Air Force and Security were focussed to the exclusion of all else to ensure that they were the successful contestant. There began a desperate scrabble to garner local intelligence in the area around the Dachau and in ever widening circles to identify any unusual event which would lead to the possibility of apprehending these harbingers of the President's wrath.

Military intelligence in Perm almost missed the significance of a citizen's report of a foreign man and a Siberian woman who were both strangers in the area who had made unusual purchases of food and more notably drums of diesel, the fuel required by the Russian made helicopters which were used by the Nuovostanis. This occurrence was reported to the

President's office and was forwarded on to the President by one of his security advisers.

As soon as Lebedev saw this intelligence he scooped up his telephone and called the Dachau. "Listen carefully to what I say." The President's voice sent a chill down the spine of the colonel who was white knuckled as he gripped the telephone. "You can get yourself out of some trouble by acting like the soldier you are supposed to be. We have an area location for the Nuovostani helicopter that the terrorists have stolen. Send somebody at once to the area and where the helicopter is parked and make sure it is secured. Do you understand me?"

"Yes Mr President," he said in an unaccustomed high falsetto voice. The phone he was holding was already dead.

Lebedev was, as always, fast on his feet and it had immediately occurred to him that the kidnappers would have captured Pelochev as an aid to their escape by using the leverage of Wilson's kidnapping to secure her cooperation. He processed the intelligence that had been passed on to him and imagined by deduction that the kidnappers had purchased fuel for the helicopter using Pelochev in the process which in turn meant that they were likely to be foreign nationals using her for local colour to prevent revealing their foreign accents. Less than an hour later he received confirmation from the colonel; the helicopter was gone from its original parking place. He ranted at the colonel and extracted from him that they did not know when the kidnapping had taken place. Pelochev and Wilson had retired to their ground floor suite shortly after 8 pm yesterday and their disappearance had only been discovered at 9 am today.

"So, colonel you are telling me that they could have disappeared at any time between 8pm last night and 9 am this morning, it is now 7 pm meaning that they could have up to a 23 hour head start." He listened for a response from the colonel but received only line static. "Return to Moscow immediately and report to the security services – immediately," he repeated before he slammed the telephone down onto its desk dock.

The President's next call was to the security services at Perm. He told them to take a detachment of men, as many as he could muster, to the country store where the purchases of food and fuel had been made and to interrogate the owner. He told them that failure to find the whereabouts of the fugitives would make them responsible for the failure of the entire mission and that they would be held responsible. At all costs it was Lebedev's intention to set up others for a fall in the event of failure.

Fifty-six

The contingent of Perm security forces descended on the nervous owner of the country store and began an inquisition without any preamble. The terrified man answered to most simple questions with fear fuelled gibberish; his terror of the consequences of saying the wrong thing was tangible. His alarm was driven by his not being an active member of the state police support, the SPS, but of taking the pay which was due only to those who were active members. The fierceness of his interrogation rendered his testimony useless; a second interrogator changed tack and used more subtle approach and began to make headway. After half an hour they had from him some more useable intelligence; a description of the two people concerned, the timing of the event and a description of the vehicle they were using. The store owner was very definite about the vehicle, his being an agricultural man, and the Land Rover being, so to speak, the Rolls Royce of farm vehicles. Their poor interrogation technique and the lack of interdepartmental cooperation lost them precious time.

Perm intelligence processed the information sent back to them from the farm store and passed it on to their Moscow counterparts who in turn passed it on to the President. He made an immediate connection; the woman concerned was obviously Pelochev and she had obviously colluded with the kidnappers in fact, he supposed, she could be the instigator of the whole scheme. This thought not only confirmed his suspicions that she could not be trusted but that she intended to renege on their original deal. It didn't occur to him that she had done to him what he had intended to do to her; paradoxically he considered it to be a betrayal of his trust, although he recognised no paradox on his part.

Decisively he picked up his telephone and told the security services to send helicopters and a convoy of secret service ground troops to the location of the store and to continue the search started unsuccessfully by the disgraced colonel for the fugitives or the helicopter or both. Security helicopters left for the newly re-equipped Bolshoye Saveno airport in Perm to set up a search of the area around the farm store to see if they could locate the helicopter or the Range Rover, which by all accounts was on its last legs and would when found be easy to capture. The ground troops and their rough terrain vehicles were loaded into transporters for their overnight journey to Perm.

Satisfied that he had taken the steps necessary to recapture Wilson using the finest of Russian troops he decided to increase the effort of the scientists to uncover the secrets of the BAM2 unit in their possession.

If the scientists could achieve this goal then Wilson and Pelochev together with whomever else was working with them could be disposed of without the necessity of a show trial. He would simply tell the people of Russia they had been eliminated as state spies and by doing so underline his ascendancy as President of New Russia.

In the quiet of his private office he allowed his mind to relish what he would arrange to do with Pelochev and the people with whom she had colluded. The anger these thoughts provoked in him recharged his depleted batteries and gave him a great deal of pleasure.

Pelochev felt paranoia. As they approached the hidden landing site of their helicopter she insisted on their making an approach to it stealthily on foot. She removed a lethal looking pistol from her coat pocket and clutched it firmly and competently in a two handed grip. With the gun extended before her she moved cautiously towards the helicopter. It looked quiet, just as they had left it.

Pettit removed his telephone from one of the many pockets in his combat fatigues and punched in a single number. He spoke rapidly when the call was answered and closed the call.

"I've spoken to Mark," he whispered to Pelochev, "he says that everything is okay."

"Maybe he speaks from being forced." Her face was pale and drawn. "All looks too quiet, maybe he is captured and forced to tell he is okay."

"You stay here and I will go and check the situation out."

"Not good idea," she sounded very agitated. "If you are also then to be forced by who is forcing Mark Lawson."

"Calm down," he cajoled her. "If there was a problem Mark would have let me know when I spoke with him. He would have called me by the wrong name or something like that."

"Not if he is being forced to cooperate."

"Okay, here's what I'll do." He punched the same single number into the telephone and waited for a response. "Mark, Irena thinks you are being held captive and trying to lure us into a trap. Give me a yes or no response, in Island speak."

"Ve- yr- gnith ho - yak" Mark responded after a moment and painfully translated the words 'everything okay' into English (Gni-shil)

"What he has said?" Pelochev enquired.

"He said 'Everything okay' in the Island language."

The side door of the rear cabin opened and Lawson emerged into the gathering gloom and walked up to them. "Where's the Land Rover," he asked, puzzled at not being able to see it.

"Let's go and get it." Pettit turned to Pelochev. "Go on board and close the door and don't open it 'til we get back."

When they returned with the Range Rover Pelochev was still pale faced and agitated. Clearly there was something on her mind which was bothering her. Once the Land Rover was secured Pettit confronted her. "What's the problem Irena, you're as nervous as a kitten in a thunder storm." He kept his voice gentle to avoid spooking her any more than she already was.

"When we leave store with food and benzinska I saw something that is not to make a quick memory in my mind but now I am having a slow memory and it is not a good one."

"What the heck does that mean?" Lawson turned to Pettit for a translation.

"It means that she saw something that didn't register immediately but on recollection what she saw was not good news," Pettit raised his eyebrows to her in search of agreement.

"Is what I said!" Her furrowed brow illustrated that she was cross.

"No matter," Pettit said to Irena, "what is it you saw?"

"Saw jacket hang on back of chair with patch on shoulder sleeve." She used the American word patch, meaning a badge.

"What was the patch?"

"Patch mean that man who own jackets is member of state support police. This are people who spy for the government and shop as well their own family to the political police. Political police is outside the law and can throw in prison for ever for no reason."

"Do you think they're on to us?"

"Not knowing for sure but could be big, big troubles."

"Okay, so we'd better get out of here ASAP while it's still dark and put some distance between us and them."

In haste they emptied the drums of diesel into the helicopters fuel tanks by syphoning and made ready to leave. Pelochev, sitting in the pilot's seat opened up her map of north east Russia and studied possible routes.

"I am think we take shortest route out of Russia. We must go Finland, is maybe fifteen hundred kilometres and will cost about four hours. We can get there just after dawn and then make more better plans." As she said this she wound up the engine in preparation for departure, she switched on the radar and watched the sweep arm showing an empty sky.

She displayed great skill in getting the machine into the air considering there, in the pitch darkness, there were no visible indicators of what was in the sky around them except for the radar scope. Everybody, except her, was nervous. The air speed indicator showed three hundred and fifty kilometres an hour and the altimeter indicated they were at five thousand metres.

"How high are the Urals?" Lawson asked Pettit, who turned to Pelochev.

"Is not to being problems, we fly away from Ural Mountains and go north of Leningrad over Lake Lodozhskoye to Joensuu in Suomi Finland. There in maybe four hours."

It was not possible for anybody to relieve Pelochev, she was the only person on board able to pilot the helicopter. Lawson went into the rear cargo deck and checked on Wilson who was beginning to recover from the tranquiliser which Pelochev had administered. He was taken from the back of the Land Rover and

345

dumped unceremoniously into one of the plastic garden seats wedged between the freight box and the fuselage.

The air over the nursery slopes of the Urals was turbulent as it fell from the summit to mix with the notionally warmer rising air from the plains. Their passage was uncomfortable in the turbulence, the helicopters airframe being designed for internal function rather than for its aerodynamics. The further they got from the high ground the less the effects of the turbulence and the more the vibration of the ponderous rotors took over. The overall result for them all, except Pelochev, was that they fell into silent contemplation and tried to ignore the total lack of any external light source and the dreadful feeling that they could run into an unseen obstacle with no hope of survival.

They were awoken from their reverie by a squeal from Pelochev who told them that radar showed that they had unwelcome company. Pettit stared at the screen and saw the sweep arm showing three blips flying in a V formation some twenty kilometres behind them.

"Change course and see what they do," Pettit said in an icily calm voice.

Pelochev did as he suggested and they watched the radar scope to see how the three blips reacted. At first nothing happened but slowly the three swung round to align themselves with a tracking course.

"Can we go any faster?" Pettit said as he continued to scrutinise the scope.

"Maybe a little."

The tone of the engine increased in pitch as she wound it up to full speed and Pettit continued to watch their pursuers. They too increased speed but could only keep pace rather than catch up.

"They're not gaining on us but how long before we reach Finland?"

"We are here." She placed a scarlet nail onto the map that Pettit was now holding pointing to a point east of Leningrad.

"We're, what, about twenty minutes from the Finish border and at this speed they're not catching us so we should be okay."

"Not okay if they have missiles to launch and not okay if they are talking to Leningrad to getting help from them." Pelochev's voice had taken on a worried edge.

"Mark, follow me." Pettit jumped hastily from his seat and dragged Lawson behind him into the cargo floor and into the Land Rover in the freight box. He spent the next few minutes talking to Lawson who shook his head frequently and looked deathly afraid.

Back on the flight deck Pelochev was coaxing every ounce of speed out of the helicopter and watched in satisfaction as she saw that they were maintaining the distance between themselves and their pursuers. Her eyes flashed between the altimeter, the radar scope and the air speed indicator.

"Silas," she shouted urgently, "we have more companies. She pointed to the radar scope.

Pettit saw that there were a further four blips approaching them from Leningrad which was to the west of them. These blips were considerably faster than the three that were following them which indicated that they were jet aircraft rather than helicopters.

"Am going to put down," Pelochev shouted in panic, "we will all be killed dead."

"Not yet, let's wait and see what they are going to do."

"If they are going to missile us it is not good to wait."

"Mark," Pettit shouted through the open door to the cargo deck. "Do what you've got to do and let's hope

347

we've got it right. If we haven't we won't know anything about it either way."

"What meaning has this?" Pelochev was both puzzled and scared.

"You'll find out soon enough."

The sound of the proximity alert was deafening in the confines of the flight deck. It was serving its intended purpose and alerting them without subtlety to the fact that other aircraft were flying in threateningly close proximity. Pelochev wrenched the control column in different directions in a vain attempt to evade the deadly onslaught that would surely come from the Mig armaments. The manoeuvres were in vain, there was no escape from what was about to happen.

Fifty-seven

The radio message from the lead pursuit helicopter which trailed Pelochev's helicopter by some fifteen kilometres had come through to the Veschevo Airport military control centre in an unstructured rush. It took the controller of information some time to unscramble the garbled message. The lead pilot sending the message had belatedly realised that they had no speed advantage over Pelochev and they were fast approaching the Finnish border after crossing which they would be untouchable. His main objective had been to capture these insurgents for the President and to reap the rewards of his success. As soon as he realised that he was not fast enough to catch up with them before crossing the border he also realised that he would bear the brunt of the President's anger if he failed to make the capture, or at the very least to blow them out of the sky.

His major difficulty was that none of the three helicopters were fitted with air to air missiles; their only armament was cannon and their range was certainly not the fifteen kilometres that separated them. So, frustratingly, he had to ask Veschevo for assistance. The assistance they gave was in the form of four intercept Migs fully loaded with air to air missiles. Within three minutes the Migs were scrambled and had their target on the radar scopes as well as the three pursuing helicopters working out of Perm.

Because the orders to attack came with the President's authority they were able to engage immediately. The Migs were on their prey within a minute and without delay the flight leader made a

349

swooping run and released a missile against the undefended and ponderous helicopter.

Pelochev was wide eyed with fear. Her insides turned to liquid as she realised that her helicopter had no defence against the Migs. She wrestled with the controls in a vain and uncontrolled attempt to try to evade the cannon shells which she could imagine travelling towards them at five times her speed. Her life did not flash before her eyes just as everybody had said it would; she felt only cold all enveloping and frustrating fear.

As the lead Mig flashed past she saw the white hot image of the twin jets as it peeled away from her; to her surprise there was no sign of cannon fire her relief was short lived when it occurred to her that what she had witnessed was a reconnaissance run to check their target. At the speed it travelled the twin points of light diminished to nothing in the absolute darkness. The respite was brief she was acutely aware that shortly after the Mig had disappeared into the distance there was a ghostly, spiralling streak in the air which was familiar to her having seen the same once before when witnessing the trials of a heat seeking missile.

The missile flew past them at several hundred metres away and she twisted in her seat and watched with dread as the missile corkscrewed around to follow their heat signature. Closing her eyes she swallowed hard and waited for that split second between existence and non-existence. It is said that under these circumstances time travels incredibly slowly and so it was with her, she suddenly realised that she was not breathing and let out an explosive breath as she opened her eyes. Pettit still sat beside her motionless as a statue with a look of complete neutrality on his chiselled features.

"What is happen, is missile brokened?" She looked askance at Pettit's immobile features.

"Just wait and you will see." Pettit nodded his head out of the port side window.

A Mig was making another pass and she watched it with trepidation as it repeated the manoeuvre of the first one. Again the twin flames of the jet's engines as it flew past and then a repeat of the missile as it corkscrewed its way behind them to follow the engines heat. The closer it came the faster it seemed to travel until without warning it disappeared in a millisecond flash. She was aware again that she had been holding her breath."

"What magicness is this," her eyes were wide open and round with surprise.

"This magic is BAM2," he said simply.

"But helicopter are not fitted with the BAM, how can this be done so?"

"We have the small unit in the Land Rover that we used to get into the Dachau. Mark Lawson did a quick reconfiguration on the control panel which allowed us to put a bubble around us to stop the missiles getting through."

"This means we cannot be hurted by anything?"

"Not while the BAM is in operation."

"What about helicopters chasing us?"

"There's nothing they can do to harm us."

"This is not what I am meaning." She assumed a look of absolute evil. "I am meaning we can turn and meet other helicopters and melt them out of the sky."

Pettit shook his head as he was once more brought up short. Her attitude would be that of many others and was why it was imperative to keep the technology out of the reach of others who would choose to use it for such purposes.

The remaining part of the journey to Suomi Finland was accomplished with comparative ease and safety. Realising that they had been outmanoeuvred the pursuing helicopters had given up the chase and landed at Veschevo to face the wrath of President Lebedev.

The Finland authorities were not happy about the unheralded arrival of a Nuovostani helicopter which was clearly on an illicit mission of some kind. There was no love lost between the Fins and a totalitarian New Russia but that did not mean they had sympathy for the Nuovostanis, whom they knew to be ruled by a renegade who was at least as undesirable as President Lebedev. For the Fins, New Russia was a threat and on their common border whereas the Nuovostanis were from remote eastern side of Russia and a different country and therefore were not an immediate threat. They decided it would be expedient to help the Nuovostanis on their way without any delay.

Before they could depart, Pettit insisted that they set up fuelling points for their eight thousand kilometre journey which would take a minimum of two days. They could not fly straight across Russia to get to Nuovostan so it was necessary for them to fly around northern Russian territories and they would need to make at least two stops for refuelling. He had insufficient local knowledge to be able to establish where they could stop safely en route.

Help came unexpectedly from Irena Pelochev, being Siberian and having until recently having the ear of high up Russian politicians she knew in some detail the relationships between the Russian government and some of the outlying territories which hankered after severing ties with their oppressive Russian masters. Two such places of interest were on her list. The first was Novaya Zemlya and the second, Severnaya Zemlya, both being islands off the north coast of New

Russia, in the Barents and Kara Seas', they enjoyed a degree of freedom brought about by the weakening of Russian bonds after the dramatic economic collapse which had influenced, for the worse, the whole world. She explained her plan which would allow them to land and refuel without alerting the Russian authorities.

The two chosen islands, together with others, were sitting on vast reserves of crude oil which gave them a great bargaining chip but neither of them could fund or afford the time to extract the oil to their advantage. Pelochev, in her world of devious plans had a scheme which would enable them to stop off in Russian territory to refuel without the central Russian government being alerted. Pettit listened to her proposals with grudging admiration and with the dawning realisation that they might actually be able to pull this off with success.

Their first stop off after leaving Suomi Finland was at Krasino on Novaya Zemlya. They were greeted by a small contingent of Novaya Zemlya Nationals, all of whom spoke English proficiently. Pelochev addressed them in Russian and they responded in English out of deference for their English speaking visitors. A fuel bowser drew up alongside the helicopter as they moved off through the snow to a collection of no frills customs buildings.

The senior member of the welcoming delegation opened up the discussion without preamble. "You want to talk to us about producing our oil products. We are interested to hear what you have to say."

"Here is Silas Pettit." Pelochev made her statement and waited for a reaction from the NZ delegation. They looked at her with blank faces. "He is chief man of Recovery Island." This got an instant reaction and they looked at Pettit as though he were from a different world, which in many respects he actually was.

"Let me explain the situation to you." Pettit decided to speed up the pace of the conversation which he thought could get bogged down by introspection. "You want to drill for oil but it is very deep and drilling down for it will take maybe years, we can do it for you in a matter of days."

"And you want what in return?" Their spokesman asked with natural suspicion.

"I am a representative of Recovery Island we would like to foster more cordial relations with you and perhaps have mutually beneficial trade arrangements." He said this with a straight face which did nothing to reveal the true purpose of their being in Novaya Zemlya which was to use the stop-over as a refuelling opportunity, this had been the kernel of Pelochev's plan.

"I don't see that we have anything you would want by way of trade."

"That's simple." Pettit got their immediate attention. "We can trade in the oil which we help you to produce."

The remaining discussions were brief and to the point and as the proposals made did not require any financial or other contributions from Novaya Zemlya, agreement was reached painlessly. Their next task was to fly to Severnaya Zemlya and to repeat the process. With both islands agreeing to the terms offered they were refuelled and on their way without undue delay. They made an additional stop at the Novosibirskiye archipelago where the same deal was cemented.

Pettit marvelled at the way Pelochev was able to manipulate the situation to her advantage and wondered whimsically if she would not be an asset to Recovery Island's aspirations. As quickly as the thought occurred to him he dismissed it; her record of duplicity was too ingrained for her to be considered trustworthy.

Fifty-eight

By the time they got back to the President's palace in Nuovostan, three days after leaving Suomi Finland, Wilson was in a bad way. The last five days of drug induced catatonia had significantly undermined his constitution and his emergence from the effects was slow and only partially successful. Since Pettit had last seen him just three years previously Wilson had aged at least twenty years in physical terms and additionally he appeared to have regressed progressively to his distant childhood. When he had recovered enough to be able to communicate he barely knew who he was and he recognised neither Pettit nor Pelochev.

Interrogating Wilson to discover the whereabouts of the documents Pettit had been charged with finding and to which Pelochev also laid claim was a fruitless task. Wilson slipped in and out of reality without warning and even then his periods of lucidity were founded in an indeterminate place. Not knowing where the full set of documents was held and not knowing how Wilson had sabotaged the information in the possession of the Russians was a problem for Pettit. The fragility of Wilson's thought processes did not preclude that he would regain his faculties to the extent where he would regain cognisance and pose a future threat to Recovery Island.

From Pettit's perspective the success of his mission lay in preventing the knowledge contained within the documents being available to any agency outside the Island. The information in the possession of the Russians was flawed and incomplete to such a degree that the uncovering of the secrets of BAM2 was all but statistically impossible. He did not know whether the

Russians were aware that the BAM unit was a dummy but it would make no difference, if they had the original BAM2 experiment notes they still posed a threat.

The fact remained that the weakness of their situation was that should Wilson recover, all their efforts to protect themselves would be in vain. It was also a fact that Pelochev's ambitions to reap the benefits of BAM2 ownership were nullified if Wilson were to regain his self-control, in which case he would reassume ownership of access to the secret, or if he were not to regain control she would not have the desired access without his collusion. Either way she was stymied as she was not so arrogant as to assume that she could control Nuovostan as President without Wilson's backing or without access to the secrets of the technology; she needed either or both of these to achieve her goals.

Pettit contacted Gilliland by satellite phone and updated him with a situation report. He felt as though he were between a basalt rock and an even harder place. The Russians were impotent to make any progress as was Pelochev but worst of all so was Recovery Island. Pettit's mission had not failed yet but neither had it been a success.

Pelochev was nervous about many things. Using the forged certificates of marriage she had would allow her to take over the Presidency but she had incurred the wrath of the Russians and she was concerned that they would mount an attack on Nuovostan which she was not in a position to repel. If she could find the information that Pettit needed she might have a bargaining chip to even up the odds by involving Recovery Island in her defence. She mobilised the rag tag of palace guards to search the palace and all its apartments for any sign of the missing documentation and threatened them with dire consequences if they did not succeed.

***

Gilliland and Crook were joined by Pickering, Tanterelli and Gray in a brainstorming session, to assess the possible actions to be taken based on Pettit's intelligence. As was becoming increasingly more frequent the two women were better equipped to come up with practical propositions which did not necessarily involve threats or implied violence. They listed what it was they were trying to achieve. Primarily they needed to remove from outside influence anything that would jeopardise the security of BAM2. The components this involved were: access to the missing research notes and the retrieval of the missing BAM unit. The first was easier than the second and more important and it was on the easier of the two components that they chose to concentrate.

Led by Tanterelli's input they devised a radical approach to the problem which would ensure that the documents if not physically found would never again see the light of day. The solution was not without its side effects which would need to be handled with care. Their proposal was communicated to Pettit with instructions to carry them out immediately.

Pettit was taken aback by the plan he was charged to implement: it was certainly radical and although easy to carry out, he would need to make careful preparations to ensure that the repercussions were minimised. He was in two minds about how to mitigate the reaction of Pelochev to carry out the plan. His first move had already been anticipated by Pelochev and a detailed search was already being undertaken by her people. Wilson was still incapable of telling them anything; he had descended into a zombie like state and his bodily and mental functions were running on automatic. He appeared to have reached the point of no return; even the voices which had been giving him direction were momentarily stilled

The search being carried out within the palace was not yielding any results. Detailed room by room inspections failed to uncover anything of value. Pelochev in her unsubtle way tried every trick in the book firstly to cajole and then to threaten the searchers; the efforts produced nothing. Against Pelochev's wishes Pettit insisted that all portable objects should be removed from the palace and dismantled to expose potential hiding places. Furniture, drapery, paintings and objet d'art were moved into an outbuilding where they were dismantled and fully inspected. This also failed and they were left with a collection of worthless components from what had been many valuable pieces. This left only the structure of the building itself and endless searches to find anything in the nooks, crannies and hollows of the structure also yielded no results.

Pelochev was devastated, not because her home had been wrecked but because they had failed to unearth the one thing which would give her the power to control her own destiny; they had run out of options. The failure of this approach left them with only one other viable solution to the conundrum. It had been established that in his last few declining months he had not left the palace and knowing that he would not entrust the documents or the piece of BAM2 that he had hidden away what they wanted, if not secreted within the structure, could only be somewhere in Wilson's personal possessions.

This was a last resort before the proposed radical plan was implemented. The last resort also, predictably, failed and they were left with no options but the final irreversible solution. Pettit decided not to let Pelochev know what the solution was, instead he distracted her by saying that an aircraft would be arriving from Recovery Island and would take Wilson back to Recovery Island where he could receive the best possible medical attention. She should accompany him and, with the aid of two Island medical personnel, take care of him during the flight. Pettit, Lawson and Carville would drive the Land Rover back to Manchuria and reconnect with their cargo plane to make their way back to Recovery Island. She readily accepted the proposal viewing it as an opportunity to inspect the Island community which Wilson had failed to take over but she, with the inside track they had presented to her, fully intended to succeed.

Fifty-nine

Pettit and his team of two watched the Apache Chieftain piloted by Adie Cox as it disappeared into the gathering gloom of evening taking with it Wilson, Pelochev and two specialist medical practitioners. He wondered why Pelochev had gone without making a fuss about something as fundamental as spiriting her and Wilson away from their homeland into what was to her an unknown society and one in which she and Wilson were considered enemies. Wilson remained semi-comatose and was completely unresponsive to social interaction. His blood pressure was high, but not dangerously so and his vital signs were feathery but not enough to cause alarm.

The Land Rover stood in the compound of the Presidents palace prepared and ready for its journey to Manchuria across the joint border with Nuovostan. Their meticulous search for the documents had not gone well, despite using every available person on the palace staff and dozens of soldiers they had been unsuccessful in their searches. To prevent the documents being stolen by a member of the search team they offered the person who found the documents a reward equivalent to a lifetime of earnings. Not finding the documents was not because of a lack of effort on the part of the searchers.

Now Tanterelli's radical solution was all that remained. Lawson entered the palace and painstakingly and made doubly sure that all personnel were clear of the building and of the palace compound and that all external doors and windows were secured against personnel infiltration. He left through the main entrance securing the main door behind him.

"All set," he said to Pettit handing to him a miniature remote control unit.

"You're absolutely sure that there's nobody left in there." Pettit was uncharacteristically hesitant.

"As sure as I'll ever be." A nervous tremor in his voice gave away that he was fully aware that any error on his part about the human evacuation of the building would be catastrophic to himself and whoever might be left inside.

"Okay, here we go then." He pressed the go button on the remote and reflexively flinched.

There was an odd tortured screech and the whole of the palace disappeared in a heap of fine particles which eddied in the light breeze. The air was permeated with an ozone laden odour reminiscent to that produced by old fashioned generators used to power fairground rides. When the dust settled the palace was gone, sheared off at ground level except for a small circular plinth in the centre of the devastation, on which sat the BAM2 unit which Lawson had removed from the Range Rover.

"Game, set and match," Pettit muttered under his breath. "If we can't find it nobody else can. Game definitely over."

Pettit surveyed the heap of finings which was all that remained of the Presidential palace and felt the same frisson of excitement he had experienced in his former military life when he had directed artillery fire from a dangerously exposed forward position and had witnessed the total destruction of his selected enemy. The feeling gave him a jolting pause for thought and he was enveloped in a cloak of sadness as he realised that despite the veneer that his years on the Island had been applied over his former lifestyle, it still lingered in the background but not as deeply in the background as he had hoped. He had felt pleasure at the wanton

361

destruction he had instigated to protect the Island from harm but did it at the same time make him as misguided as the enemies he so much despised?

Sixty

Eleven sat, as inconspicuous as he always was, in the largest of the court hearing rooms. He was there by specific random invitation to take part in a special hearing described as being of great importance but about which he had been told nothing, even as a Council member. He looked at the other occupants of the room from beneath lowered brows. There was, he noticed, a sprinkling of senior Ruling Council members who looked equally as mystified as he was himself about the reason for being there. No such meeting had ever been called before and very little warning had been given. He also noticed a peppering of non-Council members some of whom he recognised as RIR members. This did not give him cause for concern; the attendees appeared to be a cross section of Island society.

The buzz of conversation in the room tailed off as two of the four founders, Gilliland and Crook, entered the chamber and settled themselves into half of the judgement seats on the raised platform at the head of the room. An expectant hush settled in the room; it was impossible to read the intentions on the faces of the founders, they looked neither happy nor sad as they regarded those assembled before. Eleven smiled inwardly; the fourth founder was missing, what he and not many others knew, because no official announcement had been made, was that Caine was no longer living and he hoped that this would be the occasion when her demise would be released and his programme of destabilisation would begin in earnest.

Gilliland opened the proceedings. "This is an official hearing and you, as a cross section of both interested and neutral parties, have been invited to attend. The time has come to untangle the intrigue in which we have become embroiled. Some of you know of the puzzling things that have been going on." His gaze flicked towards Pickering, DK and Craddock, "and some have been rather more heavily involved." He looked this time at Lawson and Olsen.

Eleven looked uneasily at those around him, acutely aware that as well as the selection of fellow Ruling Council members there were the five RIR cell leaders whom he of course knew by name and designation but who did not know of each other, or him. He had never met but had seen in the offices of PRICE the Olsen woman whom Webber had said was a great asset to the unions cause, although she was not a radical member. He was vaguely uneasy when he noticed that both the entrance and exit doors were guarded inside and outside by two men in the uniform of Pettit's security section.

"Some of you here have knowledge of the intrigue I mentioned earlier and others are, as yet, unaware." Gilliland continued with his theme. "It came to our notice some three months ago that there was a movement afoot bent on undermining the Island's administration and our chosen way of life. We can only guess at the reasons for the formation of this movement but any guess that we make is underpinned by the presumption that whatever the reason, it is unlikely to be for the good of the Island's citizens as a whole."

Eleven shifted nervously in his seat. He wracked his brains in an attempt to see if there was some way that RIR had been discovered or infiltrated. He could think of none but was now seriously concerned about the presence of the cell leaders who of course were

364

ignorant of his identity as well as each other's. As a noted member of the Ruling Council he wondered why he hadn't been told what it was that Gilliland was planning to say and he also wondered if the other Council members were ignorant of the purpose of the meeting. He looked at them each in turn but could detect no discomfort among them.

"For those who don't know him I would like to introduce you to Mark Lawson." Gilliland indicated that Lawson should stand up and be recognised by all of those assembled. "Mark is a senior member of the control room staff and he does an excellent job of keeping us safe from attack from our recognised enemies. He also has another unheralded job for which he is admirably equipped; he is the Director of External Security and in that task he looks after the interests of the Island in respect of threats from off Island sources. He has been heavily engaged with the infiltration of other countries in order to find out if their intentions towards us are benign or malignant. As was expected he has found that there are a number of countries which do not have our welfare at heart. It will not come as a surprise to you that Nuovostan is a deadly enemy and sadly, despite our peaceful overtures, I must also tell you that the same applies to most of the Federation and latterly to Russia. There are countries within the Federation which are neutral, notably the USA and parts of Europe, parts of the Middle East, the Australasias' and Japan. All of this means that we have some powerful detractors and a number of neutral countries which would be sympathetic but of no specific help should there be any form of conflict between us and those believed to be our enemies. We do have friends in Africa, for example Nematasulu and her neighbouring countries but if there were to be a conflict they could only support us morally from the side lines, they can only offer limited non-interventional assistance.

Our isolation is only tenable because we are, as an Island, solid in our resolve to pursue our adopted way of life. At least," he paused dramatically, "until we learned that there is a group within our Island's shores which can only be described as an enemy. Their intention is to appropriate the way of life which we hold dear and change it to be compatible – dare I say as corrupt - as their own philosophy. To counter this threat it was necessary for us to take positive steps to identify those who wished us evil. Mark Lawson is the architect of the means by which we have attempted to achieve this goal. How effectively we are able to achieve it will be revealed to you a little later." Gilliland paused again and swept his gaze around the room to take in the demeanour of a selected few.

Eleven began to wriggle more uneasily in his seat. From what was being said he could only assume that Gilliland was talking about RIR. Frantically he searched his memory for anything that might have given the game away; there was nothing. The only person on the Island who might be able to identify him was Cole and possibly, but it was unlikely, Zen with whom he had recently become as spiritually close as his androgyny would allow even though they had never knowingly met face to face. Zen would certainly not give Eleven away after the way the Island administration had mistreated him. He calmed himself and awaited the unfolding outcome.

"You were told," Gilliland continued, "that I had gone on holiday when I disappeared for a few weeks. What you didn't know and what was kept from the rest of the world, was that an attempt was made to assassinate me at the airport here on the Island." Some of the listeners looked horrified and there was a sharp collective intake of breath. "We were fortunate enough to have intelligence that this was about to happen, thanks to our vigilant security procedures and our small team of agents. We were able to defuse the situation but still make it look as though the attempt was successful. Again I will tell you more about how we achieved that a little later"

This explained to Eleven the puzzling matter of the faked assassination, it was not because of a leak from either Wilson or Pelochev nor was it with the complicity of 'A'. He felt a flood of relief, his suspicions about the involvement of those he had chosen to side with being duplicitous was unfounded. The founders had been responsible for hijacking the situation by, no doubt, fitting Gilliland with a bullet proof vest – the rest was acting. His relief was all encompassing, his cohorts were not responsible for the leak – but that still didn't explain who had leaked the information.

The story that Gilliland was unfolding was uncomfortably close to the truth and continued to concern Eleven. Once more he glanced around the room at the cell leaders who sat looking relaxed which he would expect considering they did not know that he, Eleven, and by their own unrecognised association they were implicated in the events that were unfolding. Looking at each member in turn he tried to recognise by their demeanour which one could be responsible for the leaks that must have taken place for Gilliland to know so much. He could discern no visual indication and he wondered if any of them realised that RIR was instrumental by proxy in the assassination attempt.

There were no signs from any of the RIR members that they were concerned about being discovered. He searched his memory for an event that had led to the discovery of the assassination plot. Nobody came to mind, the only people who knew about the assassination apart from himself were Wilson, Pelochev and of course 'A' and there was no tangible reason why any of them would leak the information.

"There was further intrigue," Gilliland continued, "the group which had been responsible for planning my assassination also planned the execution of the UK Prime Minister." There was once more a sharp intake of breath from the listening audience. We learned that the plans made by our detractors did not end with the two assassinations there was a move to have other heads of state removed but events overtook those plans.

This added revelation was a further shock to Eleven as he realised that the carefully constructed cover for the assassinations had been compromised by means that remained a mystery to him. The assassination of the other heads of state had been conceived but not planned in any detail, so how could Gilliland possibly know about them? The common denominator in all of this had to be Wilson; he was the only one who had knowledge of the whole range of assassinations planned, maybe Wilson was not the friend he had thought and it was increasingly obvious that Wilson was rapidly losing the plot. Eleven was aware of Gilliland's voice droning on in the background but was too caught up in the betrayal scenario to absorb the words or their meaning. Maybe, he thought, it was not Wilson but Pelochev, the idea grew on him. He did not like Pelochev, she was disrespectful and calculating and incredibly self-centred as well as being self-important. He did not recognise that he and she were two sides of the same coin.

"I must tell you that a BAM2 unit was stolen and even though we thought we had fool-proof security it was spirited out of the country and sent to an enemy location."

Eleven's unease reached new heights at this revelation but comforted himself with the thought that although they knew this had happened they did not appear to be in a position to do anything about it. The stolen unit was in Russian hands and their engineers were in the process of hacking their way into the control system so that they could operate it independently. He was also comforted by the thought that his sitting in on this meeting was a sure sign that his cover had not actually been blown; they were probably fishing for information. If that was the case he placated himself with the thought that they were using the wrong bait.

Sixty-one

Gilliland surveyed the assembled citizens in the court room and continued his discourse. "You may wonder how it was possible for the assassinations to be attempted and countered. Although the attempts took place and were recorded, they are shockingly graphic and I have no intention of showing them. We were able to keep the deception secret from those who arranged the assassinations because of the sterling work of Mark Lawson and his very able undercover agent who will be introduced to you very soon. But first the assassin, the success of our mission was that we were able to sabotage the intentions of our enemies." He swept his gaze around the room.

Eleven's autonomic warning system kicked into overdrive as he followed Gilliland's gaze around the room. *'Had his gaze flickered as it swept past,'* he wondered, *'or was the brief duration of the glance a sign that Gilliland had no wish to give anything away?'* It was worrying that he claimed to have sabotaged the planned proceedings. How was that possible? At Eleven's insistence the assassin had been recommended by Paul Zen who was an avowed enemy of the Island's councillors who had treated him so badly so it was not possible for him to be working with Lawson or anyone else on the Island.

"Before we take that strand of the story forward let us consider who on the Island would want to destabilise the whole of our structure by getting rid on one or more of the founders and throwing the Ruling Council into disarray. The answer to that was once more provided by Mark Lawson. He was able to identify that there was a movement on the Island which has an agenda which relied entirely on such destabilisation; they call themselves the Recovery Island Rebels, the RIR.

Eleven found that despite his equanimity it almost impossible to control the alarm that he felt at not only their knowing that his organisation existed but also knowing it by name. His face remained totally impassive, the fact that he had been invited to this meeting indicated to him that he was not suspected of being involved, '*after all if he were a suspect they would hardly be letting him know that they were on to him.*' The feelings of unease would not however leave him despite his putting a positive spin on the revelations; he became even more uncomfortable when he recognised that he was being illogical in his thought processes to give himself fleeting comfort.

"We are a society based on freedom," Gilliland continued, "but that does not mean that any person or organisation, no matter how well supported, can override the integrity of our chosen way of life. It is evident that this is not the understanding of the self-styled RIR their aim is not clear except to say that it serves their own interests not those of the Island as a community. The temptations placed in their way by accessing the power of BAM2 are obvious, just as their reasons for stealing it are obvious. This is the very reason why we had no option but to develop our own society to prevent its misuse."

Eleven's face remained implacable but beneath that veneer he sneered at the naivety of the founders and all that they stood for. He looked around those listening to Gilliland; mostly they were wrapped up in what he was saying and were hanging on every word. His RIR members were, he noticed, beginning to look uncomfortable with the exception of Paul Zen who looked as unconcerned as Eleven had expected him to

371

be. Once more he wondered why there were so many of his people in the audience and he wondered about Zen particularly; he was after all an obvious outcast having been in court so often. Why would he have been invited?

"And so," Gilliland pursued his theme, "we are clear about the threats being made. We are also clear in our minds what needs to be done about it. We will unearth those behind the plotting of the assassinations and we will also deal with the very serious matter of a stolen BAM2 unit."

Eleven could not control an automatic body jerk at the mention of the stolen BAM2. He had a feeling of burgeoning unease at the way this dialogue was unfolding which was immediately countered by the thought that the stolen BAM2 was in the hands of Russian scientists who would surely over a hopefully short time be able to unravel the secrets of the technology at which time his plans would be nearing their conclusion.

"We know," Gilliland chased his subject relentlessly, "that the unit was stolen from the back-up storage facility at a time when an apparent accident was created as a diversion so, we know who was responsible for that incident and it is a good starting point." He paused and scanned the audience.

There was an overt reaction from Piotre Kwietakovski who immediately recognised that they had discovered his role in the deception and therefore his identity. Eleven saw the reaction clearly and was sure that others would have seen it. In his furtive mind he began to consider ways in which he could wriggle out from under the revelations which were now beginning to edge inexorably towards him.

Kwietakovski slid down in his chair in a vain attempt to become invisible but in doing so only made himself more noticeable. He was aware that people were looking around the room trying to see if anybody was reacting to what had been said. There was only one person whose eyes seemed to linger on him; it was one of the Ruling Council members whose name for the moment remained elusive to him.

Making no move to identify the perpetrator of the accident, Gilliland continued. "You may well wonder how we made the discovery about the accident being connected with the removal of a BAM2 unit; once more this is to do with the work of Mark Lawson and his agents. We presume that those who stole the unit tried to unravel its secrets and we also presume that they failed and instead decided to export it to a location where it could be worked on without secrecy or time constraints." He looked around the room at the expectant faces of the majority of his audience. "How do we know this?" He paused for dramatic effect and once more scanned the expectant faces. "There are two basic reasons involving two different people one of whom you all know and one whom you don't." The occupants of the room became very quiet as they waited with bated breath to learn who the two were. Eleven was by now beginning to actually display overt signs of apprehension. Surely, he thought, they must be on to him. Not wishing to draw attention to himself he resisted the urge to run from the room but he did look around for an escape route should it become necessary. To his added discomfort he saw that each of the exit doors were still guarded by black clad guards from Pettit's security forces, two inside and two out. He bided his time waiting to see how the situation would develop.

Sixty-two

The jury areas were thronging with desultory RIR members and the hubbub in the room grew excitedly as those still seated in the gallery talked animatedly about the startling revelations that had been made.

"This enquiry might take some time." Gilliland hushed the audience with his opening words. "We intend to uncover the process by which this despicable organisation was managed and to start the ball rolling we call Piotre Kwietakovski to the witness box to answer questions from the chair."

Kwietakovski looked drawn and sick as he made his way from the jury box to the witness box. He mounted the three steps that took him to the floor of the box and stood elevated above his surroundings so that everybody present could see him clearly. He complied with the request to identify himself in a hesitant voice.

"Mr Kwietakovski it is clear, I think you will agree that you are fully implicated in the act which led to the removal of one of the BAM2 units from its holding vault?"

"Yes," he whispered despondently, his dreams of returning home to Poland as a hero who could save his country from European tyranny were in tatters.

"I believe you said yes, please speak up so that we can all hear you."

"Yes," he repeated in a louder but still quavering voice.

"Will you tell us in your own words what happened on the night this incident took place?"

"I was told what to do, they said if I didn't follow orders I would be killed." He lied in the hope of mitigating his involvement.

"Who was it that ordered you?"

"A voice on the telephone and I couldn't recognise it because it was disguised electronically."

"Are you saying that you don't know who ordered you to carry out this crime?"

"That's what I'm saying."

"Interesting - and how long have you been a member of RIR?"

"About two years."

"And how long has RIR been in existence?"

"I don't know I'm just a member, I don't know anything about the organisation's history."

"I see from our records that you are number 15 in the organisation and that is the number you have tattooed on the inside of your large pedal digit." Gilliland smiled at his own hyperbole.

"That is correct." Kwietakovski was not as amused as the breathlessly waiting audience.

"You are the fifth member of the first cell and the leader of the cell is number 11, is that so?"

"I believe that to be so."

"If you are a member of cell number 1, does that mean that you are a member of the most important cell or that you are one of the earliest members of the organisation?"

"Both I suppose." He was unsure of where this line of questioning was leading but decided to be truthful rather than be caught in a lie.

"Both you suppose." Gilliland repeated the response in a flat voice. "You would like us to think that you are a pawn in the RIR game but you are a founder member of the premier cell and you carry out criminal activities without regard to the consequences and the way they affect other Islanders, like for example rendering a colleague unconscious?"

"I just do what I'm told."

375

"And what were you told to do on the night you arranged for the BAM2 unit to be stolen."

"I was told to distract the other guard and swap the BAM unit for a dummy box which was supplied to me in component form and once I had disabled the other guard I removed the unit to a location just outside the vault to be collected by somebody else."

"Who gave you these instructions?"

"I told you it was a voice that I didn't recognise because it was disguised electronically."

"Are you in the habit of taking orders from somebody that you don't know and breaking the law by acting on them?"

"Well no, not exactly." Although he was in an indefensible position he still had enough pride not to want to be thought of as a dumb fool. "Although I couldn't recognise the voice because it was disguised it is one I had heard many times before."

"And was it the leader of your cell, number 11?"

"Yes it was."

"Tell us who number 11 answers to."

"Eleven is the top man." He said in despair. "But I swear I don't know who he is and that is the absolute truth."

"Who else do you know in your cell?"

"I don't know anybody else. When I speak to them by telephone their voices are disguised just like mine."

"You may stand down for the moment and go back to your compatriots. You and they will be dealt with later.

The next person called to the witness box was Colleen Brogan. She was questioned about her part in the theft of the BAM2 unit and was as forthcoming as Kwietakovski had been, there seemed little point in her denying her part in the plot. She confessed that she had been unable to unlock the secrets of the unit because she feared the outcome if she got it wrong. She was, like Kwietakovski, unable to identify Eleven.

A selection of the other RIR members were questioned about their involvement in the organisation but unlike Kwietakovski and Brogan the parts they played within the organisation had not been uncovered and the general questions put to them did not lead to any further information about their involvement in the removal of and tampering with the BAM2 unit.

Eleven listened in an almost detached way to the nebulous testimony of those whom he had hoped would enable his ambitions. They would all be punished and probably exiled but that was a matter of no importance to him. He was, in that part of his brain that was not required to listen to the testimonies elicited by the inept questioning of Gilliland, considering his next moves. Zen, because of his underworld contacts, would continue to be a useful adjunct to his newly developing plans. Eleven, being a respected member of the Ruling Council was confident that he could convince whatever lame brained committee that was appointed to punish the miscreants that Zen was a victim of circumstances and had been led astray by the conniving leader of RIR and should be given an opportunity to redeem himself.

While all of this was happening he would develop the ties with Russia and Nuovostan to the point where he was indispensable to them and he could use Zen as bait for Pelochev whom he knew was more than susceptible to the charms of a young fresh bodied stud, which Zen certainly was. Eleven recognised that he was incapable of engendering such a distraction, not just for reasons of appearance but because he had no understanding of the mechanics of seduction other than that it mysteriously worked.

The listening part of his brain kicked in when Gilliland began to launch a further diatribe. "We have made a lot of progress without really getting to the nub of this matter. Unquestionably the members of the now defunct RIR are not lying but they are by no means telling the whole truth. Others of their number were involved in the processing of the stolen BAM2. Somebody collected it from where Kwietakovski secreted it after removing it from the vault. Either the same or another somebody will have tried, obviously unsuccessfully, to activate the unit, otherwise it would have been used to progress their aims. The fact that it has been removed from the Island to Russia means that they are looking for technical assistance to activate it." He paused, sighed deeply and looked around the room.

Crook took up the cudgel. "Ladies and gentlemen, this has been a long day we have as Chester indicated achieved much but there is still a long way to go. These misguided rebels," he swept his arm towards the dejected RIR members, "are a problem and cannot be allowed the freedom of the Island nor is it practical for them to be held under house arrest." He swept his gaze around the expectant audience. "You may be aware that the latest part of our Island construction has been underway for some time, the plumes of smoke and steam on the horizon are a giveaway. We have been constructing a new Island called Hold Island and these sad people will be its first guests. Hold Island is a reformatory and although it goes against our basic principles to incarcerate people it has sadly become necessary to give ourselves the wherewithal to do so." There was a general murmuring among the audience, this was a departure from the usual openness of recovery Islands administration and there would no doubt be those who were for and those against it, as is ever the case.

"These people will be taken from here and transported to hold Island by undersea Transfer Car. On

378

the Island they will be allocated individual accommodations which will not be locked. They will be free to move about the Island and will be provided with basic foodstuffs. They will have no Information Portals and recreation will comprise healthy sport and exercise and there is a learning centre with a full library of reference books. They will not be permitted to communicate in any way with anybody other than the other inmates, there will be no guards and there is no possibility of escape, the enclosing walls are thirty feet high and offer no foothold for escape. No personal effects are permitted and the incarceration starts here."

Both the group of rebels and the watching audience were stunned by the news.

Sixty-three

Hold Island was, to the thirty six inmates, a strange environment. The architecture was functional and familiar but what on the Main Island were family dwellings were here single living units comprising two rooms – a living, sleeping and dining room and a separate bathroom. The furniture was functional and the Information Portal which they were accustomed to was, in their new accommodation, a simple screen with a menu which was entirely educational and offered limited subjects from which they were permitted to choose. The other use of the screens, they soon learned, was to wake them a half an hour after dawn by sounding a deep Tibetan bell tone which continued relentlessly until the inmate was forced out of bed in order to disable it. Once the alarm was disabled they were advised through the screen of their programme for the day.

The instruction for the first morning was that they should convene in the refractory, situated in the heart of the Island, after showering and changing into prison garb. The uniforms provided for them were hung up in a locker located next to their single sleeping platform and comprised a single piece Reco-fashion suit made of lightweight material with a horizontal striped pattern of yellow and black one inch wide stripes, there was a waist length loose tabard of the same material which could be worn by those whose body shape did not display well in the body suit.

Zen stepped into his prison uniform and looked at himself in the synthetic resin mirror on the inside of the locker door. He looked like a cartoon character wearing black and yellow stripes which warned others that he was a hazard to law abiding citizens, which he supposed was the way he was considered. His physique was such that he actually looked menacing rather than comical which is how he viewed the other inmates as they made their way on foot to the refectory. Most of the others were wearing the tabards for their intended purpose of disguising their body contours and they continually tugged at the hem to hide their other attributes.

Zen made his way to the refectory as had been directed by the information screen in his room. The single storey inmate accommodation was separated from the thirty foot high external security walls by a thirty foot wide no man's land. He presumed, correctly, that the reason for the space was to prevent the roof of the single storey from being used to launch an escape over the walls by ladder – not that there was any means of acquiring a ladder. The refectory building was part of a complex in the centre of the Island and was set on a plateau some thirty feet above its surroundings. Access to the upper level was by means of zigzag stairways or alternatively ramps. Having ascended to the plateau he could see over the Island's walls to the other three peripheral Islands to the main Island. The psychology of this construction was to allow the inmates to see the freedom that lay beyond their confining walls but not to take part in the life which existed there.

Once inside the refectory he collected a compartmentalised tray of cold breakfast dispensed by a black suited security guard who made no attempt at communication from his position behind the enclosed service counter. A breakfast tray was pushed through a narrow slot at the bottom of a mesh grill which separated the guards from the inmates. He looked around the room which was furnished with plain plastic tables and benches for four people on either side; all furniture was fixed firmly to the floor. The food trays were lightweight polystyrene which offered no possibility of being used as or being turned into a weapon.

Colleen Brogan nodded agreement to him when he indicated by the tilting of his head that he wanted to join her at the table. They ate in a silence which was only broken when they had both drained their polystyrene cups of strong tea.

"Zen."

"Brogan."

"Paul."

"Colleen."

"What cell were you in?" After their taciturn introductions Zen was the first to start a meaningful conversation.

"Don't want to talk about it," she said sulkily, her Irish brogue almost entirely hidden by the Boston American accent.

"Whatever you like," Zen said dismissively. "We're all in the same boat and it really doesn't matter now. RIR is finished."

"Eleven is still out there and he will get us out of this mess."

"Did he actually say that to you?"

"No, but I know of him well enough to realise that he can and will help us if we demonstrate that we are worthy of his effort," he continued in an offhand way, in his quest to identify Eleven. "When did you last meet him?"

She frowned and looked askance at him. "I have never met him; nobody has ever met him he is a total mystery to us all. I'm surprised you don't know that, everybody else does."

"Somebody knows and I intend to find out who it is because I want to contact him so that I can get off this Island and carry on with the business in hand. If you can help me identify him I will make sure that you get out of this hell hole as well." His statement was intense.

Brogan, being a street wise Boston Irish girl, recognised when it would be advantageous to court friendship and immediately categorised Zen as being worthy, more than any others on Hold Island, of her attention. "One," she said cryptically.

"One…what?" Zen smiled in puzzlement.

"That's the cell I am in, or rather was in."

"You were in Eleven's cell. Most impressive, you must be an important part of the organisation."

"I was one of the first after Eleven. I am code number 13."

"Are you superstitious?"

"Not up until now, but after this fiasco I might become so."

"Stick with me and maybe we'll beat the superstition and get lucky."

"Not so fast, you're English, yes?" Despite her resolution to take advantage of his offer of freedom, she felt the need to feed her xenophobia.

"You can probably tell by the give-away accent," he said acerbically.

"Well, I'm Boston Irish from the old stock and us and the English don't see eye to eye exactly."

"Beggars can't be choosers," he looked at her from under raised eyebrows.

"What makes you think I'm a beggar?" Her voice took on a hard edge.

"Maybe because you are a long way up this creek and there are no paddles - except maybe the ones that I can offer you."

"I can never trust an Englishman. The English ruined my homeland and killed hundreds during the potato famine. Why should I believe what you are saying to me?"

"For somebody from a family who deserted their homeland to live in the safety and comfort of the USA you carry a mean hatred across the generations. It's a bit like me, as an Englishman, saying that I hate all Italians because two thousand odd years ago they invaded my country and destroyed its culture."

"Not the same at all." The hard edge in her voice turned to naked anger.

"Tell me how it's different?" He sat back and observed her with a faint smile.

She looked daggers at him and he could see her trying to formulate a convincing repost to his argument. After a moment of ever changing facial expressions she simply said "Because you are English." She added no explanation to the utterance, to her the statement was enough.

"OK," he changed tack. "Why don't we explore how getting to know who Eleven is can help me and maybe you?"

"I still don't trust you, English."

"I don't need your trust; I just want you to work with me. Working together is the key to getting out of here and our only choice is to rely on the strength of Eleven."

Over the next few days Zen worked hard at connecting with a selection of the inmates in much the same way as he had with Brogan. Ultimately he learned from her that she had been instructed to break into the BAM2 unit but they wanted her to work more quickly and ignore the possible dangers. She had already convinced herself that this lie was true and was not prepared to countenance the fact that she had lost her nerve at the prospect of catastrophic failure.

He was able to identify the cell leaders by their code numbers and with the exception of the illusive number Eleven he did so for the other five cells. Most of the cell members were unknown to him except for some which he recognised by sight but the other five cell leaders were all known to him at least by reputation if not in person and he had not until now realised that they were RIR members. Eleven had been careful in his selection of the leaders; they were people of some seniority and influence who had been chosen to represent most of the areas which would be of value to the organisation. They were from security, supply, airport services, technology and infrastructure and each one was prepared, for their own disparate reasons, to play a leading role in the overthrow of the Island's administration. Their motivations were many and varied ranging from greed through to those who simply wanted the thrill of dissent and all impulses in between.

Zen's intention was to inculcate a feeling of joint purpose which would enable them to break free from the confines in which they found themselves and to begin anew with the task of achieving the aims of Eleven. Most of the people he talked to were game for picking up the task once more and hinted that there were still people on the Island who harboured grudges of one kind or another and would make able foot soldiers. Within a few days of incarceration any inmate of substance had accepted that Zen was a serious player who probably represented the best chance of their being able to resume a normal life.

Contact from Eleven came unexpectedly, completely out of the blue; the means of contact was very simple. On the third evening of his incarceration he went to the refectory as usual and once more picked up his meal tray; what was unusual was that the guard serving his meal to him muttered. "Sit alone and read the message." He found an empty table away from the more popular spots in the room and placed his tray on the table as he slid into the bolted down seat.

Making sure that he was not being observed he lifted the cover off the tray and looked at the array of food and beverage before him. There was nothing unusual about the arrangement, the main ingredients of the meal were in their separate shaped compartments and the plastic capped polystyrene water cup stood on the customary paper serviette. He lifted the serviette and unfolded it; there was nothing unusual about it so he placed it on the table and searched the rest of the tray. There was nothing of interest that he could see.

Turning in his seat he looked towards the servery to see it the guard who had served him was still there thinking that he had been given the wrong tray. The guard was no longer there. Frustrated by the failure of the intended communication he began to chew the tasteless food that he had been given; it was both nutritious and totally boring. Having finished the meal he collected up the plastic components which remained and topped it with the unused paper napkin. Residual moisture from the tray on which the serviette had been placed soaked into it and as he carried the debris to the reclamation chute he saw a few words gradually appearing on the dampened surface. It read '*ill prevail. E.* '

His pulse quickened as he saw what was happening, there was a message which had been written by hand using a chemical which was unseen when dry but visible when wet. He disposed of the polystyrene components and retained the serviette for later inspection. They were not permitted to take anything with them when they left the refectory and to ensure that they were unable to do so the one piece suits they wore had no pockets and were so tight that apart from being totally embarrassing to both men and women for quite different reasons they were unable to secrete any object that could cause harm.

A guard watched him as he approached the exit and held out his hand to take the serviette from him as he left. Within three paces of the guard Zen paused and threw back his head sneezing violently causing his head to shoot forward, he blew his nose with force into the serviette which he then offered to the guard, it was a false blow but the guard was not aware of this. The guard with a look of disgust on his face took a step back and waved Zen through without confiscating the contaminated serviette.

Back in his one man accommodation he made sure that nobody was near enough to see in through the clear unbreakable plasti-glass windows before damping a hand towel and wringing it out to remove most of the moisture. Placing the smoothed out paper serviette on the damp cloth he watched the message form and appear, faintly at first then it filled out and became clear.

This instruction will remain visible for less than ten minutes and will then evaporate beyond recall. You will be brought back to the court with a selection of others and will be questioned by an official You are to say that you had no knowledge of what RIR were doing and that you were recruited to be a gofer and did not have anything to do with the stolen BAM2 unit. You will say that you regret having allowed yourself to be recruited and that you had and have no intention of causing harm to the Island or the Islanders. Do as I say and I will be able to arrange for you to be freed so that we can pursue the original aims of RIR by regrouping. Be vigilant and we w..... the message ended at the point where the serviette had been dampened earlier by the moisture originally applied to it.

Ten minutes later the message faded and was lost, Zen tried to refresh it by damping it down again and was rewarded with just a blank wet serviette.

Sixty-four

An expectant silence prevailed in the courtroom as the founders filed in to take their places in the judgement seats. Eleven watched them assume their seats and then scanned the faces of the twelve rebels as they entered the court; they comprised the five cell leaders, the five members of cell one, Preece Cole and Paul Zen.

Cole was the first to be questioned and he was so focussed on hiding his substantial illicit bank account in France that he opened up entirely and told of his knowledge of RIR which was very little when distilled to its essence. Eleven caught Preece's eye and nodded his assent to what Preece was saying; it trashed RIR but Eleven was reconciled to that being a foregone conclusion. The final question to Cole asked if he had any assets off the Island which would be of interest to the council. For the first time in his testimony he paused before answering, he glanced covertly at Eleven who shook his head imperceptibly. Cole denied any off-Island assets in a shaking voice. He realised that his precarious position could only be mitigated by the intervention of Eleven without whom he had no hope, so he elected to protect the identity of the RIR leader so that his own situation could be alleviated After being dismissed he went back to the jury box containing his fellow prisoners. He was a shaking wreck and was entirely dependent on the good will of Eleven.

The five cell 1 members and the other five cell leaders were interrogated at length but revealed only as much as Cole had done, they had clearly recognised that the court was fishing for information and elected to confirm what he had said. Most of the day was spent unproductively and it became clear to the watching and listening audience that if nothing happened soon the proceedings would get bogged down.

Zen was the last to be summoned to the witness box and the audience murmured as they recognised him as the person who had recently been pilloried by Silas Pettit."You are Paul Zen." Gilliland made it a statement rather than a question. Zen presumed that no reply was necessary. "You have recently been convicted of a felony and are bound over. Is that correct?"

"No that is not correct," Zen's denial was emphatic.

Gilliland looked puzzled and consulted the documents on the desk before him. "I have documentation that says you have been convicted of a felony. Although you are not at this time under oath you are expected to tell the truth and if you don't agree to do so we will put you under oath."

"I am telling the truth," Zen pointed a finger at the two founders. "Pettit convicted me of a misdemeanour and called it a felony to suit his own purposes and you two went along with him. He's noticeable by his absence – he's too chicken to be here in court to answer my charges"

"This man is a menace to Island security and flouts our laws without thought." Crook continued to glower at Zen.

"We will continue with our questioning but at its conclusion we will adjourn to a side chamber and enter into discussion to resolve the matter of perverting the course of justice to which you allude. That you are a member of RIR is without doubt." He watched Zen who nodded his assent. "How long have you been a member?"

"About three months."

"And what caused you to join RIR, was it perhaps dissatisfaction with some aspects of the Island?"

"No, I joined RIR because they asked me to." There was a ripple of laughter from the audience.

"Who was it that asked you to?" Gilliland asked the question with a faint smile in recognition of the response from the audience.

"It was just an anonymous voice over the telephone."

"How many conversations did you have before joining and what was it that persuaded you to join if it was not dissatisfaction."

"I was just peed off with what had happened to me in court, yes I bent the law a bit but it wasn't anything serious and Pettit got to be very antsy and threw the book at me he obviously has something against me."

"Enough Mr Zen, as I said we will deal with that matter later." He paused and shuffled the papers before him. "What tasks did you carry out for RIR."

"None," he lied thoroughly convincingly.

"I have information that you did not use your Recocard for a matter of days on several occasions. How do you explain that?" Gilliland changed tack abruptly.

Zen, realising that the plan which had been for a third party to use his Recocard during his absence from the Island to visit Pain in London and in travelling to Nuovostan, had failed and left him exposed. With lightning quick thinking he came up with a plausible excuse. "Those were days when I had a bug. It wouldn't go away completely and kept returning. I decided to stay at home and not go out and infect anybody else." He delivered the lie with a steady, almost disinterested voice.

Eleven who was watching from within the audience was mightily impressed by Zen's quick thinking and congratulated himself on picking a winner as a future 2IC.

Questions to Zen petered out and it was obvious from the look and sound of the audience that they were sympathetic to Zen and conversely could not understand why Pettit and the other founders, whom they normally respected, were being so unreasonable to Zen who was clearly a tearaway but was no serious threat to anybody. The hearing was closed and the prisoners were returned to Hold Island, with the exception of Zen who was removed from the court for private questioning.

Sixty-five

The third and, what turned out unexpectedly to be the last, day of the enquiry started, as had the others, with a summary of what had gone before. The uncovering of the RIR organisation and its supposed intentions; the complete identification of its cell members, and the method by which they had been identified and the final need to identify Eleven. The further disturbing revelation that a BAM2 unit had been stolen and then spirited out of the country now exercised the thoughts and fears of the listening audience.

Following the summary Gilliland began the day's proceedings: "In the interest of openness we have decided to let it be known how we were able to anticipate and defuse some of the methods used against us from within and outside the Island." This caused a stir of interest within the audience as they waited with baited breath for the revelations.

Eleven sat, unnoticed, at the rear of the courtroom in a corner away from the bright lights that otherwise illuminated the room. Like the rest of the audience he was waiting with baited breath to hear the revelations, but for a different reason; he wanted to make sure that the same weaknesses that led to the discovery of RIR could be avoided the second time around. He sat expectantly in his chosen inconspicuous part of the room where he was anonymous among people whom he did not recognise and who would not recognise him. His interest quickened as those he now thought of as the defendants filed into the well of the court, among them was Zen who seemed none the worse for having been singled out at the previous hearing.

"We will not be calling on the testimony of these ex-RIR members unless the need arises through the testimony of others. In the interest of giving this hearing the full attention of the founders we will be joined by our third and fourth members: Director Caine and Director Pettit."

Eleven visibly started at this announcement. He had seen evidence with his own eyes that she had been assassinated during her visit to the Azores. He had seen the bullet strike her in the temple he had seen her taken away in a body bag. What was happening was beyond his comprehension, how could he be wrong? He had used Pain to pull the trigger, he had personally supplied the rifle and its ammunition he had seen the moving images, yet here she was, alive and kicking.

A sympathetic murmur filled the room as Penny Caine entered the room and assumed her place with the other three founders. Her face was pale and drawn on one side but on the other, the right side, there was a riot of colour, reds, blues, yellows and many in between shades; her right eye was closed and badly swollen.

Gilliland waited until the murmuring died down before continuing with the address. "Penny Caine was the victim of an assassination attempt. The third of three failed attempts. We were aware of the attempts on myself and James Creswell, as I will explain later, in advance and were able to manage them. Penny Caine's survival is attributable in its entirety to Ed Pickering" The listening public gasped, with the exception of Eleven who simply looked alarmed. "The incident took place in the Azores during the testing of the car which we hope will give us the freedom of travel in complete safety in otherwise unsafe areas. What the assassins did not know and what was only known by Ed Pickering and nobody else who was at the test, was that apart from protection using a BAM2 shield a secondary feature was being tested. Using BAM2 as a defence is not subtle. Anything the protective shield comes into contact with is totally compromised. This is not a feature to be employed lightly because, for example, if our protected vehicle was to be involved in a collision with another vehicle, a person, or any solid matter - our vehicle would be unscathed but whatever it came into contact with would be deconstructed, turned into unglued atoms." He tried to keep the description simple, not wishing to demand too much of his audience. "This is, of course, in direct contravention of our philosophy of non-aggression so Ed came up with an intermediate solution should our vehicle be attacked by fire arms when the shield is down for safety or any other reasons. He developed a fully transparent molecular polymer skin which is so strong that it is proof against any small arms projectile. This feature was put to the acid test before what was our intended testing programme could be carried out. Fortunately Ed is an engineering genius and his design was not found wanting." He looked with amusement at the rapt attention of the listeners, noting that there was one face in the audience that was less than enthusiastic about his discourse.

"Before the Jaguar used for the test was shipped out to the Azores, Ed did some night work. He spray coated the interior of the car with the polymer, including the windows, in which there was already a polymer sandwich with a view to allowing it to set hard over a number of weeks so that it could be tested here on our Islands on its return from the Azores." He paused dramatically. "But fate intervened and somebody that we have since been able to trace thanks to our friends in the Azores was able to make an assassination attempt. Under any other circumstances Director Caine would have been killed but thanks to Ed's good work the bullet which was fired smashed the toughened window of the car but did not penetrate the polymer membranes, unfortunately the membrane was not fully set and as a consequence it distorted when it was hit and it allowed the bullet to hit the Director on the temple with enough force to render her unconscious and she was in fact comatose for three days. Fortunately by the time the bullet struck its energy had been largely depleted. We are eternally grateful to Ed for his forethought and his expertise which saved the Director's life." There was a roar of approval from the audience and they applauded both Pickering and Caine."

Eleven was nonplussed by the turn of events. Three attempts had been made at assassination and all three had failed; a lesser focussed man would have been tearing his hair out but not Eleven. He continued to learn and plot; he still didn't fully understand why the first two assassinations had failed but at least he now had a full understanding about why his carefully assembled plan had failed; it was because of something he didn't and couldn't know about which excused him, in his own mind, from blame. Eleven tuned back into what Gilliland was saying.

"The reason Director Caine is appearing in the hearing before she had fully recovered from her injuries will now be explained to you. There are two pivotal people who have been deeply involved in the execution of the defence of our country. I would like to introduce you to the first of these two important people." He looked expectantly towards the door of the jury retiring room which opened on cue and revealed a tall off Islander wearing casual off Island clothes. He filled the doorway with his physique and his presence. "May I introduce you to the man responsible for the first two 'assassinations'." He tweaked the first two fingers of each hand in the air. "The assassinations of both myself and the British Prime Minister, but not of Director Caine." He paused and allowed the murmuring of the audience to die down as 'A' entered the room and mounted the witness box.

Eleven's belief in his anonymity from what was transpiring began to leave him and he watched, in a snake-and-mongoose-like state of hypnotism, as 'A' entered the box and placed his huge hands on the rail running around the top. 'A' nodded to the founders and turned towards the watching audience with a friendly smile. The watchers were bemused by the spectacle and were waiting with anticipation to learning about the confusion of assassinations which were not assassinations and an assassin who was welcomed by the founders and who looked upon the court with friendly amusement.

"Ladies and gentlemen, it gives me great pleasure to introduce you to a man who is not a domiciled Islander but has been made an honorary Recovery Island National for his invaluable help during the difficult times we have been enduring of late. This is Simon Caine and if the name rings a bell it's because he is one of the twin brothers' of our own Penny Caine."

There was a rumble of excited conversation around the court room. Eleven absorbed the information in disbelief. He could not comprehend the tortuous path of the enquiry but he understood now how 'A' had eluded the spy who had followed him from his home in Colorado; clearly his identical twin had been used as a decoy. The assassin 'A' being Caine's brother told him forcefully that there was a traitor in the very heart of the RIR operation and he could not fathom who it might be. Being out of control was not familiar territory for him and once more he congratulated himself on the wisdom of keeping his identity a secret. The only

397

person who did know his identity was Cole and Eleven had been able, because of his membership of the Ruling Council, to get a few discrete moments with Cole before he had been transported to Hold Island. He used the few moments to full effect saying to Cole that if he revealed Eleven's identity for any reason not only would he lose his substantial bank account in Paris but he would be fully implicated in three assassination attempts. The penalty for being found guilty of these crimes alone would mean a lifetime of incarceration at best and his own assassination at worst. Cole had immediately and irrevocably acquiesced.

He did not rejoice in his understanding of the assassinations now that Simon Caine had been revealed as a double agent; a chill ran down his spine as he realised that they had used Simon Caine as 'A' to transport the BAM2 unit to Russia. Obviously he would not have taken the genuine article with him; he must have substituted a dummy unit. This also meant that the Russians would discover that they had been duped when they managed to open the box, as he was sure they would, and blame for the duplicity would be attributed by the Russians to the RIR and therefore to Eleven.

Simon Caine was not questioned; he was simply asked to outline his part in recent events and was invited to sit in the witness box or if he preferred to join the founders in the judgement seats to make his part in events known. He chose the judgement seats and sat next to his sister and before sitting down he planted a kiss on the top of her head keeping well away from her injuries. She smiled wanly at him.

"I will try to be clear about these events but they are complex and if I become too obtuse or I wander into unprepared territory I would like you to stop me, through the chair of course." There were no signs of dissent from the audience. "When it was learned by Mark Lawson, by means which I'm sure he will explain to you, that somebody on the Island was looking for an assassin, he made contact with me and asked me to help out. I was until quite recently a member of Delta Force the American equivalent to the SAS and SBS in Great Britain, so I had the necessary training to carry out the job of 'assassination'. It had to look real and so I went underground and got tied up with two groups one was the Nuovostanis and the other was RIR. The Nuovostanis were easy to recognise and were quite open about what they wanted done, they were the ones who instructed me on the task and they were the paymasters. The RIR was a different matter they were and are more secretive about their part in this and no names were given and none of the members revealed their faces to me. It was they who arranged for me to be smuggled onto the Island in a freight aircraft and it was they who provided me with the gun to carry out the task. The rifle I used was a 4S, sub sonic snipers special, manufactured in Nuovostan. The providers of the gun fitted a digital movie camera in the rifle butt because they wanted to witness the kill shot. I had a modification of my own made to the fire arm; I had a voice transmitter fitted along with a gel pack detonator sensor which was tied in to the trigger mechanism. Next I modified the bullet by taking out the business end and plugging the open end of the cartridge with wadding. The final pieces of equipment were the blood gel packs fitted under the shirts of the victims and an ear buds for them to wear during the great deception. After that it was quite simple." He paused again and looked at his audience. "There is an old saying which I have lived all of my military life by. *"Complicated planning leads to a simple solution. Conversely, simple planning leads to a complicated solution.* What I have just described is the complicated planning. The simple solution was just that - simple. At the appropriate time and with all the preparations in place I took aim and switched on the camera and the recording device. Fractionally before firing I said 'bang', this prepared the targets, through their ear buds, to react a fraction after I squeezed the trigger. The gel packs were detonated automatically the blood was produced, the shirts were bloodied and the victims fell as though dead. The recorder recorded and the pictures were a masterpiece of deception."

There was fascination on the faces of the audience when he finished and there was a moment of absolute silence before an outbreak of excited babbling. Eleven used this moment to gather his thoughts. The assassin had not made mention of Eleven so he began to feel a little easier. Of the members of RIR who were present, apart from Cole who he had frightened into submission, nobody would suspect his identity. The issue now was whether Simon Caine had realised that he, Eleven, had been in Nuovostan at the same time as him, it appeared that he did not realise it, on reflection Simon Caine had been anxious to hide his own identity so he probably had not registered Eleven's face.

Eleven's situation was becoming more precarious by the minute, the slender thread of his salvation grew ever thinner as disturbing revelation after disturbing revelation was uncovered. The one salvation was his androgyny which also retarded the feelings of panic that might be experienced by those without his condition. He continued to escape exposure because he had covered his tracks by a cloak of anonymity and he had plugged the one source of weakness by muzzling Cole Preece.

"Was the identity of number 11 ever discussed when you were in Nuovostan?" Gilliland enquired.

"Not openly and I was careful to keep my identity confidential. I took photographs of the meeting but from outside the room and I only managed to get shots of the back of Eleven and a profile of Jack Pain – you all know him as Jacques Pantin." There was a rumble of dissent among those members of the audience who were on the Island when Pantin, by his actions, branded himself as a traitor. "The only name reference I heard was Mr Da Neel but there is nobody of that name on the Island, so presumably it is a code name."

On hearing this name Eleven stiffened imperceptibly. It was his name mispronounced by Pelochev using her bizarre form of English. Fortunately, he thought, these stupid people did not have the intelligence to work out the value of this clue.

The enquiry resumed when Simon Caine left the witness box to be replaced by Mark Lawson who was known by everybody as being responsible for the safety of the inhabitants by watching the sea and sky for enemy action. They had only learned during the course of this enquiry that he was also the head of Intelligence and they regarded him in a new and even more respectful light.

"We first became aware of the nature of this problem when, as part of our normal security precautions, we intercepted a careless radio message. The message structure was such that its clumsiness warned us that it was a coded communication of some kind. We applied the best brains available to decipher the message using the latest cryptology programmes, but had no success. The code being used was so basic that it slipped under the net of detection by the usual means; it was actually solved by one of our team who writes crossword puzzles containing, among other things, anagrams and cryptograms. What we found when we decrypted the message was that an

401

organisation calling itself RIR, situated on the Island, was looking for a professional assassin. You can imagine that it got us very interested. By its very nature this request which would normally only be deciphered by the recipient would take some time to fulfil and check for suitability so we decided to try to get into RIR through the back door and circumvent the hiring process."

Crook interrupted the delivery. "Mark is being very modest, when he says that we decided to get to RIR by the back door he means he decided; the 'we' didn't really come in to it."

Lawson gave Crook an embarrassed look and continued. "We, or if you like - I, talked to the founders about the opportunity. Director Caine came up with the idea of using her brother whose background fitted in with his being convincing as an assassin. The next layer of the deception was to introduce the assassin to RIR convincingly and this was a genuine joint effort with the founders; we decided to infiltrate the ranks of RIR with one of our own."

Eleven was boiling beneath the surface at the duplicitous nature of what was unfolding. He wondered at the stupidity of his minions who had used such an insecure method of searching for a hired assassin, as it turned out unsuccessfully, and in so doing allowed the damning message to bypass their normally secure methods of communication. Just as he was sure he could secure the release of Zen and Cole from incarceration he could also ensure that the idiots who fouled up a simple request would rot in jail for a long time. Still he was secure in the knowledge that his identity was protected.

"That, in simple terms was one segment of the work we undertook. Another segment was to deal with the stolen BAM2 unit. You have already been told about how it was stolen and by whom, at this point we were blessed with poetic justice and we had a further stroke of good luck of the kind that all successful missions ultimately rely on. Simon Caine in the guise of a US ambassador visited the Island and was recognised by a member of RIR as being 'A'. The luck is that RIR had not got the expertise to access the BAM2 unit and were looking for a way to get it to engineers in Russia who thought they could uncover its secrets. They hired 'A', Simon, to take it to Russia in an imaginary diplomatic bag which he did. Once its receipt had been confirmed and 'A' had been paid a serious sum of money he escaped from Russian clutches and returned to the USA. What RIR, the Nuovostanis and Russia did not know was that the unit which was passed to Simon for inclusion in the supposed diplomatic bag was exchanged for a dummy which was reconfigured so that it could not possibly work." There was a ripple of applause from the listening audience.

Eleven closed his eyes, as his fears were confirmed, and he wondered how it would be possible for things to get worse. His organisation had been decimated, he had spent millions on assassinations which were a fiction and now he had lost his only bargaining chip, a working BAM2 unit. The only thing he could now cling on to was his fully protected anonymity. He didn't know who yet but somebody was going to pay for this very dearly.

There was a sudden flurry of activity in the judgement seats which immediately got the attention of the audience. Silas Pettit signalled to Lawson to halt the proceedings and went into a huddle with his fellow founders; there ensued harsh whispers which were indecipherable to the other occupants in the room but the urgency of the sounds intrigued them. The huddle broke and Lawson was beckoned to join the founders

403

for a further bout of whispering; he returned to the witness box.Eleven was as much in the dark about what was going on as any other member of the audience. There was no other facet of this enquiry that could uncover any other of his secrets. Everything had been exposed and destroyed.

A large digital screen was deployed on the wall of the courtroom above the heads of the founders; the photograph which came into focus was a sheet of crumpled paper in what looked like a fish tank. The audience looked at it without being able to comprehend why it was being shown.

"We have an interesting experiment to show you but first I should give you some background and explain why it is so important. That there is another agent involved in the work we have been doing has already been mentioned. We were going to ask this person to give testimony to this hearing but we have decided that for the person to remain effective in taking care of our security the testimony should be given incognito. The agent will address you by radio from another part of the complex and the voice will be electronically distorted for the same reasons of anonymity."

There was a white noise sound from the speakers hidden within the walls of the court which terminated with a click and then a momentary silence and then the voice, disguised in such a way as to register gender without definition, broke the silence. "The task of tracking down the leader of RIR has proved to be impossible."

Eleven felt the, for him unaccustomed, tension which had been building up in his whole body, let go in a flood of relief. He had confirmation that he had not been discovered; at least that was what he thought.

The disembodied voice continued. "That is until three factors came to light one of them is in the form of a message which was smuggled into the Hold Island complex where the RIR prisoners are being held. We were able to acquire this document which the sender believes to be indecipherable by the use of specific degenerating chemical ink."

The digital screen sprang into life and the crumpled paper was enveloped in a mist of gasses. Slowly a message began to appear on the surface of the square of paper; after a few moments the chemical mist was ventilated from the tank and the paper was removed by hands clad in surgical gloves and placed on a table top where it was smoothed flat. The message read:

This instruction will remain visible for less than ten minutes and will then evaporate rendering it beyond recognition. You will be brought back to the court with a selection of others and will be questioned by an official You are to say that you had no knowledge of what RIR were doing and that you were recruited to be a gofer and did not have anything to do with the stolen BAM2 unit. You will say that you regret having allowed yourself to be recruited and that you had and have no intention of causing harm to the Island or the Islanders. Do as I say and I will be able to arrange for you to be freed so that we can pursue the original aims of RIR by regrouping. Be vigilant and we will prevail. E

"The hand writing is neat and our hand writing expert is unable to determine if it is written by a man or a woman the sign off is E, that is not conclusive it could be Elaine or Edward or it could be E for 11; there is no way from this document that we can tell. What it does tell us is that this person male or female is high up in the Island as well as being high up, probably the leader of RIR." This news elicited a collective groan from the audience which was not echoed by Eleven.

The RIR leader showed no visible emotion although inside he was jubilant. He had lost his organisation to

405

this inferior breed of people but at least he was free and clear – free to start again and make sure that the mistakes of others which had brought his organisation down were not repeated. His newly emerging plan was still on track; he would arrange, in as understated way as possible, to have Zen released and with him he would plan a new and more dynamic organisation to fulfil the original aim of controlling the BAM technology and the Island.

***

A door at the back of the court room opened a fraction and the person inside peered out through the crack. Seeing that the alley onto which it opened was clear he stepped out and allowed the door to close and lock behind him. He had an appointment with Mark Lawson at the Atlantean Club for a debriefing. He took a Transfer Car to the foot of the slopes which climbed to the crest of Central Mountain.

The two men greeted with familiarity and shook hands as they met in the small private meeting room in which Lawson had met with Silas Pettit to be given the job of External Security supremo. "Take a seat and let's talk," he said to his surreptitious visitor.

They both sat and admired the view to the western horizon through the old fashioned picture windows which were so right for this location.

"You can relax now, it's all over. It must have been hell for you." Lawson's tone was sympathetic.

"I could do with a long tension free holiday but the truth is, although the tension was unbearable I got a kick out of it. What do you think Doctor Tanterelli would think about that?"

"She'd probably sit you in a chair, shine a bright light in your eyes and give you a third degree."

"The icing on this cake was Simon Caine. We were struggling to make the nebulous handwriting thing stick, it was only identified by comparing it with an inconclusive sample of Eleven's writing that was questionable; the only samples we had on file of his hand writing was in upper case – the note to me was in long hand. It simply wasn't enough to be one hundred per cent conclusive. Fortunately there are two factors which give us a great deal of help. One of them was unearthed this morning by Simon Caine who recalled conversations with Irena Pelochev, the consort of President Wilson of Nuovostan. Her command of the English language contains a number of structural mutilations which are both painful and amusing and she has a tendency to use epithet of Mr when using only a given name. Her misuse of the language and the use of a specialist in comparative handwriting proves to us that Mr Da Neel is Mr Daniel and the writing has been identified as that of Daniel Pierson."

"There is another clincher." Lawson removed a photograph from his breast pocket and slid it over to Zen." This was taken by Katya some time ago; it is of a man acting very strangely in one of the east side cafes, strangely enough to attract her attention."

Zen peered at the photograph and frowned. "This could be anybody, what is it supposed to prove?"

"We took Cole aside and talked to him about optical surgery we discovered by interrogation what he was carrying out and it turned out to be to implant something called Spy-Eye. It's a thing of genius invented and used by Pierson, it enables him to see remotely what other implanted recipients are seeing and hearing. What we believe drew Katya to take the photograph was Pierson testing the apparatus and being uncharacteristically distracted by it. If you look carefully at the photograph you can see that he has the same build and posture as Pierson and, even though it's indistinct he has the same disassociated look about him."

"Simon working out the Da Neel connection was pure genius. When you add the indications from Katya's photograph the whole thing is being drawn together." Zen buried his face in his hands as he spoke and looked a picture of a worn out man.

"Why don't you take a long holiday, you could go anywhere in the world and enjoy yourself?"

"There's more to be done. If I'm going to continue working with you to keep the Island safe I need to keep up the pretence of being a bad boy. To do that I'm going to have to go back to Hold Island and I'm going to have to go back into court and face the music over my criminal activity. All I ask for this time is that I don't get Silas as my judge, he gave me a torrid time on the last occasion." He laughed at his own joke.

"You really do like being a bad boy don't you? Maybe I should tell Carlina and she can brain wash it out of you."

"There's so much still to do." Zen lifted an eyebrow to Lawson, "we may have stopped RIR but there is still the danger of PRICE. Your girlfriend Beverley is involved, as secretary to the union, with hundreds of people who are disgruntled about the workings of the Island and it would be better to keep PRICE going and have them keep all their eggs in one basket, where we can see them.

The tension of the last few months of deceit and of managing his multiple identities as Paul Zen, member of the Recovery Island external security squad, Paul Zen rebel dissident and Anton Wright supposed journalist - had played havoc with his personality. He had been mixing with some desperate homicidal people. Carlina Tanterelli had warned him of the knife edge on which he would be living where one slip out of character of the persona he was using could have spelt disaster for him.

Like Lawson, Zen had entered into the fray with his eyes wide open and accepted that he might not survive the dangerous game of spying. Acceptance did not absolve him from the privations of his shadowy existence. Now that his primary task had been completed he accepted that he would continue to work for the safety of the Island and had suggested to both Lawson and Pettit that he should maintain his bad boy image and work with Daniel Pierson, rather than exposing him, and by being on the inside feed intelligence to the Lawson's security operation. They had both blanched at not throwing the book at Pierson but they accepted that his proposal would give them the best chance of securing for themselves a rebel free future.

To all intents and purposes Pierson would become his own Trojan horse.

Sixty-six

During the flight of Pelochev and Wilson from Nuovostan to Recovery Island, Pelochev ruminated on the unexpected situation in which she found herself. She was, for the moment, safe from the repercussions that she was sure Lebedev had in mind for her. Wilson was no longer a threat to her aspirations of taking over the Presidency of Nuovostan and she had the documents which would enable her to realise that ambition. The documents recording her marriage to Wilson would stand the closest of scrutiny and were in her name, Irena Petrova Pelochev-Wilson.

She looked at Wilson as he slept, induced by powerful drugs, on a sky stretcher which was anchored to the floor of the cabin and in which Wilson was restrained by bindings. She made this journey as ipso facto President of Nuovostan and it felt good. The crew afforded her the accolades due to the President of a sovereign country and she basked in the attention she was given. The journey was long and involved a refuelling stop which was too brief to allow her to leave the aircraft and stretch her legs. They arrived at Recovery Island in the middle of a warm summer's day descending from a cloudless sky.

The aircraft made a circuit of the Island, banking gently as it did so, so as not to disturb the sleeping President Emeritus. This move was to give their VIP guest, the President in waiting, the courtesy of a preview of the Island before finally landing. She was impressed by the Island and by the way she was being treated. Within that instant any thoughts of her taking over the Island in furtherance of Wilsons aims were dismissed. In her own mind, as President of Nuovostan, her aims now concentrated on developing Nuovostan so that it could become a great and glorious nation under her governance. Her priorities had reversed, she now wanted the patronage of Recovery Island to protect her against the probable aggression of New Russia; she would propose a pact of non-aggression with the Islanders and remove one of the Island's major concerns about their own security.

The stretcher was removed from the aircraft using a medic-hoist which kept it level, which would not have been the case had it been carried down the sloping steps. The two VIP visitors were transported to the medical centre by a specially equipped Transfer Car, through the system of subterranean TC tunnels which served all areas of the Island.

This was Pelochev's second visit to the Island; her first visit was to give evidence to the British secret service which led to the absolution of their PM James Creswell who was charged with corruption and treason. Her observations this time were differently focussed: Then she had been nervous about being interrogated by the secret service, now she viewed the Island and its inhabitants as a visiting President who had helped the Island's causes by supporting Pettit and his team to meet their objectives.

On arrival at the hospital they were greeted by a stunning and strangely disturbing woman who was introduced as Doctor Carlina Tanterelli. She wore her signature wardrobe of black and scarlet Island fashion which Pelochev found to be fascinating and immediately considered adopting this fashion in her own country. Such clothing would suit Pelochev because she had a figure which would be displayed to advantage by the unforgiving, clinging material and give her greater presence.

Tanterelli transferred Wilson immediately to one of the examining rooms. Without delay she gave him an initial appraisal after which she shook her head and pursed her lips as she surveyed his inert form. She looked at the notes, which had been kept by the crew during the journey, which recorded the medication which had been administered.

She decided to revive him by administering an antidote to the drugs he had been given and almost immediately he began to stir. His eyes flickered open and he stared blankly at the ceiling, he showed no signs of comprehension.

"Can you hear me Mr Wilson?" she whispered gently into his ear.

Pelochev was about to interrupt, as was her normal reaction to people not addressing him by his title of President, when she suddenly changed her mind and remained silent. Instead she watched Wilson's complete lack of response to Tanterelli's enquiry. She also glanced at Tanterelli and saw on her face a look of genuine concern for her patient.

"He is OK, no?" Pelochev asked Tanterelli.

Tanterelli looked at Pelochev with as much concern as she had Wilson. "From my initial observations and those of the medical crew on your flight in, the prognosis is not good."

"What is meaning prognosis?" Pelochev frowned at the unfamiliar word although she could guess with some accuracy what it meant.

"It is not possible for me to predict the outcome of his position but it would appear that Mr Wilson is very sick."

"Da," she nodded her head.

"Normally, here on the Island we do not use intrusive medical intervention, we employ the healing capabilities of the mind to repair ailments but from what I observe and have heard, Mr Wilson does not have the necessary thought processes to allow us to use these techniques. We will need to treat him with drugs to stabilise him but I doubt he will recover his faculties well enough to affect his own cure. He is too far gone, but I will do my best."

Treatment began immediately and with a speed which was determined by the understanding that Wilson's decline was happening at breakneck speed and that it might already be an impossible task. After the infusion of nutrients dictated as being essential by blood tests he was put into an induced coma to facilitate as much natural repair as possible. He was given physiotherapy, in his supine state to aid circulation and to keep his joints comparatively supple. It soon became obvious that his dissolute life style had caught up with him physically. When he was awoken from his coma it became almost immediately clear that his physical deterioration was matched and bettered by his mental condition.

When he was fully awake he displayed a complete lack of rational interaction. He recognised Pelochev as somebody he had met before but he could not recall her name. The name Recovery Island meant nothing to him and Nuovostan was familiar but he didn't know why. Tanterelli tried every known world standard medical intervention technique to restore at least some of his comprehension of the past but it was to no avail. She did at least manage to halt the decline but repair to his damaged mental power was impossible.

To her surprise Pelochev was touched by this childlike Wilson just as she was by the selfless dedication of Dr Tanterelli and her team. The founders showed a compassion which she found puzzling in view of the threats Wilson had made against them and it made her stop and think about her own position. The people around her, here on the Island, were supportive in a way which made her rethink her own selfish philosophy. She would, she decided, rule Nuovostan in a less harsh way than Wilson; she would restore some of the cultural freedoms which he had curtailed. She would, of course, not allow any other person than herself to take the presidency even though it was based on the lie of her marriage to Wilson. To achieve these aims she needed help on the one hand to control the Nuovostani people so that they would not see her transformation as weakness and on the other hand she needed help to keep the Russians at bay.

The latter of these two requirements occupied her most; maybe the people could be persuaded to give her their support by the simple expedient of money. The Nuovostani population was small and the money Wilson had amassed was truly huge but of course not endless. The requirement of protection against the Russians was an entirely different matter, there was not enough money in the world to buy them off. Her fertile brain came up with a plan to stave off the attention of the Russians and perhaps even satisfy the Nuovostanis without sacrificing her ill-gotten fortune. She put the plan into being immediately.

Sixty-seven

When Wilson was patched up as much as he could ever be, he was discharged from hospital and given accommodation on the west side of the island with views out over the Gardens of Remembrance to the Atlantic horizons. He had full time attendants who looked after every need; he was by now incapable of any logical thought or action, his every want was administered by voluntary medical staff. He could no longer walk unsupported and was unable to hold a conversation, in fact the only time he spoke at all was when some memory, probably horrific, would surface momentarily and he would become furious at not being mobile or in command of his own movements. When he was not consumed with corrosive anger he looked almost cherubic in a primitive way and would spend hours watching a spider spin its web or simply staring at the horizon as the sun began to sink beyond sight.

Pelochev spent some time with him but he failed to recognise her or to converse with her. She surprised herself by actually caring about his condition and regretting that they could no longer spark off each other in a way which time had made her believe, incorrectly, was a constructive way. When she was not with him she was canvassing support for her Nuovostani ambitions from any founder or Ruling Council member who would listen.

Slowly she built up an ever growing support as she doggedly hammered away at the resistance she met, but progress was slow and sometimes ground to a halt. Support came to her from an unexpected quarter. DK and Caroline Pelham visited the Island to report on the world PR progress they were making. They too were

415

having a difficult time garnering support for the Island's humanitarian cause. During the course of their brief visit they teamed up with Pelochev and became a trio of off-Islanders. Pelochev listened to their problems and her fertile mind once more came up with a plan which would help the Islanders in their quest for acceptance but most importantly would benefit her.

Caroline Pelham had not been able to enlist the aid of her husband, a minister of HM government to further their cause because it was not compatible with his aims of advancement in government circles. One of the more junior members of parliament was sympathetic to their cause but his lack of seniority had rendered his help ineffectual. They had briefly considered using James Creswell the British Prime Minister who had close ties with the Island but decided against it in case his involvement failed to succeed, which would make his position as PM untenable. They were not making sufficient headway.

Pelochev observed their disappointment at the lack of progress. DK had written some eloquent articles on the subject but to no avail – what they needed was a good focal article to which ordinary people could relate. She made a proposition to them: "Maybe can be of helping you." She smiled in a way which would not have been possible just a few short days before. "Island is look after Cullin, he is in very big sickness. People of Island should not be to helping Cullin. He has not been kindness to them in the past ago. But people of Island is good to him because they are all gentleman even all of the ladies and look after him at no cost because are all big humans. Peoples of world should knowing this and I will telling. Of course I will be of need to help with words English which you can do, yes."

Caroline looked puzzled. "What did she just say?" She turned to DK for an answer.

416

"I think what she just said makes a lot of sense." He explained to her the gist of the proposal. "I'll write a piece based on what she's just said and I think I can interest all of the broad sheets with it and I think I can also interest the tabloids." His use of the terms broadsheet and tabloid were generic as newspapers no longer existed – all news was digital both audio and visual.

Pelochev was happy with the article that DK wrote even though she understood less than a tenth of it. The writing of it had served her purpose well she now had the grateful ear of the founders and the Ruling Council. She met with the founders and told them that she, unlike Wilson, had no designs on either the Island or its technology. Her task was to modernise Nuovostan and give to its people greater freedom than had been enjoyed at any previous time. To do this it would be necessary to defend themselves against Russian aggression and as Nuovostan had no armed forces except for the palace guard and some very unsavoury secret agents whose sole task was, it seemed, to terrorise their own citizens rather than to defend the country against incursion, an aim which could only be met with external help. Like for example Recovery Island technology. Much to her surprise they did not refuse immediately but said to her that they would consider her request. She waited for the rest of the day on tenterhooks and occupied herself with assisting the medical staff with tending to Wilson. At the end of the day she joined DK and Caroline for dinner at the Atlantean club where she was subdued in contrast with her two companions who were bubbling over with the excitement that the international reception given to his carefully crafted documentary on the beneficence of the Islanders with their humanitarian support for Wilson, who should have been their sworn enemy.

417

At the conclusion of their meal they were joined by Pettit who was back to normal after the harrowing experiences in the New Russian territories. He shook hands with DK and kissed Caroline's proffered cheek; Pelochev was taken aback when he also kissed her cheeks three times as was the Eastern European way. She felt suddenly very special as she sat with people whom for the first time in her life she felt she could call friends and she had conversations which had no other purpose than to exchange views of friendship. The feeling was unexpected and alien to her. They took her breath away.

Pettit's real reason for joining them was not one spurred on by friendship although that was what he felt; he had a proposition for Pelochev which he was happy to share with the two people who were striving so hard to help the Islanders. "Irena, I have discussed with my fellow founders what you propose and I must tell you that there is no way we will share our technology with you." He held his hand up, palm out as he saw her face fall at his words. "However, we will help you in the same way that we offered to help other nations but which they have rejected." He was amused by the look of abject relief on her face when she realised what it was he had said. With a whoosh she let out the breath that she was not aware she had been holding.

She stood up almost knocking her chair over and tried to do something she had never tried before; she tried to demonstrate unbridled excitement but she only succeeded in clenching her fists and shuddering from head to toe. "You are really to helping me?" She said in disbelief, still shuddering. "You really will be to saving me from the Russian powerfulness?"

Pettit laughed at her unaccustomed excitement. "We will help you defend yourself against all enemies but the BAM2 technology will only be used for the purposed of defence and peaceful use but the technology will be operated only by chosen Recovery Island personnel."

She was beside herself and turned in uncoordinated circles where she stood rather like a dog meeting up with its master after a long absence. She rushed around the table and hugged Pettit with a spiritual way which was alien to her. Caroline Pelham was caught up in the moment and hugged her and joined in her dance for joy, they were both joined by DK and they continued to dance round in circles.

When they finally calmed down, Pettit bade his farewells and left them to enjoy what remained of their evening together. Pelochev finally subsided onto her chair and buried her face in her hands and wailed as if in great pain. She looked up at her two companions through a blur of tears and confessed in a choked voice. "Have not crying since little girl in Siberia." Returning her face to the covering of her hands her shoulders jerked with unchecked sobs which grew louder and louder as full realisation dawned. She released the unshed tears of a lifetime and for the first time in her life was able to display emotion openly and freely.

There was no question of Wilson being able to leave the Island, he was too far out of touch with reality to be able to live an independent life and there were no facilities in Nuovostan where he could reside in safety. He was an empty husk, a hollow shell, devoid of all emotion and expression. He was not in pain; his discomfort was entirely taken care of by medication but he was no longer continually sentient. As far as could be told he was, in his own limited way, content; he no longer felt anger, he no longer coveted power and was no longer driven by the urge to destroy that which he could not possess. In short he felt nothing but, thankfully he was not aware of any of this. His last

419

days would be spent in the care of the Islanders he had tried to destroy and he would benefit from their compassion, which in the spirit of the Island's ethos was so freely given

Pelochev had much to be thankful for. In her newly emerging humanitarian state she was even able to express those thanks. She had successfully negotiated the supply of a BAM2 unit and its operating team to help her to rebuild and restructure Nuovostan. Just in case her good intentions slipped the BAM2 unit was fitted with extra self-destruct capabilities which engaged naturally as soon as the wrong biometrics were used to gain access to or to operate the unit. Any attempt made to disable the unit would lead to its automatic and irreversible destruction. These restrictions did not bother her in the least. She had changed so dramatically over the last few days and it was her avowed intention to unravel the tangled web which Wilson had woven and to make Nuovostan a better and more productive place for its citizens and of course herself. However, the change was not entirely benevolent; she still intended to take the presidency illicitly, using her forged certificate of marriage and letter of succession and she still intended to continue to amass a greater fortune that she had inherited from Wilson. None of that had changed.

She departed the Island leaving Wilson behind. When she had said goodbye to him he had looked at her as though she were a stranger and made no response to her farewell. The sadness she felt was transient and soon she was building in her mind a new life as undisputed President of Nuovostan, unopposed - omnipotent. There was the matter of the destroyed presidential palace to be considered. The first job of the BAM2 team would be to rebuild the palace but this time more to her liking than the original designed by

420

Wilson. Her palace would not be plain like Wilson's, she would adopt a more traditional Russian design based perhaps on the cathedral of St Basil in Red Square – but hers would be more colourful, more ornate and have more gold decoration, more swirling domes. It would reflect her colourful newly benevolent personality.

Sixty-eight

With all that had been going on - the assassination attempts, the illicit organisations bent on destroying the Island's structure, Nuovostan's territorial and proprietorial ambitions, focus was lost. They had survived the attempts at assassination and insurrection within the Islands, without resorting to violence, by focussing on their continually developing philosophy but at the same time they were distracted and had not been monitoring the bigger picture. The bigger picture, once they cleared their minds enough to comprehend it had progressed undetected, slowly and inexorably over a protracted period. They had beaten off the advances of the Federation and all its hangers-on as well as the new Russian Alliance. The Nuovostan threat had been emasculated using the same tactic of non-violent infiltration into the heart of the enemy and then by secreting Wilson away from harm on the Island which served a dual purpose; it took him out of the picture and also allowed treatment for his ailments that would not be available anywhere else on earth..

They were, however, still isolated and despite their best and continued attempts to make BAM2 available to the rest of the world they were still unable to believe that any society other than their own could contain the attendant destructive power and resist the urge to use it for the acquisition of dominant power. Helping the rest of the world, mostly the poorer nations, was still being achieved partially, but only by administering rigid control of the technology.

Mountains had literally been moved, rivers diverted, swamps drained, deserts irrigated. Sea defences had been constructed; underground treasures had been accessed and harvested. Undersea tunnels giving access between islands and continents by road or high speed train had been constructed. Notwithstanding all of these bounties, given freely to deserving countries, vested interests still prevented the intended dissemination of the bounties of the technology. The Federation and Russia still had designs on the closely protected technology but had long since abandoned overt overtures both legal and illegal, having been ultimately and expensively thwarted at every turn.

Projects were carried out with increasing frequency all over the world; even in locations which until recent intervention had been virtually unknown, they were no longer the lost civilisations; care was taken to ensure that such civilisations were assisted by the technological offerings without extinguishing the simple philosophy of their society.

Workload increased exponentially and the manpower needed to carry it out kept pace severely stretching the resources of what was now the Recovery Archipelago. This was countered by rethinking the plan for Island development. The original Island, now renamed Home Island, was no longer big enough to accommodate the burgeoning workforce and further Islands were constructed to cater for the increase.

A second accommodation Island was constructed and was named Newhome Island which was considerably bigger than the original and housed twice as many of the population. Farm Island was likewise increased in size by two hundred per cent, an expansion of this magnitude had been allowed for in the original construction but its development had been considerably accelerated.

To aid integration a further island, adding to the developing string stretching to the north east of Main

Island, was constructed for the purpose of recreation; Holiday Island. Originally it had been intended for the exclusive use of the Islanders but with the acceleration of their programme of hoped for integration into the world community it too was expanded to allow non-Islanders the opportunity to enjoy luxurious holidays – and promote the advantages of co-existence with the Islanders. Holiday Island boasted its own airport and a deep water port suitable for ocean going cruise liners. Their financial strength allowed the cost of holidaying to be ultra-competitive.

Industry needed a home and one was built. Industry Island gave a home to the latest in technology some of which was imported from other nations but most of which was home grown. Ed Pickering's department now numbered some eight thousand personnel, split between research, maintenance and manufacturing. It was by far the biggest of the Ruling Councils many ministries, followed closely by Carla Tanterelli's medical research team of around seven thousand.

All of this and more had been evolving in times of great turmoil and uncertainty for the Islanders. The global financial collapse which had led to the inception of the Recovery project had long since ceased to be the all-pervading problem. BAM2 had enabled the promotion of a global prosperity based not on power or wealth but on the ability to harness the natural powers of the planet. But still it remained under the supervision of Recovery Island. The ruling council were acutely aware that the dissemination of the technology across the globe threatened the absolute security to which they were so committed. The secret was to balance the unease with the resultant benefits and units used outside the Island were protected by the most sophisticated means that could be devised and continually updated.

The founders, guided by Caine, gave a great deal of thought to the reasons why their peaceful overtures were so universally unsuccessful and reached a basic but meaningful conclusion: The reason for its lack of success was that nations greater in size than the nation of Recovery deduced that the radical changes that the BAM technology would cause in their evolved society was unacceptable because of the egalitarian nature of its evolution. Without doubt there was a desire to use the technology, in some of the developed nations, for the ascendancy it would give them. For others however, developed or not there was a genuine fear that the changes would destroy the fundamental root of their society which had taken hundreds if not thousands of years to establish.

Back in the sanctuary of the apartment he shared with Juilietta Gray, realisation dawned with a jolt and Pettit felt cold fingers of apprehension crawling up his spine. In the melee of chasing their dreams they had failed to spot the obvious. The fight against overwhelmingly superior odds and their focus on getting their philosophy across had blurred the direction that they had unconsciously taken. Thoughts tumbled through his mind as he sat in the reflection room of their apartment which looked west, towards the setting sun. His sudden chilling thought was prompted by a simple question from Gray.

"Where do we go from here?" she asked.

His mind extrapolated the apparently simple question; he considered where they had come from and where they appeared to be going. The early beginnings, when as a small group they had used the peaceful skills and shrewd anticipation to enable the construction of Recovery Island, he listed in his mind the litany of their progression:

425

The 'coming out' when they had revealed themselves to a sceptical world.

The attempts they had made to offer their bounties freely to the rest of the world and which had been so roundly rejected.

The desperate defence they had made when the Island was invaded by Wilson and the Chinese in the guise of the Federation.

The countering of the attempted assassinations.

The negative spin which had been visited upon their inventions, even though they were universally beneficial.

The way they had chosen after the failure of their negotiations with the Federation, to ignore the rest of the world and take their own path to a future which offered them the chance of so much promise.

The unconscious reasons for their development of vehicle protection which allowed them the generally unusable ability to travel, if they so wished, within areas of the world where they were considered to be pariahs.

His reverie was broken by Gray who looked at him indulgently. "Is there anybody home?" She tapped her loosely folded knuckle on the top of a coffee table, sending minute ripples of coffee across the surface of the two cups of cooling liquid.

"Sorry darling, you asked something simple but which is, I've only just realised, very complex."

"Where do we go from here - is complex?" She looked startled. "It was meant to be uncomplicated."

"Just think about it," he listed for her all of the thoughts he had just had. "If I extrapolate them they lead to a conclusion which I find even more frightening than the early days of our struggle."

"Do you want to share your apprehensions with me?" She wrinkled her brow in puzzlement.

"Not until I've thought them through; they are too important to expose until I've considered everything."

"Just a hint?" she asked coquettishly.

"Not now, the thoughts I'm having are frightening me because I fear that we might have become the very thing we have spent all this time fighting against."

On the following day, having slept uneasily as he wrestled with his thoughts, Pettit sat with Gilliland and Crook and reviewed his thoughts with them. They were less troubled than him by the conclusions he had reached, simply because they had reached the same conclusion as he had but earlier and had elected to keep quiet about it until they could break the news to the Ruling Council in a way that would not instil the discomfort that Pettit felt.

"Silas, both Bruce and I agree with your findings. We've been agonising over this with Penny and she has considered the psychological aspects of where we are and where we can go. It is her considered opinion that this is a good news and bad news situation. The good news is that we are capable of keeping a cap on the use of the technology. The bad news is that we are tied to doing so for at least our lifetimes and we are alone in this, and any other world that can be envisaged. We are the only people who can keep guard over it; more bad news is that we must pass the dilemma on, at least to the next generation, to run the Island; we have assumed responsibility for the wellbeing of the whole world, it is a burden that we cannot ignore."

"What you're saying," Pettit looked horrified as the chilling burden settled down around him, "is that we've become the very thing we are fighting against. We have become, like it or not - a super power."

"Precisely," they echoed in reply.

427

After all the tribulations they had endured Gilliland, as had Pettit, wondered what kind of legacy they would bequeath to mankind, he needed to give it substance.

They had pioneered so many innovations which served individuals: Surgery which did not require the crude cutting open of the corporeal body. Giving visual hearing and speech to the fundamentally deaf - allowing the visually impaired to hear see.

They had benefited other countries, rich and poor alike, with their mining and drilling capabilities; their civil engineering accomplishments – the raising of coastal defences and the provision of underground storage facilities for water, gas and rapidly disappearing fossil fuels, the building of whole towns and city infrastructures where formerly there had been none. At a stroke they were able to provide at low or no cost homes with limitless energy being available for everybody.

Furthermore they had benefitted the whole world by providing practical defence against the next ice age and against meteor or comet strike, these were the more obvious of their accomplishment and there were many less spectacular discoveries which improved the lot of mankind in more subtle ways.

But what would their legacy be and how could it be communicated to the rest of the suspicious world? Everything had been made possible by using the beneficent power of BAM2 but would they leave behind a legacy of *any* kind? They had subjugated the destructive power of their great technology using it only for defence, carefully nurturing its prodigious benefits. Still, after having scoured the whole of the globe, they were unable to find a suitable guardian for the secret of BAM2. What, they continued to wonder, could possibly be their legacy? These questions spiralled around in his brain in a confusion of indecision.

The very thing which gave them freedom held them captive. Protection of the technology was the greatest of all the efforts they made. It took up disproportionately more time and manpower than any other single element of Island life. Paradoxically the more time and manpower was applied to it the greater was the danger of failure, by dilution, of their efforts. And then of course there was one of mankind's great dilemmas, *who would watch the watcher?*

It seemed impossible for him to resolve in his own mind the form the legacy could take. It would not be the healing powers or its ability to give substance to the lives of those who would otherwise be without hope although of course these things were too important to be overlooked. It would not be the protection it offered against attack whether they were terrestrial or extra-terrestrial. It would not be the easy life that it offered. These, undoubtedly desirable, things were transient it would need be something more ethereal, more fragile perhaps even spiritual. *But what?* He wondered as he continued to think in fruitless circles.

Sixty-nine

The hubbub of the Ruling Council subsided in reverential respect. It was some time since he had attended the chamber in person. The Island was celebrating its centenary and the Council members looked at the sole remaining founder with a mixture of affection and reverence. He returned their gaze and wondered at the faces of the young people who now held positions of influence within the Island's administration. Bright young people, some of whom were fourth generation Islanders, had taken over the tasks of governance. To him some of them looked strange, not just because they were wearing Reco-fashions which he still found alien, but because they had assumed the evolved look of a RIN, a Recovery Island National. He was surprised at how little time it had taken for the Islanders to change both physically and attitudinally to become recognisably RIN even before they started speaking with strangely accented English which had evolved through the development of their alternative Island language.

Nationalities throughout the world are visually identified by their build and skin colour. An Australian Maori can be differentiated from a South African Bushman, not by the colour of his skin or his stature, but by his facial structure. They can both be distinguished from a Zulu not by skin colour or facial structure but by the simple factor of height. The Islanders, in a very short time span had evolved in a way which had taken other nationalities hundreds if not thousands of years.

RINs' had evolved within a few generations into being generally taller than other races from the same root by the simple expedient of not having suffered the same pollution and general ravages as those who had led a less beneficially protected life. They were not subjected to childhood illnesses because of processes which had been introduced by the Tanterelli Foundation and therefore did not suffer from the deformities either physical or mental that such illnesses left behind. They were straight of limb and back because of the exercise and diet to which they were introduced at a very beginning stage in their development.

Every RIN received a specifically tailored education which optimised their natural academic or vocational abilities. Not everybody could be an Einstein or Hawking or Brunel and not everybody wanted to be. The Island recognised that its own needs relative to its residents were diverse. There was no such thing as a menial task; the most important thing anybody could do was what they were now doing. If not then they should be doing whatever was more important This did not mean that there was no time to relax, sometimes relaxing is more beneficial than activity, as is the correct amount and quality of sleep. This was inculcated by the Tanterelli Foundation and Dr Carla Tanterelli continued to teach and develop her ideas, despite her advancing age, in the continually developing society.

These things were his observations but were not the legacy which he had been trying to formulate for so long. The Ruling Council members indulged him his reverie. He was revered not only for his great age but for the startling flashes of wisdom with which he was still imbued. He held in his hand a simple wooden box on the lid of which was carved the silhouette of the Island that had become the equivalent of their national emblem, they did not support the jingoism of a national flag.

Holding the box as high overhead as his age restricted limbs would allow he addressed the assembled council in a voice quivering with emotion, placing the box on the table before him. He addressed the council. "We have fought so hard to help those who have been turned against our offerings. Our intention to help has been met with rejection, suspicion and disbelief; disbelief that the good that BAM2 can do, can be theirs without strings attached. The fact remains that, much as we might wish, we cannot allow free access to the technology because it is irrefutable that the power it brings will be used ultimately for the wrong reasons. It has always been so. Just as it was with nuclear fission, back in the twentieth century, which had great benefits in the provision of limitless cheap energy but which arose from the wish to develop a of a weapon of mass destruction. It was ultimately this dark purpose which prevailed. We have, much against our natural inclinations, become a super power - by the simple virtue of our ownership of BAM2. Small as we still are we must take complete responsibility for the security of what could become a weapon capable of destroying our world and all who inhabit it, were it to fall into the wrong other hands. That frightening scenario almost played out when the RIR almost succeeded in capturing a BAM2 unit all those years ago. Fortunately our vigilance won the day. I know that there are those among you who, despite the risk, would still like to share the capability of the technology. I do not share that view and never will, my experience of world politics is too painful and promises given are too easily withdrawn or simply overruled. The legacy that I intend will not satisfy those people – BAM2 must

432

always remain under the control of the Island and of the Island only. There is no substitute for this philosophy."

There was a muttering around the table from those who did not share his view and nods of assent from those who did.

He smiled sadly to himself and took a deep breath. "The legacy I bestow on you is burdensome. In this box," he tapped its lid, "there is a full account of the development and workings of BAM2 technology. This is the only copy and it will be locked away in such a place that it will be secure against external interference. The secrets lie at the moment with me alone; upon my demise this," he tapped the box again, "will be the only remaining record of the secret. Your responsibility is this: You, the council members, will have sole access to the contents of the box. All forty five of you will be required to take a collective oath to access the contents only after my death, until that time I will have sole access to its secrets. At the appropriate time you, the council, will be advised of the details of the security and of how it may be accessed in a way which involves the agreement of every one of the forty five members, or however many there might be at the time, must agree to take the sacred oath that the secrets will never be revealed to any other, person, people or organisation of any kind, within or outside of the Island. Actual access to the secrets within the will be limited to the Leader of the Ruling Council and his Deputy and to no other person." He finished and sat down slowly, looking worn and tired.

The members around the table were at a loss for words, they had hoped that the legacy would be one of great wisdom and which would magically benefit them all.

"Question?" One of the new young members, whom he did not know, raised a finger. "What if we don't want to do it that way maybe the council will decide at some time in the future that it would be appropriate to share the technology and become a fully paid up member of the rest of the world?"

"You could of course do that at any time." He paused when there was great dissent around the table and the majority of the councillors, who shared his views of exclusivity, were shocked by his words. "All you would have to do is persuade one hundred per cent of the council to agree with you – there can be no abstentions, an abstention would default to being a no and a single no would be a collective no."

"That's hardly a democratic way of handling the situation." The young man was indignant.

"You are quite right. This Island is not run on traditionally democratic lines because democracy has brought us nothing but war and famine and ultimately democracy will democratise itself to a popularly voted self-destructing death." He continued philosophically. "We are now at the third incarnation. Firstly there was the discovery of the technology. Secondly there was the development of our philosophy of life and wellbeing and thirdly and perhaps most importantly there is the legacy. The legacy is the beginning of the end of the road which provides two options: One branch takes us to salvation the other leads to oblivion. Be sure that you understand this, it is vitally important. It is to you and your successors that will be responsible for determining the future of mankind. Should neither of these options be chosen there is a third option and that is to destroy the legacy and to hope that nobody else is able to discover the root of this awesome power." He took the legacy box, turned and left the room without looking back. There was no sound to fill the vacuum he left behind him.

After all the trials, triumphs, disappointments and heartbreaks the legacy turned out to be an illusion. Years of toil and uncertainty on the part of the founders and the Islanders condensed down to a simple wooden box in which their future hopes and aspirations for themselves, and the rest of the world, lay. The legacy box, as it was soon dubbed by those who knew of it, would be locked away and guarded so that, should it fall into the wrong hands, it would self-destruct and its power would be lost for ever. The Island had become a super power with an enormous amount of influence and all that could be seen for them was isolation because of the absolute power they alone possessed. The legacy which they had hoped would provide an instantly better world society gave nothing more than expectation of a future in which equanimity would enable the development of the potential so readily available in controlled circumstances, but at least it did not preclude hope.

He would discover much, much later, that the legacy he had described to the Ruling Council would not be as he had envisioned. It would become, paradoxically, both deep and at the same time prosaic. When this ultimately dawned on him it would change his thoughts about the legacy completely and forever.

Seventy

A solitary figure stood inland of the western shore of Main Island watching the sunset. The stratified clouds were in glorious colours; red, pink, peach, blue and mauve with all their countless subtle shades and variations; the last rays of the sun lanced through the clouds and spread as they descended towards the sea where they came to rest and died in a never again to be emulated incandescent display of shimmering random light.

The figure was tall and slender, shoulders slightly stooped. His head was dipped forward and from the back he could have been mistaken for a headless apparition, silhouetted as he was against the deep red orb of the sun. He raised his head, as though suddenly aware of the beauty of the scene before him, as he did so his shock of silvery white hair was illuminated by the sunset in a sudden spangled halo of ethereal light.

Sitting on a stone bench he gazed once more out to sea, this time looking over the gardens of remembrance with their lines of markers identifying the last resting place of the first generations of Islanders. He focussed his attention on a group of three markers in a reversed L shape; the top left hand space which would make the arrangement symmetrical was unmarked. He looked at it reflectively and tiredly passed his hands over his finely lined sun kissed face. The unfilled place was for him and he accepted that it would soon be his time to give symmetry to the incomplete pattern.

With a sharp intake of breath he thought of his wife and the struggles and joys they had experienced together and with their close companions; the tear that glistened in the corner of his eye was a testament to the life they had enjoyed but that he alone now remembered. They would, he prayed, be together again soon enough when his time finally came. The tear escaped and ran down his cheek, he wanted to be with her and his departed friends but he felt that he had more to do on this earth; his whole life had been a mission and the mission had almost been fulfilled, but not quite.

He smiled wistfully at the fortunes and misfortunes of his one hundred and thirty two years on this earth. When this all started he had not thought he would be fortunate enough to live this long but thanks to Island technology his ailments had been attended to and his health restored several times by the healing techniques developed on the Island by the brilliant Doctor Carlina Tanterelli.

For the first thirty years of his existence he had lived the old life; eating bad food taking crude corrosive medicines and breathing in the toxic fumes of a profligate self-destructive society. The damage done to his body during those formative years could not be entirely mitigated by his new lifestyle, the toxins had done their irreparable damage and he would not live the span that his successors might have the opportunity enjoy.

Wistful sadness prevailed once more as he revisited memories of old other world friends flooded into his mind. Without the benefit of the Islands special healing gifts they had lived normal life spans and were now long dead. He felt as though he had failed his fellow man, friends and as well, enemies. Second generation Islanders were as healthy as off Islanders less than half their age. Only time would tell but he fully expected the second generation to live until one hundred and fifty and more, as for subsequent generations who could guess?

He grew weary and continued to move away from the bench cautiously straightening his reluctant arthritic back before attempting to walk with any pretence of gusto. He slowly rotated his shoulders as he stumbled unsteadily towards the Transfer Car station at which he joined the queue of young people who had just left the new Institute of Technology building which overlooked the beautiful western approaches. The assembled youth grew quiet as he joined them. He was after all the most famous face on the Island, being the only remaining founder. Putting them at their ease he smiled gently at them and wished them a good evening.

"Sir," One of the young girls who appointed herself spokesperson, addressed him with deference. "It is a great honour for us to see you and perhaps to have an opportunity to talk to you if you would permit?"

He looked at her open smiling face; she had adopted the look and fashion of the Island's modern youth which he viewed with amusement. Her harlequin like costume clung provocatively to her young body and, as was the fashion, she had depilated all body hair and had intricate swirling tattoos on her hair free head.

Looking at her lively and slightly excited face he knew in an instant that the course of action he would take would ensure the continuation of the society which he had been instrumental, sometimes unwittingly, in forming. "Young lady and your young friends," he turned to encompass them in his gaze. "The honour of speaking to you is all mine."

The legacy he wished to leave was not, as he had thought, the legacy box; that was just an empty icon. It was, it suddenly occurred to him, the realisation of their ideals in and for the rest of the world. It was a daunting task but one he would pursue for as long as he was sentient. He owed it to the memory of his fellow founders, he owed it to his fellow Islanders and he owed it as a contribution to the harmonious reinvigoration of humanity. Here was his epiphany; the realisation that he could at last fulfil the destiny that had until now eluded him.

The future he decided, would be an exciting challenge and he had become suddenly aware that standing before him was the generation which had it within their power to realise the dreams upon which their nation was originally founded. They, the young people, were the true vibrant legacy of which he had dreamed because within this, their cloistered Island environment their aspirations were pure and had not been tainted by the corrosive influences of the outside world. They were the illusive legacy, the whole of the legacy and they would, if nurtured, be the architects of a new and glorious Genesis.

Lightning Source UK Ltd.
Milton Keynes UK
UKOW03f1624250314

228781UK00002B/4/P

9 781910 162637